The Price of Honor

By T. S. Dawson

Acknowledgements

First, and foremost, thank you to Wesley, my little muse that keeps me inspired to write. I hope he grows up seeing through my example that it is never too late to try something new or to learn something new. And, thank you to my husband for trying to help me set these good examples for Wesley.

As I recently said at the Decatur Book Festival, these books are a team effort. Thank you to the T.S. Dawson team, John Bryan, Donna Goss, Christie Johnson, Annette Saunders, Jill Rowland and Susan Kavanaugh. John is our computer guru. Donna, Christie and Annette edit and Jill and Susan help spread the word. Without you all I wouldn't get very far with these books.

Thank you to the ladies of SWW, my day job, who have supported all of my artistic efforts.

Thank you to the store owners at Genuine Georgia in Greensboro, Georgia, The Book Worm in Louisville, Georgia, Paper Soiree on Lake Oconee, Olio Cottage in Wrens, Georgia and The Paisley Bag also in Wrens, Georgia. Thank you all for carrying my books and helping me get the word out about them.

I would like to especially thank you, my readers, for giving your time to my writing. I appreciate your support and feedback and I enjoy hearing from you whether through reviews on Amazon.com or emails. Without your feedback, I won't know if I am doing well or if there are things I may need to improve on. I welcome your opinion.

T.S. Dawson

"The truth about Aunt Gayle was that she was suffering from a twenty year old broken heart. The one boy she ever loved had died in front of her when they were in high school. They were swimming with some friends at the rock quarry near Sparta when he dove in water that was too shallow. Some people would look at her life as a waste, but not me; especially since I was a product of that life."

-Amelia Anderson Hewitt

It was the first clear day we had had in what seemed like a month. It had rained so much that winter that we rivaled Seattle for record rainfall totals. Today was a break from the pouring gloom and my niece, Millie, drove over from Milledgeville with her two daughters. While her husband was working, she brought the babies to visit and to check on the construction at the property she owned near mine.

We took the two girls out to the front porch swing and began to glide back and forth with the breeze. I held one and Millie held the other. The magnolias in the yard were in bloom and the scent, well, it smelled like spring. Earlier in the day I let up all of the windows in the house and while the wind floated in and the sound of the Judds on the radio floated out. How fitting that WTHO, just about the only radio station that came in clearly out in these parts, was playing "Rockin' With the Rhythm of the Rain" at that time.

Poor Millie, the girls were about six months apart in age, not twins and thank goodness for it since both had battled colic. The youngest, George-Anne was still battling and it was just about her witching hour when we took our conversation to the front porch swing.

Between the Mylicon and the movement of the swing, Millie managed to calm George-Anne enough for me to hear what she was saying. "You know Mr. Graham is going to propose to you soon."

"I know," I sighed as I pulled my hair from Gabby's little fist. Gabby was the older of the two girls and she liked to play with my hair, but sometimes she got a little overzealous.

"Aunt Gayle, I'm grown now and I don't need you to take care of me anymore." Millie patted George-Anne's bottom and tried to keep her settled as we talked.

"I know that, too."

The swing went back and forth and my feet barely touched the porch beneath it as we went. I looked over at Millie. She was married with two children of her own now. She was quite grown. I had helped take care of her almost all of her life and almost all of my adult life. Looking at her I thought surely she had heard the story before and surely she didn't think...

"Millie, you know taking care of you isn't the reason I never married, right?"

"I guess." Millie looked at me with wonder. I thought she had heard the story, but she hadn't heard the entire story and she hadn't heard my side of it as we had never spoken of it before.

The truth was that it was my choice not to marry. My choice had nothing to do with Millie and all to do with my own broken heart. Some say it is better to have loved and lost than to have never loved at all, but I have never been sure if I agreed with that statement.

CHAPTER 1

It was July 16, 1976. It was two weeks after our country celebrated its bicentennial, the two hundredth anniversary of the signing of the Declaration of Independence, and the day after Jimmy Carter, the governor of Georgia, became the Democrat Party's nomination for President. Many Georgian's were thrilled to pieces that our governor was going to run for President, that we might actually, finally, have a President that was from our state. It was all over the local news, but all I cared about was Noah Walden and the fact that it was his birthday.

My mother dropped me off around noon at my best friend's house. She lived on Highway 1 on the outskirts of Wrens headed toward Louisville. Her house was huge compared to ours. Mother said it looked like a funeral home, but my opinion was that Judy's "funeral home" made our brick ranch look like a rat trap.

Mother continued through the circular driveway and back toward Wrens after slowing down just long enough for me to jump out. While she was gone to get her hair permed at Mrs. Cornelia's beauty shop, I was going to spend the afternoon laying out with Judy. As soon as mother was safely down the road, I threw off that one piece that she bought me and put on one of Judy's bikinis.

Judy and I hauled a quilt and a radio out to the front yard and threw it out in a spot where the sun was beating down the most. I was pale and needed a tan so badly. We decided to start out on our stomachs and rotate every thirty minutes. As soon as we were settled on the quilt, the real girl talk began.

"So, Noah is home this weekend, right?" Judy asked.

"Yes!" I squealed.

"How long has it been since you saw him?"

"About three months," I replied as I adjusted the top of the suit. It was a little big on me, but other than that I liked it. I wasn't allowed to have two piece suits and my mother would have died if she knew what I was wearing now. It was by far the most revealing thing I had ever had on.

"I don't know if I could go that long without seeing Doug. I don't know how you do it." Judy had been dating Doug Mathis since long before we were old enough to date. I think they had been matched since birth.

Our conversation tapered off and we just laid there listening to the radio. WBBQ was coming in loud and clear out of Augusta. They were doing an oldies hour and playing songs from the fifties and sixties. Considering what I was planning for my date that night with Noah, it was fitting that the song, "Will You Still Love Me Tomorrow" by the Shirelles, was playing. As I listened to the song I thought about everything leading up to my decision.

I thought about the day I met Noah. It was at my brother's funeral. It was early summer. The day was unusually cool for that time of year. I remembered every detail right down to the smell of honeysuckle that floated in the air from the bushes that separated the cemetery from the woods. The honeysuckle was in full bloom and overpowered the scent from the sprays of roses, carnations and lilies that surrounded the coffin.

The first three notes rang out across the cemetery. Most everyone else at the grave site hung their heads or looked straight ahead at Andy's casket and the flag draped over it. I did not hang my head and I had seen enough of that casket to last me a lifetime. I looked for the origin of the music. Where was the bugle that whined so beautifully to honor my brother?

I searched the graveyard until I found a lone soldier standing near the wood line that bordered the cemetery. He was so stiff and serious. I could not take my eyes off of him. He held the bugle with only one hand and played it with such pride. Just when I thought my heart could not have been broken more, it was. And who knew a song of only twenty-one notes could do that?

The last note was blown and my attention was snatched away by the cries of my niece. I glanced to Baby Millie in the arms of her mother, a woman I had despised since I first laid eyes on her. My fury got the better of me and I forgot the soldier for a moment. When I looked back to the soldier again he was gone and I was disappointed.

The other two soldiers that were sent up from Dobbins Air Force Base finished out the funeral with the folding of the flag from the coffin. I looked at Andy's widow as she accepted the flag and I knew before she left the graveyard I was going to let her know exactly what I thought of her. She didn't deserve that flag. She was the reason my brother was dead. No one deserved that flag because my brother did not deserve to be dead.

The final prayer was said and the song "I'll Fly Away" was sung by Mr. McGahee, one of Daddy's good friends. As everyone took their turns again telling my parents how sorry they were for their loss. Rhonda Thigpen, as she would always be known to me even though she called herself Natalie when she married my brother, took that opportunity to slip away. She gave Millie to her mother and just walked off toward the parked cars. She was almost to hers and I almost had a hand on her shoulder. I was to the point of reaching out to her with the intention of grabbing her and slinging her around to face me when a car door slung open and knocked the wind right out of me.

The next thing I knew I was feet in the air and flat on my back. I couldn't see anything but a figure standing over me with the sun behind him like an eclipse.

"Miss, I'm so sorry. Are you alright?" a soft deep voice asked as he extended a hand to help me up.

"I am fine!" Other than having had the breath knocked out of me and my skirt being nearly over my head. Thankfully, I was wearing a black dress with a full skirt and crinoline underneath. The most this mystery figure saw was the white crinoline and not my panties. I scrambled to jump up and push my dress down still not taking notice of just who was in front of me.

"Are you sure you're okay? I didn't mean to hit you that hard," he said leaning in to help me brush down my dress.

I jerked away. I was disappointed that I hadn't been able to give the Widow Anderson a piece of my mind. I was highly irritated and his words hit a nerve as well. I stood as tall as I could and I looked up to him. "You didn't mean to hit me that hard! That kind of implies that you did mean to hit me."

He hung his head and looked down at what was in his hands. It was the bugle. I had not noticed his uniform. In the heat of the moment I had taken for granted that the gentleman before me was wearing just another blue suit like the other men in attendance at the funeral, not actual dress blues.

My face was suddenly flushed and I was embarrassed. I wasn't mad anymore, but still curious as to why he hit me with the door.

As he fiddled with the bugle he began to explain, "I saw you coming, storming after that woman. I know what you're going through is rough for you and your parents. I just thought that if you were in your right mind and thinking clearly that you would use your better judgment and..."

"Not make a scene at a funeral and embarrass my family?" I was suddenly ashamed of myself. I bit my lip and I was the one hanging my head and staring wishing for something to do with my hands. I settled for clasping them behind my back. "Thank you for stopping me and thank you for playing so beautifully for my brother today. He would have loved it."

"Shucks, ma'am, it's the least I can do. I'm real sorry about your brother. I didn't know him of course, but from what all was said here today, he sounded like a real fine man."

I could feel the tears coming again. "He was the best."

I paused and there was an awkward silence between us. When the last note of "Taps" rang out before I was distracted by Millie crying, my thought was that I wanted to meet that soldier and now here I was standing face to face with him. Well, almost face to face. He was about four inches taller than I was.

"I'm Abbigayle Anderson, but everyone calls me Gayle." I extended my hand and he looked up from the bugle and the dirt he had been pushing around with his patent leather shoe.

Before taking my hand, he removed his cap and transferred it to the hand that was holding his instrument. "I'm Senior Airman Noah Walden, but you can call me Noah."

My heart fluttered and I trembled a little when he took my hand. I hoped he didn't notice. Senior Airman Noah Walden was the best looking man I had ever seen. He had dark brown hair that had a slight wave to it and he had blue eyes, ice blue like the color of my prom dress this year.

People were getting in cars all around us and leaving the cemetery and the two other members of the color guard were approaching. Stupid me, I snatched back my hand before they could notice. Nothing inappropriate was going on except for in my own head. In my head I was picking out the names of our children and wondering how I would sign my name, Mrs. Noah Walden or Mrs. Gayle Walden?

Noah turned his attention to the members of his team that were nearly to us and I noticed that they saluted him and he saluted back. He was the senior officer. Witnessing this helped me make the choice, definitely signing as Mrs. Noah Walden. I blushed at the thought, but quickly came to my senses. If he left now, I would never see him again and meeting him had been the one bright spot in the last three days.

"The church is providing dinner for the family. It is only right around the corner, in the fellowship hall. There'll be plenty of food." I looked right at Noah as I continued, "Y'all are welcome to come. If y'all have the time, you can get a home cooked meal before you go back."

Noah didn't have time to answer before the guy with the least amount of décor on his uniform replied. "Sir, what-da-ya say? I couldn't tell you when I last had home cooking."

I remember that being one of Andy's complaints in the letters he sent home to Mother during the two years he was in the Air Force. There was no cooking of any kind where he was stationed and Mother often packed up corn-bread patties and fried peach tarts and shipped them to Vietnam. She said they might be molded and stale by the time they got there, but at least he would know she loved him

13

enough to try. Didn't that just beat all? Andy served a tour in Vietnam as a medic and died less than a mile from his house in a car wreck?

Noah wasn't answering fast enough for my liking so I sweetened the offer by describing what all would be on the table. "There'll be fried chicken, creamed corn, green beans, chocolate cake, fried pies. You name it, it'll probably be there. All homemade."

I was hardly finished with my list before the two guys were begging Noah. He looked at me and shook his head from side to side. "We'll make the time."

"Good." I tried to sound demure, but I was giddy inside.

Mama and Daddy were still seeing to guests by the grave, but I went ahead to the fellowship hall with Noah and the boys from the color guard marching close behind. We turned the corner of the church and the youngest looking one of the bunch announced, "I can smell that fried chicken already. Ma'am, I might love you."

I smiled bashfully at him. He looked like a sweet boy, about my age, but I only had eyes for Noah.

Noah punched the guy. "Stop or you'll make her regret inviting us."

There were about ten of my family members already going through the buffet line when we entered the hall. Aunt Ruth and Uncle Bud were working their way down the buffet with their son, Dixon. Dixon was raising a stink about not wanting his food to touch as Aunt Ruth made his plate and hers. Aunt Ruth was my daddy's youngest sister.

Daddy's older sister, Aunt Dot, and her husband, Uncle Jim, were just sitting down at a table, but their son, Ben, and his fiancé, Connie, were in line behind Aunt Ruth and Uncle Bud. There were also a couple of great aunts from my mother's side in line as well. Everyone turned and spoke to me again, told me they were sorry for my loss.

The other boys were too busy salivating over the sight of the food to notice the exchange between Noah and myself. Each time someone told me how sorry they were or offered me any sort of condolence, I teared up all over again.

I dabbed the corner of my eyes with the tips of my finger attempting to stop any more from escaping. I did not want him to see me cry. I was not a pretty crier.

"I want to give you my condolences, but I think you may have heard that enough today," Noah said as he handed me a handkerchief.

"Thank you." I took the handkerchief and it worked better than my fingers for drying up the tears. "I meant thank you for your condolence as well as this."

I offered it back to him, but he told me to, "Just keep it. I have a couple of dozen of them."

I smiled back at him and took a couple of steps toward the beginning of the table. Noah and the boys followed. I passed them all a plate as we neared the head of the line.

I took a couple steps more and started to add a drumstick to my plate. I leaned back to Noah and handed him the tongs. I whispered, "See that stuff on the red platter?"

"Yes," he whispered back.

"It looks like a harmless lime Jello mold with some fruit in it, but it isn't."

"Oh, it sure looks like a lime Jello mold."

"That's Mrs. Collins' signature dish. She's a little too fond of moth balls in her house and it tastes like what you would imagine moth balls to taste like. Trust me."

Noah heeded my warning and skipped the lime Jello mold. The two other airmen did not get my warning and they piled their plates high with everything including the Jello mold.

15

As we made our way to the end of the buffet line and picked up our glasses of sweet tea, I scanned the room for a table with enough spaces for me and the airmen. There were plenty of tables in the fellowship hall that were still vacant, but I didn't dare choose one of them. I knew better than to be seen at church of all places entertaining three boys I had only just met. That would surely set tongues wagging. It would be all over town by sundown that I had picked up three boys at my brother's funeral. I would be the talk and the tart of the town.

Connie and Ben were headed across the room in front of us. Lucky for me there was no love lost between Connie and Aunt Dot. That should have been Ben's first indication that something was off about that girl because everyone got along with Aunt Dot. Instead of sitting with his mama, Connie led Ben over to the table where Aunt Ruth, Uncle Bud and Dixon had just sat down.

Connie's choice of seating worked out great for me. Aunt Dot's table had the perfect number of chairs still available and I knew sitting with Aunt Dot and Uncle Jim would spare any tarnish to my reputation.

I led with Noah and the other two close behind. Although I knew the answer, I did the polite thing and asked if we could sit with them. "Aunt Dot, Uncle Jim, this is Senior Airman Noah Walden and..."

I looked to the other two realizing I had not been properly introduced to them and had no idea what their names were. Thank the Lord they had name tags on which I quickly read aloud. "And, Airmen Rosier and Wilson."

Noah smiled knowingly at me. I think I made a good save, but it appeared he knew that I scrambled to name them. Aunt Dot and Uncle Jim were quick to shake hands with the guys and while they were shaking, each guy insisted that their first name be used. Rosier's first name was Robby and Wilson's first name was Lewis.

"Do you mind if we sit with y'all?" I asked once the boys finished the introductions for me.

Aunt Dot and Uncle Jim were always so hospitable. "Of course," they answered in unison.

I put my plate and tea down in front of the seat next to Aunt Dot and started to pull out the chair. Noah quickly sat down his food and his drink at the chair on the other side of me and reached for my chair. "I'll get that."

Noah pulled my chair out for me. Regardless of all of the "I'm sorry's" or condolences I received, Noah pulling out my chair was one of the nicest things anyone had done for me.

We took our seats, me by Aunt Dot. Noah was on the other side of me followed by Wilson, then Rosier, Uncle Jim and back around to Aunt Dot.

Uncle Jim was always more reserved than Aunt Dot. They were the definition of opposites attracting when it came to personalities. Regarding looks, they were spot on. She had been the homecoming queen at Stapleton High and Uncle Jim had been on the junior Olympic swimming team. He credited that to saving him in the war when he had to swim ashore and storm the beach at Normandy.

The years had been kind to the both of them. They had both gained a little weight, but were still proportionate to one another. They were in their late forties and her hair was still its natural brown and his was salt and pepper gray.

Usually Aunt Dot reserved most of the embarrassing stuff that she did for Uncle Jim, but today I fell victim.

"Don't you just love a man in uniform? I do," she said in her whisper voice which was not a whisper at all.

I was embarrassed to the point of mortification. Everyone one of the airmen looked my way as if they were waiting on my answer.

Uncle Jim saved me by changing the subject. "Oh, Lord, Dixon just wiped his nose down our future daughter-in-law's arm. Our poor boy is in for it with that one."

More than what Uncle Jim said, attention was called to Connie violently wiping her arm and storming off from the table. "That boy needs a leash! I cannot eat after that!"

My parents were just entering the door of the fellowship hall when Connie nearly mowed them over to get out. Ben chased after her, but all eyes turned back to Dixon. He started singing, "If you're happy and you know it, clap your hands." The look on my mother's face said she was not amused, but Aunt Dot was. Aunt Dot was very amused about Connie's misfortune and untimely departure. She was so amused that she clapped her hands to little Dixon's song and gave him a big thumbs up. Dixon smiled gleefully from ear to ear.

While we all went back to eating, I leaned in Noah's direction. I felt an explanation was in order. "The brunette that just stormed out is my cousin Ben's finance. Cousin Ben is Uncle Jim and Aunt Dot's son. Connie and Aunt Dot don't really get along. She doesn't like Aunt Dot very much. In fact, I don't think she likes much of anyone in our family."

I wondered what he must think of us since, were it not for him, this would be the second spectacle he had witnessed at my brother's funeral.

I glanced over at him from pushing the butter beans around my plate. "You must think we're awful people bent on making scenes." I begged in my head for him to reassure me that he thought nothing of the sort.

Uncle Jim was engaging the other boys with comparisons with his time in the Army and their time in the Air Force. This left Noah able to have a conversation with me without all ears listening.

"This is nothing. Tame even compared to some of the stuff we've seen," Noah assured me as I had hoped he would.

"Really?" To me it was a pretty big deal. It wasn't every day that we were treated to Connie and I had never thought about picking a fight with someone until today.

Noah put his fork down and looked at me, gently shaking his head from side to side. "Oh, definitely. At our last funeral the deceased's children from the first wife and the children from his

18

second wife started fighting. I'm not talking about little kids. These were people in their forties duking it out beneath the canopy. Wilson barely got off his knee from presenting the flag to the widow, who was actually the third wife, when obscenities and fists went flying. There wasn't time for us to break it up before one of the daughters was thrown over the casket and into the open grave. She took half the flowers in with her. So, you see, this is nothing."

I had not realized until she started snickering, but Aunt Dot was listening to Noah's story the whole time. I tried not to laugh myself, but I could just picture Rhonda scratching and clawing her way out of the open grave.

"And that's not even the worst," Noah added.

"There's worse?" Aunt Dot snorted. She shook a little all over as she snorted and laughed about it.

"Yeah, my all-time favorite is from about a year ago. We were presenting at a funeral down around Cordele. I had a bit of a cold so there was another guy playing "Taps" and I was one of the guys on flag duty. The family was so cheap that they didn't spring for a tent for everyone to sit under. So, there's my buddy Marshall in the distance blowing the trumpet. You know how it is; everything's still as a stone and quiet as the notes ring out. Well, he's about midway through and this flock of geese..."

Aunt Dot put down her fork and covered her mouth. She saw where this story was going before I did.

Noah went on, "Marshall was just about to the end when the geese were directly over the heads of those at the service. The geese let loose in mid-air and there wasn't a dry person in the group save me and Wilson and that was just a miracle. Everyone was just sitting there scared to move and our jaws were on the ground when this woman stands up from the back row and says, and pardon the language, 'Ittin' it just fittin' he shit on me in life and now he's shit on me in death.' The woman turned and stormed off. Turned out she was his mistress and no one knew. So, yeah, y'all's family is pretty tame."

Aunt Dot was still laughing when Uncle Jim brought our conversation back around to a more appropriate topic. "So, Noah, where are you from and how long have you been in the service?"

I was thrilled. Uncle Jim asked the questions that I had been dying to ask myself, but had not wanted to seem forward. I listened attentively, but continued to take bites of my food as Noah answered.

"I'm from just a little ways down the road from here. I'm sure y'all have heard of Blythe, Georgia. I graduated from school there and a week later went straight into the service. This makes my third year."

I did the math in my head. That would make him roughly twenty or twenty-one and he was from right down the road.

Uncle Jim continued with the questions. "That's real close to Matthews. Are you related to any of the Waldens from down around there?"

"That's some of my distant cousins."

"Well ain't it a small world?" Aunt Dot winked at me and I gave her a face that begged for her to stop.

I could not add anything more to the conversation because I was busy thinking about how we were related to everyone in the county, but thank goodness we weren't related to the Waldens from Matthews.

Courtesy of Uncle Jim and Aunt Dot by the end of lunch I had learned a great deal about Noah Walden. He had two brothers and no sisters. His mom's name was Linda and his dad's name was Royce and the farthest away from home that he had been with the Air Force was Fort Darby.

"Fort Darby is in Italy, about six miles south of Pisa and on a clear day you can see the leaning tower," he described. He was fascinating and I had always wanted to go to Italy.

I was learning things about the other two guys when Mama and Daddy finished fixing their plates and stopped by on the way to their table.

"We could pull up a couple of chairs." Uncle Jim stood and started for the empty table behind them. Noah, Wilson and Rosier stood as well.

"No, no," Daddy stopped him and gestured over to the preacher and his wife who were finishing up with the buffet line. "Thanks for the offer, but we're gonna sit with Pastor Phil and Mrs. Peggy. I just wanted to stop by and tell the boys here how much we appreciated them. Andy would have loved it. Short of the few weeks he had practicing as a doctor, he loved nothing more than serving his country. Thank you so much for coming up and helping us to honor him. We really appreciate it."

Daddy extended his hand to Noah first and Mama, who was standing right behind him, asked Noah, "Are you the one that played? It was so beautiful. Thank you so much."

I felt so sorry for my parents. They had held up so well, but I could feel my own tears coming on again as I witnessed them thank the guys for playing for Andy. They had been so strong and I didn't want them to see me cry again so I excused myself from the table. I put my plate away and walked outside for some fresh air.

I did not think about what I would see as I walked back down the route I had used to lead the boys to the fellowship hall earlier. When I turned the corner around the back of the church and looked across the cemetery. The men were working to lower Andy's casket into the grave. It wasn't like it did not hit me the night we got the call about the accident, but it really hit then and I lost it. I would never see him again. The sobs were coming and my knees were going weak and I turned back to bury my face in my hands, but Noah was there and I buried my face in his chest instead. I sobbed for what seemed like an eternity and he didn't say a word. He just held me.

I finally composed myself enough to be embarrassed. I eased back from him, but somehow managed to end up holding his hands. "I'm so sorry. I think I've gotten makeup all over your uniform."

"Don't worry about that."

I said it again anyway. "I'm so sorry." I sniffed to clear my nose. "You hardly know me and here I am crying all over you. I'm not a crier. Oh, that's a lie..."

"You don't have to explain anything to me."

"I just came out to get some fresh air and well I just didn't expect to see..."

"Hey, it's going to get better. I promise. Why don't we walk around to the front of the church? I have a feeling the air may be fresher around there." Noah smiled at me and he had the prettiest teeth of any guy I had ever seen. Just looking at him somehow made me forget a little of what I had just seen. I would never forget Andy, but perhaps he had been the one that sent Noah to me.

Noah turned to walk through the corridor between the church and the fellowship hall and he realized about the same time I did that he was still holding my hand.

"Oh, um, sorry about that." I didn't know what else to say as I eased my hand from his.

The way I felt right then, I could have gone on holding his hand indefinitely, but what would people say and I certainly did not want his buddies to see. Noah smiled a pursed smile at me. I hoped I hadn't hurt his feelings by taking my hand back. We walked the rest of the way around the building in silence.

When we made it to the front of the church and as we approached the steps I asked him, "Do you mind just sitting here with me for a few minutes?"

The steps of the church stretched across the entire front porch. I picked the third step from the bottom and brushed off a spot and sat down. Noah sat on the same step, but about an arm's length away, an appropriate distance for near strangers.

Noah slumped over and propped his elbows on his knees. I sat more ladylike and crossed my legs.

"May I ask you a question?" he asked.

22

I cut my eyes in his direction. "Sure."

"How old are you?"

"Seventeen," I know I sounded like the wind had been let out of my sails when I answered. I hadn't wanted to tell him my age. He was clearly older than me and why would he be interested in a high school girl? I hoped he was interested and hadn't just been being kind.

I thought he was going to be disappointed with my response. I expected to see it written on his face, but it wasn't.

"So you are still in high school?"

"Yes. I'm a senior." again I answered with caution.

There was a bit of a lull in the conversation until he broke the silence again. "I'm going to have to be going soon, but I was wondering if you would mind if I wrote to you?"

"You want to write to me?"

"Well, I put in for a transfer a while back and my orders came through. I am being sent back to Camp Darby in two weeks and I won't be back for at least six months. I've enjoyed meeting you today and, I mean, you aren't under any obligation."

Now the wind really was out of my sails. I was getting my hopes up to date him and he was being transferred over-seas for six months. It was as if I was heartbroken all over again. What was I to say? "I have enjoyed meeting you too and I think I would like it if you would write to me. You can tell me all about your travels while I am stuck here."

"I don't know that there will be that much to tell in the way of travels, but if there are any, I will write to you and tell you every detail."

I smiled politely at him.

"I guess I better get you back inside before anyone starts to get worried about you." Noah stood and offered his hand to help me up. He was such a gentleman and I liked it. The boys around here barely held doors for girls anymore.

I took his hand and he helped me to my feet. His hands were soft. They reminded me of Andy's hands. That thought rushed in before I could stop it and I immediately took my hand back. I pressed the corners of my eyes to try to squash the tears. I didn't want my time with him to end, but I really didn't want to cry in front of him again. This time he didn't seem to notice and I was relieved.

I followed behind Noah by only a couple of paces as he led us back to the fellowship hall. Just inside the door I excused myself to fetch a pen and paper so I could give him my address. He would need that if he was going to write to me. When I returned I found him seated back in his chair at the table with the other guys. The three of them appeared to be riveted by Uncle Jim's story of storming the beach at Normandy.

I approached the table wondering how I would slip my address to Noah discretely. His hat was on the table next to my seat and it occurred to me to slip the note into the hat. Everyone including Aunt Dot was engrossed in Uncle Jim's story. I had heard it all my life, but it never failed to hold my attention. Uncle Jim really was an American war hero and he was our American war hero.   I ended up just laying the folded paper next to Noah's hat as I listened to Uncle Jim.

When Uncle Jim finished telling us about laying with the dead for three days until the Red Cross came through and found him and saved him, Noah thanked us for allowing them to have lunch with us, but then insisted they must get on the road. "It's a fair piece back to Warner Robins and we are due back no later than 7:00 p.m. so we've got to get on the road."

"Of course," Aunt Dot and Uncle Jim responded in unison.

Aunt Dot continued, "You boys did a great job today and, Mr. Walden, you are very talented with that bugle. My nephew would have been very proud to have you play for him today."

"Thank you, ma'am. It really was the least we could do not only on behalf of a grateful nation, but on behalf of all of us who serve, including myself. From what I have heard, your nephew was a fine man and he will be sorely missed." Noah looked my way, "Again, I am so sorry for your loss."

Everyone at the table stood as the three airmen did. Noah reached for his hat and noticed the paper. He picked it up with his hat and no one seemed the wiser. Aunt Dot, Uncle Jim and I walked them out and within a few minutes I was left standing there with them watching Noah, Rosier and Wilson drive away. As the government issued Chevy Nova that they were driving faded in the distance, I wondered if I would ever see Noah Walden again.

To me, lunch together at Briar Creek Baptist Church after the funeral, was our first date, but to Noah that didn't count. To him, the official first date was the one he asked me on that took place six months and one week later. He had been a wonderful distraction from the reality that was my life that day.

I had been lost in my thoughts until Judy poked me. "Time to turn over."

I rolled over on my back and closed my eyes again. I always liked Judy best of all of my friends. She was an only child and appreciated quiet. We could just sit together for hours and not say anything.

CHAPTER 2

I could feel the sun beating down on my chest, face and legs. I was fair skinned and if this were earlier in the summer I would have been burned already, but since I got that sunburn back in late May, this was just a matter of working on my tan. I wanted the perfect tan and to look my best that night for Noah.

Judy sang along to the Monkees' "Day Dream Believer" and I continued to daydream about Noah. I remembered every line of every letter he wrote to me during the six months that he was stationed at Camp Darby in Italy. I thought about that first letter and how it came three weeks after we had met at Andy's funeral.

I ran to the mailbox every day as soon as I got home on my lunch break from the feed and seed store in Stapleton. I snatched open the flap door on the mailbox and peered in hoping for a letter or a postcard or anything to let me know that Noah Walden thought of me at least once since I met him. Bills for my dad, sales papers, the Avon catalogue for my mother, correspondence from people still sending their condolences over Andy, things like that came day after day. I had almost given up on Noah. I began to think he had just been being kind to the country girl who had lost her brother. For all I knew, he got all of the girls' addresses at funerals. Then the letter arrived.

Thank goodness no one was passing along the road when I jumped up and down and danced a jig in the ditch as I walked back toward the house from the mailbox.

"ITALY!!!" I screamed and scared the horse in the pasture next to our house. The horse neighed and then took off running for the barn.

The letter arrived in a small envelope, three inches by five inches, and it was shipped from an APO address in Italy. I tore open the envelope as soon as I regained my composure from my dance and the scream. The letter inside was folded into eighths. I unfolded it and devoured every word starting with the date he wrote it.

26

Dear Abbigayle,

I hope this letter finds you well. I am so sorry it took me so long to write and I apologize if you had given up on me. To tell you the truth, if I were much of a writer you would have received a letter from me over a week ago. I have attempted to write every day since I arrived at camp, but I wasn't sure what to say.

I arrived at Camp Darby last week. I mentioned to you that I put in for this assignment a few months ago. This is my second deployment to this particular base. I was stationed here for a short term assignment last year and it was amazing. People ask me all the time why I joined the Air Force and aside of my family being a family of airmen; I am third generation Air Force, I wanted to see the world. Now, here I am in Italy again.

During my first trip over, I did not travel off of the base much. There really wasn't time due to my assignment and that's why I requested to be sent back. Of course now that I am here, I am rethinking it. Don't get me wrong, I love it here, but I miss my family. I came back so I could see the sights, but what fun is sight-seeing if there's no one to enjoy it with you? I suppose that's just my case of homesickness talking.

It was sunny here today. It was clear and I spent a fair portion of the day when I wasn't working looking north. I could see the Leaning Tower of Pisa. I didn't go last time I was here, but this time I am going. I don't care if I have to walk the six miles there. I will walk and when I do, I will send you pictures of the place. In fact, I will send you pictures of everywhere I go. I wonder if you would like it here? Do you like to travel? If I ask too many questions, please tell me.

I suppose I will wrap this letter up by telling you, I hate the circumstances under which we met, but I am glad I met you and I hope you will see fit to write me back. I will understand if you decide that you don't want to commit your time to writing to someone who is half a world away when you could be doing *meaningful activities with boys your own age and who live within driving distance. Please know that if I were not all the way over there, I would ask you out for this very weekend.*

If for some reason you decide not to respond to my letter, I hope you have a great life and may you never know pain like you felt with the loss of your brother. I wish you the best.

Yours truly,

Noah O. Walden

I read Noah's letter to the point that the paper tore apart at the folds and had to be taped back together. I squealed with delight each time I read it. My favorite part was when he mentioned that he wanted to ask me out on a date.

I had been conflicted about my feelings and how easily I became distracted the day of Andy's funeral. I felt guilty that I had lost focus of mourning my brother that day, but at the same time, being asked out by Noah had been the stuff my dreams had been made of since I met him. I had heard of people getting dates at weddings before, but I was the horrible girl that wished she had come away from her own brother's funeral with a date.

Of course, I discussed the letter and everything with Judy. Judy was so much wiser in the ways of the world than I was. I had never even been on a date before.

"You do not want to appear desperate so don't write back straight away," she said. "And, as for guilt, after how Andy's life was cut so short, how can you have room in your life for guilt? Have you learned nothing? You must seize the day. Would Andy want you to miss any opportunity because you were mourning him?"

Although Judy's advice was a complete contradiction, "don't write to him right away, but seize the day?" Luckily, I understood what she was trying to tell me. I didn't want to be disrespectful to Andy's memory, but I knew my brother well enough to know that he would not want me to stop living just because he did.

I managed to wait a whole three days. I probably should have waited longer, but that was a stretch for me. I figured the quicker I responded to him the quicker he would write to me again. I wanted another letter from him so badly. Beyond that, I wished he was back at Robins Air Force Base. I had asked my father after the funeral how far the color guard guys had to drive back and he said their base was about two hours away. Two hours was sure better than the distance to Italy.

Noah's letter had been so thoughtful, wishing me a great life even if I chose not to write back to him. He was so sweet. I wasn't sure what to say back to him so I first focused on addressing the question he posed, "Do you like to travel?"

August 8, 1975

Dear Noah,

Thank you so much for your letter. I hope you are enjoying your time at Camp Darby and that you make it to the Leaning Tower of Pisa. You asked if I like to travel and the answer is yes. In fact, I envy you being in Italy and I appreciate your offer to send photos from your travels.

There are a million places in the world that I would like to see, but my mother has never been keen on leaving home. She seems to think that everything we will ever need is located within a ten mile radius of our house. We take vacations every year, but we go to the camping club that my parents are members of on Clark Hill. I love it there, but I would love to see the beach at Panama City and the Gulf of Mexico, the White House, the Pacific Ocean and the Vatican.

I envy you. You could go to the Vatican. I'm not Catholic, but I love art and the photos I have seen of Vatican City amaze me. One day, I am going to go there. Maybe I will go after I graduate from veterinary school.

I don't mean to sound like such a simpleton when it comes to traveling, but I guess I am. The farthest away from home I have been is Savannah, Tybee Island to be exact. Andy insisted that I see the ocean and he took me last year. He woke me up at three in the morning and we made it to the beach in time to see the sunrise over the Atlantic. He treated me to dinner at Williams' Seafood. I had never had swordfish before. It was amazing.

I don't want to unload my troubles on you, but I miss my brother. I miss him so very badly. He was so much older than I was and he wasn't around that much, but when he was, he was the best. My parents were in their thirties when I came along and sometimes they came across more like grandparents to me so Andy filled in the gaps as they got older and more complacent. My dad loves cars, but it was Andy that taught me to drive. He taught me to hit a baseball and shoot a gun, too.

There's not a day that goes by that I don't think about him and everything reminds me of him. For a moment last week, I forgot that he was gone. It was Thursday and that was the day that Andy usually drove out and cut the grass for Daddy. Can you imagine; he had just started his first job as a doctor at a hospital, yet he still made time to come out once a week and cut the yard? The windows were up in the house and there was a little breeze. No sooner did I hear the tractor fire up, I smelled the fresh cut grass floating through the house. The smell hit me and I went running outside to see him and there was Daddy up on the tractor. My heart broke all over again as I remembered.

I know my parents are grieving and I don't want to talk to them about this. I don't want to burden them or make things about me. I know there's no greater loss than the loss of a child.

Anyway, I don't mean to unload all of this on you. I should probably get a diary for this sort of stuff. Sorry. If you should choose to write to me again, I promise I will not be such a downer.

I sincerely hope this letter finds you well and safe so far away from home. Also, just curious, what does the O. stand for in your name?

Sincerely,

Abbigayle J. Anderson

As I put the letter in the mail to Noah, I prayed he would write to me again. I imagined all the stories he would have to tell about being stationed in Italy. I knew he was there for work, but he said he was going to see the sights and I could not wait to hear all about them. I was sure he would have a ton to tell me about, but I worried what I would tell him in my replies. Most of the time, my life was boring. Each day was like the day before; I got up and I went to work at the feed and seed store and then I came home. I was off on Wednesdays and those broke the monotony only enough for me to clean the house for Mama and then go visit Judy.

As it turned out, I had worried about keeping up my end of the letter writing for nothing. Saturday morning arrived and life suddenly became a little more interesting.

Mama was making a trip to the church to replace flowers on Andy's grave so I asked if I could tag along. We took Daddy's truck, the Chevy C-10, so we could pick up feed for the horses on the way back. Mama told me not to tell him and she would let me drive it. She didn't have to worry about me telling. Everybody knew everybody and any number of them that we saw along the way would happily report back, but I did not remind her of that.

Another reason Mama didn't have to worry about me telling is because I loved cars as much as my father. I loved them more than most anyone else around. Daddy was sort of a collector. He bought cars and fixed them up as a hobby. He sold some to make a little extra money, but every now and then he would do such a good job fixing one up that he would keep it. Rarely did Daddy buy a new truck, but this blue C-10 caught his eye over at Wrens Chevrolet back in 1968. It was pretty and it might not have matched Mama's Dart, but it looked real good sitting up next to the old Ford Thunderbird that he had restored. It was probably going to look real nice with the '57 Chevy Bel Air that he was fixing up right now. Daddy took excellent care of everything that belonged to him, but nothing more so than his automobiles. This truck looked as good today as it did the day it rolled off of the showroom floor.

The church was about four miles from our house on Gene Howard Road out toward the Thomson Highway. The clutch was a little stiff on the truck and I struggled to get it going when I made the left turn at the four-way stop. The truck jerked a little and I thought it was going to shut off on me. With the jerking and the slickness of white leather seats, Mama was nearly thrown into the floorboard. Daddy shined those seats as if they were a pair of patent leather shoes.

"Have you heard from that boy you met at Andy's funeral?" I wasn't sure if she had noticed me at the funeral at all that day and when she spoke, I thought Mama was going to say something about my driving skills. I was caught a little off guard.

"He has written to me twice," I replied as I shifted from second to third and we picked up a little speed.

"You know your father wants you focused on your studies and would not be happy with you dating," Mama cautioned.

Daddy's opinion was that there would be plenty of time for dating after I finished school. It was unclear if his opinion only extended to high school or did he mean for me not to date until I was finished with college as well? Daddy was usually a fair and reasonable man, but this was one subject he did not budge on.

The one consolation is that Daddy had been the same way about his rules with my brother. Andy had plenty of offers, but as far as anyone knew he did not date until he was in the service. And, boy, did he date when he was in medical school. Perhaps if Daddy had kept with his rules as long as Andy was in any school then I wouldn't have Rhonda, or whatever her name is this week, as a relation. The thought of her provided what I thought was a great response to my mother's warning.

"Well, Daddy doesn't have to worry about me dating Noah since he's currently stationed in Italy for six months. Not to mention, if Daddy had stuck with his guns on Andy not dating as long as he was in school perhaps some white-trash wouldn't have gotten her claws in him. I wonder what she's up to these days. Have you even heard from her since the funeral? Who's watching baby Millie?"

"Abbigayle Jane Anderson, you need to watch that smart mouth of yours." Mama cut her eyes at me and I knew she was not impressed with my answer.

I did need to watch myself. At the very least she would make me pull over and she wouldn't let me drive anymore. At the most she was liable to reach over and pop me in my mouth. On the other hand, it had been over a month since the funeral and I wondered if Mama had had any word on the baby other than what gossip might be going around.

I took a different tone when I asked the question again. "Have you heard from her?"

We were just about to the turn for the church when my mother turned her head so I would not see tears in her eyes. She looked out the window. I didn't need to see her face, I could hear it in her voice when she replied. She had not heard from Rhonda since the funeral.

I should have put on the blinker for the turn, but instead I kept going and passed right by the turn for the church.

"What are you doing?" Mama asked as she dabbed her eyes and looked back to see the road to the church was now behind us.

"We're going to find out how my niece is doing?"

"What?!! We can't just show up over there unannounced."

I looked over at her like she had three heads. "You think that girl is going to judge us on our manners?"

Mama shook her head, but didn't say a word. I was surprised she didn't insist that I turn around right then, but she didn't and I drove on.

First I drove us over to the house where Andy and Rhonda had been living. I took the back roads, six miles of which were on a dirt road and I was going to have to wash the truck that afternoon or Daddy was going to have my head. Washing the truck was a small price to pay for Daddy not being mad and Mama not having to see the intersection where Andy got killed again.

33

Rhonda's red Nova wasn't in the yard or under the car shed that sat off to the side of the house. We pulled up in the driveway. I didn't have to get out of the truck to tell the house was empty. I guess mother just couldn't believe it.

"Stop," she ordered me. I had barely rolled to a stop and was putting it in reverse to leave.

"Why?" I asked.

"I'm going to the door."

I asked again, "Why?" The place was obviously empty. There were no curtains in the windows and the chairs that Andy had put on the front porch of the little green house were gone. Everything was gone.

Mama didn't say anything else. She just looked at me and I stopped the truck. She shook the truck when she slammed the door behind her. She stomped through the yard and up the steps to the porch and right to the front door. I thought she was going to knock, but there would have been no need for that. She just stood there for a moment, shook her head in what appeared to be disbelief, and then she went over and peered into the windows.

On her way back to the truck, I was scared Mama's feelings were hurt, but that wasn't the case. Jane Anderson, my mother, was a woman who rarely said a cross word about anyone, but when she snatched open the truck door and got in she had some choice words to say about her former daughter-in-law.

"Do you know the way to Rhonda's parents' house?" Mama gritted her teeth and asked in a huff.

"Yes, ma'am." I put the truck in reverse and turned it around. Back out on the dirt road we went.

"Gayle, you can make this thing go faster."

My eyes went wide. I gave it the gas and shifted through all of the gears in record time. Usually when I drove with her she continually insisted that I slow down and she used the invisible brakes on her side of the vehicle time and again. After riding with me I often thought she would jump out of the car and kiss the ground when we made it back home safely.

"How could she do this?" Mama rang her hands. "What did she do with everything?"

"Mama, what do you mean?" She was scaring me. I could tell she was both hurt and mad.

"I want to know what she did with Andy's things? Where is his diploma from high school, college and medical school? Where are his football trophies? What did she do with his Air Force Uniform? She practically killed him and now she didn't even bother to tell us she was moving and cleaning out the house. He bought that house."

"Are you sure you want to go over there like this?"

"Like this? Yes, because the alternative is that we go home and I get my gun. Andy's not around anymore so I don't have to kill her with kindness anymore."

"What happened to not showing up unannounced or uninvited?"

"Gayle, just drive the damn truck!"

The rest of the ride to the home of Mr. and Mrs. Thigpen, Rhonda's parents, was in silence. There was a bit of a straight away that led up to their house and from a quarter mile we could see that Rhonda's car was not in the driveway. I didn't say anything and pulled the truck into the driveway.

I barely had it stopped when Mama jumped out and headed to the door. There was a big old crafty sign by the front door that said, "Back door guests are best!"

Mama took one look at that sign and then started around the trailer to find the back door. She looked over her shoulder at me as she went. "They'll probably want to take that sign down after we leave."

If I wasn't worried before, I was then. I wanted to tell Rhonda off since I found out that she trapped my brother into marrying her. Heck, I had wanted to kill her with my bare hands the day of his funeral.

When Andy first met the girl that he introduced to us as "Natalie," he had a girlfriend. Then along came "Natalie." The look on all of our faces was priceless when he showed up with Natalie for Sunday lunch instead of Linda Carpenter, the real nice girl from Louisville that he had been dating for over a year.

We had not been long arrived home from church when Andy pulled up that Sunday afternoon. Not only were we shocked that Linda was not with him, Mama and Daddy were mortified over Natalie's attire. We were all in our Sunday best; Daddy still in his suit from church, Mama in a floral dress and her best cooking apron and I had changed into button up blouse and some dungarees. Andy was dressed like someone who had been raised to show some modesty as well. Natalie, on the other hand, had put all of her goodies out on display. Daddy said she looked like a "pin-up girl". She was wearing a shirt so tight and so low cut that each of us, not just the men folk, was distracted. I could not even look at her when I asked her to pass the fried chicken.

Natalie really got Andy's attention and poof within a month of meeting her he knew what "real love was" and then poof! She was pregnant. Four months after meeting her we were all ushered down to the biggest church in Augusta and with all of fifteen other people, mostly our family, we witnessed Andy marry what I knew was the biggest tramp I had ever seen. I think Daddy tried to talk him out of it, but we all know how that worked out. Andy didn't come around for a while. It wasn't until she gave birth and we saw her wrist band in the hospital that we knew her real name. Andy didn't even know her real name until then either. From then on we called her Rhonda and she never failed to try to correct us.

Mama found the back door of the Thigpen's and knocked urgently. We could hear baby Millie screaming while we waited. The cries came louder as we heard footsteps from inside coming to the door. My mother just looked back at me and shook her head.

"Rhonda ain't here!" Mrs. Thigpen said before Mama even asked to see her.

Mrs. Thigpen had Millie on her hip and Millie's little face was beat red and she continued to scream. Millie had never spent all that much time with Mama and Daddy, but she held out her little arms for Mama to take her. Mama reached for her and Mrs. Thigpen did not put up any protest at all. She practically gave Millie to Mama then turned around and went back inside. The door of the trailer was still open so Mama went inside and I followed.

The stench of cigarette smoke and a cat's litter box slapped us in the face as soon as the back door closed behind us. It was about twenty degrees hotter inside the trailer than it was outside. Between the heat and the stink, I thought I was going to be sick.

"If you have any diapers, I will change her. She's soaking wet." My mother was becoming more disgusted by the minute and it was showing in her voice.

Mrs. Thigpen wandered over to an end table in the living room and picked up her cigarette case and lighter. She motioned to a box of diapers sitting against the wall on the other side of the room as she lit the cigarette and took a puff.

Mama looked at me and I got the diaper. I covered my mouth to try to breathe as I moved through the place. Right next to the box of diapers was the litter box. On the wall above the box was another one of those painted sayings. This one said, "Home is where the heart is." In this case, home was where the stink was.

It was awful in there and I felt so sorry for Millie. I had never seen her cry before and I had never seen any baby cry like she was crying when we showed up.

Mama pushed some newspapers to the other end of the couch so she could sit down and change Millie. All the while Mama tried to comfort Millie. "Nanny's here. It's okay, baby. It's okay."

Mama looked at Mrs. Thigpen in complete disgust, but Mrs. Thigpen still had her back to us and was focusing on her smokes.

"Where is this child's mother?" Mama tried to keep her tone in check as to not upset the baby further.

"Your guess is as good as mine," Mrs. Thigpen said dismissively. "She dropped this rug rat off with me a week ago and said she'd be back. She ain't come back yet."

Mama was fuming, but seized the opportunity. "You look like you could use a break. Why don't I take Millie with me until Rhonda comes back."

"I don't know…"

"Nonsense. I'm her grandmother too and I think it's only fair that I share some of the burden."

I raised my eyebrow to my mother and she shook her head at me, warning me not to say a word. All the while her two grandmothers talked, Millie continued to cry. She shoved her little fist in her mouth and sucked on it and cried some more.

"Well," Mrs. Thigpen started as she put out the cigarette in an ashtray that should have been emptied a month ago, "let me just get her things."

"Don't trouble yourself. Gayle and I were just on our way to Augusta to go shopping and thought we would stop by. I'll just treat our granddaughter here to her first shopping spree. You won't mind will you?" I understood what Mama meant. She meant she didn't want anything from that nasty place.

"I guess, if you don't mind," Mrs. Thigpen scratched her head at us taking Millie shopping. "She's a handful."

Mama patronized her just little more so that we could get out of there with Millie. "Oh, don't worry about at thing. I've got plenty of experience."

The truck doors were barely closed behind us when again my mother told me to, "Give it the gas Gayle, before she changes her mind."

She didn't have to tell me twice. I floored it and spun the tires in the dirt on the way out of the Thigpen driveway.

We didn't go straight to Augusta that day. Mama insisted that we go to Peggy's restaurant in Wrens. Peggy's was a popular spot for home cooked meals, meat and two vegetable type of place. Mama said it was the closest place that we could get vegetables that were already cooked. I wasn't real sure what she was up to since we had just had breakfast before we got on the road and it wasn't quite time for us to eat again.

When we got to the restaurant Mama held Millie and sent me through the cafeteria line. "Get a child's plate of turkey, mashed potatoes and green beans," she told me.

The one thing we had taken with us from Mrs. Thigpen's house was a bottle and that's only because Millie had it in her hand the whole time. It was empty as empty could be so Mama asked one of the waitresses to fill it with milk. The waitress arrived at the table with the milk about the time that I came back with the plate.

Poor little Millie sucked down the bottle like she hadn't had anything in days. Her crying was tapering off. Mama then started feeding her the mashed potatoes and Millie swallowed them down as fast as Mama could get them on to the spoon. Baby Millie smacked her gums after each mouthful and begged for more.

"The poor thing was starving," Mama observed as she fed Millie. Mama was furious at the thought of Millie not being fed properly.

After about five spoonfuls of mashed potatoes, Mama started mixing in the turkey with it. Millie didn't even seem to notice the difference as she gobbled it down and still begged for Mama to keep feeding her. Mama continued on with the turkey and mashed potato mixture until it was about half gone. Mama chopped up the green beans and then switched to them. Millie noticed and she was not a fan of the green beans. She spit them out. Mama tried the green beans again before giving up and sending me back to the line for carrots. The carrots were almost as big of a hit as the mashed potatoes and turkey.

The whole time Mama was feeding Millie the servers and town's people who were in the restaurant stopped by our table.

"This must be your granddaughter," one after another said and Mama politely introduced them.

Mama held her head high, but I know she was embarrassed. She would have died before she would have let Andy or I out looking like Millie did. Her clothes looked like third generation hand-me-downs. Not that there was anything wrong with hand-me-downs, I wore plenty of them. The difference with my hand-me-downs and what my poor niece had on was mine did not look like they had been thrown away as hers did. She was dressed in little more than rags and she smelled like stale cigarette smoke.

Mama used to scold Andy and me if we put on something that she felt was unsuitable, "I won't have you leaving my house looking like no one cares about you."

My heart broke for Millie. Seeing Millie I understood what Mama was saying about looking like no one cared about you. My heart broke for my brother because he loved his little girl so much and now here she was looking like no one in the world cared for her.

After we finished feeding Millie, Mama did exactly as I knew she would. She marched us right down the street to Anderson's department store where she bought almost every outfit they had in size nine months. After Anderson's, we went to Bill's Dollar store and Mama purchased every baby essential they had.

We finally made it back home that afternoon around 3:00 p.m. I pulled the truck over to the side of the car port and parked it. Daddy came running out as we were getting out of the truck. He was sick with worry since we were only supposed to have been gone about an hour and instead we were gone for about five hours.

"Gayle, take Millie inside and give her a bath. You can do that in the kitchen sink." Mama handed Millie to me along with all of the shopping bags. "I've got to have a few words with your father, but I'll be there in a few minutes."

As soon as the screen door closed behind me, Mama started telling Daddy the condition Millie was in when we found her. He was

40

fit to be tied. My Daddy wasn't one to use profanity, but I heard a word or two from his mouth and I was all the way inside with the door shut. If they were trying to spare Millie and me hearing their conversation they failed at that. I heard everything as I got everything together for Millie's bath. Perhaps they forgot that it was summer and all of the windows were up in the house.

Mama was hurt and mad about finding Rhonda, or Natalie or whatever she was now calling herself, had up and abandoned Andy's house and Millie, but Daddy was just plain furious. None of us had liked her, but Mama tried to get along with her as long as Andy was alive. Daddy only tried the first day and then he was done.

Rhonda had a way of turning up her nose at people she thought were poor and her nose was so far in the air that she couldn't be bothered to fake a smile for Daddy. The entire time he tried to talk to her, she looked at him as if she smelled something sour. Little did she know my daddy owned half the land in the town and could buy and sell her ten times over any day of the week. After all, who did she think paid for Andy's schooling? It wasn't Andy. It was Daddy and the Air Force. Luckily the nearest neighbors were about a tenth of a mile down the road, because Daddy called Rhonda every name in the book that evening.

***

"Gayle? Gayle? Hello?" Judy poked me. "It's time to rotate. You don't want an uneven tan or to burn on one side."

"Right, sorry." I rolled over.

The radio had stopped playing music and the news was on.

"Do you think Governor Carter stands a chance against all those other guys?" Judy asked in conjunction to what the D.J. was reporting on the radio.

"I don't know. My Daddy sure hopes he doesn't." I reached for the radio to try to see if I could get another station to come in.

"Really? Why's that?" Judy was truly confused looking. "I think it would be awesome to have someone like us in the White House."

41

"Daddy doesn't think he's like us."

"Do you listen to everything your daddy says? Never mind, I know the answer."

"That's not true. He just knows more about politics than I do."

"You really should start thinking for yourself. You know you get to vote next year. If you don't, then your dad might as well just vote twice and save you the trip to the poll."

The voting poll was in the gym at our high school so it wasn't much of a trip to make considering I would still be in school when my first chance to vote came. It would only be a matter of me walking from the main building where classes were across the breezeway, but maybe she was right. Maybe I needed to start becoming more informed on my own and not relying on my dad to provide me an opinion.

CHAPTER 3

My next letter arrived from Noah about a week after Millie came to live with us. I could not wait to tell him all about her.

The day his letter came was one of those strange days when we actually got rain in the summer, but that did not deter me. As usual, I rushed to the mailbox as soon as I got home for lunch. It was pouring cats and dogs as I snatched open the box and pulled out the mail. I recognized the envelope immediately. He always used the same kind, white envelope with red, white and blue stripes all around the edges. Today, it wasn't just raining. Lightening was popping all around so I tucked the mail under my arm and ran back to the house even faster than I had run to the mailbox.

Once back inside, I tore open the top of the envelope anxious to find out what he had to say. When the letter slid out so did something extra which fell to the floor. I bent over to pick it up. From the back it looked like a little white card, but once turned over I found that Noah had sent me a picture of himself.

I screamed with delight and jumped around the living room looking at it. Thank the Lord Mama and Daddy weren't home. They would have thought I lost my mind.

In the photograph, Noah was wearing his dress uniform and he looked exactly as I remembered him, but with the hat on. His eyes were so blue and lips so red. His skin was pale and, my goodness, he could have played Dracula in a movie. He was so handsome. I looked at the picture the entire time I made my lunch and ate it. I nearly forgot to read the letter for looking at his picture.

August 15, 1975

Dear Abbigayle,

Thank you so much for your letter. It arrived just in time for my birthday. In case you were wondering, my birthday is

August 10, 1955. I turned 22 this year. And, to answer your question, my full name is Noah Oliver Walden. Of course now I am curious about your middle name. What does the J. stand for? Also, I noticed on the note where you wrote your address that your name is Abbigayle. That's an unusual spelling and I wondered; is there a story behind why it is spelled like that?

I have not made it to the Leaning Tower yet so I have not been able to take any pictures yet, but I am enclosing a picture of myself and I hope that will do for now. I will do my best to make it off of the base and take some pictures to send to you by the next time I write.

I am struggling for things to write about so I thought I would tell you all of the things about me that I would like to know about you.

First of all, I was born on August 10, 1955. You already know my parents' names and that I have two brothers. Nicholas is my oldest brother and Nathaniel, we call him Nate, is between me and Nick. I am the youngest. There's three years between each of us.

We have all been in the Air Force, but I am the only one that has been stationed abroad. I am also the only one that's still enlisted.

Nicholas is married and his wife is named Hannah. They met while Nick was in the service. He is the fool that dated the Captain's daughter. Lucky for him it worked out.

Nick and Hannah live just down the road from my parents, but still on the farm. They have a son named after her brother that was killed in Vietnam, Sammy. He's five and a real spit-fire. He's the light of all of our lives.

Nate isn't married and he would give me a run for my money when it comes to you. He'd try anyway. Mom and Dad are worried that he's going to be a bachelor for life even though it would take him little or no effort to find a wife. He looks like my mother's side of the family and Nick and I look like Dad. He's by far the best looking of the three of us. We joke and say he's the mailman's kid.

Both Nick and Nate work with my dad on the farm. Nick is a good farmer. He can tell you anything you want to know about planting and he's been working on tractors ever since he was old enough to hold a wrench.

Nate is more business minded and mathematically inclined, so not only is he the best looking, he's always gotten the best grades of the three of us. Not only does Nate work on the farm full-time, but as soon as he left the service he enrolled in Augusta College and he's supposed to finish up a degree in accounting this year. He's talking about getting his Master's and Mom and Dad are extremely proud of him. They are proud of me and Nick too, but Nate's, well, Nate.

There's a bit of animosity between Nick and Nate because Nate's a natural to replace Dad when he retires. He can take the farm into the future and not just keep it from struggling, but if there's anyone who could figure out how to make a profit, Nate could. He has business sense and Nick's just a farmer.

Nick and Hannah seem to think that Nick should be in charge because he's the oldest. Hannah hasn't said anything outright, but she comes across like she is trying to protect Sammy's inheritance. That's just a feeling I get. I like her, but I don't like that aspect of her. I could be wrong.

Personality wise, Nick and I are the most alike, but if I got a vote, Nate would be the one in charge. In case you are wondering, I have no desire to be a farmer. I wish them the best of luck, but farming isn't for me. They can have it, all of it. Until I met you, I didn't care if I ever saw that part of the country again. As far as I was concerned my family could come visit me where ever I was stationed.

"Oh my God!" I coughed. I nearly choked on my PB and J sandwich when I read the part where he said he didn't want to come back home until he met me. Those words would stay with me for the foreseeable future.

"Oh my God! Oh my God! Oh my God!" I gasped three more times before I threw the rest of the sandwich in the trash and picked up right where I left off.

I guess I should tell you, the farm produces peanuts, cotton and there's also a grove of pecan trees. Cotton is our biggest producer. Every now and then we rotate the crops and plant corn as the weather permits. Daddy also plants a ten acre garden of vegetables for Mama to can and freeze.

There's five hundred acres, a barn dedicated to harvest each item and there's a barn for the equipment. It's located between Blythe and Keysville. It is bordered by the main road on one side and there's a dirt road that cuts through a third of it.

The house Nick and Hannah live in was my grandparent's house. We call it "The White House" only because it's big and white and my grandmother always wanted to see the White House. The house was just a brown, wood house for years until granddaddy painted it white one day and told her, "Now you have seen the white house."

You can see the white house from the main road and the small house that sits next to it. The small house to the left is the one I grew up in. It's a little Jim Walter house that Mom and Dad had built when they first got married and was the first Jim Walter home around. We moved out of that house when I was in the eighth grade. Nick lives there now.

I found your last letter amusing when you said that your mother thinks that all you could need is within a ten mile radius. I think of my parents the same way except their radius is smaller. Everything they need is on the farm with the exception of what they can order from the Sears Roebuck catalogue. I swear if they could order meat from it and not have to trade with Mr. Lindley down the road they would.

Please don't mistake me. I love my family dearly, I just want more from life than living on the same piece of land where I was born and raised. I know it is strange that I mentioned in my last letter that I get homesick, but here I am writing about wanting to get away from home. You must forgive me if I sound like a contradiction.

Enough about me, there's so much I want to know about you. Right now, the main thing I know about you is that you are

46

the most beautiful girl I have ever seen. No one else compares and I could never get the words out in person, but just in case I never see you again, I wanted you to know. I know times are hard on you lately with the loss of your brother, but if you are ever feeling lonely I hope you will look at my photo and know that I am thinking of you fondly and would give most anything just to sit next to you on a set of church steps again.

I hope I am not being too terribly forward when I tell you that I look forward to your letters and I have never been one for writing, but I enjoy writing to you. I hope you will write again and although I would love to know all about you, please feel free to write about anything you like.

It is getting late here so I am going to sign off. As always, I hope this letter finds you well.

Yours truly,

Noah Oliver Walden

Thank the Lord I had the good sense to stop eating and throw the rest of the sandwich away or I would have surely choked to death when I read the part in the letter where he told me I was the most beautiful girl. My mother would have arrived home from work to find me dead, keeled over at the kitchen table.

I cherished every word. I folded the letter and put it in the pocket of my jeans and carried it back to work with me. Every chance I got, I snuck behind the shelves at the far end of the stockroom at the feed and seed store and re-read it. I also snuck peeks at his picture every chance I got. That night, after reading it for the hundredth time, I put the letter under my pillow and right before I cut my bedside lamp off, I kissed his photo and put it under my pillow as well.

I dreamed of kissing Noah that night. His lips were soft and sweet. Waking up the next morning, realizing it was only a dream, was heart breaking. I barely knew him and I missed him to the point of being sick.

The next day was Wednesday, my day off. Daddy asked me if I wanted to ride to Augusta with him. Daddy had to go and pick up parts for the tractor and he offered to take me to lunch at Sunshine Bakery on Broad Street. He knew it was my favorite place for lunch in Augusta and normally I would have jumped at the chance to go, but I declined. I wanted to stay home and write back to Noah as quickly as possible. Daddy probably thought I was ill and in a way I was. I was heartsick! Falling for a boy that I had only met once and now was a world away.

It took me all day to compose the letter. How could I keep from telling him everything I was feeling? How could I heed Judy's warning about playing my cards close to my vest when I felt like this?

I tried all morning to write the perfect letter. A letter that was both honest yet not completely forthcoming. I had so many re-writes that I filled my bedroom trashcan with wadded up balls of paper evidencing my attempts. It seemed hopeless until I stopped trying. My final attempt was from my heart.

August 28, 1975

Dear Noah,

I don't know where to begin other than to tell you thank you for your photograph. It is exactly the way I remember you. Not to worry, I would much rather have photos of family and friends than places any day.

School starts back soon. I am so excited to start my senior year and to get it behind me. I know I sound like I am wishing my life away, but I have dreamed of being a vet all my life. I too grew up on a farm except we raise animals, grow timber and lease our land for kaolin mining. Maybe one day I will tell you how many acres we have, but, for now, I will just say, it's a lot.

Since my last letter my niece, Andy's daughter, Millie, has come to live with us. Every time I think I cannot despise my former sister-in-law more, I find out that I am wrong. I can indeed despise her more. I know that is not an attractive quality; confessing that I loathe someone, so I will explain.

It is pretty safe to say that no one is ever good enough for one's son or brother. This was especially true for the way we felt about Rhonda being a match for Andy. She openly bragged to us

48

that the only reason she went to college and got a nursing degree was so that she could work where doctors were and marry one. I haven't seen one, but according to Uncle Jim she looked like the centerfold from a men's magazine. Everything about her suggested she was cheap.

Regardless of all that, Andy chose her. And we had to live with it and we did our best. They were married within months of meeting. Of course, she was pregnant. As soon as they were married, they moved into a house that Andy bought just across the county line into Jefferson County. There's a dirt road that runs along the edge of Fort Gordon just across Briar Creek and the house was down that road. It was small and not at all what Rhonda had in mind. After all, it was only about five miles from where she was born and raised and her goal in life, beyond marrying a doctor, was to get far away from that place. They moved in before Millie was born and they fought about it all the time. Nothing was ever good enough for Rhonda.

I know I sound like I am gossiping, but I am leading up to something, so please bear with me. I also apologize if you feel as though I am using you as my diary. Looking back over this letter, I guess it sounds a little like it should have started, "Dear Diary," as opposed to "Dear (nice boy that says he would like to take me out on a date) Noah."

Anyway, from what my dad found out from one of the doctors that worked with Andy, there were rumors around the hospital that Rhonda was fooling around with one of the higher-ups in the hospital. We think that Andy found out and confronted her.

My brother never drank openly until he met her. The only thing she told my parents was that he was drinking and they fought. Andy got in his car and left. That was the night he got killed. She let him get in his car and drive off. He was really drunk according to the coroner's report. He was way too drunk to ever get behind the wheel of a car, but she let him and she has yet to show an ounce of remorse. I wonder would she have even cared if Millie had been in the car with him or would it have been two birds with one stone for her? She would have been free of the both of them then.

49

They fought and he got in his car and sped down the road. The road they lived off of dead-ended into highway one. There's a stop sign, but Andy never stopped. They said there were no marks to even suggest that he hit the brakes. There was a transfer truck headed toward Augusta and it never slowed up either. The driver survived and according to the police he was so shaken up that he could hardly speak. All they could get out of him is that he never saw Andy, never saw the car coming, just felt the impact.

There's not an hour that goes by that I don't miss Andy and there's not a day that goes by that I don't hate my former sister-in-law. Have you ever hated someone that much? I know it's wrong to hate. I know for the sake of my own soul that I should forgive her, but then I look at Millie and the fact that she is living with us now and there's been no word from Rhonda and I feel justified in my hate. Does this make me a terrible person? Sorry, there I went with the "Dear Diary" stuff again.

I would very much like for you to ask me on a date once you get back to the states and, I promise that between now and then, I will try to get past this. I will try to find more interesting subject matter to talk about. I'll do my best, but for now, you said you wanted to know everything about me and this is the biggest part of me right now. I hope this isn't being too forward, but thinking of you is the only thing that really takes my mind off of thinking about how Andy's life was wasted and blaming his wife for that.

I almost forgot. The reason my name is spelled Abbigayle, with the "y." My mother's maiden name is Gay. All of her friends were naming their children their maiden names so this is what she came up with; misspelling my name just so she could try to be like everyone else. There are three other girls in our town named Abbigail and I guess she never thought I might like to be like them or everyone else with this name. Different isn't always that good, sometimes, it's just different.

I should also apologize that I have not bothered to tell you sooner. Most people call me Gayle. They have since I was a child. In fact, the only person that called me by my whole name was Granny Anderson and I think she only did it to get at my mother. You are certainly welcome to continue to call me Abbigayle if you like. I just thought I would mention it.

As always, I hope you are having fun in Italy and that God brings you home safely.

Yours truly,

Abbigayle Jane Anderson

Before I sealed the envelope, I searched my mother's box of photos until I found the one in which I thought I looked my best. It was from Easter this year. I was standing on the steps of the church. It was so sunny that day and warm. My Easter dress was blue gingham, kind of like Dorothy's from the Wizard of Oz. The dress looked like a fitted, collared blouse with thick white belt and a flowing skirt. The hem of the dress hit near my shins. It was the most sophisticated article of clothing I had ever owned.

My hair was blowing a little in the breeze and the sunlight shining through it made it look a little more blonde than it typically appeared. I had on my mother's pearls, white, high-heeled sandals and a matching purse. I looked nothing like Judy Garland, but I felt like a movie star that day.

The look captured on my face was priceless. Daddy had been picking at me and I was cutting my eyes at him and smiling. You couldn't see him in the picture and I gave no explanation in my letter about the photo.

I closed my eyes and made a wish that Noah would like the photograph of me as much as I liked the one of him. I slipped it into the envelope and sealed it. I carried Millie with me as I went to the mailbox, stuck it in and flipped up the flag.

I skipped back to the house singing to Millie. I am sure that poor child thought I was crazy. I was excited about mailing my letter to Noah. I threw caution to the wind and ignored Judy's advice. I did not confess that I was falling in love with a boy that I had only met once, but I did tell him that I thought about him all the time. I'm sure she would have been disappointed in me.

51

"Gayle, time to flip." Judy stopped singing along with the radio long enough to announce. I hardly heard her so she gave me a nudge. "Are you asleep over there?"

"No." I didn't lie. I wasn't asleep. I was relishing the sunshine and the time just to lay there and daydream.

Judy and I both rolled over simultaneously. "I think we should untie our tops. Don't you think it would be a thrill not to have a tan line."

I gasped and turned my head toward her. "We can't do that! We are in the front yard! God only knows who would see!"

"I guess you have a point." Judy rolled her eyes.

"I do have a point. I am already risking my hide wearing this bikini of yours."

"You are about to leave for college. Surely you aren't still letting your mother tell you what to wear?"

"I surely am. You know the saying," I did my best to mock my mother's voice as I finished the sentence, "As long as you're under my roof, you'll do as I say, young lady."

"Right. I just cannot imagine my mother forbidding me to wear something."

"Your mother and my mother are a far cry from being anything alike!" This time I was the one rolling my eyes.

We were facing the road, but Judy crawled around on the quilt and turned so that her back was to the road. Judy untied the back of her bikini and laid her top to the side. I left the strings of mine right where they were. I looked away. I had never seen another girl topless before.

"What if someone sees?" I asked with my face still looking off at the magnolia trees to the far side of the yard.

52

"Sees what? My back?" She reached and set the timer again and I went back to my daydreaming.

I could not believe she did that. "People can see you from the side as they approach."

"If their eyes are that good, then I say they deserve to see."

I laid back on the quilt. I continued to try to not look at Judy.

This time when I returned to my daydreaming, I didn't dwell on my letters from Noah. My mind flashed back to the Tuesday after Labor Day 1975.

I started my senior year of high school that morning. It started like most other school days, especially those that marked the beginning of the school year. I awoke to the smell of bacon. My mother went out of her way to make me a full breakfast each year on my first day of school. She had been doing that ever since I started kindergarten and the menu was always the same: bacon, cheese and eggs, grits and biscuits.

After I polished off all of my favorite breakfast foods, I put on my favorite outfit from my new lot of school clothes. This was the first year girls were allowed to wear jeans to school and I seized the opportunity. I matched my jeans with a white collared blouse and a blue scarf tied around my neck for school colors.

I pin curled my hair the night before and pulled it back into two barrettes and away from my face. After finishing my hair, I went to the front porch and waited for Judy show up.

Judy pulled into our driveway at a quarter 'til eight. She was driving her new orange VW station wagon. She wanted a Bug, but her dad got a good deal on "The Pumpkin," that's what we called it.

Since we got our driver's licenses, on Tuesdays and Thursdays I rode to school with Judy. I was allowed to take Daddy's Dodge Dart on Mondays, Wednesdays and Fridays. The only reason I was allowed to drive the Dart was so that neither him nor Mama would have to come pick me up after work at the feed store. It was the color of chicken manure, but it was better than nothing.

It was funny, Judy's family was related to the folks that owned the Chevy car lot in town, but her parents were the only people I knew who bought foreign cars. Thank goodness Daddy had a meeting that morning with the big-wigs at the kaolin plant in Sandersville so he left well before we expected Judy to arrive. None of us wanted to experience another of his tirades about how he fought the Japs and the Germans and lost some of the best guys he ever knew and now everyone had just forgotten.

"I wouldn't spend a damn dime on anything that wasn't American made. Patriotism is just dead, I tell you." If it were up to Daddy we would go back to isolationism as a form of foreign policy. I had been hearing his opinion of trade policies long before Judy's new car came into the picture.

To some degree I understood where Daddy was coming from, but I really liked Pumpkin. It was fun to ride in with Judy even though she could not get the hand of the manual transmission. The way she grinded the gears always announced our pending arrival.

It was out of her way for Judy to pick me up and I tried to give her gas money, but she wouldn't hear of it. Judy didn't start school at Stapleton until ninth grade. Ordinarily she would have continued high school at Wrens, but she got expelled there. Her dad made a sizeable donation to Stapleton High to allow her to enroll with us. I was her first friend. I was actually assigned to be her buddy for the first week of school and we had been best friends ever since.

We were sitting at lunch the Friday of the first week I met her. I was dying to know so, over school issued pizza, I asked her, "Why did you get expelled from Wrens High?"

Judy pulled her purse open and showed me what was inside.

"There's a brick in there! You have a brick in your purse!" I gasped in a loud whisper.

"Shhhh!" She snatched the purse shut. "If everyone knows, it won't be as effective."

"Effective at what?" I didn't know why anyone would need to carry a brick in their purse. I had never seen the like in all my days.

Judy was a bit filled out for a ninth grader and she gestured to her chest as she answered, "I'm tired of the boys getting so handsie with me."

"What? Is that how..." I covered my mouth with my hands.

"Yep. I told that big ol' Lewis boy to keep his hands to himself. I even tried to tell the ladies in the school office, but their opinion was 'boys 'll be boys' so I took care of him myself."

"What did you do?" I shrieked through my fingers which were still covering my mouth.

"I knocked him out with this here brick!" She flipped her hair as she answered. She was proud of herself.

"No you didn't!"

"I did and I'd do it again!" Judy snickered. "I think that's why they expelled me because they knew I would do it again. He probably won't do it again, but I would."

I knew in that moment she was either the bravest person I knew or the dumbest. Either way, I was certain I had found a friend for life. I also knew that as long as she was around, no one better ever mess with me.

When the release bell rang I walked the few blocks from the school to where my mother parked her car outside of The Stapleton Garment Company. There were a number of us who walked in the afternoons and it was like a parade for the old folks who lived along School Street and Main Street in Stapleton. They all made their way out to the rocking chairs and swings on their front porches to watch. Everyone knew everyone to the point that one day when I was out sick they noticed I was missing and called my mother that evening to check on me.

I was one of the last few to reach my destination which was the parking lot of the factory. The factory was at the corner of

Harvey and Main streets and the parking lot was on the opposite side from Harvey Street. On the days that I didn't drive, Mama drove the Dart. She always parked in the same spot, so I climbed up on the back of it and started my homework.

It seemed like I had hardly gotten comfortable and cracked my English book when the quitting time bell rang for Stapleton Garment Company. Mama was not one for diddling around or chatting it up with co-workers after work. She would be out in a matter of minutes and she would be ready to get home to start supper so I packed up my things and got in the car.

"How was your day?" Mama asked as she opened the driver's side door and handed her purse to me.

"It was great. Judy and I are in all but one class together," I replied as I sat her purse on the floorboard between my feet.

"Well, that's nice, but how about your teachers?" Mama put the key in the ignition and fired up the Dart.

"I don't know why you ask. You know all of them and you know how they are." I looked out the passenger's side window to make sure no cars were coming as we started out onto Main Street.

When I looked back at Mama she was smiling. She knew I was right there had been no real need for her to even ask. It's not like I was starting a new school or anything.

"So Debra..."

"You mean Mrs. Tenley?"

"Yes," Mama cut her eyes at me.

I knew what she was going to ask so I went ahead with the answer. "She's still the school gossip and I still know not to tell her anything that I would not want the entire world to know. You trained me about that years ago."

"That's my girl," Mama winked at me.

Debra Tenley was famous around the county for spreading any and everything she heard. Somehow she knew everyone's secrets, but they didn't stay secrets for long. There had been a number of marriages broken up and maybe even one murder on her word alone. She was known as "Telegraph Tenley" behind her back. I was allowed to be cordial and say "hello" to her, but that was it.

We pulled out onto Main Street and zig-zagged over to the McDonald's for our one and only stop on the way home. Mrs. McDonald took care of Millie while Mama was at work. I ran in to get her and then we headed on home.

When I returned to the car with Baby Millie I immediately reported to Mama all that Mrs. McDonald had to say about Millie's day.

"They said she tried pulling up on the coffee table today. I hate that I missed seeing her." I was excited about anything Millie did, but I was disappointed that I didn't get to witness it.

I pulled the car door shut as Mama was assuring me that Millie would probably try again tonight if we let her.

We continued to discuss Millie and her accomplishments all the way home.

"I wish Andy could see her." Millie never did anything without Mama making that statement. Every thought of Andy broke my mother's heart including those that involved Millie.

"I'm sure he's looking down from heaven on all of us." I always did my best to comfort her.

We didn't live too far off of Highway 296 on Gene Howard Road, so when Mama made the turn we could easily see what looked like every Sheriff's Department car in Jefferson County in our driveway. One of the cars still had the blue lights blaring.

"Sweet Jesus, what is going on?!!" I could hear the panic in Mama's voice as she gave the car the gas.

"I hope nothing's happened to Daddy!" I could not think of any other reason they would be at the house.

Mama was never one to drive recklessly, but she took the turn into the driveway on two wheels and slammed the brakes of the Dart. We slid to a stop just behind the last of the deputies' vehicles.

Mama jumped out of the car and ran to the house. I had not seen my mother run but once in my life and that was when she saw the rattle snake in the garden that time. I grabbed Millie and followed as quickly as I could.

I arrived in the house to find my mother being man-handled by one of the deputies, one from the far end of the county that did not know us, and my Daddy sitting on the living room couch in handcuffs. There was quite a commotion in the room.

"Be still, ma'am!" the deputy ordered Mama.

"Please, she didn't do anything," Daddy begged the deputy to let go of Mama.

I was not sure what happened with my mother in the few seconds before I walked in the house or what happened with Daddy before we arrived, but just as I demanded to know "What's the meaning of all of this?" I noticed Rhonda. "What are you doing here?"

All eyes turned to me and Millie started to cry over the commotion.

"That's my baby!" Rhonda started screaming repeatedly and she started for me.

I turned to shield Millie and the deputy got between us. One deputy was still holding on to Mama, one standing over Daddy and the one between me and Rhonda was a fellow that went to our church, Deputy Rowland. He was a big guy and Rhonda was fighting to get around him.

I started taking steps back toward the door. I meant to protect Millie from whatever it was that was going on in there.

"Ma'am, ma'am," the deputy tried to get Rhonda to calm down.

Everything was happening so fast. Rhonda was still screaming. "Let me have my daughter! They kidnapped my baby!"

I tried not to scream back since I had Millie in my arms and she was already hysterical enough for the both of us. It seemed like no one else was concerned with terrifying her, but me.

My tone was that of a growling lion, but I didn't raise my voice, "We didn't kidnap anyone! Your mother was all too eager to give her to us and that was three weeks ago!"

Deputy Rowland turned and looked at Rhonda. The deputy that had a hold of Mama immediately loosened his grip and Mama snatched away from him. All three deputies turned toward Rhonda.

"Mrs. Anderson..." Deputy Rowland addressed her.

Rhonda being called that was offensive to my ears. My nostrils flared and I cut him off. "My mother is Mrs. Anderson and my daddy's mother was Mrs. Anderson, but she's no Mrs. Anderson! She's just the poor white trash my brother got knocked up and married. She doesn't even take care of her own child. She left her baby with her mother over a month ago and she's just now finding out we had the baby and accusing us of kidnapping? How dare you! You are no Anderson at all!"

Rhonda grabbed her breath in a big huff as if I had insulted her. I meant to insult her and if I had that brick from Judy's pocketbook in mine, I would have done more than insult her.

"I didn't tell them they could take her!" Rhonda shouted.

Deputy Rowland cleared his throat as I was about to throw another jab Rhonda's way. "Mrs. Anderson," he started again, "Is it true you left the child with your mother approximately one month ago?"

Rhonda looked away, trying to come up with a reasonable sounding excuse. "Ummm..."

"She did!" I answered for her in a snap.

"Abbigayle," Daddy said in that tone that let me know I needed to just stop talking.

I was about to tell them all that she could get the first college degree in her family and the first store bought boobs in the county, but she'd never be anything but poor white trash. On Daddy's mention of my name I held my tongue.

Evidently Deputy Rowland was the senior officer since he asked the other two to take Mrs. Natalie Anderson outside and wait.

"You mean Rhonda Thigpen!" I could not help myself as I again turned Millie away so the mean look on my face wouldn't scare her. I had just bounced side to side enough and patted her bottom while speaking to get her to calm down a little.

"But I want my baby!" Rhonda protested.

Apparently my mother could not hold her tongue either. "You could have fooled me!" That was the first time I had ever seen my mother roll her eyes.

"Mrs. Anderson, we've heard your side of things already, now if you will step into the yard so we can get this sorted out, I would appreciate it." Deputy Rowland took a tone himself. I think he was beginning to smell the stink he had been served.

The two other deputies escorted Rhonda on to the porch. When the front door closed behind them, Deputy Rowland removed the cuffs from Daddy. "I'm so sorry about that Mr. Anderson. Martin there gets a little over eager. He's a bit on the Barney Fyfe side. Now, why don't you all tell me what's going on here?"

Daddy looked to Mama and she began, "We had not heard from Rhonda or Natalie or whatever she calls herself since our son's funeral so Gayle and I decided to go visit her and my granddaughter one Saturday morning."

Mama reached to take Millie from me as she continued to tell how we came to have Millie. "We drove to the house that Andy owned near where the accident happened. When we got there the whole place was empty and deserted. I didn't know what to think. I just could not imagine that she moved and didn't tell us."

Mama shook her head still in disbelief of what we found that morning. Daddy hung his head. He felt the same way.

Mama went on and the deputy listened and jotted down some things in a little notebook that he took out of his front breast pocket. "I knew where her parents lived so we drove over there."

I interrupted Mama, "Millie was barely dressed in rags and starving when we got there."

"Abbigayle." Daddy cut his eyes at me and again I went silent on his mention of my name.

Mama picked up where I left off. "Millie was starving and she looked as if she had been in the same little nightgown for a week. According to Mrs. Thigpen, her daughter had left the child with her two weeks prior and she hadn't heard from her since."

I spoke up again, "Mama offered to take Millie and for us to watch her for a while and Mrs. Thigpen sure didn't have to be asked twice."

"One more word Abbigayle Jane Anderson." He used my full name in his warning.

"Yes, sir," I hung my head.

Millie stirred in Mama's arms, but she continued. "Gayle's right. Mrs. Thigpen was all too eager to give Millie up and we have not heard from her once or her daughter. We've had our granddaughter for over three weeks and this is the first we are hearing from any of them. We were beginning to think she had been left for us to raise and we are more than fine with that. In fact, based on what we've seen from those people thus far, I would prefer it."

Daddy finally asked the questions that were burning in my mind and probably Mama's too. "Exactly how did y'all end up involved in this? I assume my daughter-in-law called you, but what'd she say? Did she really accuse us of kidnapping our grandchild?"

"We got a call about 1:30 p.m. this afternoon. It was Mrs. Anderson," Deputy Rowland looked to me to correct him as he called her that, but this time I didn't say anything and he carried on.

"She appeared genuinely concerned and panic-stricken about her daughter. She told us that y'all took the child. That's when I was dispatched to the home of her parents along with 'Fyfe'."

"It took little to nothing for her to convince him, batted her eyelashes and what not. Anyway, we headed over here with her to find out what was going on."

"And you had to put handcuffs on my Daddy to find that out?" That time Daddy didn't say a word over me speaking up.

"I apologize, that could have been handled a little differently." Deputy Rowland appeared embarrassed.

"I'd say," added Mama.

"Here's the thing," Deputy Rowland scratched his head. "I know this isn't ideal. I've seen that house her parents live in just this afternoon and I can imagine the child not being in the best of care over there, but y'all don't have any sort of custody arrangement with Mrs. Anderson so, legally, I have to have y'all turn the baby over to her."

Immediately tears filled my eyes and Mama screamed, "No!"

Daddy jumped up from where he was sitting on the couch and grabbed Mama as Deputy Rowland took Millie from her. I wiped my eyes, but it wasn't enough to keep the tears from streaming down my face. Poor Millie started screaming and reaching for me and Mama. That just compounded the heartbreak of the situation.

"I hate her! First she killed my brother and now who knows what she will do to my niece! And she just bats her lashes at your deputy and y'all come rushing over her to arrest my dad? What is wrong you people?" Everything I had wanted to say to her at the funeral before Noah stopped me was coming out then and more.

"You're not helping," Daddy whispered in my direction.

Mama and Daddy said goodbye to Millie, but I just couldn't. They tried to no avail to calm Millie down, but we could hear her wailing all the way to the car. There wasn't a dry eye in our house as they drove away with her.

"They didn't even let me give them Millie's things," Mama sobbed. "It's like losing Andy all over again."

Daddy just held Mama tighter. "I know. I know."

I felt so sorry for them. I felt even sorrier for Millie. I had never felt more useless in all my life. There was nothing I could do for any of them.

CHAPTER 4

Days passed and my parents and I were in a fog. My mother had never called in sick to work before that she wasn't really and truly sick, but she called in the three days following Millie being taken away. She stayed in bed and Daddy stayed in the fields.

I got up and went to school, but I could not repeat a thing any of my teachers had said the rest of that week. Everyone noticed the change in me. It showed in my face, my clothes, even in my hair. I forgot to brush my hair one day and that was not me at all. Judy and the rest of my friends tried to pull me out of it. My teachers and the men that I worked with at the feed and seed store were concerned about me.

Friday evening, I arrived home from work to find another car in our yard. It was a big navy blue Buick and it was blocking the carport. I didn't recognize the car. I went around and parked the Dart next to it so whoever it was could back out. I got out of the car and I drug myself inside as I did every day since they took Millie away.

The house had not been the same without her. I could see her sweet smile as she looked up from the playpen when I went to get her up in the mornings. I could hear her giggle as she rolled in the floor when I would tickle her. I could even hear her in the yard as I got out of my car. My mother had been trying to get her to say Gran, that's what mother wanted Millie to call her, and the day they drug her away she screamed for Mama. I had watched from the window as they loaded her in the Sheriff's Department car.

"Gran!!! Gran!!! Gran!!!" at the top of Millie's little lungs and right through the walls of our brick house her first words came. It sounded more like the word ran, but we all knew what she meant and who she wanted to save her.

To be honest, it nearly killed my parents when Andy died, not just my mother, but both of them, and Millie brought them back to life. Apparently, Rhonda Thigpen hadn't quite killed Daddy again. The car in the yard was that of Attorney Bell.

Attorney Bell was one of the few lawyers in the county and his office was in Wrens. Attorney Bell was a man of about forty, salt and pepper gray hair and about six foot four when he was standing. He came to Wrens just after he finished law school and took over his uncle's practice. Daddy had been one of his first clients. He oversaw all of the dealings with the leases and mineral rights to our land with the chalk mines. Over the years Daddy and Attorney Bell had become friends, but this was his first house call.

It wasn't land leases or mineral rights they were discussing when I found Attorney Bell seated with Mama and Daddy at the kitchen table that night. He was still dressed in his suit and seated in Daddy's spot at the head of the table. Mama was in her usual seat and Daddy was in mine. I could see them, but they didn't notice me in the doorway so I stood there and listened for a moment. They were discussing the possibility of the suing Rhonda for custody of Millie. Mama was the first to notice my presence.

"Gayle, would you mind stirring that?" Mama pointed to the pot that was simmering on the only eye of the stove that was still lit.

"Yes, ma'am." I turned and, as I swirled the spoon around in the black-eyed peas, I listened. I arrived in the middle of the conversation. I was so happy to see Mama up and about and Daddy not sweat stained from the garden that evening that I would have done absolutely anything they asked me to.

"I'm gonna just let y'all know: It's dang near impossible for a mother to lose custody of her child," Attorney Bell advised them. He put down his pen from where he had been making notes on what all Mama and Daddy had told him so far and shook his head.

"Are you saying you won't help us?"

"No, Mrs. Jane, I'm just saying it's an uphill battle. A steep uphill battle," he replied. "I think what we should do is start by seeking visitation. I'll write her a letter this week."

"We don't even know where she's living and I'm not afraid of an uphill battle. This is my granddaughter we are talking about and I don't care if I had to push a boulder up Bald Mountain in January, I'd do it and I am not worried about the expense." Daddy might have been a man of few words normally, but that night he really said what was on his mind. He was also not one to throw around money.

"Maybe that's where you should start?" Attorney Bell contemplated.

"What do you mean?" Mama asked.

I looked around curiously. I had a feeling I knew what he was suggesting and when he spoke, I found out I was right.

"The one thing y'all have always communicated about your daughter-in-law is that she was money hungry. Have you considered making her an offer?"

"What?!" Mama was offended.

Daddy piped up, "Are you suggesting I offer to buy my granddaughter from her mother?"

"Of course not. That's illegal. I am suggesting that you offer to help her with her expenses for a while and let y'all take care of the baby while she recovers from the death of her husband. You know, it can take a while to get over such things as you are aware." He all but winked at them and I almost snickered.

Mama held her head in her hands and Daddy shook his head. "The last thing I want to do is give that girl one red cent."

"But, you would do it for your granddaughter," Attorney Bell nodded his head up and down.

Daddy let out a breath of exasperation and I answered for him, "Yes, he would!" I wanted Millie back as badly as they did and I really would have done anything.

The three of them turned to look at me each more shocked than the other that I had been listening.

"You can use my college fund if it means that Millie is safe," I added and I meant it. The sight of her, when we picked her up that

Saturday morning from her other grandparents, was fresh in my mind all week. I hated to think of her like that.

"That won't be necessary, Gayle," Daddy replied and I turned back around to the stove. It was clear I had stuck my nose in where it didn't belong.

Daddy continued, his voice as about as stern as it had been with me. "Why don't we start with a letter asking for visitation? You can vaguely offer to help her with Millie's expenses. I don't mind providing food and clothing for my granddaughter, but I will not subsidize the lifestyle of that tramp."

"That's fine," Attorney Bell agreed. "Where should I send the letter?"

"Send it to her parents. I'm sure they will get it to her," Daddy instructed.

Mama called to me, "Gayle, bring me the address book from my purse."

"Yes, ma'am." I put down the spoon and left to find her purse.

I found Mama's purse and right next to it was the mail. There was a large envelope in the stack, and it was of the style that Noah usually used with the red, white and blue border. I slid it past the rest of the envelopes and had a look. It was addressed to me and the return addressee was Noah O. Walden. I had not expected another letter from him this soon. My last letter had not even had time to reach him yet. I became so distracted that I forgot my mission and was about to rip it open when Mama called my name.

"Coming!" I yelled back. I tucked the envelope under my arm, reached in her purse and dug out the address book and then I nearly ran back to the kitchen to give it to her.

I handed Mama the address book and already had my back to her before she could say "Thank you."

I was nearly to the kitchen door when Mama reminded me, "Gayle, stir the peas and would you mind starting the chicken? I floured it and it's in the bag in the refrigerator."

I turned back and just looked at her. She didn't notice. The honest to God's truth was that I did mind, but it wasn't a question for which she required an answer other than me starting the chicken. It was just Mama's polite way of telling me to get on with cooking dinner.

I sat the envelope on top of the refrigerator as I took out the chicken. The last thing I wanted was to get chicken grease on it. After reading Noah's letters to the point of their fragility, I stored them among the pages of my favorite book. Instead of opening To Kill A Mockingbird and finding pressed flowers, anyone opening the book would find his letters.

Not only did I fry the chicken, but I heated up the mashed potatoes and made the biscuits and a peach cobbler as well. The only thing Mama had managed before I got home was the black-eyed peas and cucumber salad.

Attorney Bell stayed for dinner and he was full of compliments. "Miss Gayle, I don't know how you knew, but peach cobbler is my favorite and I think this is one of the best I have ever put in my mouth."

I was probably speaking out of turn again, but I said it anyway, "If you get my niece back for me, I'll bake you one of these cobblers every week for the rest of your life or mine."

"You're a sweet girl. That's some of the best incentive I've been given in a long time. I would love nothing better than one of these cobblers every week, but I can't guarantee anything. I can tell you that I will do my utmost to work something out."

Working something out wasn't exactly what I had in mind, but it would do for now. I thanked him and began clearing the dishes while Mama and Daddy finished up with him. It was nearly 8:30 before Attorney Bell left.

I washed the dishes as quickly as I could and then realized I had forgotten where I put the envelope. I turned the kitchen upside down as discretely as possible. I did not want Mama and Daddy to help me look for it because along with their help came their questions. I just wanted to find my letter and go to my room to read it.

When they went outside to walk Attorney Bell to his car I turned over every pot and pan and dish in the kitchen. I even looked between the stove and the counter to make sure it hadn't fallen between them. I strained my eyes looking in the dark space between the crack beside the counter and underneath the stove itself only finding crumbs from twenty years-worth of dinners. I stood up and spun around, slapped myself on the forehead and it was like lightening hit. I saw the envelope barely hanging over the freezer door of the refrigerator.

I snatched that envelope down, threw off my apron and ran out of the kitchen and down the hallway. Two doors down and to the left I went. I threw myself backward on my bed, feet in the air and giggled with anticipation as I opened the envelope. Out of the envelope fell a whole stack of photos. All over the bed they went. I only barely glanced at them. I unfolded the letter and began to read.

Noah's letter came just when I needed it most, just when I needed something more than Attorney Bell's promise to "work something out". I needed something that genuinely gave me hope. I looked forward to Millie coming back to us, but each letter from Noah brought me closer to the day I would see him again. There was a light at the end of the tunnel that was his service in Italy, but there was no light at the end of the tunnel that was us without Millie.

August 27, 1975

Dear Abbigayle,

By the time you read this you will have noticed the photographs. You can see I finally made it to Pisa. It really is only six miles from Camp Darby. I cannot believe I have not been before.

69

A few of the guys and I went to Pisa the day after I mailed your last letter. I promised the fellas in the communications department that I would have someone back home send them a case of Chips Ahoy cookies if they would develop the photos for me double-time. As soon as I finish with this letter I will be writing to my mother to send her copies of the photos and ask her to fulfill my promise of Chips Ahoy cookies.

We went to the Leaning Tower of Pisa first. You will see there are photos of the exterior and looking out from the top. I climbed all the way to the top, 297 steps, according to the guide. It really is a bit of a challenge for fear of it actually tipping over. It only leans less than a six degree angle, but, yes, I admit it, I was a little scared.

There had not been a day since I arrived at Camp Darby that I did not spend a fair portion of my day looking north and admiring the tower. When I got to the top, I searched the horizon to see if I could see the camp. I leaned against the marble railing. I could not get over how smooth it was as I caught glimpse of the camp. I could barely make it out, but it was there. It wasn't quite the view looking south as it was looking north but it was still awe inspiring. There was a breeze in the air and like every place else in Italy, someone was cooking something with garlic. Every one of my senses was awake at the top of the tower.

Do you know the history of the Leaning Tower? I didn't until I went there. As I mentioned before, we had a guide and he told us all sorts of details. The Italian name for it is Torre Pendente di Pisa. There are four buildings in the cathedral complex in Pisa, the tower is one of the four.

The construction of the tower began in August 1173 and continued for 200 years. They noticed the leaning when they built the second level. Due to wars between the providence of Pisa and everywhere else, they stopped construction. When construction began again, I forgot how many years later he said, the soil had settled enough that they were able to continue. Also, when they started again, they built each level of the side that it was leaning toward taller to try to compensate for the degree of which it was leaning. Due to that side being taller, the tower isn't straight, but it

70

curves. I could not see the curve from looking at it. I'll just have to take their word for it.

Another interesting thing is that name of the original architect is a mystery. I find that just crazy, that they don't know who designed it. It's so amazing. How could they not know that? They have several names of who they suspect, but for one reason or another there's doubt about each one.

Anyhow, the whole complex is called Campo dei Miracoli or Piazza dei Miracoli. In English that means "Field of Miracles." I can't explain it, but there's a feeling that came over me while standing there looking at all of the buildings and I think that was the closest to God I have ever been. It is just a marvel that they built such things and they didn't have the modern tools that we have now. It really is nothing short of a miracle. I guess if I measure miracles by architecture, then the whole country is speckled with one miracle after another.

The other thing I thought was interesting is that on one side of the piazza is a burial ground with earth reputedly brought back during the Crusades from Golotha. Golotha is the hill where Jesus was crucified. The significance of this is that it allows Pisans to rest on holy ground. Can you imagine?

As for the tower, I think it looks like a giant wedding cake. It's made of white marble and has many arches. My mother loves to bake and decorate cakes. She would be in awe of it looking like a cake, too. I think it is so much more beautiful in person than in the pictures. I hope you and my mother get to see it in person one day. Not together, I mean, if you wanted to go together that would be fine. I should stop.

You will see that I sent more than just photos of the tower. I wanted you to get a feel for the whole place. You'll see there's so much more to Pisa than the tower, but all the world knows of the town is the tower and the fact that it leans. I guess without the tower, it would just be another forgotten town in Italy.

The guys in communications were not done with the photographs I took in Rome yet so I will send another letter and *enclose those. It should be about a week so keep checking your mailbox.*

I know by the time this letter finds you, school will have started back. I am curious, what is your favorite subject in school? In case you cannot tell, mine was history. I love history. I love knowing the why and how behind things.

Well, I should wrap this up and get to bed. Next time I will tell you about Camp Darby as it has just occurred to me that I have yet to tell you much about it. Congratulations on your senior year and I hope you are living every minute of it to the fullest.

Yours truly,

Noah O. Walden

About a fourth of the way through the letter, I shifted my position on the bed from flat on my back and grabbed the photo of Noah that had been on the night stand by my bed since the day it arrived in the mail. I returned to crisscross apple sauce seated position on my bed, kissed his photo and returned to reading. All the while I read, I glanced down at his picture and to the pictures that he sent me.

Of course I appreciated the effort he went to in sending the photographs of Pisa to me, but, to my disappointment, there wasn't a single photo that he was in. Picture after picture, I searched for him, but he wasn't there. I would have loved to have seen him, to have something of him beyond the stiff, posed, military yearbook-looking portrait that he had sent earlier. It would not have solved any of the issues of my week, but it would have been so nice, another image of him to fill my dreams.

The photos of Pisa were amazing. There were so many photos. There were also photos of native Italians, one was clearly the guide he spoke of and others were just people doing everyday things.

One of the photos he took from outside of the tower looked like he must have been lying on the ground to take it. It was a shot looking up through a patch of flowers. I loved that one, but my favorite was a picture that he took along what appeared to be along the river. I didn't know the name of the river that ran through Pisa, but it looked as if it ran all the way through the town like it ran through the middle of the photograph. The top half of the photograph showed the actual buildings and the bottom half was the mirror image in the river of the top. It was artistic in a way, like something out of National Geographic.

There was a picture of a door. It was a plain wooden door with what appeared to be an iron hinge and brace across the bottom and top. It wasn't much different from a door you might see on an old warehouse, but there was just something about it. Perhaps everything was better in Italy.

As I looked at each and every one of them, I let my mind run away with me. I imagined being there with him. There were things that were set in motion with Andy's death that were prompting me to grow up so much faster than I should have, but I still had the mind of a teenage girl and I could not help myself. I imagined these were photos of our honeymoon. What a dream that would be and so far from the reality that I was living, but the moments I lost myself to my dream were the best moments I had had all week.

I read the letter again and again and looked at the photos until nearly quarter 'til ten. It was a blessing in disguise that my parents had enough on their plates that night that they didn't bother with me. They didn't check on me when I didn't come out for our usual television time or that I didn't head for my bath at my usual time. There was only one bathroom in the house and I was usually the first to go, but that night I missed my spot and had to wait until after Daddy who typically went last. Lights out was at ten, per his strict orders and I was scarcely out of the bath in time. I couldn't recall the last time I was up past ten.

The whole time I was in the bath all I could think about was Noah. I bathed as quickly as possible, threw on my nightgown and jumped into bed all with the hopes of seeing more of him in my dreams. Despite lingering on reading his letters and looking at the pictures, I could not wait to go to sleep. Dreaming of him, as I knew I would, was sure to be the highlight of my day. As I looked at each and every one of them, I let my mind run away with me.

73

That night I did dream of Noah. It was interesting that I had my first kiss in a dream. We were at the top of the Leaning Tower of Pisa and the view in my dream was just that from his photos. The sun was shining and there were clouds floating by like bales of cotton in the sky. There was the scent of baking garlic bread floating up from a local restaurant. I was leaning on the railing and it was just as smooth to my touch as he had described it, white and slick and his hands were on mine.

Just moments before I had been looking at his camp in the distance from the top of the Leaning Tower of Pisa when I leaned back to him and whispered, "It's just like you said it was."

I smiled slightly as his left hand left mine and slid into my hair that hung around my neck. With just a touch he directed the tilt of my head and even in my dream I was caught off guard by the kiss. His lips were the combination of soft and firm and he tasted like mint chocolate chip ice cream.

I awoke with the feeling as if I had really been there. I could still feel him pressed against my back as firm as I could feel the mattress beneath me. Even though I was alone in my room I blushed at the thought of his lips still on mine.

I laid there in bed reliving my unreal moment. "Mint chocolate chip ice cream?" I asked out loud. "Where did that come from?"

Dreams can be so random. I had not had that flavor of ice cream in months and months. It wasn't something that they carried at the grocery store in Stapleton that you could buy by the scoop for a dime like you could chocolate or vanilla so that part of the dream was weird.

Daylight was creeping through the curtains and at the Anderson house there was never a day for sleeping in. There were always chores to be done; animals to be fed, toilets to be scrubbed and all sorts of other fun things that filled my Saturdays. Lounging in bed until 8:00 a.m. was unheard of no matter what day of the week it was. I couldn't believe neither of my parents had come in to wake me and set me about my usual tasks, but here I was catnapping to thoughts of Noah.

Finally the sun got to be too much. It amplified the light yellow paint on my walls and it was impossible to continue to drift in and out of sleep and that disappointed me. Beyond the walls, the bright spot was that there was no noise in the house at all. I began to suspect that Mama and Daddy might have gone somewhere. It was unlike them not to tell me they were leaving, but I didn't dwell on that.

Before I even rolled out of bed, I leaned over to my nightstand and pulled out my notebook paper and a pen. I started writing a letter responding to Noah's latest, a letter that turned out to be a very large thank you note.

September 11, 1975

Dear Noah,

Thank you so much for the present I received in the mail yesterday. I will not bore you with the details, but it was just what I needed after the week I have had. I will only sum up by saying that my niece has been reclaimed by her horrible mother and we have lost her. Now, enough of that.

I hope this letter finds you well and you will forward half of the contents of this package to your friends in the communications department. Please pass along my sincere gratitude for helping you show me the world. The other half of the contents of the package is yours to do with as you like. I hope you all are not disappointed that I am not forwarding Chips Ahoy, but homemade chocolate chip cookies instead. It's my grandmother's recipe and I hope you all enjoy them.

I apologize for making this letter short, but I need to finish the baking and get these to the Post Office before it closes at noon. I am crossing my fingers that these make it to you while they are still somewhat fresh.

Thank you again and I will write again soon to tell you just how much I love the photographs and the thought behind them.

With Love,

Abbigayle

I signed my name and jumped out of the bed. I didn't even bother to make it. I just ran to the kitchen stopping by the bathroom only long enough to grab a rubber band to tie back my hair. I tore open the cabinets and drug out all of the ingredients. I was in luck. We had every single item listed on the recipe and an abundance of it.

There was no sign of my parents and that was a good thing. I don't think either of them would have minded me making cookies for our troops, but explaining my every move was never something I liked to do.

Once in the kitchen I turned the dial on the oven to preheat it. Next I took out the biggest mixing bowl that my mother owned and the measuring cups. I memorized the recipe years ago so I started adding flour, brown sugar, plain sugar, baking soda, butter, eggs, a little salt, vanilla flavoring and chocolate chips. I doubled the recipe as I went and once everything was in the bowl I rolled up the sleeves to my night gown and dug in, mixing by hand.

I washed my hands, took out the cookie sheets and greased them with butter. I balled the cookies out and started the first pan in the oven. I set the egg timer so I could go and get dressed while the cookies baked and would not burn them.

I managed to throw on some clothes during that first batch. The next batch I brushed my teeth and applied a little makeup. The third batch I redid my ponytail.

Half way through the batter, I added chopped pecans. Now there would be chocolate chip cookies and chocolate chip pecan cookies. While the next batch baked, I amended my letter.

P.S. Half of the cookies have pecans and the other half does not. The pecans come from our grove. I believe I recall from one of your previous letters you said your family has a pecan grove as well. So, I know you own a grove of your own, but I'm not sure if you are a pecan connoisseur or if you even like pecans. If you do, you might notice that this year's batch from our grove is a little sweeter than your average pecan.

Anyway, hope you like the cookies; with or without pecans.

-Gayle

I finished packaging the cookies and boxed them up for shipping to Noah. I saved one pan of the cookies for my parents, wherever they were. I still had not found a note or anything saying where they were and I hated to leave home without telling them, but it was getting on toward 10:00 a.m. and I did not want to wait around just in case they did not come back by lunch time.

I started my cleaning chores while I waited. I cleaned the entire bathroom in the hour between when the last pan came out of the oven and the coo-coo clock went off again. Wherever my parents went, they didn't take the Dart so I did. I left a note and away I went to mail a box full of love to Noah.

When I returned, my parents were back.

"We didn't want to worry you, but your cousin Dixon went missing," Daddy explained over the ham sandwiches Mama put together for lunch.

"What?!" I covered my mouth at the horror.

"Oh, he's fine now." Mama chewed discretely, trying to salvage her manners as she spoke with her mouth full.

I looked at Daddy for further clarification.

"You've heard the stories about him sleep walking..." Daddy began.

Hastily, I added, "Right, last week Uncle Bud awoke to find Dixon making peanut butter and jelly sandwiches at 2:00 a.m. while completely asleep."

"Well, this time it was a bit more severe. They left the doors open to let the air circulate and cool the house as they have always done, but Bud or Ruth, one, forgot to latch the screen door. Sometime during the night, Dixon got out. Ruth went in to check on him around 4:00 and found him gone."

"Oh my word!"

"I can't believe you didn't hear the phone ring." Mama looked at me curiously.

The truth was I was sleeping and dreaming so hard that I wouldn't have heard a bomb go off if it had been under my bed. I almost giggled at my thought.

"You know your Aunt Ruth," Daddy shook his head.

"She called everyone in the tri-county area at 4:00 a.m.?" I asked.

Mama nodded up and down with a pursed smile.

Daddy went on, "Well, we didn't find him until around 9:00 this morning and you can imagine..."

"Everyone was absolutely beside themselves, I'm sure. He's such a little fella."

"Right, well they found him about a mile through the woods and across the creek. He was lost. It got a little cold during the night last night so luckily that old coon dog of Bud's followed him. Half the county turned out to help hunt for him and Barney Murphy found the coon dog cuddled up around Dixon and both of them were asleep against a tree. Mr. Murphy brought them both back home safe."

Mama looked over at me, "If I would have been your Aunt Ruth, that would have taken ten years off of my life." She just shook her head still in disbelief.

"I guess they'll make sure to lock their doors from now on." I passed the plate of my cookies to each of them.

CHAPTER 5

"Gayle," Judy nudged me. "It's time to wake up!" Judy gave me a little pinch. "I don't want you to burn!"

"What?" I struggled to come to. Apparently, I wasn't just day dreaming anymore. I had been really dreaming.

Judy was putting her bikini top back on and truckers were honking. That was a sure fire way to wake me up.

"Oh my God! They can see you!" Never did I take the Lord's name in vein so much as when I was with Judy.

"Let them look," she smirked. "There's going to come a day when no one wants to look."

"You are a bad influence!"

"I know. It's my job in life, to be a bad influence on you."

Once her top was back on, Judy and I started packing up the quilt. We needed to get inside and get my one piece back on before my mother arrived to pick me up. Awake or not, I could not stop thinking about the last year and how everything had gone with Noah, everything leading up to tonight.

I wandered inside following Judy. She carried the quilt and I carried the radio. It was operating on batteries and I didn't bother to cut it off for the trip across the yard. "Hooked on a Feeling" by Blue Suede was coming on. I sang along and Judy did the "Ouga Chuga" part as we danced our way to the house.

We kept on singing all the way into the house. I grabbed my suit and the top clothes I had worn over and headed to the guest bathroom. We only had one bathroom at our house, but Judy's big house had three. It was a modern marvel to me, especially the bathroom in her parents' room. It was huge, bigger than any bathroom at any of my relatives' houses. It was the size of my parents' whole bedroom. The tub was the size of the baby pool at the

Wrens Country Club and I only knew that because Judy's dad had a membership there and she took me there a few times every summer.

Her parents' bathroom was also the most colorful bathroom I had ever seen. It matched the bedspread in their bedroom perfectly. My mother's matched the walls in the bathroom too, but hers was a solid white Chenille spread and the walls were white, too. Both her mother's spread and the bathroom were all shades of pink, and Pepto Bismol pink was the dominate shade.

After escorting me back to her room to get my clothes, Judy followed me. She was on her way to the kitchen to find us something to snack on. As we walked back down the hall past her parents' room, I tilted my head with a nod toward the room. "I don't know how your father stands it. I'm sure mine never could."

"What do you mean?" Judy seemed confused.

"So much pink. It ain't exactly a man's color," I explained.

"Oh, my daddy would do anything for my mother. Decorating their bedroom pink is just the tip of that iceberg."

I stopped just inside the door to the bathroom that I was going to use. "Must be nice. I mean that, not in that snarky way that people say 'must be nice'. I mean it, it must be nice to have a man that would do absolutely anything for you."

"Awe, Gayle, you do have a man like that," Judy hugged me and I did not expect that at all. "Your daddy would do anything for your mama and Noah would do anything for you."

I held on tight to her. "How do you know?"

Judy leaned back to look at my face, "Because no man would write to a girl the way he has written to you all these months and done all of the other things he's done for you in the last year. What more proof do you need?"

"Nothing, I guess." I let go of her and backed away.

"I know you've had a hard time since Andy died, but you need to accept that good things can happen to you. You deserve good things."

"Yeah, but Andy's the prime example of bad things happening to good people."

"Well, Gayle Anderson, I absolutely forbid you to go on living your life as if you are waiting for the next bad thing to happen. Stop it! I'm not hearing any more of this nonsense." With those words Judy ended the conversation completely and left me to get changed and I wandered into the bathroom.

I sat down on the toilet lid to slip off my bottoms, but before I made a dent in changing my clothes, my mind started to wander. I was back in the midst of my memories of Noah and his time in Italy.

By mid-September Noah's letters were coming more frequently. Our letters began crossing in the mail and I looked forward to every single one that I received from Noah.

The photos of Rome arrived and they came with the longest letter thus far. He explained every detail of every picture. I did not know how he knew all of the history on every one of the places and buildings in the photographs, but he did. I checked the set of encyclopedias that Andy had left on the bookcase in our living room. It's not that I didn't believe him. I just couldn't believe he knew so much. I was intimidated about how smart he seemed.

No sooner did I mail a letter in reply to his photos of Rome than did the great big thank you letter for the homemade chocolate chip cookies arrived. He was as impressed with my cooking as I was with his knowledge of the historical buildings of Rome and Pisa. Reading his letter and remembering from a prior letter that he liked history, gave me an idea. I quickly wrote a letter back to him because I thought if he looked forward to my letters as much as I looked forward to his, then he would be expecting one pretty soon and what I had in mind would take a little while to put together.

I called Judy that day and asked her to help me. She had a better camera than I did and she was glad to loan it to me. My plan was to take pictures around the county of places I thought might be of historic significance. Admittedly, they were not as old as the buildings in Rome, but it was hard for anywhere in our country to compete with that. Everywhere I went for the next week, I took photo after photo and then I had to send off for them to be developed.

October 25, 1975

Dear Noah,

I have so enjoyed your photographs from Italy that I decided to follow your lead and take photos depicting some of the history of where I live. I apologize for the quality of photos that you will find enclosed. Unfortunately, I do not have the backing of the United States Air Force's Communications Department which I liken to the photography development department of National Geographic.

I have taken the liberty of labeling some of the photos and below is a brief description or history of the subject of each photograph.

1) *The Jefferson County Courthouse...Many do not know it, but Louisville was the first permanent capital of Georgia as temporary ones were first at Savannah and then at Augusta. The current courthouse, pictured in the photo, was built in 1904 and sits on the location of the original capital building which was destroyed by fire.*

2) *This is the Norton House now, but it was first built by the founding father of the city of Wrens, Mr. W.J. Wrens. I love the big porch and the white columns. To me, it is everything that one thinks of when they think of a Georgia mansion even if it was built after Sherman's march to the sea and thank God for that. Anyway, I know it's too big for any one person to keep clean, but I have always loved it and I am going to buy it or one just like it one day.*

3) *The Woodrow Wilson Home—This is the house that our former president lived in during his childhood in Augusta.*

I have enclosed some other pictures, but they aren't historically significant. The brick house with the white shutters is where I live. My room is the first window on the left at the far end of the house. It was Andy's room before it was mine. I swear last week I saw him standing, looking out of the window. It was Saturday morning. The light was coming through the curtains. It's always so bright in there that I am awakened by it at dawn and this particular morning, I rolled over to look at the window as I always do and there he was. His back was to me and he was looking out the window.

I know I sound crazy, but I don't think I was dreaming. You're the first person I've told and I pray you don't think I am losing my mind. I can't tell my parents about this. My mother would be in there trying to talk to him and see him. It would just break her heart all over again. Daddy wouldn't believe me. He doesn't believe in ghosts, but it's my opinion that where there's smoke there's fire. I think too many people claim to have seen them for them not to exist.

Anyway, I enclosed a picture of my school and creek in the woods behind our house. That big rock in the middle of the creek is my favorite place in the world. I wade out there and sit on it. I have read half of your letters while sitting on that rock. The trickling of the water is music to my ears. One day, I will take you there and if it isn't too boring for you, we can just sit and talk about whatever you would like to talk about.

I look forward to the day we can talk in person again. I enjoy reading your letters, but I would much rather talk to you. I hope I am not being too forward when I say, I would like to hear your voice again.

I should probably sign off on this letter. It is getting late here and I promised myself I would get these pictures in the mail to you tomorrow. I hope you enjoy them and I am sorry there aren't more.

I hope you are having fun in Italy.

With Love,

Abbigayle

I don't know what I was thinking, but I took the letter and pictures out of my purse in home economics class and showed them to Judy. She asked to see the envelope so I handed it to her for what I thought was going to be a closer inspection. I was wrong, she took out the perfume from her purse and before I could stop her, she sprayed the envelope. She doused it good.

"Chanel No. 5, Marylyn Monroe said she slept in this and nothing else." Judy raised a sly eyebrow as she fanned it around a little and then handed it back to me.

I was mortified. The scent filled the whole class room. Talk about going over-board. My letter now smelled like a harlot.

That afternoon the bell to let school out at Stapleton High rang at 3:15 p.m. and, as soon as it did, I walked the couple of blocks over to the post office. I hugged the envelope tight to my chest, closed my eyes and wiped it up and down my blouse. It still smelled to high heaven and I tried to get as much of the perfume off of the envelope and on to me as I could. I prayed all the way to the post office that I would be able to tone the smell down a little bit, but I'm not sure if it worked or not.

The wind picked up as I opened the flap of the big blue mailbox out in front of the Stapleton Post Office. I had just dropped the envelope in when the wind whipped my hair all around my face and my skirt went swirling up as well. I let go of the box to push down my skirt in an attempt to avoid flashing any passing cars and the men across the street at the feed and seed store.

I managed to get a hold of my skirt with one hand and brush back my hair with the other. As soon as I could see again, I saw my hair and skirt had not been the only thing the wind had taken. I saw my letter sliding away on the gales of a monsoon and headed down the sidewalk in the direction of Avera, which was pretty amazing considering the thing took three stamps due to the weight of the pictures. It was a good twenty yards ahead of me when I first noticed it and I don't think I had ever run that fast in my saddle-oxfords before. Those chunky shoes made such a racket as I chased after the letter that I was surprised my mother did not get off her job at the Stapleton Garment Company and come out there and tell me to start acting like a lady.

I had fifteen more minutes before my mother was scheduled to get off work and I did not need her clocking out early to deal with me as someone from the building would surely see me from the window and tell her. After a few minutes of cat and mouse with the wind and the letter, I finally caught it. Returned to the mailbox and slid it in. I closed the box behind the letter and I made a mental note to myself that I would mail all future letters from the box out in front of our house.

Things at the Anderson house moved on as they usually did for the rest of October and into November. We had dinner every night at 6:00 p.m. We went to church every time the doors opened. I went to work three evenings out of the week and every other Saturday and school every day. I rushed home every day and checked the mailbox, but no letter came from Noah: however, one did arrive from my brother's widow.

The letter from Rhonda came just as I was beginning to worry about Noah. I had not heard from him in three weeks. The letters had been coming at a rate of every week to week and half so when they stopped, it was alarming.

The letter was addressed to Daddy and the return address was apparently Rhonda's new residence. I did not know a whole ton about addresses in Augusta, but I knew most any address on Walton Way, especially if it was in the hill section, was expensive. The fact that that woman had moved on at all galled me.

I could not wait to give the letter to Daddy as soon as he came home from the Woodmen of the World meeting he had been to that night. We didn't dare open any mail that did not have our name on it and we especially did not open anything addressed to Daddy, so Mama and I had been waiting with baited breath all night. We were dying to find out what Rhonda wanted and how Millie was.

Mama was sitting in her spot on the couch and I was in the leather rocker in the back of the living room. Mama was putting the backing onto a quilt and the loom was all set out in front of her. I was propped sideways with my back against one arm of the chair and my legs draped over the other. The TV was playing in the background. I liked "Welcome Back, Kotter," but Mama insisted on watching "The Waltons" even though neither of us was really watching. She turned it up loud so she could hear, but that didn't matter. We both heard Daddy's key turn in the lock.

Mama and I both jumped to our feet. The letter from Rhonda was lying on the coffee table and I got to it first. As soon as Daddy opened the front door I had my arm stretched out handing him the envelope.

"It's from Natalie." Mama said as Daddy took the envelope from me.

Mama still called her that and I rolled my eyes. That wasn't her name any more than it was mine.

Daddy was hardly in the door good, but he took the letter. In a huff, he cut his eyes at Mama. "Seems like she should have directed her correspondence to Attorney Bell as that's what I've paid him to deal with."

Mama and I waited while Daddy tore the letter open and read it, but we didn't dare say anything until he was done. When he was done, as much as one could slam down something that had the weight of a feather, he slammed it down and left the room for the kitchen.

"Well, what does it say?" I followed him and Mama followed me.

Daddy snatched open the refrigerator, "Where's the God forsaken milk?" He slammed about in the refrigerator.

I backed off and Mama gently eased forward. She knew better than to bother with her usual line, "If it was a snake it would have bitten you." She always said that when something was right in front of our faces and we couldn't find it. This time she didn't dare, she just reached to the top shelf on the door, where the milk was always kept, and handed it to Daddy.

Daddy turned up the milk jug like most men would turn up a liquor bottle. No glass, he just took a gulp, a minute long gulp, straight from the jug. That was shocking and totally unlike my father. I don't think I had ever seen him forget his manners like that before. When he was done, there was no milk left.

Daddy sat the empty jug on the counter and propped himself up with his hands against the sink, staring out the window. We gave him a couple of minutes. It was clear he wasn't going to talk until he was good and ready and pressing him would only direct his wrath toward us. There was no way Mama or I wanted to be the substitute and get what Rhonda had coming.

Finally, Daddy let out a deep breath and whirled around to Mama and me. I stepped back. The veins were bulging from his head and his face was red. The redness of his face made his hair appear so much whiter than it actually was. He looked a lot like me when I got mad.

"I swear, that's girl's going to cause me to lose my religion!" He shook his head with a look of utter disgust. "She had the audacity to ask me for money and not once, not one single time, did she mention Millie. Two pages of what a hard time she's having and not one damn word did she say about the child."

My contribution at that point was the word, "Typical."

Mama shushed me, but Daddy corrected her. "No, Gayle's right. This is so typical and if she thinks I am giving her one red cent, she is sadly mistaken."

Daddy paused for a moment and turned his sights directly toward me. "Thank the Lord your brother had the good sense to name Millie the beneficiary to his life insurance policy and not leave his sorry excuse for a wife as the trustee. That's the one smart thing he did in regard to that girl."

"Now, you just wait a minute." Mama got her back up. "You leave Andy out of this. Whatever she's said in that letter, that's her words, not his and he's not here to defend himself."

87

Mama was not happy, but neither was Daddy.

"She says she doesn't have money for rent. Funny considering there's a perfectly good house sitting empty over in Matthews that Andy paid cash for. Oh, but she wants to live in Augusta."

I might have only been seventeen, but I was quite familiar with sarcasm and it oozed from my lips as I made another observation. "Well, everyone knows you're no one unless you live in the big city."

"Gayle." Mama spoke my name in disapproval.

"That's how she always acted when she was around us," I defended.

"Perhaps if we offer to take Millie until she can get on her feet." I thought Mama had a point. All any of us cared about was Millie and if Rhonda was so strapped for cash, then maybe she might let us have Millie.

That's when Daddy said the most crass thing I had ever heard him say. "I hate to break it to you, but girls like that aren't interested in getting on their feet."

Mama didn't get it and it should have been over my head as well, but perhaps I had received too much of an education from Judy. I knew exactly what Daddy was getting at, but the fact that the statement came from him was almost too much. I quickly looked away so he did not see by the look on my face that I was embarrassed by realizing exactly what he was saying.

"There's no need in us discussing this further. I'll take this into town tomorrow and see what Attorney Bell wants to do next." We all just stood there for a moment until Daddy spoke again, "Gayle, isn't it about your bedtime?"

"Yes, sir."

"Then you need to get to it."

Mama was still worried about Millie. We all were, but Daddy was done with the conversation and there was no need pressing him further.

By Wednesday of the following week, I still had not received a letter from Noah and I was past worrying. My heart was broken. It had been three weeks since my last letter from him and I just knew I would never hear from him again. I didn't know why he hadn't written and although I was desperate to know, it seemed like I would never know. I didn't think there was anything that could cheer me up until I arrived home that night after my shift at the feed and seed store.

This time it was me that turned the key in the lock and then found a surprise on the other side of the door. I found Mama holding Millie and I dropped everything in my arms. My purse, school books and the sack of dog food that I had brought home from the store all hit the floor so I could free my arms to take her.

"She's gotten so big! And look, she's got more teeth." I twirled her around and she giggled as I listed my every observance of her. "Look at her hair. It's the same color as mine, the same color as Andy's. Look how it's filling in and how long it is. And, her eyes are just like his and look she has that mole on the side of her cheek just like he had and just like Daddy has. She's so pretty."

I hugged her as tightly as I could without hurting her. It suddenly occurred to me, "She's a year old. Her birthday was two days ago! Oh my goodness! She's one already. Is she walking?" I asked Mama.

My mother's face was full of pride. She was every bit as happy as I was. I had never doubted that Millie belonged with us and even though we could never replace Andy, the house felt more like home with Millie there than it had since he died.

All of these thoughts raced through my head and then they stopped. They stopped by the realization that I could not write to Noah and share this with him. It would be forward of me to write to him after this long of not hearing from him and as excited as I was to have Millie back, I was absolutely heartbroken over Noah. I shook off those thoughts so Mama and Daddy would not notice something was wrong with me. I had done so well to hide it from them this far, I did not want them to see it now. I did not want anything to put a damper on their joy to have Millie back.

Mama and Daddy divided their attention between watching Donnie and Marie and watching Millie and me. I crawled around the floor chasing her as she toddled around the coffee table. I ducked behind the table and then popped up to Millie's delight. She loved playing hide and seek.

I didn't want to stop playing with her for a moment, but there were questions eating at me. I looked over my shoulder to where Daddy was sitting in his recliner.

"How did we end up with Millie?" I asked Daddy.

Mama answered as Daddy looked at me over his glasses. "Just be glad she's here. That's all you need to worry yourself with."

"Well how long is she staying? I hope she stays forever." I smiled and made faces at Millie and she put her hands over her face and played peek-a-boo at me.

"Gayle, just be glad she's here," Mama answered again.

"Is it some sort of secret?" I knew that comment would get Daddy talking. He loathed secrets.

I was right. Daddy jumped right into the conversation then. "We don't have secrets in this family."

I had heard that line a thousand times.

Daddy continued. "Attorney Bell worked out a custody arrangement with Rhonda. We get Millie every Wednesday night and every other weekend."

"Like a divorced family?" I raised an eyebrow.

"Something like that." Daddy tried to turn his attention back to the Donnie and Marie Show.

I thought I was just making a joke when I asked, "So are we paying child support too? So much for not giving her one red cent."

"My finances are none of your business!"

His tone let me know I had hit a nerve and I was right. Daddy was paying her so we could see Millie. I bet that was eating at him something fierce. As soon as I figured it out, it ate at me. It was funny, Daddy kept her from getting Andy's money and now she was getting his. I was curious as to how much he was giving her, but I didn't dare ask. All I knew was, maybe Rhonda wasn't as dense as I thought she was. She cut out the middle man and went straight to the source. Daddy was worth way more than Andy was, even though he was a doctor.

It was 10:00 p.m. and Millie had been asleep in my arms for about thirty minutes. I played with Millie right up until she fell asleep. I rocked and rocked and rocked her and it was the most peaceful feeling I had ever felt. I tried to forget that Rhonda was getting another one over on our family. I did my best to enjoy being with her. Feeling her breath against my chest was so sweet. I loved her more than just about anything.

I did not want to wake her, but staying up this late was unusual so I asked, "Is she spending the night?"

"Yes," Mama said. "Daddy's going to take her back in the morning."

At that point, I got up and took Millie and put her in my bed. Mama and Daddy didn't say a word. That night Millie slept in the bed with me and I snuggled with her. She was restless and cried out several times. I felt so sorry for her. She seemed too tiny to have nightmares, but I think that was what was going on.

The next morning I got up and got ready for school. I played with Millie the whole time and tried to make the most of what time I had left with her. Mama tried to get her away from me, but I would have none of it. Millie worked wonders for keeping my mind off of Noah.

When I left for school that morning with Judy, I kissed Millie good bye and she held her arms out to me, begging me to take her with me. I knew she wouldn't be there when I got home from school and that brought tears to my eyes. I did my best not to let her see that I was sad, as Mama took her back inside and I got in the car.

As we headed toward Stapleton High, Judy tried to take my mind off of things. "Was your mom able to finish the alterations to your homecoming dress?"

I dabbed the corners of my eyes to stuff the tears back in. "I don't know. I guess."

"Well you better have a dress that fits considering you're in the homecoming court." Judy grinded the gears and we puttered off from Gene Howard Road onto the highway that led in to town.

"I really couldn't care less about any of that," I replied.

"I care. That dress needs to be taken in. You haven't got the twins to hold it up like some of us and I can't have all eyes on your bosom as they are crowning me homecoming queen." Judy tried everything she could to make me laugh, but I was having none of it.

"Perhaps we could talk about this later on today. I'm just not in the mood this morning."

All day long I wondered if we would see Millie again or if Rhonda would just take Daddy's money and that would be that. I also wondered if I would ever hear from Noah again. I drifted through the day in a daze.

When I got home that evening, I checked the mailbox as I had been doing for the last three months. There was nothing in it at all. Until I was inside and saw the spot on the table where my parents put the mail when they got it, I crossed my fingers that they had already picked it up and that there would be a letter from Noah. There was nothing on the kitchen table at all.

That night the three of us tried to carry on as if we all weren't missing something. We all missed Millie, but no one said a word about it. We went about our night.

Mama and I worked on my homecoming dress and by the end of the night, my "twins" as Judy put it, were not on the loose. They were thoroughly concealed in the confines of the blue taffeta dress. Mama also hemmed it.

"Now I won't trip and break my neck in front of everyone," I told Mama as I stepped down from where I had been standing in the dining room chair.

Instead of pinning it and having me take it off to hem it, Mama just whip stitched it as I stood there. Mama was a very talented seamstress.

"Well we don't want that."

"No, we don't. As if it isn't bad enough that my escort is my cousin, I really don't want to fall on my face while appearing to date one of my relatives."

Not that I wanted to date anyone other than Noah, I certainly didn't want to date my cousin, Billy. He was from Sandersville and whenever I needed an escort, Daddy called Aunt Gladys and recruited her son Billy. I always felt like such a social pariah, but Daddy didn't care about that. The simple fact was that I was not allowed to date as long as I was in school and there was no room for discussion on the subject. Reflecting on that rule, I thought that maybe things ending with Noah were for the best. I don't know how I would have gotten around Daddy and I certainly did not want to have to explain to Noah about the rule. Who was I kidding? I would have figured something out to get around that outdated rule.

I snapped back to the reality of my afternoon with Judy. Daydreaming was fun. Daydreaming about Noah was even more fun, but Mama would be there to pick me up at any second and I needed to be free of that teenie-winnie bikini of Judy's or Mama would have my hide!

I finished putting on my clothes and took Judy's bikini and put it in her hamper. All the while I continued to think of Noah and how tonight would be so much more significant than the Homecoming at Stapleton High had been last year.

CHAPTER 6

It was nearly 4:00 p.m. when Mama pulled into the driveway at the "Wren Mausoleum" as she referred to it. Lying in the sun had exhausted me even though I spent a fair portion of that time napping. Apparently, that did not matter. I fell asleep almost as soon as we pulled out of the driveway.

Not only did I fall asleep, I fell right back into the night of the 1975 Homecoming football game at Stapleton High. I was a member of the homecoming court and, like Judy had mentioned, my dress had been altered to the point of almost having to be remade.

On one hand I was lucky my mother was a great seamstress, but on the other hand I was unlucky. I was unlucky because it had been a battle for her to allow me to buy a dress, let alone a dress of that expense. She made me use my own money and even then she criticized me that I had completely wasted the money. As she reminded me on multiple occasions, she was fully capable of making a dress for me. After all, she had made the majority of my wardrobe every year of my life. Making a formal for me would have been of little or no effort for her and Mama so much as told me so with every rip, cut and re-stitch she made to the dress I bought at J.B. Whites.

I fell in love with the dress the moment I saw it. It was royal blue, school colors, and all of the members of the court were wearing it. It was strapless and both Mama and I worried what Daddy would think when he saw it. She came close to forbidding me to buy it and we argued in the store.

"Buy it if you want Missy. I dare you and you'll be the one that explains it to your father." She thought she was going to scare me with threats of Daddy, but little did she know, I was as stubborn as he was.

"Fine!" I remember telling her as I drug the entire ball gown from the rack and headed off to the cashier. "I'll take my chances."

It was my size so I didn't bother trying it on at the store and there were no returns on formal wear. Of course it was too big up top and too long., but after she gave me a good, "I told you so," Mama worked her magic on it. I even convinced her to make a gold sash to go with it instead of the one that came with the dress. Gold was the other school color and this would surely set me apart from the other girls in the court.

The night finally arrived and so did cousin, Billy. I made it out of the house with little more than a raised eyebrow from Daddy over my dress. Mama, on the other hand, gave me quite a look. The sash she made was rather thick so I draped it over my shoulders like a cape and it worked. As soon as the front door shut behind me, I snatched the sash off and tied it around my waist with a bow on the side.

I felt I had had a victory until I stepped in the yard and saw my chariot. It was a Gremlin and what paint was left on it was lime green. I wanted to call the whole thing off and go back inside. It even made the Dart look appealing.

"I just bought this. What do you think?" Billy asked as he opened the passenger's side door for me.

What I thought was that he bought it at a junk yard and I thought about reminding him that this wasn't a date. I thought about telling him he didn't have to open doors for me, but I was distracted by the fact that the passenger's seat was a lawn chair, one of the aluminum folding kind with the nylon straps. If he hadn't been my cousin and I hadn't known him all of my life, I would have told him to get his serial killer car out of my yard before I called the police. Ringing in my ears were the words, "I just bought it," like that was something to be proud of.

"Go on, get in. It's ok. I welded the bottom of the chair to the frame of the car," he held out a hand to motion me in.

I just stood there. I was trying desperately to think of any way out of having to get in that car, but none came to mind that did not involve another encounter with my dad. On top of that, I really didn't think that one could weld aluminum. That just didn't sound right.

I looked back at him. I'm sure I had a look of smelling something foul and curious at the same time.

"What?" Billy was losing patience with me. "You wanna go to your stupid football game, don't you?"

I didn't make a sound other than letting out a huge sigh of disappointment and defeat. Reluctantly, I scooped up all of the fabric of my dress and did my best to get it stuffed into the aluminum lawn chair.

I didn't utter a word out loud the whole way there. Thank goodness Billy couldn't read my mind. My thoughts would have surely hurt his feelings, then he would have told on me and I would have been grounded. My main thought: I knew I had my fair share of boy trouble, but if Cousin Billy was able to get a date and get one to ride in this heap, I would be amazed. In fact, I shudder to think what sort of fool that wasn't related to him would go for this. The Gremlin was so horrible that I made him park across the street in the vacant lot next to Mrs. Barrow's house.

"All the kids park here. We're just early," I told him while pointing to the turn in for the lot. I wasn't typically this shallow, but, again, it would be bad enough if anyone found out he was my cousin, let alone that we came in that hideous thing. I crossed my fingers and prayed to God no one saw us.

I waited for him to come around and realized when he didn't that he only opened the door earlier on the off chance that Daddy was watching from the window. I reached over for the door handle to let myself out. Not only was I shocked when the lawn chair came un-welded and I slipped into the uncarpeted floorboard, but also when I found there was no interior door handle. No wonder he only got dates with his cousins. This really was a serial killer car and he didn't have the good sense to know it.

Once I got the chair uncrumpled from around me and myself off of the floor, I started banging on the window, knocking and screaming as loudly as I could for him to come back. I was pretty mad at the entire situation and I took out my frustration on that car window.

I swear he was nearly across the street from where I made him park before he realized I wasn't with him. He must have been deaf not to have heard the pounding on the window. In those moments when I banged and banged, I made up my mind that I was getting another ride home. Sure, I could have crawled across. I could have tried the driver's side door or even the back hatch, but that was complicated by the formerly welded down lawn chair that was snagged among the layers upon layers of ruffles that made up the bottom half of my dress. I was going to kill him if my dress was ripped.

Billy sauntered back over to the car door.

"Please let me out!" I tried to ask calmly.

He began trying the door handle, but it wasn't budging. "Crawl across." He pointed toward the driver's side.

"NO! You better open this car door!" I screamed at him.

Billy looked like a lion had roared in his face and he tried jerking the handle harder until it came off in his hand. I thought I was going to cry.

"Open it!" I shouted and flailed about double fisted on the window.

"Hey, take it easy on her!" Billy said in a huff as if I could actually hurt that thing.

"It's not a 'her!' No self-respecting woman would ever look like this piece of crap car! Seriously, it must have been Hitler or Mussolini in its former life to have been beaten to hell and back like this! Now get me out of it!" The wisps of hair that I had hanging around my face were now full on clumps that had fallen from all of my struggles and fit throwing to get me out of the car.

Billy stuck his face up to the window and screamed back, "CRAWL ACROSS IF YOU WANT OUT!"

I shook my head at him in disgust. I could not believe I was in the running for Homecoming Queen and I had my idiot cousin as my date and I had to crawl across the driver's seat in the most beautiful, most expensive dress I had ever owned, just to get out of the car. I just could not believe this. On top of all of it, I had to do it while mortified that one of my friends or classmates would see me.

Luckily the driver's door had a handle and it worked. I was able to get out. Once I pulled all of my dress out behind me after snatching it loose from the stick shift that I whacked my knee on as I climbed over it, I slammed the door shut to the point that the whole little Gremlin shook. I looked over the top of the car to where Billy was still standing on the passenger's side.

"Just go home." I turned up one side of my nose at him.

"What? Don't you need an escort?" He actually sounded disappointed.

I shook my head from side to side and sighed. I would rather go alone than go with my cousin who I made park across the street because I was ashamed. "Just go home."

"But Uncle George will kill me if he finds out that I left you."

"He's going to kill you when I tell him about the lawn chair that you made me ride in, but I won't tell him if you will just get out of here."

"I drove all the way out here..."

"And now you can drive all the way home. Just go home." I was as polite as I could possibly be. I didn't want him to hate me and I didn't want to hate him, but I really hated this situation. This is not what I wanted for my high school memories. I wanted what all the other girls had, normal dating experiences.

I turned and started walking toward the school and I continued all the way there by myself. I never looked back, but I heard the Gremlin fire up and drive away. I kept walking and I didn't know what I was going to do. I don't know of anyone who had ever been in the homecoming court without an escort. I had to do something. I pulled my hair down out of the bun and let it fall down my back as I walked.

I strutted on toward the crowd that was forming outside of the gym when I spotted my friend Joseph. Joseph was in ROTC and a member of the color guard that presented the flag at the games. We had been friends since kindergarten. I could ask him to be my escort. I was sure he would do it and there wouldn't be any awkwardness.

It just so happened, Joseph saw me coming and I was just lifting my hand to wave at him when a voice called my name. The voice came from behind me and I didn't really recognize it, but I turned to see who it was.

"I thought you worked at the feed and seed store on Friday nights." I was still trying to take in what my eyes were telling me as he spoke. I completely forgot about Joseph as I nearly fainted at the sight. It was Noah. I could not respond. I was speechless. I was in shock. All I could do was stand there in awe.

"Gayle, are you alright?" He paused for a moment as if he was taking in the full sight of me. "You are the most beautiful thing I have ever seen."

I could not believe he was here or that he said that. I wasn't alright. I was so happy that I thought I was going to jump out of my skin. I still could not believe my eyes, but I mustered the words. "I thought you forgot me."

He seemed wounded by my statement. "How could you think that?"

"Your letters stopped."

"What? I wrote to you two weeks ago and told you I was being deployed to an aircraft carrier for training and I explained that I would not be able to get mail out as regularly, but I never stopped."

The wonder in my eyes said it all, but I asked for reassurance, "So you didn't..."

Noah took my hands and stopped my words with his touch. "Of course not," he assured me.

There was a flush of relief that came over me. The moment didn't last. It ended with what sounded like a jet plane coming in for a landing while dragging a string of a thousand tin cans behind it. Both Noah and I turned toward the source of the sound and I recognized it immediately. The Gremlin was back and turning into the parking lot where we were standing. It thumped and rattled and roared up toward us. I held tighter to Noah's hand and he stepped between me and the approaching car.

At the last possible moment, Billy cut the wheels of the car and the pulled up next to us. All in a huff he rolled down the driver's side window.

"You forgot your corsage!" Billy screamed and threw the boxed flower out of the window at me.

Noah caught the box with one hand and I shielded myself behind him.

From the look of things, Billy meant to make a grand scene. It didn't work so well for him since it was obvious he couldn't get the window to roll back up. Oh he struggled and struggled before he gave up and slammed down on the gas and sped away the same way he had come in.

"What was that about?" Noah didn't look back at me, but I could tell he clearly didn't know what to think of that spectacle.

"That was my cousin, Billy, the village idiot of Sandersville, Georgia. He was supposed to be my escort for the homecoming court." I explained as Noah turned back around to me. I also felt the need to explain that it was not a date. "My dad arranged it. I'm not supposed to..."

Noah didn't allow me to finish the statement. "So, let me get this straight. You don't have a date for homecoming now or an escort?"

Noah was about five inches taller than I was so I looked up at him and admitted my predicament. "No date. No escort," I sighed with no expectation at all.

"Will I do? I came all this way and all."

100

"You're not really dressed for a formal." I hated to point out the obvious, but he was wearing a blue collared, button down shirt, which brought out the color in his eyes to the point that I could hardly look at him, and he had on a pair of Levi's jeans. He was stunning, just the thing to make anyone who saw me pull up in the Gremlin forget.

My knees knocked when he said my name earlier and I just about fainted at the sight of him. His hair was longer than it was when I met him at Andy's funeral. There was more of it now so I guess that's what made it seem darker, almost black, and he was taller than I remembered.

I had dreamed of him every single night since I met him. I had wished for him to come home from Italy as soon as possible. I dreamed of him and wished for him more times than I could count. Every time I was sad about losing my brother or missing Millie, I comforted myself with thoughts of Noah Walden. Now, here he was in front of me and I was worried about what he was wearing. Maybe I was the village idiot of Stapleton, Georgia.

"I have my uniform in the car," Noah gestured toward the 1969 Camaro that was parked about fifty feet away from where we were standing.

"Now that's a chariot!" The words escaped my lips.

It was black as black could be and the street lights in the parking lot reflected off of it like stars in the night sky. It shined and sparkled and was the absolute definition of American muscle cars. I had never had sex before, but I knew that's what it looked like on wheels. Just, wow!

I looked back at Noah, if I wasn't in love before, I was then. The fact that he was standing there with me offering to be my date for homecoming was enough to make my pulse race, but looking at him and the car, imagining his arm around me and his hand on my shoulder as he drove, that made my heart stop, my knees weak and I started to perspire. It was occurring to me that I had found my ride home and I was on my first date. I would have to answer to Daddy when I got home, but right now I was getting my wish to be normal, to make normal high school memories.

"A chariot?" Noah laughed.

"Yeah," I cut my eyes at him. "Beats the snot out of the Gremlin that just rattled its way out of here."

Noah laughed again.

I guess I needed reassurance. "You don't mind being my escort for the night?"

"I would prefer to be your date," Noah corrected my wording. "Come on, if you want me to change."

All I could do was smile and follow him to his car. I could not take my eyes off of him. When he wasn't looking, I pinched myself to make sure this was really happening; that this wasn't just another dream about him. The result of the pinch told me he was really there.

After he grabbed the garment bag from the back seat of the Camaro we started back for the gym. Reaching in the car was the first time he had let go of my hand since I first saw him. I liked it.

"I don't mean to rush you, but I still have to let the gentlemen in the announcer's booth know to take my idiot Cousin Billy's name off as my escort and to add yours. We don't really have time to wait around for the football players to clear out of the boy's locker room and the restrooms aren't unlocked until game time. I'll stand guard if you don't mind changing in the girl's locker room. The cheerleaders all get dressed at home before the game so there won't be anyone in there."

"I guess that will have to do," he smiled at me. "I must admit, it will be the first time I've been in a girl's locker room."

"Well, if you've ever been curious, now's your chance."

We passed through the crowd that was steadily increasing in size outside of the gym and there was little more than a wave from everyone. Joseph was still a member of the group and I would have been fine with him as my escort, but having Noah here was so much better.

Other girls in the homecoming court and their dates were starting to arrive and had joined the crowd. The girls were fawning over one another, but Judy wasn't one of them. For a change, I was grateful that she tended to run a little late to most everything. I really didn't have time for the introduction and fuss she would make over Noah.

We continued to the door of the gym and Noah held it open for me. The girls' room was on the far side of the gym, opposite of the football field and the door where we entered. I took the lead and pulled Noah by the hand as I picked up my pace across the gym. My dress floated along the floor as I went and made a swishing sound.

"Did I mention that I love that dress on you?" Noah asked.

I gave him a look over my shoulder and cut my eyes at him. I smiled slightly and bit my bottom lip.

"Please don't look at me like that," he sounded so serious.

I slowed my pace as I replied. "Look at you like how?"

"You know how." I could feel his breath on my neck and his arm slide around my waist.

I hesitated because I wanted to be in his arms so badly, but we really needed to get going. I spun around and slipped loose of him. "Locker room, please." I drew out the words as I almost ran away.

"If you think I won't chase you, you're wrong. I've come around the world for you so chasing you across a basketball court is nothing and you aren't going to get far in that gown."

I giggled as Noah did as he said and ran after me. I stopped shy of the door and Noah grabbed me and whirled me around. I screamed like Millie does when I spin her.

When he stopped spinning me, I was nearly breathless from giggling. "Here we are. You've got to get changed. We're supposed to be on the field in a few minutes. Wait a second and I'll check to make sure no one's in there."

I went in. I called around and no one answered. To be double sure, I pushed open all of the stall doors. I came back out and Noah was still there. I held the door for him and he squeezed past me through the doorway.

"I'll just stand here in the door so I can let you know if anyone is coming." I nodded my head.

"Okay." Noah continued on into one of the stalls and started getting changed.

There was a moment of silence before he called out from the stall. "Isn't there usually a dance after these things?"

"Yes, there's a homecoming dance." I looked back toward the direction of his voice as I answered. It was instinct to look at who I was talking to, but I quickly turned my head, afraid I would see some part of him that would make me blush even more than guarding the door as he changed was making me.

"Are we staying for the dance?" Again his voice came from the stall. This time it was a little muffled. It sounded like he was pulling his shirt over his head.

"I don't know. Are we?" I placed emphasis on the word "we" and tried to play coy, but my insides were doing flips at the thought of dancing with him.

"I figure I came all this way, the least I can have is a dance with you." I had to fan myself over that statement.

"That reminds me, why are you here and how did you know where to find me?"

Noah said something, but there was a group of football players passing by and I could not understand him. Their cleats on the gym floor made such a loud racket that it drowned out everything else.

"Don't you look pretty, Ice Princess," one of them said to me.

I didn't respond. I just looked away, turning my head and praying none of them heard Noah and I prayed that he didn't speak again until they were well past me. My prayers were answered and they kept walking. I didn't look back toward them until they were exiting the gym door on the football field side of the building. I watched them until the last one passed through the door and at the same time I heard the sound of dress shoes on the wooden floor approaching from behind me.

Noah was dressed and he looked almost exactly the way I remembered him. The suit was sleek and freshly pressed. Even without the cap on, it made him look taller than he had looked in his civilian clothes. I did not know what the colors across the lapel signified or the three stripes up the arms, but I knew there were more of them now than when I first met him. He was so handsome it took my breath away. Just looking at him made me feel the need to fan myself again. I thought to fight that urge by asking Noah what he said, but before I could ask him anything, he was the one doing the asking.

"Why did he call you 'Ice Princess'? It didn't sound like a compliment." Noah slid his hand down my arm to find my hand as he asked.

There we were again in the doorway of the girls' locker room and here was my moment of truth. Time to confess. "I'm not allowed to date. All of the boys have asked me out, but I've always had to turn them down. I'm not supposed to date as long as I am in school." I hung my head and bit my lip. I figured this would be my first and probably my last date with Noah and I braced myself for the news.

I knew he was enough of a gentleman to at least stay and be my escort, but I thought surely he would run. I just knew he would not want to waste his time with a high school girl whose parents were so prehistoric that they would not allow her to date.

"Well that just eliminated the competition." He genuinely looked pleased with my answer and I could not believe my eyes or my ears.

"What? I'm confused."

105

"I was going to wait until later to tell you, but I guess now's as good of time as any. The reason I'm here is because they have extended my stay in Italy. I wanted to tell you in person so I used some of my leave that I had saved up. I will be stationed there until May."

All the while Noah spoke he moved closer into me. There was no place for me to go. We were in the doorway of the ladies' locker room and my back was against the left side door jam. I did not notice when he let his bag of clothes drop to the floor, but it was gone as he placed one hand above, propping himself up while still holding his cap. His other hand was sliding through the length of my hair between two of his fingers all the way down until he reached my bare shoulder.

"I wanted to beg you to wait for me, but it doesn't appear that you have a choice."

Noah smiled like he had won a prize and I peered up at him through my lashes and returned the gesture. I wanted him to kiss me right then and there. I had imagined that moment so many times. I just knew this was it. Chill bumps ran down my arms in anticipation as he inched closer still.

Noah bent down toward me and his nose was caressing mine when the gym door was snatched open.

"Gayle Anderson, you look amazing! I love that dress!" Judy came running as fast as she could in her tight fitting dress. Her dress was the same color as mine and strapless, but different from mine, very nontraditional.

Noah and I quickly composed ourselves and the moment passed without fulfilling my dream of kissing him. Judy dashed right between us as if Noah wasn't standing there at all. She grabbed both of my hands and held them out to fully inspect me. I half way expected her to instruct me to twirl around.

Noah stepped to the side as Judy went on. I kept looking at him and mouthing the words, "I'm so sorry."

Finally I interrupted Judy, "This is Noah." I took back one of my hands from hers and motioned to him.

Judy whirled around on her heels. "What?!" Her mouth fell open and she quickly let go of me to cover her mouth with both hands. She cut her eyes back to me. Despite her hands, I could tell her jaw was still on the floor.

"Noah, this is my best friend, Judy Wren." I introduced them.

"It's nice to meet you, Miss Wren," Noah said and Judy blushed.

"Nice to meet you, too." She uncovered her mouth just enough to speak and smile at me.

"Judy, we were just on our way to get Noah signed up as my...date." I paused for a moment as not to use the word "escort" and have him correct me.

"What happened to your cousin, Billy?" Judy was quick to inquire.

I did not want to rehash the evens of the serial killer car in front of Noah. "I'll tell you about it later."

Judy took my cue and did not press me further. "Y'all excuse me. I've got to use the little girls' room and then I'll come find you on the field. Save me and Doug a seat, okay?" Judy was always the social butterfly and she made sure to include. "It was real nice to meet you, Noah. I've heard so much about you and I expect to hear all about Italy tonight."

"I'll be glad to tell you whatever I can."

Judy headed into the locker room and we headed out to the announcer's booth. Hiking up the bleachers to the top where the announcer's booth was located was challenging in a ball gown, but Noah held out his hand and helped me. I scooped as much of my dress up with my free hand as I could and up the bleachers we went. Once at the booth, I explained to Mr. Ralph that there had been a change in my escort for the evening. I apologized for any inconvenience this might cause, but begged him to cross out Billy Carpenter and add Noah Walden. Not only did I add Noah's name to the list as my escort, but I had to provide his parents' names as well. I did well to recall their names from memory and he appeared impressed that I remembered.

When we were finished in the booth, Noah helped me down the bleachers. It was tricky on the way down. I just knew I was going to get my foot caught in the hem of my dress and go tumbling the rest of the way down. I slipped once and thought that was it, but Noah caught me. Again, a moment when I was so close to achieving my first kiss and someone interrupted the moment.

"Gayle," Mr. Ralph called from the booth and we turned back, "Is your dad coming tonight?"

I would have melted into a puddle if Noah had kissed me, but the mention of my dad coming sent a different kind of chill through my body. The truth was, "I don't know if he's coming or not. Sorry."

"Alright, Hun, good luck tonight. Us fellas in the booth are pullin' for ya." Mr. Ralph gave me a double thumbs-up.

Noah and I were almost halfway down the bleachers when Mr. Ralph called my name. After he wished me luck, I let go of Noah and scooped up my dress and ran back up and gave Mr. Ralph a giant hug. "Thank you so much!"

I knew Mama was coming, but I wasn't sure about Daddy. He hadn't been to any of the football games this year. The only time he and Andy missed a football game was when Andy was stationed in the Air Force. Football was their thing and since Andy died, Daddy hadn't been to a game. He didn't even watch it on T.V. I think it was a painful reminder of the loss of Andy so I really didn't expect to see him in the crowd tonight. With Noah there, it was probably for the best that Daddy didn't come.

I dashed back to Noah, grabbed his hand and down we went. We were supposed to be in our seats on the sidelines of the football field no later than 7:45. Kick off for the game was at 8:00. Turns out, there wasn't a huge need to rush after all.

My feet touched the ground and my stomach growled. "Have you had dinner?" I asked him because I hadn't.

"No, but don't you want to hang out with your friends before the game?" He seemed concerned.

"I can hang out with them anytime. Come with me." I took Noah to the concession stand.

"Hey, Gayle! What could I get for you?" Jenny Martin beamed from behind the counter of the concession stand.

I looked back to Noah. "Do you like hot dogs?"

"Yes."

"Can we have two hot dogs, two Cokes and," I looked to Noah again, "do you like cake?"

"Of course."

"The Home-Ec class provides the cakes and I made the red velvet and the double chocolate one. Which one would you like?"

"Either one. You choose."

"Jenny, can we have one piece of the red velvet cake and one of the chocolate?"

As Jenny gathered up our order, Noah took out his wallet.

"Put that away," I told him.

"You don't seriously think I'm going to let you pay, do you?"

"No, that's not what I meant." I explained while Jenny finished sitting the slices of cake on the counter.

"Can I get y'all anything else?" Jenny offered. She noticed his wallet as well and essentially told him the same thing I did. "Your money's no good here if you are treating Gayle."

"Seriously?" He raised an eyebrow at me and Jenny.

"No lie," she shook her head.

"Thanks so much, Jenny, but you really didn't have to." I always told her that and she always refused my money.

Noah and I gathered our items and started toward our seats.

"What was that about?" I knew he was going to ask.

"Her name is Jenny Martin. Her brother is in my grade. He used to beat up on her all the time. It was so bad that he broke her ankle one time."

"Dear Lord, that's terrible!"

"I know. I think she tried to tell her parents and I told my parents and my mother even tried to talk to her mother about it. Do you know what her mother said?"

Noah got a curious look on his face as we continued to walk.

"Their mother told my mother that this was just something siblings needed to work out among themselves. Can you imagine? Well, they walked the same route as I did after school every day and almost every day he started taking out his frustrations on her as soon as our feet left school property."

"What happened?" Noah's mouth was full of a bite of the hot dog, but I could understand him just fine.

"We were in ninth grade at the time and I was the same size as him. Jenny was two years younger than us and tiny. One afternoon as we started the walk from school, I decided it was time for him to pick on someone his own size. As soon as we were off school property, he drew back to hit her and she was still in a cast and on crutches from the broken ankle he gave her. He never saw it coming. I punched him right in the nose, kicked him in the...never mind about that, and pushed him into the ditch. Needless to say he went down holding both ends. I also insisted that Jenny give him a few kicks with that cast of hers while he was down. All of the old people that sit on their porches who watch us go by day after day, stood and cheered for me and Jenny. It was exhilarating. I know that sounds terrible to say and unladylike, but as far as I know, that's the last day he messed with her. Maybe he believed me when I threatened him that there was more where that came from if he ever touched her again. Jenny's worked the concession stand for the last two years and she never lets me pay. I've tried and tried and she hasn't let me yet. She finally told me to stop trying that my money

110

was no good because she could never repay me for teaching her that it was okay to fight back."

"Wow! I just don't know what to think of you."

I laughed. "You know what's funny? He's twice the size of me now and he's still scared."

We were the first ones to take our seats on the field and we still had five minutes to spare. We sat down about midway through my story about Jenny and continued to eat as we spoke. Noah finished his hot dog first and in between bites, I begged him to tell me something about him.

"You know so much about me. I want to know more about you."

"Like what?" He wiped his mouth with his napkin.

I looked to the sky and back at him and shrugged my shoulders, "I don't know, something more significant than your favorite food or color."

Noah chuckled. "Fried shrimp and navy blue and my brother Nathan had climbed up one of the Magnolia trees in our yard when an afternoon rain set in. He was fourteen. It was one of those flash floods that we get during the summers, you know, a five minute downpour and then it's over. He decided to sit in the tree and wait out the rain, but suddenly a bolt of lightning hit the tree. It went right through Nathan and exited his leg. It threw him out of the tree and by all intents and purposes, he was dead. My mother and I were the only ones at home. She gave me a crash course in CPR and we rotated performing CPR on Nathan until the ambulance came. It's a miracle that he's with us, but the doctors and everyone credit Mama and me with saving him. Other than the huge scar on his left leg and some heart palpitations every now and then, Nathan's fine."

There were other couples starting to take their seats as Noah finished his story, but we paid them no attention. With the exception of their chatter, it was as if we were alone.

I scooted my chair a little closer to Noah. If he had set out to impress me with how he saved his brother, he had succeeded. "Tell me something no one knows about you," I said as I took his hand and cradled it in my lap among the ruffles of my dress.

"Something no one else knows? Let me think." Noah waited a few moments appearing to ponder the request. "That I am in the States."

"What?"

"Everyone was at work still when I picked up my car this afternoon and came straight on to find you."

I smiled and blushed.

We were seconds from game time. Short of my consistently late best friend, everyone in the homecoming court was in their seat. The color guard was taking the field for the presentation of the flag as Judy and Doug came running and slid into their seats, Judy next to me and Doug on the other side of her. Judy on one side and Noah on the other, this was going to be one interesting night.

Noah removed his cap for the anthem and, although, I should have been looking at the flag, I could not take my eyes off of him. I still could not get over Noah being there and I couldn't seem to tear my eyes off of him. He had paid me several compliments throughout the evening and I could not recall if I had returned the favor. After all, how could I put into words that he was the best looking man I had ever laid eyes on? There's no way I could convey that without drooling all over him and completely embarrassing myself. Thinking these things as I looked at him made my cheeks warm. Little did I know when I put on my makeup that afternoon, I would not need rouge at all.

Noah must have felt me staring at him. As the trumpet played the tune that went with the words, "And the rocket's red glare," Noah turned his glance to me. I was caught.

"What?" Noah whispered.

I didn't know what to say and replied as much. "Nothing."

Embarrassed, I turned my attention away from him. I looked to the stands for my family. The Star Spangled Banner was coming to a close as I spotted Mama, Aunt Dot, Uncle Jim, Aunt Ruth, Uncle Bud and little cousin Dixon in the bleachers. They were centered to the fifty yard line and about two rows from the top.

I looked and looked, but didn't see Daddy anywhere. Almost everyone in the family was there except him. I guess he still hadn't worked up the courage to return to the football field, not even for me. As much as I feared Daddy getting on to me about my strapless dress, more than that I wanted him there to see me in the homecoming court. I wanted him to get past things, get past his grief, and put me first, but that wasn't happening.

These thoughts about not being enough for Daddy were making me sad. I held Noah's hand a little tighter, giving it a squeeze as we returned to our seats.

Noah felt the squeeze. He leaned into me and again complemented me on my looks. His timing was perfect. I needed whatever boost of self-confidence I could get. I had always been Daddy's girl, but since Andy died I was second fiddle to a ghost. I had never been jealous of Andy before, but I was finding myself a little jealous of his memory.

I laid my head against Noah's shoulder. The material of the jacket to his uniform could have been softer. It was scratchy from the starch, but it was still the most amazing feeling. My hand in his, my heart pounding and the breeze in the air that allowed me to breathe him in. He smelled like fabric softener and pine trees, my new favorite scents.

The players burst through the banner and everyone stood and cheered including me and Noah. We clapped and clapped along with the crowd. From the corner of my eye I saw Judy watching us. I turned to her and she whispered to me, "I am so happy for you."

"What do you think?" I asked her.

"He's amazing!" she gushed. Although I wanted to live the night to the fullest, I was stuck between not wanting it to ever end to not being able to wait to tell Judy everything.

Mine and Judy's conversation was cut short. As the players ran passed us, Noah turned to me. "I can't remember the last time I went to a high school football game, any game for that matter."

He smiled at me and for the first time I noticed how the lines formed around his mouth. Noah had dimples and the bigger his smile, the more adorable they were. They were sexy and endearing. Who knew dimples could be sexy?

Noah's letters were wonderful, but they were nothing compared to sitting there next to him. None of his letters would ever singe the sight of his blue eyes or the depth of his dimples into my mind. Letters, no matter how many words, no matter how well written, could not burn his smell into my memory. No matter how long I lived, I knew I would never forget a single detail of this night.

***

I snapped out of my daydreaming when I realized Mama didn't make the turn onto Highway 17 and head toward the traffic circle. We weren't headed home. We were headed in the opposite direction. I turned my head from where I had been staring aimlessly out of the passenger side window and looked to Mama for an explanation.

Mama could tell what I was asking just by the look on my face. I didn't have to say a word, but she answered me anyway.

"I forgot that I needed to run by Flemings."

Flemings was the drug store in Wrens. "I forgot I need to pick up some diapers for Millie. Your Daddy should be picking her up now and you know how that sorry mother of hers never sends anything with her. I swear she doesn't spend a dime on the child."

"Why should she when she's got you and Daddy for that?" It wasn't so much of a question that I was asking as a statement I was making.

Mama didn't bother to disagree with me. She knew I was right.

114

CHAPTER 7

The car rolled to a stop at the red light at the intersection of Broad and Main in downtown Wrens. Fleming's Drug Store was on the next block up from Anderson's Department Store on Broad Street. Mama had the blinker on and it was the only sound in the car. I gazed down the street toward our destination. I was nearly back in my own world, homecoming night 1975, when Mama broke the silence.

"You can come in or wait in the car if you like."

I turned to face her while I gave my answer. I became distracted by her hair. I could not believe I had not noticed it when I first got in the car with her in Judy's driveway. Mrs. Cornelia had done it again. She had dyed Mam's hair pink again and Mama didn't even realize it.

Mrs. Cornelia was getting older, she had to be getting on toward seventy and she was still doing hair; putting in perms, coloring and giving cuts. Mama's hair cut was the same it always was, but when the sun hit her just right there was no question that ash blonde was not the color Mrs. Cornelia had mixed in that tiny little sink in the corner of the bathroom in her beauty parlor. When the sunlight hit her, Mama looked like she had a giant ball of cotton candy on her head. The spinning vat of sugar at the fair could not have done it better, but I wasn't about to say a word. This time, I was going to let Daddy do the honors.

"What is it?" Mama noticed the look on my face. The look said something was amiss.

I tried to reign in my thoughts. The light changed. "Mama, the light's green." I pointed to the traffic light and it was enough to get her attention off of me.

Mama gave the car the gas and made the turn onto Broad Street.

"I'll just wait in the car, if that's okay."

115

"That's fine." Mama pulled into one of the spots out in front of the drug store. "I promise I will only be a minute."

Mama got out of the car. I smiled knowingly at her. She was never only a minute.

I watched her disappear down the sidewalk and into the front door of the drug store as I rolled down my window. I put my arms across the window sill and laid my chin on top of them and drifted back into my dream. Within seconds, I was back on Noah's arm as our names were called to take our place on the football field.

"Miss Abbigayle Anderson, daughter of Mr. and Mrs. George Anderson. Miss Anderson is being escorted by Staff Sargent Noah Walden of Blythe, Georgia." Mr. Ralph went on to list my high school accomplishments as Noah and I walked to our designated spot on the field.

I did not hear one word Mr. Ralph said past Noah's name because I spotted my family in the stands again. Aunt Ruth, Uncle Bud, and Uncle Jim were all clapping for me. Aunt Dot was screaming my name and clapping. She always made a big fuss over me and she was my favorite relative aside of my parents, of course. I would have waved to her or acknowledged her somehow, but instead I saw my mother.

I had been nervous about whether Mama would be upset with me that I was with Noah instead of Cousin Billy. I was shocked to see that she didn't appear mad at all. I dare say, Mama was cheering for me as loudly as Aunt Dot. Mama wasn't usually the jump up and down and shout type. She wasn't one to make a spectacle, but she always had a way of coming through for me when I needed her and when I least expected it. This time, I waved to her and all of my smiles were for her in that moment. Maybe she was trying to make up for Daddy not being there. I looked up and down the stands and up and down the fence that lined the field. I didn't see Daddy anywhere.

"Look." I nudged Noah. "There's my mom and most of my aunts and uncles that you met at the funeral that day."

There were his dimples again and his eyes shone brightly from the lights on the field. He did as I instructed and looked until he spotted my family. Noah tipped his cap to Mama and paused a moment to salute Uncle Jim. From the stands Uncle Jim returned the salute, releasing Noah for us to continue our march.

I loved being on Noah's arm and I loved that my family looked so proud of us. This was the most magical night of my life and it only kept getting better.

Judy was crowned homecoming queen. When Noah tried to console me about not winning, I almost laughed. I knew I was never really in the running to win.

"Oh, please don't worry about that," I went on. "I only ran so that I would have something else to put on my college application."

Noah looked puzzled by my response. We returned to our seats on the sidelines as our conversation continued.

"I applied to The University of Georgia. I told you already that I want to be a vet. There are no female vets around our area and I want to be the first."

"You are very determined, aren't you?" Noah was clearly intrigued.

"Yes, I am."

"How are your grades?"

"I am in the top three, but they won't tell us who the valedictorian is yet."

"You may be the valedictorian?" Noah didn't expect that.

"I might be, but I really think it's going to be Clifton Beasley. He's super smart and it doesn't hurt that his mother is one of the teachers here."

"Maybe you'll be salutatorian." I wondered if those words tasted like vinegar coming out of his mouth because they sounded like they should have.

I turned up my nose on instinct and I was quick to respond. "I don't want to be salutatorian!"

Noah was taken aback. I didn't mean to snap at him, but before I could apologize or explain my position a voice came from the row behind us.

"Hey, Ice Princess," Mickey Martin barked, "can you keep it down? I'm trying to watch the game."

I never paid much attention or let the name calling offend me, but Noah wasn't like me. He was highly offended. He jerked around in his chair and addressed Mickey.

"Insult my girl one more time and you'll watch the rest of the game through black and blue eye sockets! Do I make myself clear?" Noah was so calm in his threat, so intimidating, that Mickey Martin apologized to me.

My eyes were as big as saucers and I cut them to Judy. She had seen the entire thing. She was looking at Noah and fanning herself. She exhaled slowly before whispering to me.

"Gayle, he's hot."

I was thinking the same thing she was. "I know," I whispered back.

The final score of the game was Stapleton 35 and Gibson 21. The crowd in the home stands went wild as soon as the buzzer went off at the end of the fourth quarter. People were up and moving everywhere. I wanted to find my family and show off Noah, but at the same time I didn't want to press my luck. There was still a very real possibility that Mama would insist that I go home with her. She knew Daddy's rules as well as I did.

Instead of searching for my family, I opted to go to the ladies' room before the dance. I led Noah off the field and we were exiting the gate hand in hand when there with all of the other parents waiting for members of the homecoming court was my father. My heart would have sunk except the look on his face was that of pride. He had been watching the whole time. I could not stop the

118

smile that spread across my face. Despite the risk of being sent home, I was still overjoyed to see him.

I stepped forward and hugged Daddy. "I didn't think you were going to make it, but I'm so glad you did. I love you so much, Daddy."

"Are you kidding me? I wouldn't miss it for the world."

Daddy held me tightly for what seemed like an unusually long time. Finally Daddy loosened his grip. "I had not planned on coming so early, but when Billy came back by the house and told me you needed to be taught a lesson about insulting a man's car, I came straight on. I figured you needed an escort, but it looks like you did just fine finding one on your own."

Daddy nodded his head to Noah.

"Good evening, Mr. Anderson. It's good to see you again." Noah extended his hand.

"Likewise, Staff Sargent Walden," Daddy replied as he took Noah's hand.

"Sir, please call me Noah."

"Well, Noah, what brings you to our fine city? I thought you were stationed in Italy these days."

I was puzzled. I had not told Daddy a thing about Noah. I thought I had done well to catch all of his letters before Daddy saw them and I knew I had not said a word about him being in Italy. My curiosity as to how he found out was written all over my face.

"Gayle, don't look so shocked. Your mother can't keep a secret from me to save her neck. I know the two of you have been corresponding for some time now."

"Sir, I hope you don't mind. I would very much like to escort your daughter to the homecoming dance." Noah was certainly brave.

I had explained the rules to Noah and I was terrified that Daddy was about to explain them as well and drag me home at that point. I decided to plead my case for being allowed to stay for the dance with Noah.

"Daddy, I've done everything you ever asked me to do and I have been a good student, scratch that, I have been a great student. And, this is probably a onetime thing since Noah's tour at Camp Darby has been extended until the summer. So, please Daddy may we please stay for the dance?"

What I failed to tell him was that if he didn't let me stay for the dance, I was going to ask Noah back to the house. One way or another, I was getting my time with Noah even if it had to take place while sitting on our front porch.

Daddy thought on my argument for a moment and Noah tried to convince him. "Sir, I will have her home by midnight and you won't have to come back out and get her. I have a safe driving record, no wrecks or tickets or anything. I assure you, sir, I will be the perfect gentleman."

"Midnight? Son, you are pushing it. Make it 11:00 p.m. and not one minute later."

"Yes, sir," Noah and I said in unison.

"Thank you, Daddy!" I jumped in his arms and hugged him and kissed him on his cheeks. "Thank you! Thank you!"

"Go on now, before I change my mind." Daddy said as he released me and shooed me away.

Daddy didn't have to tell me twice. I reached back for Noah's hand as he thanked Daddy as well and then we were on our way.

Inside the gym we found Judy and Doug. The place was so loud with music and the roar of the football players still cheering over their win. Noah and I stood around and talked with Judy and Doug and things started to settle down. Noah told Judy and Doug all about his time in Italy and Doug pretended to be interested in joining the Air Force, but Judy and I knew that was just an act. Doug was one of those guys that had no ambition to see anything beyond the tri-county area. He would likely get a job at the chalk mines straight out of high school or start farming with his dad.

All the while Noah gave the details of all of the places he had toured while overseas, I listened intently, but all I could think about was getting him to myself again. I wanted to finish what we had started in the door jam of the girls' locker room before Judy interrupted us.

Finally, the DJ played a slow song, "The Best of My Love," by the Eagles.

I tugged Noah's hand to get his attention without fully interrupting him. It worked and he looked my way.

"How about that dance you mentioned earlier?" I bit my bottom lip. It was a habit of mine that I did when I was nervous. Even though I desperately wanted to dance with him, the thought made me extremely nervous. What if I was terrible? I had never danced with anyone other than Andy at his wedding reception and that was more like a lesson in how to dance, my only dance lesson.

We excused ourselves from Judy and Doug and Noah led me to the dance floor. My stomach was swirling like a swarm of bees was loose inside of it as Noah stopped in the middle of the floor. I guess he realized I didn't know exactly what to do with myself so he didn't let go of my hand until he had draped it around his neck. He slid his hand back down my arm and continued on until he found the small of my back.

We swayed with the rhythm of the song, slowly back and forth. The song played on and the longer it went the closer Noah drew me to him. He sang along softly along with The Eagles to the point that Glen Fry was drowned out and all I could hear was Noah in my ear.

The song was winding down and Noah broke with the lyrics. "Would you mind if we got out of here?"

I leaned back to see his face. "Okay." I said softly.

Noah smiled. "Can you hang out with your friends and let me change back into my civilian clothes? Do you mind?"

"I like you in the uniform, but, no, I don't mind."

121

Noah kissed my hand. "I'll walk you over to them and then I'll go get changed."

We found Doug and Judy right where we left them. Doug wasn't a dancer so I did not have to worry about losing Judy to the dance floor. While Noah went to get changed Judy and I went to the ladies' room. I wanted to take that opportunity to tell her everything, but half of the school was in there and I didn't like to spill my guts in front of everyone.

"Get out!" she ordered the other girls who were several grades younger than us.

They were intimidated by Judy and they scurried. As soon as they were out the door, Judy squealed, "Tell me everything! Spare no detail!"

"There's nothing to tell yet."

"Has he kissed you?"

"Not yet!"

"But, you think it will happen? Oh, it will definitely happen! I am so excited for you!"

"I am nervous! He's so good looking. I can't stop thinking about that. Every single time I look at him the words, 'He's so good looking!' run through my head and I know I become flushed. I can feel it. I hope he can't tell. Stupid strapless dress!"

"Stupid strapless dress? Are you kidding me?" Judy looked me up and down and then grabbed the top of my dress and started straightening it. "Let the girls work for you. Show a little cleavage. I know you have some in there somewhere."

I smacked her hands. "Stop that! This dress shows enough without your help."

"Good Lord, if I were as pretty as you are Gayle, he wouldn't stand a chance." Judy shook her head. "Gayle, he is just as perfect looking as you are. I just hope he is as nice as you are."

"Stop being ridiculous, Judy Wren. You're going to give me an ego."

"You couldn't get an ego if you bought one!"

Judy was right. I cannot imagine anyone who could get an ego up next to her. She was my best friend and I trusted her completely, but she was the apple of every guy's eyes in school. Even though I trusted her, I would not want her as competition for Noah's affections.

Why she thought I was prettier than she was; that was beyond me. Not only was she naturally pretty, but her makeup was always pristine. What little makeup I was allowed to wear, a little blush, a little lipstick and the slightest bit of mascara, was from the small assortment they carried at the IGA and on rare occasions I got some of the leftovers from Avon that Aunt Ruth couldn't sell.

Judy's makeup was the same kind her mother wore and it came from J.B. Whites. No expense was spared and it showed on her face, foundation, powder, blush, mascara, eyeliner and lipstick, the works.

It also didn't hurt that Judy had the best hair of anyone I knew. My hair was blonde and thick and it wouldn't curl worth anything. Judy's hair was almost the opposite. Hers was light brown. She had to blow dry it just to get it to straighten at all and even then any moisture in the air caused it to form ringlets.

Judy and I finished up in the restroom and headed back to find our dates.

"Do you think he has a girl in every port?" I asked her as we spotted the boys talking like old friends.

"Awe, Gayle, don't think like that. Just enjoy him while he's here and don't think about that nonsense." Judy took my hand and pulled me close to her side as we walked.

"You know how they warn us about getting mixed up with the boys from Fort Gordon. It's got to be the same with guys from any branch of the military. Wouldn't you think?"

123

"You are just borrowing trouble, now stop it! I have watched him look at you all night and it makes me envious. I don't know that Doug has ever looked at me like that."

What does one say to that? I said nothing. We were within feet of being back in the presence of Noah and Doug so there was no time to continue that conversation.

Noah was back in his civilian clothes and he was just as good looking in those as he was in the Air Force uniform. His cap was gone and I really loved his hair. It was longer than Andy ever had his while he was in the service. It was long enough that it parted on the left and fell to the side. The sides and back were still kept short and tight to his head. Maybe one day I would get to run my hands through it. Maybe that day would be today.

"Are you ready to go?" Noah held out his hand to me.

There was some disco song that I wasn't familiar with blaring above all of the noise the crowd was making. I could barely hear myself think the entire time we were in there. I could barely make out what Judy was saying when I was talking to her on the way back from the ladies' room. I could hardly hear myself think, but I understood what Noah was asking and the answer was, "Yes, please," for more reasons than one.

I could not contain the smile on my face as I answered him. My insides were dancing at the thought of being alone with him, of having him to myself. He took my hand and led me out of the gym and away from the roar of the homecoming dance. I guess most girls would have wanted to dance with him all night, but not me. I just wanted to sit in a quiet spot and look at him and listen to him as he talked about anything and everything.

Noah escorted me to his car, the black Camaro that was by far the best looking car in the parking lot of Stapleton High School that night. There wasn't a car there that even came close and even though he was just leading me to that car, I would have followed him anywhere.

As we got closer to the car, I had flashbacks to the Gremlin from earlier. There was just no comparison between the cars or the two boys who had accompanied me that night. In fact, Noah was not a boy at all. Everything about him was all man. It was evident in everything about him from the way he carried himself to the condition of that car. Not that there was any competition, but everything about Noah made poor Cousin Billy pale in comparison.

Not a word was spoken between us during the walk to the car. I was so nervous and excited that I was scared if I made a sound at all it would be a scream of glee. I wondered if Noah felt the same. Was he as excited about the possibility of being alone with me as I was of him?

Around to the passenger's side door, Noah walked with me close behind. I could see our reflections in the paint on the door. Although the paint job was as black as it could be, our reflections were as clear as a mirror.

Noah paused to open the car door for me and held it until I was safely seated inside. He closed the door and while he made his way around to the driver's side, I assessed the interior of the car. It was as pristine as the exterior. Black leather covered the seats and the dash. I ran my hand across the dash and I was marveling at how smooth it was when Noah opened the driver's side door. Noah got in, but did not notice as I snatched my hand back from the dash. This was my dream car, but I didn't want him to catch me groping it.

Noah shut the door and stuck the key in the ignition before looking over to me. "Where do you want to go? I'll take you anywhere."

I didn't know what to say. I had not thought that far in advance. All I had thought about was being with him and I didn't really care where. The football field and the gym had been fine, but I wanted time where I didn't have to share him or wonder who was watching and would report back to my parents. Now was my chance to have that and my mind was drawing a blank. Thanks to my curfew we couldn't go far.

I was stumped and Noah could tell. "How about we just go for a drive."

"Okay."

Noah turned the key and fired up the engine. When he gave it the gas, the Camaro roared and we took off. Out of the parking lot of the school, he made a right and headed back to the intersection of School Street and Highway 102. Noah stopped and looked both ways at the stop sign. I looked as well.

He nodded to the left. "I know what's that way so let's go see what's over this way."

Right in the middle of the turn out onto the highway, Noah gave it the gas again. This time he really let down on it. Not only did the engine roar again, it made this, "Womm-womm---womm-wom-wom-wom," sound when it did and the backend fishtailed. I screamed with delight as the force of taking off pinned me against the seat.

Noah laughed. "You liked that?"

What was I to say to that? I confessed. "I love cars. It runs in my family. My dad buys them and restores them as a hobby. I would kill for a car like this!"

"You know, I loved everything about this car until tonight." Noah shifted gears as he described his new grievance with the Camaro. "I thought it was perfect, but now I realize I wish it had a bench seat instead of these buckets."

I looked curiously at him and he explained further. "So you could sit next to me and I could put my arm around you."

"Oh."

We continued on in silence for a couple of miles, but I could not take my eyes off of him. He had to know I was looking, but he didn't seem to mind.

Within minutes we were in the town of Avera, Georgia. It was five miles from Stapleton. As we passed under the red caution light in the center of town it occurred to me where we could go.

"About a quarter mile ahead, make a left onto Montlow Hill Road." A quarter mile came quick and I pointed to the turn. "See the R.C. Cola sign? Turn there."

Noah did like I asked and away we went up the road past Mrs. Raley's store.

"When the road ends, make a right and when you come to the fork take the left side."

With each turn Noah pushed down on the gas, my insides turned over. I didn't just hear the rumbling of the engine; I felt the vibration all the way through my seat.

There was nothing but woods, rows and rows of planted pines, on each side of the road. It was pitch black out there except for the stars and the headlights of the car. The last street light we passed was at Mrs. Raley's store. We had gone about a two miles when I pointed out our next turn.

"There's a mailbox coming up on your left and a driveway just past it. Turn there."

"Someone lives way out here?"

"Lots of someones live way out here, just not where we are going."

Noah made the turn and we followed the tire tracks down the driveway.

"Deer!" I shouted.

Noah shouted too. "Oh my God!" He slammed the brakes and threw out his right arm to block me like my mother would do to keep me from flying forward.

As Noah ended up with a handful of my right breast, a buck followed by a doe crossed right in front of us and we had barely missed them.

"Oh, no, I'm so sorry about that!" This time it wasn't me that had embarrassed themselves.

"Yeah, I think it's a little soon for that." I tried to laugh it off.

Noah tried to do the same. "Right. I like to think my moves are a little smoother than that."

"So you have moves?"

"Uhhh, no, I mean..."

We both laughed and Noah let off the brake. It wasn't much farther until the headlights lit up the front of an old antebellum house. I felt I needed to explain about the house.

"Remember my friend Judy from earlier?"

"Who could forget?" Noah answered offhandedly.

I pursed my lips and looked sideways at him. "Well, she has a cousin, Allison, who was also in our grade. Allison's dad and Judy's mom are brother and sister. Anyway Allison's dad works with Goodyear and he got transferred to Birmingham. Her dad says they have to sell the house, but her mother wants to hang on to it in case they get to move back."

"It looks like an amazing house."

"It is. Judy and I used to come over here all the time." I opened my car door. It took me a moment to peel all of my attire out of the car, but it didn't take me nearly as long to get out of Noah's Camaro as it did Cousin Billy's Gremlin.

Once out of the car, I leaned down and looked back in at Noah. "What do you say we sit on the front porch and pretend it's mine?"

"Maybe we could pretend it's ours?" I had just been joking about pretending it was mine, but Noah's words made the butterflies in my stomach go nuts.

The huge grin was back on my face. "Okay. Leave the headlights on and follow me."

It occurred to me when I stood back up that I might have given him a show with the top of my dress when I leaned over. I closed my eyes and tried not to think of that in an attempt to ward off my being completely embarrassed again.

I picked up the sides of my dress so I could walk a little easier and met Noah at the front of the car.

Noah had grabbed the jacket to his uniform and as he draped it over my shoulders, I looked at his face and did everything to make a mental note of it. If he had noticed my cleavage earlier, he wasn't letting on now.

"I still can't believe you're here." I reached up and touched his face. I slid my hand gently against his cheek. I could feel the slightest hint of stubble.

"I can't believe I am here with you and you look like this." I wasn't the only one with a grin plastered across their face. Noah's was more of a sly grin, like he knew something I didn't.

He reached up to his face and took my hand. "Come on let's go sit on our front porch."

The rocking chairs were still on the porch and the curtains were still in the windows. The place looked like the inhabitants had just turned off the lights and gone to bed, but I knew there hadn't been anyone living there in quite a while. The car was far enough away from the house that the headlights weren't beating down on us. It was a soft light that shown across us and the façade of the Greek Revival house. Our shadows were cast against the house and they looked so much larger than life.

Noah took two steps up and turned to help me up. I thought he was just afraid I would trip on the hem of my dress, but I was wrong.

Once I was on the same step as him, Noah released my hand and eased his hand around my back and pulled me closer to him. "Can I ask you something?"

I braced myself with my hands against his arms. I really didn't know what to do with myself. I could smell the scent of a fire burning in the distance like the one that was burning in the pit of my stomach. I had never felt like this before.

There was no need for him to whisper yet he did. We were alone. Being this close to him made me breathless. I bit my bottom lip and whispered back. "Anything."

Noah pressed his forehead to mine, his nose to mine. His hand was still on my back, holding me against him. With his other hand, he grazed my hair back over my shoulder. "I know, good girls aren't supposed to kiss on the first date, but I want to kiss you. I don't want to hug you goodnight on your parents' front porch. I want to kiss you here on our front porch."

I lifted my head slightly. I would have melted into a puddle right there if he had not received the signal I was giving. I wanted to kiss him so badly and I wanted him to kiss me.

I didn't think we could be any closer, but his hands gripped gently around the small of my back and in my hair against the back of my neck. Noah pulled me into him, closer still, as his lips touched mine.

Noah's lips were soft and firm at the same time. It was my first kiss and I didn't know what I was doing. On TV, they close their eyes when they kiss, but I could hardly stand to close mine. I wanted to look at him and take in every bit of that moment.

I was puzzled that I could breathe as easily as I could. I leaned back for a moment, in awe of what it was like kissing him and being kissed by him. My chest heaved and I was thankful for his jacket to hide the effect this seemed to be having on me. I swear when I first put my dress on that afternoon the top fit perfectly, but now it felt as though I was going to bust out of it.

Noah pulled me back into him. My hands found their way to the back of his neck and as much as he pulled me into him, I did the same.

Finally, Noah eased back only enough so that words could escape his lips. His forehead was still gently pressed to mine when he spoke. "I have dreamed of this moment since I first laid eyes on you."

⏌

Noah kissed me again and my knees were weak, but I knew he would never let me fall. I felt completely safe with him. The truth was that I had dreamed of that moment since I first saw him as well.

I paused for a moment and just marveled over him. "Thank you," I breathed against his Adam's apple.

"For what?" He seemed surprised by my gratitude.

"For my first kiss."

"Really? I didn't realize." He was stunned, but pleased.

"There's never been anyone else." I hung my head, looking farther down.

"Would you mind if we did it again?" Noah lifted my chin.

Of course I wanted to, but I didn't want him to think less of me. I referred to his earlier reference, "Good girls shouldn't and..."

"Gayle, you are the best girl I know."

I gave a sort of snicker in response. I was a good girl, but in that moment, if kissing Noah made me bad or if the thoughts I had about him made me bad, then I was a definitely bad. I rationalized that I was only that way for him, not every boy in town so that should count for something.

Bad or not, I knew we needed to settle down for a moment. Beyond not being bad in the context of kissing Noah, I did not think of anything else. I took a step back from him. "Would you like to see inside the house?"

Noah looked skeptical.

"I know where the key is. Judy's parents are the caretakers and they certainly aren't coming out here at this time of night."

"Of course I want to go in. Who wouldn't, but what if we got caught?"

"You're probably right, but I know that if anyone else showed up out here at this time of night they would be up to no good."

131

Noah furrowed his forehead and raised his right eyebrow. "Isn't that what we are up to?"

It was a challenge by him to see how I would respond and I rose to the occasion. "I'm not sure about you, Mr. Walden, but I'm a prospective buyer."

Noah struggled to stifle a snicker. "At this time of night?"

I picked up the skirt of my dress and continued up the remaining steps to the porch. Noah followed me across the porch and stood peeping through the windows that surrounded the front door. While he got a peek inside, I raised up the black standing urn that was still next to the front door. Allison's mother typically sat giant ferns in the urn during the summer time, but right now it was empty and easy for me to tilt to the side. I reached under it and grabbed the key.

"So, we're really going in?" Noah asked as I started around to the door.

"Unless you are scared." I stuck the key in the lock and gave it a turn.

"Hold on a minute." I thought he was cautioning me as I felt the latch in the lock give.

Before I could utter another word about him being a chicken, Noah scooped me up. I was not expecting that and I gasped.

"If we are pretending, we might as well go all out!" Using his foot, Noah gave the old wooden door a stern push and it swung wide open and smacked the wall behind it.

I squealed and laughed. "Dear goodness!"

"That's not how I pictured that going." Noah put me down. "I didn't put a hole in the wall over there or anything did I?"

The house was dark, but the headlights of the car beamed right through the windows and lit up the hallway that ran the length of the house. There was enough light for us to see there was no hole in the wall.

"Would you like a tour?" I didn't really want to give him a tour. I really just wanted to kiss him again. I wanted to kiss him in every room of that house. As I offered him my hand to guide him through the house, I wondered if it would be too forward of me to tell him that.

"Sure."

"Follow me."

I turned to walk toward the living room and Noah pulled me back. My feet got caught in the crinoline in my skirt when he spun me around. Falling into his arms took my breath away.

Noah cradled my face in his hands. "Gayle, I would follow you anywhere."

"Would it be forward of me to ask you kiss me again?" The words escaped my lips as I gazed up at him. The perfect combination of moonlight and headlights lit up his face. I could not take my eyes off of his. They were so blue and all consuming.

Noah leaned down closer to me and whispered as he did. "Not forward at all."

There was a burning sensation in the pit of my stomach as he kissed me. I was pressed so completely against him, but it was like it wasn't close enough. This kiss was deeper and more passionate than the first and I had not imagined that possible, but it was.

My heart was pounding out of my chest and again I felt as if I should have rethought the strapless dress. It felt too small, like I had an abundance of cleavage, which was unusual for me. I held tight, fistfuls of his collar in my hands. Closer and closer we pulled each other, until finally Noah snatched back from me.

"What is it? Did I do something wrong?" Noah's sudden movement frightened me.

Noah wiped his face with his hand before rejoining his with mine. "You didn't do anything, but we need to get on with the tour. We still have to worry about your curfew."

"Oh. Right."

I led Noah from room to room. There was a piece of furniture here and there, but most of the rooms were empty. We continued our pretending with a discussion of where we would place furniture in the rooms.

In the living room we decided that it would be best to put my piano in there as opposed to the study which was across the hall. We joked about the wallpaper in the living room.

"Mrs. Arrington, Allison's mom, said it's real wallpaper, not the stuff my mama has on the wall in our bathroom. This stuff's from France. She said it was priceless." I did my best snobby voice and flopped my hand about and batted my eyes the way Mrs. Arrington did when she put on airs about the tacky tempura paint that was flaking off all over the place.

"Priceless, huh? She's right. I wouldn't give a plug nickel for this mess. It's terrible looking. It would have to go."

Still in character, I pranced to the kitchen acting now as if I was Mrs. Arrington giving the tour. "And in here we have the kitchen."

We were barely in the room when Noah leaned me against the counter top and braced my head against the cabinets. Earlier in the night I had wished for a normal high school experience with dating and what not and now I was getting just that and it was amazing.

My fingers found the back of his head and strolled through his hair as he kissed me. I could feel his chest move against mine as he breathed. There was something wondrous about just being near him and playing this game.

I eased my hands down his neck and down his shoulders and then this time it was me that cut things short. "Come on, I'll show you the upstairs."

***

I was just remembering finishing up the tour of the house with Noah when Mama returned from the drug store. I was so deep in thought that it startled me when she opened the car door and I screamed. A man walking down the street heard me and he jumped and turned to see where the noise came from. I guess I scared him as much as Mama scared me.

"Dear Lord, child, the devil must be after you if you scare that easily." Mama huffed as she loaded her purchases into the backseat.

"Sorry. I was just about asleep." I dare not tell her I was sitting there reliving my first kiss while I waited on her.

"What's got you so tired that you're sleeping during the middle of the afternoon and in broad daylight?" Mama cranked the Dart and reminded me that we weren't really the napping kind. For us, there was always something to be done.

"Oh, nothing."

The truth of the matter was another subject that I dare not approach with Mama. In fact, what I had planned for the evening, for Noah's real birthday present, was not a subject that I felt comfortable sharing with anyone.

Mama just looked at me. She could tell when I was lying, but she didn't press me. She was not the most secure driver and she had all she could handle with the traffic on Broad Street. Friday afternoons in downtown Wrens had a tendency to be crowded so navigating through all of the other cars and making the U-turn to head back toward Stapleton took all of her focus. Thank God.

135

On the ride home I fell back into my day dreams. I rested my head on my arm which I had folded over the open window. The wind blew in my face and it was the best breeze I had felt all day. The faster Mama went, the better the breeze.

All the way home I remembered the remainder of my date with Noah on homecoming night. I remembered the feel of his stubble on his cheek, the firmness of his lips and the taste of his kisses. I blushed at the thoughts I was having while riding in the car with my mother just inches away from me. She might have been able to tell when I was lying, but thank goodness she'd never mastered reading my mind.

I remembered the conversation Noah and I had that ended the tour and brought to light my own insecurities. I had walked him through every room in the house and fulfilled my wish of kissing him in most of them. I told him about the time I spent playing Barbies in Allison's room when we were little. I explained that I had actually known Allison before I met Judy and ever since the first time I was invited to play at her house, I knew that I wanted a house just like hers one day.

We finally came to the master bedroom. I stopped just inside the door. Roaming the rest of the house felt fine, but this room gave me the vibe that it was off limits.

I could feel Noah ease an arm around my waist. I wrapped my arms around his and held on to him. The house was warmer inside than it was out so I had left his uniform jacket hanging on the banister at the bottom of the stairs. My shoulders were bare except for my hair that fell down my back. Noah moved all of my hair over one of my shoulders leaving the other completely exposed.

"It really is my dream house and I am going to buy it one day."

"This could be our room." I could feel his breath against my skin as he spoke.

I leaned back into him and closed my eyes.

"Dare I let myself imagine life here with you?" Noah sighed and placed soft kisses along my bare shoulder as he spoke.

For me, this wasn't a part of the game we had been playing. This wasn't me pretending. This room was a game changer.

"One day, this isn't going to be pretend, Gayle. I promise. We could buy it," Noah whispered in between each kiss.

I turned around to face him. "I'm not pretending anymore."

Noah brushed his hand gently against my face. I'm not pretending either. We could buy this house, if you want it."

I was dumbfounded. I didn't know what to say. I could tell he was serious and he went on to tell me as much.

"I haven't spent a dime of my military pay and I could make an offer as soon as you tell me it's for sale." His eyes were so intense, so convincing, but it scared me and I eased out of his hold.

I could not help it. A million thoughts flooded my mind. Minutes before I had been worried about being too forward with him and hours before I had been worried that I would never see him again. Now this. What was he implying?

"We should probably go." I started down the stairs. This was the first time all night that I didn't have his hand in mine, pulling him along behind me. This time I only had hands full of my dress and I was picking up the pace as I went down the steps.

Noah called after me and I could hear his footsteps bounding down the stairs after me. "Gayle, what's wrong? Wait!"

I didn't stop until I hit the porch. I was promptly reminded that it was November. There was a chill in the air and I had left his jacket hanging on the bottom post of the staircase. I held my arms and rubbed them together for the heat of friction.

Noah was right behind me in stepping onto the porch. He had thought to grab his coat on the way out and as he draped it over me from behind he begged, "Did I say something wrong?"

This time, I didn't turn around. I couldn't face him. "I got accepted into the University of Georgia. I'll be the first woman in my family to ever attend college."

"That's great, Gayle!" Noah reached his arms around me again.

"I want to be a vet. I always have. That's four more years of school. The acceptance letter came a week and a half ago. I've worked for this my whole life."

I held on tight to Noah's arms around me. "Don't you think this is a little fast?"

I didn't give Noah a chance to answer, I just kept going. "I'm not even out of high school yet. This was my first kiss tonight and I feel like I could go on kissing you forever. My heart races every time I open my mailbox now. I'm elated each time I find a letter in it and I'm equally devastated when I don't."

I stopped to catch my breath, worried that I had said too much.

Noah's voice was soft and patient when he responded. "Gayle, we've been something a kin to pen pals for nearly five months. I've known for some time now that I would never be satisfied with being your pen pal or as you have put it, your diary. As far as I'm concerned, you have been my girl since I laid eyes on you. Since your photograph arrived in the mail that day, yours is the first face I see when I wake up each morning."

"I'm sorry if you feel I'm rushing things. We can take as much time as you like, but I'm serious."

Noah turned me around and took my face in his hands. "I would do absolutely anything for you," he assured me.

I stood there wide-eyed over everything he was saying. I just couldn't believe he felt this way about me. I never thought there was anything special about me. I thought most boys just asked me out so they could tease me about being the Ice Princess. I never thought anyone could be serious about me like this.

Ever since I met Noah at Andy's funeral and all the while he wrote to me, I mainly thought he was just paying charity to the girl whose brother died. I daydreamed about him, too, but I always held onto the thought that he was too good to be true.

Daddy always said, "If it seems too good to be true then it usually is." He gave the example of Andy's wife and once I overheard him tell Mama, "She may be built like a brick shit house, but she's still a shit house." Daddy was never wrong and his voice in my head keeps reminding me, "He's too good to be true." What was I supposed to think? He was so beyond what I ever thought possible for me.

Did he not see that I was the tall lanky girl who still behaved a lot like a puppy that grew too fast and didn't know how to handle itself? Did he not notice how many times I had tripped in my heels and dress tonight? I was a fumbling giant standing five foot ten inches tall and towering over most of my friends.

"We hardly know each other, Noah, and..."

"Tell me you don't feel something for me. I know you do. Have you doubted me all night when I told you that you were the most beautiful girl I've ever seen? How could I ever look at anyone else or kiss anyone else or feel as comfortable talking to anyone else as I do with you? Gayle Anderson, you've ruined me for any other girl."

I blushed and hung my head. "I know you think you mean that, but there's no telling. They could sell this house tomorrow. You could go back to Italy and some Italian girl could turn your head..."

"Tell me you don't feel something and I will take you home right now."

"No, I can't tell you that."

139

"I'll wait for you, Gayle. I'll wait 'til May when you graduate and when I get shipped back stateside. 'Til you graduate from college. I'll wait. I always thought I would be a career military man, retire from it, but since I met you all I can think about is getting back here to you. It's funny, you fear some foreign girl turning my head and I fear some local boy turning yours. Maybe it's because I've seen some of what the world has to offer that makes me know that there's no one I would rather call mine than you."

I heard everything he said, but my head was still spinning. Our game of pretend had turned onto a game of cat and mouse in my head. How easy it would have been to tell him I wanted him, but what did I know about wanting a man? He continued to offer more than just kissing, but kissing was all I was prepared for.

I opted for changing the subject. I gestured toward his car, "You know, you might should cut the lights off to the car before the battery dies."

Noah agreed and promptly went to the car and back.

"Why don't we sit?" Noah motioned toward the steps of the porch as he approached.

"Okay," I replied and I took a seat on the top step.

Once Noah was seated beside me and had my hand in his, I started the conversation again about our future, specifically his future.

"I've told you about my plans for college, but beyond saying that your feelings about staying in the Air Force have changed since you met me, you haven't told me what your plans are. Have you thought about what you would do if you got out of the service?" Noah made circles across my hand with his thumb as I spoke.

"I think I mentioned in one of my letters that I might join the family business and start farming with my brothers and my dad."

"What I remember of the letters is that you had never intended to farm and that you had no interest in it." I paused and scooted closer to him. "If you could do anything you wanted, what would it be?"

Noah wrapped his arm around me. "I like to fly. I've earned my wings and I've have enough flight time to transition into a commercial pilot, but I also enjoy taking pictures and history. The thing is there's not much of a calling for a pilot slash photographer slash history buff in the CSRA." I felt Noah shrug his shoulders.

"Have you thought about going to college?"

"Not really."

"Why not?"

"I really hadn't planned all of this out. I thought I knew my path in life."

"So you've changed your entire path for a girl you've kissed six times? She must be one heck of a kisser." I could barely say that with a straight face.

"The best." Noah was all teeth and smiles when he looked at me.

I leaned my head against his shoulder and kind of nudged him. We both laughed. For the next thirty minutes Noah and I continued to talk and laugh and test his theory about me being the best kisser.

On the ride home Noah mentioned again how he hated bucket seats, but I didn't mind so much. It gave me time to settle down and hopefully not look flushed when I got home. I knew Mama and Daddy would be waiting up on me and I didn't want them to see me all worked up over Noah.

My house was along a straight away on Gene Howard Road and I could see it was lit up like a runway as soon as we turned down the road. Noah noticed it as well. "Let me guess, that's your house?"

I shook my head and rolled my eyes. "Yep. That would be the one."

"I've seen aircraft carriers with less lights."

Noah pulled into the driveway and the rumble of the engine made our horses run in the pasture. We were ten minutes early for my curfew. It gave us a few more minutes to talk as we had already agreed that we should not push our luck with a good night kiss there in the yard. Noah had been the perfect gentleman as he had promised Daddy he would be. I knew Daddy would be watching from the window. We might not see him, but I knew he would see us so now was not the time to give him a bad impression of Noah.

"Do you think it would be pressing my luck if I invited you to Sunday dinner?" Noah didn't wait for my answer. He got out of the Camaro and came around to open my car door.

He held out his hand to help me out of the car. "My mother cooks all day and the whole family comes. You could come too and meet everyone."

Noah and I walked hand in hand to the front porch. "I don't know what my Dad would say, but I don't suppose it would hurt to ask."

"I came all this way to see you and I'd like to spend as much time as possible with you, but I understand that your dad has rules and as long as you live in his house we have to respect those rules."

The front porch light flickered off and on. I rolled my eyes.

"I'll call you tomorrow," Noah promised me before he returned to the Camaro.

He fired that car up and the roar of the engine made the porch beneath my feet tremble. Although, I didn't let him know, I loved him and I loved that car of his, too.

Of course Mama and Daddy were waiting. The living room was just as lit up as the outside of the house and the yard had been. The television was playing and the Channel Six news was on. It was way past their bedtimes, but there they were.

Mama was in her spot on the far end of the couch. She was knitting another blanket for Millie. Daddy was in his rocker and peeling an orange and eating it. Someone had flipped the switch on the porch light, but neither of them appeared to have moved a muscle. In fact, if I didn't know the time, I would have thought it was about 8:00 p.m. because they were doing the type of things they would have been doing at 8:00 not 11:00.

"You're late." Daddy didn't even lift his eyes from the orange when he spoke.

"Late?" I gasped. "I was early by five minutes."

Mama cut her eyes from me to Daddy as I protested.

"Young lady, I broke the rules for you. You were to be in the house by 11:00 p.m."

"But I was in the yar..."

"In the house and in the yard are two different things."

"You didn't say in the house. You said home by 11:00..."

Daddy cut me off again, "I know what I said."

I had never argued with Daddy like this before, but I stood my ground. "You might know what you said, but you should also know that 'Home' extends to the yard and I know you knew I was in the yard. I know you looked, no, I know you made Mama look."

"Don't sass me!"

"I'm not sassing you, but you're being unreasonable. I did like you said I'm just pointing out that if you're going to be such a stickler then so am I."

Neither one of us was backing down and, as usual, Mama intervened. She slammed down her knitting on the end table and stood up with a commotion. "It's past my bedtime and I'm not staying up to listen to you two argue! I suggest y'all get to bed as well."

I followed Mama's lead and went to my room. I was barely in my night gown when Mama knocked on my door and eased it open.

The whole house was quiet and that could've been why she whispered, but I think she whispered in order to make sure Daddy didn't hear her. "Gayle, I know you think he's being unreasonable, but, for your Daddy, this was a major step."

"I know, Mama, but that was ridiculous, y'all knew I was in the yard. Noah's car is so loud that you could hear it coming from a half mile down the road so I know Daddy heard us turn in. So, he's just picking on me by saying I was late and that's not right."

"Just hang in there. He doesn't have Andy to split his focus and, that's not your fault, but all of his focus is going to be on you. He's just trying to keep you safe so cut him some slack. Alright?"

"Fine." I drew out that word as if it had a dozen syllables.

"Good night, my sweet girl." Mama hugged me before I climbed into bed.

"Good night, Mama. I love you."

"I love you too. Now, get some sleep."

Morning came too soon. Usually it was the light through the windows that woke me up on Saturday mornings, but not this morning. This morning I was woken from my dreams by the ringing of the phone followed by Mama's voice calling me.

"Gayle, the telephone."

I fell out of bed and staggered down the hall. The only phone in the house hung in the cut through between the living room and the kitchen.

For the life of me I could not imagine why anyone would be calling me that early on a Saturday morning. My first thought was that it was Judy calling for the details of the rest of my night, but that thought was wrong.

"Hello," I answered in a still groggy voice. I had slept so hard that I felt like I had only been asleep for a half hour. In actuality, I had slept a full eight hours.

144

"Good morning, sleepy head," came the voice on the other end of the line.

"Noah?" Was he really calling me? I looked around to the kookoo clock that hung above the couch in the living room to find out the time. It was 8:00 a.m.

From the clock I cut my eyes to Mama who was standing there listening as Noah answered. "I thought I would give you a wakeup call."

I giggled and shooed Mama way for some privacy. She shook her head at me, but she left the room all the same.

"Thank you. My alarm clock was going to go off any second, but I would much rather wake up like this."

"I want you to know that I did hear you last night, but you could wakeup to my voice every morning if you like. I'm just sayin'."

"You are persistent, Mr. Walden."

"Yes, I am, but please don't call me 'Mr. Walden.' It makes me think of my dad."

I slinked back against the wall that held the phone and I bit my bottom lip as I asked, "What do you like to think about?"

"You."

I had to stifle the urge to squeal. "Surely you have better subjects to occupy your mind that me."

"We really are going to have to work on this self-esteem problem of yours, Gayle. If you don't have any plans for later we can begin working on this problem right away."

"I don't have a problem and I have to work today."

"Right, the feed and seed store."

"Yes, the feed store."

"Well surely you aren't working there all day and all night."

145

"No, we close at 2:00 p.m. and then I have to help Daddy cut grass."

"It's a little late in the year to still be cutting grass."

The banter between Noah and I went back and forth like rapid fire. "If you had been here the last few months, you would know that this has been about the hottest fall on record so the grass still hadn't stopped growing. And, we've got a very big yard."

"Ah, and once you finish cutting grass?"

"I don't know. I don't know how long it will take for us to finish the grass."

"I don't suppose we could convince your dad to break his rules for a second night in a row?"

I hated to answer that one after how Daddy had been to me when he accused me of being late the night before. As bad as I wanted to go out with Noah again, I was afraid to ask Daddy. Plus, he was already out and gone that morning so there was no chance for me to ask him and that's ultimately what I told Noah.

"Okay, well, consider this a standing invitation to go out with me tonight. Let me give you my number."

"Oh, Daddy would never allow me to call you. Girls calling boys, that's a big no-no. Sorry."

"I will just have to call you this afternoon after you get off work. I am persistent, you know." Noah laughed as he used my words to describe himself.

"Right, persistent. I should go get ready for work, I guess."

"If you must."

"I must."

"Then what are you still doing here on the phone with me."

"I'm going."

146

"Really? Are you sure?"

"Yes, I'm going. Goodbye, Noah."

"I'll see you later, Gayle."

"Don't you mean, you'll talk to me later?"

"Maybe."

"You are bad."

"I am and you are going to be late for work."

It was so fun to talk to him and the way my heart fluttered when he said my name, I never wanted to hang up with him. "I really do have to get dressed for work. I'll ask my dad about going out tonight and I'll talk to you later. Bye."

"Bye, Gayle, and have a good day at work."

I'm sure Mama heard every word, but she didn't say anything other than to warn me that I better get a move on if I was going to be on time for work. I was due at work at 9:00 a.m. and it wasn't hard to pick up the pace. The call from Noah was like a shot of adrenaline to start my day. Even the most remote thought of seeing him that evening put a spring in my step.

I had to run from the car to the time clock, but I punched into work with one minute to spare. Once there, I found Mrs. Smith waiting on me. She wanted to know all about the young man who came in there looking for me the night before, the one she saw on the field with me as my escort for the homecoming court.

"Lordy, Lordy," Mrs. Smith shook her head. "I did not know you had a beau, Miss Gayle. Where did you meet him?"

I guess Mrs. Smith was right. I had a beau and I blushed at the thought and at her questions. I stalled before answering her question and pulled my hair up into a ponytail.

"You must tell me all the details," she insisted.

Mrs. Smith thought of herself as one of my friends. She was sweet, but I think she was a little delusional, thinking we were somehow the same age and girlfriends. In actuality, she was a woman in her early forties who had married a man twenty something years her senior. He aged her before her time and she was now trying to regain her youth. They had been married twenty years, but the ladies around town never took to her because Mr. Smith, the owner of the feed and seed store and my boss, didn't wait the appropriate amount of time after his first wife died before he remarried. Everyone knew it was customary to wait a year moving on, everyone but Mr. Smith and the Mrs. Smith that I knew now.

"I met him at Andy's funeral. I don't know if you remember the boys from the Air Force that presented the flag to Mama and Daddy." I proceeded from the time clock near the back door toward the front to unlock the door and turn the "Open" sign around. Mrs. Smith followed me all the way and our conversation continued.

"Yes, who could forget? It was the most beautiful version of "Taps" I had ever heard. Walter and I commented on it all the way home. Walter wants a sendoff just like that. He's starting to talk more and more about going to meet our Lord, but I've tried to tell him that we don't need to talk about such things."

Mrs. Smith tended to ramble, but I got her refocused. "Anyway, he was the one that played the bugle. He played "Taps."

"Oh my." Mrs. Smith fanned herself. "Ohhhh my."

I wouldn't see Judy before school on Monday and I had to tell someone so I confided in Mrs. Smith. Any other lady her age would rush to tell my mother, but not her. Like everyone else, Mama had never given Mrs. Smith the time of day. They weren't enemies, but they certainly weren't friends.

I was allowed to pour my heart out to Mrs. Smith and she was allowed to live vicariously through me. The conversation about Noah lasted my entire shift and it sure made quitting time come a lot sooner than it would have if I had not had her. Before I knew it, it was time to clock out and head home.

On the ride home, I thought about what Mrs. Smith had imparted to me. "Follow your dreams," she told me. "If your dreams are to get married and start a family right out of high school and you love this boy, then do that. Of course, don't tell your Mama and Daddy I told you to do that. Now, if your dreams are to become a veterinarian, like you have told me a million times, then don't let some boy get in the way of that. If he is the right one, he will want you to follow your dreams. If you compromise your dreams, stay home, marry him, you will resent him and it won't last. Don't let someone else make you think their dreams are yours. It won't end well. I should know. That's exactly how my first marriage went."

I thought it was pretty good advice that she gave me. Despite what others thought, Mrs. Smith was more than Aqua Net, fake eyelashes and an overly pronounced twisty walk.

I was deep in thought, but when I made the turn and our house came into view, I could see Noah's black Camaro sitting in the yard. My stomach dropped and swirled about all at the same time. What was he doing there?

So much for planning how I would look the next time I saw him. Thanks to my choice of blue jeans, t-shirt and smock, which just realized I forgot to leave at the feed store, that decision was moot. I was mortified at the thought of seeing him in my current state. It wasn't the outfit that was the problem so much as the fact that I reeked of manure.

Junior Williams, the boy that works with me, and usually does all of the heavy lifting, called in sick today. With Junior out, I had to pitch in and help Mr. Smith with some of the loading. As if that wasn't bad enough, one of the bags of fertilizer busted and went all over me. I was somewhat fortunate in that the manure accident happened only about thirty minutes before we closed. I needed a shower in the worst way and I certainly didn't want to see anyone, let alone Noah, while I was like this. It was even in my hair.

It was too late, but I rolled down the car window. I prayed that the stink would blow off of me in the last two hundred yards before my driveway.

As I came closer to the house I noticed Daddy on the riding mower. It first seemed odd to me that Daddy would be outside moving the yard with company over, but then I spotted Noah on the far side of the yard. He had the same build as Andy and was shirtless with the push mower. For a moment, I saw a ghost.

My heart nearly burst out of my chest and as quickly as it did, I came back to my senses. I was happy to see Noah, but devastated that it wasn't Andy.

Noah was going back and forth through the ditch that separated the yard from the field where Daddy planted corn. November had been unusually warm and the grass had to start dying off for the winter. Noah was glistening in the sun as he pushed the mower up and down through the ditch. It had been cool at night, but the days were still in the eighties. Today was the same.

Daddy lifted his straw hat and waved at me as I passed by. I pulled in the driveway and parked the Dart alongside Noah's car. I rolled up the window and got out. The entire yard smelled like fresh cut grass and wild onions. The scent was so strong that I could no longer smell the manure on me.

Noah noticed me and shut the push mower off. I met him halfway from the driveway to the ditch.

"What are you doing here?" I asked him as I smiled from ear to ear.

I wanted to hug him, but showed the proper restraint that was dictated to me all my life by the words in the back of my head whispering, "What would Mama and Daddy say?" That voice was quieted when Noah took both of my hands in his. He was as genuinely happy to see me as I was him. It showed all over his face, the smile, the dimples in his cheeks, the light in his eyes.

"You told me this morning that you had to come home and help cut grass. You didn't think you would be able to do anything tonight because you didn't know what time you'd be finished with the grass so I thought I would help solve that problem."

Some might have been distracted by the fact that he was shirtless, but not me. I was fascinated by his face and I hung on his

150

every word. The way he looked at me as he spoke made every thought leave my head and all I could do was bite my bottom lip. I wanted to kiss him so badly that I totally forgot about the scent of animal waste that was all over me.

I tried to maintain the conversation and not go completely speechless as I looked at him. "So you are mowing the grass in my place? You didn't have to do that."

"Yeah, I know, but your dad seemed glad to get the help. I think I might have made some brownie points too."

"I bet you did." I could not erase the giddy grin from my face long enough to hold up my end.

"Why are you looking at me like that?" He noticed and I was embarrassed.

I hung my head and kicked the dirt with my Keds. "You are full of surprises. I don't know what to make of you. No one's ever been like this..."

"Gayle, look at me." Noah, let go with his right hand and lifted my chin forcing me to look him in the face again.

"Let me explain something to you, when I was seven I wanted a bicycle and I got it. When I was twelve I wanted a go cart and I got it. When I was seventeen I wanted that car and I got it." With a slight tilt, he nodded his head toward his car. "I worked hard for those things. Now, I want you and I am not above working hard to get you."

I thought I was going to faint. If I was Scarlett O'Hara I would have needed some smelling salts. That was hot, but who says stuff like that to girls? How was I supposed to respond to that? My mother would die if she heard him talk to me like that. My face was hot, but not like when I got mad. It was the same kind of heat that took over me when he kissed me.

The fact of the matter was he was the magnificent combination of sweet and cocky and I liked it. I really liked it. The other fact of the matter was that he had me. He had me from the day of the funeral, but I wanted more out of life than to just get married. I guess I was a real odd bird for these parts. I knew this was the dream of every girl in my high school, for a boy they loved to ask them to marry them, sweep them off their feet and, poof, everything about their lives would be wrapped up with a bow on top. What was I going to do with him?

Judy had warned me a while back about the chase. "Once the chase is done, they're done, so be careful."

My stomach was doing flips, but I gathered my nerves. "You are so bad. You probably say that to all the girls. I'm going to get changed."

"You keep thinking that."

I was almost to the front door when I glanced back to Noah. He was leaning over to pull the engine cord on the mower. He gave it a swift snatch and I could see every muscle in his back and his arms. I remember thinking when I was first driving up that he and Andy had the same shape, but I was wrong. Of course I never looked at my brother like this, but I knew Andy was not built like Noah. Andy was lean, but Noah could have been the body double for Leonardo Da Vinci's Vitruvian Man, the drawing he did on proportions, I learned about it in art class.

Earlier, I envisioned wearing my favorite dress the next time I saw Noah. I pulled it out of my closet, but putting that on now seemed a little presumptuous. Also, I didn't know what the night held, but the afternoon still held about an hour worth of mowing for Noah so putting a dress on just to wait and see if we were even allowed to go out was silly. I grabbed a fresh pair of jeans and my favorite blouse, the one I had worn on my first day of school this year.

I finished my shower. I was clean and smelled more like myself. I finished my hair and makeup and wandered to the kitchen. I looked out of the kitchen window and I could see Daddy and Noah standing over the push mower. Daddy had his straw hat in his one of his hands, both of which were perched on his hips. The mower was smoking and Noah was shaking his head. I was too far away to hear what they were saying and I was curious. I grabbed a couple of glasses and hurriedly made ice water and carried it out to them.

"Hey, what's going on?" I asked as I approached them.

Daddy was the first to turn around, but it was Noah's face that got my attention. All cockiness was gone.

"Well, looks like the old mower has given up the ghost," Daddy sighed.

"I'm so sorry." I got the distinct impression that that wasn't the first time Noah said those words. He looked so sincere.

"Dang, Noah, you broke our mower?" I almost laughed as I handed them each a glass of water.

"Thanks, Gayle, and, if he didn't want to mow, you could have just said so." Daddy took my lead.

"Thank you, but I swear, I didn't..."

I could not hold it in any longer. "Noah, don't worry about it. That mower's been on the fritz for years. It's almost as old as I am." I cracked up.

Daddy slapped him on the back. "It was on borrowed time. Don't worry about it. Come on, let's go get cleaned up. I'll buy your dinner tonight for helping me out."

Daddy started toward the house and Noah and I followed.

"Sir, you really don't have to do that."

"I insist."

I mouthed the words, "brownie points" at Noah and he winked at me. I think we were both a little shocked by Daddy's offer. Noah grazed my hand, but he didn't press his luck and take my hand in that close of proximity to Daddy.

Daddy looked over his shoulder to Noah and we immediately snapped our heads forward. "I'm guessing you brought a change of clothes in hopes that I agreed to allow you to take my daughter out."

"Umm..." Noah was cautious and stalled to try to decide whether to admit it.

Daddy paused for a moment and turned directly at Noah. "It's okay, son. I was once young, too. I'm not saying I'll let you take her out, but you can go ahead and grab your things from your car."

Noah didn't wait around for Daddy to change his mind. He asked me to hold his glass of ice water and then he went straight to the Camaro and pulled out the same duffel bag he had last night. I waited on him by the front door while Daddy went ahead inside the house.

When Noah and I made it inside we found Daddy standing there with his wallet. "I said I would buy you dinner so I was thinking that after you got washed up and changed, you and Gayle might run out to Raley's and pick us all up a shrimp dinner."

"I can call it in while Noah showers," I offered.

Daddy shook his head back and forth. "No, that won't do. Place the order once you get there so it will still be hot when you get back with it."

Without realizing what I had done, I cocked my head to the side and looked at Daddy like, "Are you sure?"

"You know, I can't abide cold French Fries, Gayle. Now, go show Noah where the bathroom is."

I'm sure I still had a curious look on my face, but I didn't say anything other than, "Yes, sir."

Halfway to the bathroom it occurred to me. Daddy was breaking the rules for me, but didn't want to be so obvious about it. How would he look to me and Mama if he was suddenly lightening up? I nearly laughed out loud at the thought.

Mama wasn't back from her day out with Aunt Ruth, but within twenty minutes Noah was out of the shower and ready to give me a ride to Raley's Restaurant. Daddy handed me a twenty dollar bill. "Pick up a plate for your mama as well. You know what she likes."

"Yes, sir, fried shrimp, hush puppies and a baked potato with butter only."

I tucked the bill into my pocket as Daddy modified his order. Noah waited patiently for me by the front door with his bag in his hand.

"I feel like a steak tonight. Noah, get yourself a steak too if you like." Daddy handed me an extra five dollar bill and I folded it and stuck in my pocket as well.

I hugged Daddy and started toward the door. Noah held the door for me. He knew as well as I did what Daddy was up to. "Thank you, sir." Noah told him.

As soon as the door shut behind us I felt as if I was going to jump out of my skin over the excitement of being alone with Noah again. I could hardly wait for him to kiss me and I prayed he wouldn't wait to do it. It was like I was desperate to feel his lips on mine. That had been one of my prevailing thoughts all day long.

I gave Noah directions to head back toward Stapleton and then toward Avera. "This is back toward our house, right?"

"Yes, it is." I said, obvious that I was impressed that he remembered. I liked that he called it our house despite me warding him off last night.

"Do you think we have time to swing by there so I can see it in the daylight?"

I bit my bottom lip. "I think we have time, but we'll have to be quick."

I didn't have to give Noah the rest of the directions to the house. He remembered the whole way, right down to which trail-looking driveway off of Hadden Pond Road to take.

The sun was still beating down like a summer day, but the colors of the foliage around the house were all fall. The yard could

155

stand a good raking, but it was beautiful. The house stood out like a white angel among all of the red and orange and yellow that framed it.

Noah let the Camaro roll to a stop and cut the engine off. "It was pretty at night, but I never imagined anything like this. Gayle, I see why this is your dream."

Noah opened his car door. "Wait there. I'll come around." He had yet to fail to open a door for me.

Noah led me to the steps of the front porch, holding my hand the entire way. He stopped there on the steps and looked out across the yard. "I didn't even realize there was a barn over there. It was so dark last night, I guess I couldn't see it."

"Yeah, it's a big barn. I've always imagined fixing it up a little and running my vet practice out of it. It has enough stalls for eight horses."

"That sounds like a good plan." I'm sure my face told the story that I liked having his approval.

"You can't see it from here, but through the woods behind the barn is a ten acre pond. The road is named after it, Hadden Pond. The water in the pond is so still that they named the house here Still Water Plantation when it was built."

"Really? Our house has a name? I don't remember you mentioning that last night."

"It has a name, a great deal of land and a history. I'll have to tell you about that another time. We should get going."

"Before we go," Noah paused and brushed my hair from my face. With that same hand he took my chin and gave me what I had been dreaming of all day long, a kiss. It was just enough to weaken my knees and make me swoon for him.

Noah eased his lips from mine and rested his forehead against my forehead. He wasn't too terribly much taller than I was, but I wasn't ready to stop and I stretched up to him. Standing on my tip toes, I aimed to continue.

"I could kiss you for days if you let me, but you said yourself that we need to be going."

I slinked back down onto my flat feet in disappointment.

"Come on." Noah took my hand to pull me toward the car.

I resisted just as we reached my car door.

"What is it?" he asked.

"Noah, I know we could be happy here. I know, I told you I have dreams of college, but, well, maybe I shouldn't tell you..."

Noah seemed delighted, but waited with baited breath as to what it was I really meant to say. "You can tell me anything."

"I just didn't want you to think that I didn't have dreams of you too."

***

Our driveway wasn't paved, so I was jolted back to my seat in the car with my mother when she turned in and we rumbled over the gravel. I looked at my watch. It was 4:00 p.m. and Noah was supposed to pick me up at 6:00. I had two hours to get ready for our date.

CHAPTER 9

I took my time getting ready for Noah. I couldn't believe it had been so long since I had seen him. I thought back about the rest of the week he was home on leave and the last time I saw him before he returned to Italy in November. I thought about when he came back in June and then was gone again.

I stood in front of my closet attempting to choose an outfit for the night and before I knew it I was down to one hour to shower, dry my hair, put on what little makeup I tended to wear and get dressed. My mind drifted back to Thanksgiving. Noah was such a gentleman and at every turn he showed respect to Daddy for breaking the rules for him to court me. It really was more of a courtship than dating, as well as dating was in the 1970s.

Noah wanted to invite me to his parents' house for Thanksgiving, but he dared not do it by just asking me outright. In fact, the way he went about getting Daddy to allow me to come to Thanksgiving and meet his family was downright genius on his part.

When we got back from picking up dinner from Raley's, Noah brought up the subject of Thanksgiving. "Can you imagine that Thanksgiving is just a week away?" Noah started.

It was almost as if Mama and I were not seated at the table next to each of them the way the conversation went.

"Oh, I know," Daddy replied. "It's been so warm this year that it doesn't seem like November at all."

"Being in Italy all this time and then coming here with the humidity, it's really thrown my sense of the seasons off." Noah added. "That doesn't mean I would turn down some sweet potato pie, mind you. I haven't had a good sweet potato pie since my grandmother died four years ago."

"Well, you are in luck. Jane here's Cousin Dawn, makes the best sweet potato pie you ever put in your mouth."

"That's Mama's cousin on the Landrum side of the family," I added. It also struck me odd that Daddy had just invited Noah to Thanksgiving. I didn't say anything as I was thrilled to think of Noah joining us.

"Is there more than one Dawn?" asked Noah. He nudged me under the table. He knew he had gotten the invite as well. The only person that didn't seem to know it was Daddy.

"Lord, there's three of them. We've got about as many Dawn's on her side as there are Linda's in most other families." Daddy snickered and Mama looked at him above her glasses as she took another bite of her hushpuppy.

After dinner, Noah and I took a walk. Behind our house was the barn where Daddy restored cars and kept the tractor. I threw open the doors to the barn. I reached and felt for the switch, flipped it and a string of lights running the length of the barn flickered on until they reached full power.

Along with stacks upon stacks of hay, there were two cars currently parked in the barn. Andy's brand new Corvette was stashed in the back. Daddy was hiding it from the former Mrs. Anderson and saving it for Millie. Daddy was also working on a 1955 Thunderbird and it was sitting in the middle of the barn.

The prior owner of the Thunderbird had abused it and Daddy got it for a steal. He had been working on it for a few months off and on. So far, it had new tires and a tune-up to the engine, which Daddy had found in pretty good shape. The paint was stripped and a new convertible top was on order.

"Wow, now that's a car even in this condition!" admired Noah as he left my hand to run his down the length of the car, along the trunk and made a circle to back around to where I was at the front. He didn't even notice the Corvette in the back.

The interior of the car looked fine so I asked Noah if he would like to sit in it.

"No." He said just above a whisper and who would have thought that word could ever sound so sexy, but it could and it did.

Noah backed me into the hood of the car. "Remember what I told you we would continue later?"

"Yes," I exhaled as he pressed into me. I could feel the length of him against me.

Noah's eyes burned into me and he didn't break that connection while in one swift move he lifted me and sat me on the hood of the T-bird. Daddy would die if he caught me sitting on the car like that, but worrying about my father in that moment never entered my head.

"Do you mind?" Noah asked as he placed his hands on my knees and started to widen the space between them. Who could mind? I could hardly think at all.

Before I was completely finished shaking my head "no," Noah reached around me, slipped his hands into my back pockets and pulled me closer to him. I could feel every inch of him against me and, in this position, *every* inch pressed into me. I had never felt such before and that fact alone sent me into a frenzy of hormones. For the first time, I knew what it was to want a man. If I had been more like Judy, and not at all like myself, I would have satisfied that want right there on the hood of that old car.

My arms were around his shoulders, firm, muscular shoulders, and my fingers found the line where his hair met his neck. Despite its short length, Noah's hair was fine and soft. I gripped the back of his head and I pulled him deeper into the kiss. This was so much more than an action. It was every bit of emotion that had built up in me all day long, all week long. Every bit of anticipation that had been pushed off earlier in the evening was exploding into him now.

Noah eased his hands from my pockets up my back, climbing until he found my hair. Simultaneously, Noah eased his mouth from mine and with one hand he gripped me around my waist and with the other he swept my hair back to expose my left ear. He drew circles around my ear with his tongue and it sent chills down both of my legs.

I let go of his neck and braced myself with my palms against the hood of the car. On instinct I sighed and tilted my head arching my back. This was the best feeling I had ever experienced and it continued with Noah inching his tongue down my neck. The chill bumps were not letting up.

Noah found that divot in my neck, that little spot in the center that sinks in between my collar bones, and he sucked. I thought my eyes were going to roll back in my head.

"Oh, God, Noah!" Breathlessly and like a quiet scream, I said his name again, "Noah!" I exhaled three sharp little breaths. He was the master of kissing. Not in my wildest dreams could I have imagined this feeling, burning and chills and sweat and breathlessness all at once.

Noah eased back from me, but I didn't let him go far. I had never kissed anyone before this last week. I really didn't know what I was doing, so I did my best to follow his lead. First I took his mouth with mine again. I explored his mouth until I pulled his tongue into mine and applied a little suction of my own. At the same time, I let go of the hood of the car and ran my hands up his arms feeling every muscle as I went. I traced the neck of his t-shirt with my index fingers and then with my tongue.

I believe Noah was about as overcome with the moment as I was because I could feel him shake off a shiver. "We are going to have to cool this down, Gayle." His stare was so serious. "Do you know what you do to me?"

I broke eye contact and looked sideways toward the floor of the barn. I shook my head. I didn't know. I only hoped I did to him what he did to me. I hope I had set him on fire like he did me. His touch, his kiss, they were the striking of a match that lit a bonfire in the pit of my belly that burned all the way to my soul.

"You drive me insane. I think of nothing else, but you lately. I don't know how I'm going to endure months without seeing you."

161

Noah lifted my chin. "Months without kissing you. I lie awake at night wondering what you're doing and wondering if you think of me. This is not me."

I smiled. I leaned into Noah and rested my head against his ear. The house was a good fifty yards from the barn and there was no one to hear us, but I whispered anyway, letting him in on my secret. "I dream of you even when I am awake. There's not a day that goes by that I don't miss you."

Noah held onto me tightly. "What are we going to do? I've never been this way over anyone before, Gayle. No one."

"Good." The thought of him like this over anyone else made my stomach churn so hearing that I was special to him just made me want to forget who I was, forget that I wasn't like Judy, forget that my parents could pop into the barn at any moment.

"Good?" Noah laughed quietly.

Was this the point where I told him I loved him? Was it alright to do that? He had essentially asked me to marry him last night so surely, I could tell him. I wanted to say the words. I wanted to hear him say them back, but I didn't get the chance. I was interrupted by the faint sound of Mama calling my name and the moment passed.

"I guess we better be getting back," Noah backed away and offered his hand to help me down.

"Yeah, we've been out of sight for a while now and they probably prefer to keep an eye on us."

I cut the lights off in the barn and Noah helped me with the doors before we walked back to the house. We found Mama waiting at the front door. Before she could say anything, I explained to Mama that I was showing Noah the T-bird. She wasn't stupid and the look on her face reaffirmed that notion. There was no getting anything past her or Daddy.

The rest of the evening Noah and I sat in the porch swing and talked about any and everything. Before he left for the night, Noah stuck his head inside and said good night to Mama and Daddy.

"Thank you all for having me tonight and I wanted to ask your permission to call Gayle during the week," Noah asked.

Although I could not see Mama and Daddy, I could hear everything they said. Mama spoke first. "Noah, how long are you home on leave?"

"Until the Friday after Thanksgiving, ma'am."

"So, next Friday?"

"Yes, ma'am."

Daddy chimed in and answered Noah's initial question. "You are welcome to call Gayle on Wednesday night. I can't have you calling her every night as she has school work to focus on."

"Of course," Noah nodded his head. "Thank you, sir, and again, thank you both for having me for dinner."

"It was the least we could do after you helped George with the yard this afternoon. And, if it's alright with your family, we would love to have you for Thanksgiving." I was thrilled that Mama extended the invitation to Noah. This meant no awkward discussion with Daddy to make sure he had meant to invite him while we were at dinner earlier.

"Thank you, but my mother has already informed me that I was only allowed to have Thanksgiving lunch with Gayle if Gayle and I were at her table that evening. She said there was no way I was coming all the way from Italy and not spending some portion of Thanksgiving with her. I hope you understand and don't take that as me trying to negotiate. Those really were my mother's words."

"I'm sure I would be the same way," Mama replied, but neither she nor Daddy consented to me going to Thanksgiving dinner at Noah's parents' house.

Knowing that my parents were watching, Noah wrapped his arms around me on the steps of the porch. He buried his head in my hair.

"I will miss you all week. It's bad enough to leave you tonight. I don't know how I'm going to go back to Camp Darby next week."

"I don't know how I'm going to let you go." I actually felt tears coming at the thought of him leaving even though it was a week away.

The week drug by and the only thing that made it bearable was giving Judy the play by play of my weekend. She made me tell her every detail and in telling her I was able to relive my time with Noah.

Wednesday came and I rushed home from school not knowing when Noah might call. I was desperate not to miss that call. I was dying to hear his voice. I wanted to stay home from Wednesday night service at the church, but Mama wouldn't hear of it and Daddy said I needed to get my priorities straight. He reminded me that the Lord came first. I figured the Lord would understand.

I was miserable and distracted the entire time we were at church. I just wanted to go home and as soon as the closing prayer was said, I was out the door and waiting in the car. As it turned out, Noah counted on us going to church and he didn't call until after 8:30 p.m.

Noah understood that our only phone was right there in the room with Mama and Daddy. The phone situation at his parents' house was the same. His mother and father were there in the room with him, listening to our conversation as much as mine were.

"Do you think I could see you on Friday night?" Noah asked.

"I have to work, but I get off at 7:00 p.m. I guess, if you don't mind waiting for me until 7:30. Let me ask to make sure."

I put my hand over the phone and asked. I was stunned that again Daddy broke the rules. He said he would need to know our plans, but he would agree for Noah to pick me up after work as long as he had me home by 10:30 p.m. I relayed that to Noah.

"Then I will see you on Friday night."

Friday came and it was great!

When Noah picked me up we went the opposite way from my house, away from Stapleton. As soon as we reached the stop sign at the intersection with the Warrenton Highway, Noah put the Camaro in park.

"We need to take care of some business, if you don't mind," he said as he leaned over to me.

With his index finger, he tucked the hair that had been dangling in my face behind my ear. His finger gently grazed my cheek and it sent chills down my legs. From my ear, his whole hand went through my hair and to the back of my head, near the base, and he pulled me toward him. I was wearing a skirt and thought he would notice the chill bumps, but he didn't. As he guided me closer, he held my gaze.

I had dreamed of that moment a million times since I slid down from the top of the Thunderbird last Saturday night. As Noah's lips caressed mine, my stomach flipped and fluttered with butterflies.

Ever since Noah mentioned being apart for months there was something as heartbreaking as it was exhilarating when we touched. Like a storm brewing and I tried to shrug off the dread of constantly knowing that our days were numbered by his return to Italy.

I don't know how long we would have sat there if Reverend Pickle from Pleasant Grove hadn't pulled up behind us and honked when he got tired of waiting. Noah rolled down his window and motioned the Reverend around as I hid my face with embarrassment.

"We should probably get on to dinner," I mumbled knowing all the while I would gladly skip dinner just to stay enveloped by him. I would much prefer the taste of Noah as to any food at that moment.

We had dinner at The Dairy Barn in Wrens. After dinner we met up with Judy and Doug at Doug's house. We played pool and Noah beat the snot out of all of us. I pretended I didn't know how to play, but I did. Noah's arms around me, teaching me how to hold the stick and aim, all of that just made me want more time alone with him. Short of riding in the car, there really wasn't any alone time with Noah that night.

Saturday night was the complete opposite from Friday. Daddy allowed us to go out again.

I made a picnic and we ate it while sitting on the top step of the porch of what we had jokingly referred to as "our house" at Stillwater Plantation. Dinner was going well and Noah was mostly done with his sandwich when he stopped. He put what was left of it down on his napkin and just looked at me.

"What?" I asked curiously.

Noah put his hands to his head and scruffed at his hair before falling back. His knees were up on the step and his torso landed flat against the boards of the porch. He stared up at the ceiling for a moment and I asked again, "What is it?"

"I've only been here twice and ever since then, each time I ask you out, I hope that you want to come here again." Noah rolled to his side, to face me. "I look forward to coming here with you."

I was in the middle of chewing a bite of my sandwich and had not expected him to say that. I blushed and struggled to swallow without choking. I was sure my face turned as red as the shirt I was wearing.

"Are you alright?" Noah sat up quickly.

I could not answer him. I had not succeeded. I was choking. I tried coughing, but nothing was happened. I just couldn't get air. I was panicking.

Noah jumped into action as I continued to try to cough, to get a breath. Within seconds, he was wrapped around me, jerking me to my feet and giving me the Heimlich maneuver. With one snatch, the bread from my ham sandwich popped loose. Noah let go of me, giving me space to regain my composure. It wasn't very ladylike, but I spit out into the yard and gasped for air. I doubled over with my head between my knees and continued to try to catch my breath.

"Gayle, are you okay?"

I still could not answer. My only sound in return was a few coughing hacks, still trying to make sure my windpipe was clear.

Noah reached over and held my hair back. Perhaps he thought I was going to throw up. I took a couple of more deep breaths and finally things were back to normal. I stood up and there was a genuine look of concern on Noah's face.

"I'm sorry I scared you." I fell into his arms and hugged him for all I was worth. Noah had saved my life. That was the closest I had ever come to choking to death. "I cannot thank you enough."

"No, no, it's okay." Noah cradled my head and ran his hands through my hair. "I have less than a week before I have to go back to Italy and I can't stand the thought of leaving you. I'm not sure what I would do if something happened to you."

I could feel the collar of his shirt against my cheek. It was blue and soft and my eyes rolled back as it distracted me from the scratching in my throat. Beneath the shirt, he was firm and I tilted my head to rest on his neck. "I love you," I whispered in a voice that sounded nothing like my own.

Noah held me tighter. A minute, maybe two passed in silence. In that time I wondered if he heard me, but I didn't worry if he would say it back. I didn't care if he said it back. I hadn't planned on saying it, it just came out.

Noah took a deep breath. He didn't reciprocate. Noah didn't return the line to me. Instead, Noah lifted my chin. "Look at me."

I did as he instructed me. When our eyes met, he held my gaze for a moment to gain emphasis on what he said. I thought he was going to reciprocate, but instead, he just looked at me. His eyes had never been bluer. The corners of his mouth turned up slightly and there was a hint of a smile. I blinked nervously still not knowing if he had actually heard me, the hesitant internal dialogue that escaped my lips and confessed my feelings.

167

Gently, Noah ran his fingers from my forehead down my cheek and tucked the wisps of stray hairs behind my ear. As he grazed my check, I leaned into his touch and closed my eyes. "You're so beautiful. I want to give you something."

Noah reached in front pocket of his blue jeans. "I've never given this to anyone. I hardly wore it." With his free hand he took mine and opened it as he spoke. "It's yours and you can put wax in it and wear it on your finger or you can wear it on a chain. If you want a chain for it, I'll get you one."

I looked at him in amazement and down to the ring. It was his class ring and he slipped it on my middle finger. He was right, I needed wax in it if I was going to wear it.

I held out my hand to admire it. "Are you sure about this?" I blinked up at him. It was pretty compared to mine and so bulky. His was the traditional man's ring, heavy, white gold with the big, round ruby in the center and it sparkled. The thing that really caught my eye the most was his name that was carved down one side of the ring.

"I'm sure. Plus, it's something so you won't forget me and so everyone else will know you're mine."

"It's really pretty," I said, continuing to turn my hand to admire it. On the opposite side of his name, there was a football player carved in it.

"One day, I'll get you something more suitable for telling everyone you're mine."

"This is perfectly suitable."

"It will do for now."

Noah pulled me close to him. "Wait," I leaned back from him. I pulled off my own class ring and handed it to him.

"You don't have to do that," Noah said as he took my ring in the palm of his hand.

"It's only fair."

My ring was tiny compared to his. Noah's was white gold and mine was yellow. The blue stone in mine was rectangular shaped with the school name engraved in the band of the ring. My graduating year, '76, was carved into one side and an "A" for my name, my real name, Abbigayle, was carved in the other. I loved that ring. It took six months of my salary from the feed store to pay for it. It was the most expensive thing I had ever purchased, but it felt right to give it to him.

The rest of our date was spent lying on the picnic blanket. After we finished the brownie I had made us for dessert, we drug the blanket into the front yard. The moon was full that night and there was enough light we could still see one another.

We were side by side, my hand intertwined in his, staring at the stars. There was nothing but the sound of crickets and a howling coyote in the distance. It was as quiet as the middle of the woods could be at night. We were probably lying like that for fifteen minutes or so before Noah rolled over on his side to me.

"Do you think if we lived here we would ever come out and lay in the yard like this?"

I rolled over toward him. I was struck by how amazing he looked in the moonlight. The way the shadows fell across one side and he looked like he was in black and white. "Our parents have yards. Do you think they ever go out in the yard just to enjoy each other's company or watch the stars?"

"I don't think my parents have enjoyed one another's company in years," Noah sighed.

"Really? I think my parents still love one another." I reached and touched his face. There was a hint of stubble and it tickled my fingers.

"It must be nice to have a good example of how to love. I love my parents, but they are no kind of example of a marriage." I could feel Noah's breath beneath my touch and his eyes drifted shut as he started his next sentence. "I promise I will marry you some day and we won't be like them. We will be a great example for our children."

I scooted closer to him. I forgot about college and everything else. He was wearing me down. "How many children are we going to have?"

Almost every time Noah started to kiss me, he pressed his forehead to mine first and lingered for a moment. This time was no different, except this time instead of taking that moment in silence he exhaled and with it came his answer, "As many you want."

His nose pressed to the side of mine and his lips lured mine open. It always seemed like instinct to close my eyes, but I didn't want to miss a moment of seeing him and I peeked. I opened my eyes to get a look at him. It was disbelief that made me do it. I still could not believe I was here with him. That it was my leg that his hand was easing up and pulling over his. Slowly, deliberately, patiently, gently, he rolled me to my back. I could not believe this was happening to me as his chest pressed to mine.

I'm not even sure how he did it, but Noah parted my legs. It didn't matter how. It also didn't matter how he balanced on top of me and kept from bearing his weight on me. He was definitely more experienced than I was, but none of that mattered. What mattered was that my thoughts were lost in him. Noah was the fulfillment of a dream I didn't even know I had had.

My heart raced and I'm sure Noah could feel my pulse pounding in my neck as he kissed me there. From ear to ear by way of my neck he left a trail that sent chill bumps from the last hair on the base of my skull all the way down each of my legs. I clasped his hands, our fingers locked together above my head.

Using his nose, Noah inched my collar open and planted kissed farther down to my first button on my blouse. I tilted my head back and gave in to his touch. I was breathless. I could feel a heat for him all the way to my core. Good girls fought the burn in their loins that I was feeling for him, but I didn't know how long I could fight it.

Noah let go of my hands and started to unbutton the top button of my shirt. His eyes caught mine and I struggled to say anything to stop him. With one flick, that button was free. The next button down rested between my breast and Noah ran a finger down my bare skin. It tickled and I squirmed, coming to my senses.

"Noah," I heaved, "A good girl would stop you and I'm..."

"It's okay, Gayle," Noah didn't take his eyes from mine. "We don't have to do anything you don't want to do. We don't have to rush anything."

"You aren't mad that..."

Noah gently eased my hair out of my face. "There's nothing to be mad about."

Noah rolled back to his side and on to his back, pulling me over on top of him. I sat up on him and braced myself against his chest. He was more muscular than most of the boys in school and I could see almost all of his muscles by the outline of his shirt.

I don't know what possessed me to ask, but the question was out before I could stop myself. "Have you ever been like this with anyone else?"

Noah hardly looked phased. "I've already told you that I've never felt like this about anyone before."

"I didn't mean..."

"Oh, you mean, have I ever..."

I didn't allow him to finish the sentence. I wasn't sure if I wanted to know the answer after all. "You don't have to answer."

"It's okay. I don't mind. The answer is that I've been with one other person."

"Oh."

"And you?"

"Seriously?"

"Seriously."

Surely he already knew my answer. "No one. Not ever."

Noah smiled like he had won a prize. He was already playing with my hands, caressing them as they pressed into his chest to help me with my balance.

"So were you with her a lot and how long has it been over?"

"It's been over for a long time and it was pretty serious for a while so ..."

I cut him off. "Never mind. I don't want to know. I don't want to think of you with anyone else. I'm sorry I asked."

"Gayle, I don't see her anymore and it's not anything I would ever want again."

I was happy with Noah's response. I don't know what possessed me, but I pulled one of his hands up and inserted one of his fingers into my mouth. I whirled my tongue around his finger. I watched Noah's face as I played with his index finger in my mouth.

Noah's eyes almost rolled back in his head before he snatched his finger back. "No, Gayle. You don't know what you're doing."

I had an indication I knew what I was doing. I could feel that he was more erect under me. There was something about sitting in that position, on top of him, and feeling the change I had inflicted on him, that made me want him more. My mind told me to stop, but my body, my own organs were pushing me on.

"Stop, Gayle!" Noah scrambled. "Get up. We have to go."

I wasn't sure what I had done wrong. Noah was quickly grabbing the blanket and the picnic basket, but I stood there puzzled.

"Gayle, look!" Noah pointed toward the driveway. "Headlights."

I scrambled with Noah. We grabbed everything and ran for his car. We made it to the car and that was the only time thus far that Noah had not opened my car door for me. My heart was racing as Noah cranked the car. Although we weren't really doing anything, both Noah and I knew that being back there alone did not look good to anyone who discovered us.

Noah floored the gas, spun the tires and fish-tailed the back end of the Camaro around and down the driveway we sped. I held on to the side of the seats fearing we were going to hit the person with the headlights head-on. What Noah realized long before I did, was that whomever had turned down there was only using the driveway to turn around and Noah was actually showing off in the car for me. It was thrilling enough just kissing him, but I had a thing for fast cars and this was just another thing about him that revved my engine for him.

***

For a moment I blinked and found myself standing beneath the running water of my shower. The water was hot, but I barely felt the sting while it pelted down on me. Physically, I was in the shower, but mentally, I was reliving Thanksgiving.

CHAPTER 10

I daydreamed the whole way through my shower. My heart fluttered in my chest as I thought of Noah and all that led to Thanksgiving with him.

My mind was back in the aftermath of our date. I could feel the front door against the palms of my hands as I shut it behind me and fell against it. I closed my eyes and took a deep breath. I could still taste Noah's goodnight kiss on my lips. It was sweet from the cherry chap-stick that he used. I could feel Mama and Daddy staring at me. There they sat in their spots in the living room waiting on me to make my curfew.

I exhaled and peeled myself off of the back of our front door. I glanced down at Noah's class ring that I had been careful not to let slip off of my finder all night. "Wax," I thought and off to scour the kitchen in search of it I went.

I was so proud of his ring. All of my other possessions paled in comparison to it and it was elevated to the status of my most prized possession. I found the wax and melted a little of it. I fixed it to the inside of the ring and with the wax I resized the ring to fit my finger.

As soon as Noah's class ring was firm on my finger, I skipped back into the living room where I found Daddy shutting off the TV and Mama putting away her quilting and picking up Millie's toys. Millie was with us that weekend, but she was already fast asleep.

I pranced into the living room bent on showing the ring to Mama and Daddy.

"Look what I got," I held out my hand, fingers spread wide, for Mama to admire it with me.

Mama took a good look and cut her eyes to Daddy. Immediately, I skipped across the living room over to him.

"See." I said as I held out my hand for him just as I had done for Mama. "It's so big."

I turned my hand to different positions, flashing the ring all about and Daddy looked. "I can hardly make a fist when I am wearing it." I tried to make a fist, but the ring was so bulky on my hand that I trouble closing my hand.

I was completely oblivious to the looks flying between Mama and Daddy. I was also completely oblivious to the steam coming off of my father. I stood there gushing over the ring and still trying to make a fist when Daddy's displeasure at the situation was brought to my attention.

Daddy didn't raise his voice, but the stern sound of it always let me know that he was not pleased. "Young lady, don't you think you're moving a little fast with this boy?"

I was totally caught off guard. "What?"

The fluctuation in Mama's voice signified a correction, "Sir?"

The word, "What" had not been the proper response and I was digging a deeper hole with the disrespect I showed Daddy when using it.

"Sir. I mean, sir?" I was quick to rephrase. "I've been writing back and forth with Noah for months. I thought you liked him."

Mama ran interference. "We're sure he's a fine boy, but whether or not we like him is not the point, Gayle."

"I don't understand." I still did not see what the problem was.

Daddy's face was beat red and he was fuming. He started to speak, but Mama cut him off.

"Your father was kind enough to bend the rules for you and Noah, Gayle, but you must see how you have taken advantage of the situation."

I didn't see how I had taken advantage, but I knew better than to inquire further.

175

Mama continued, "You might consider putting that away before your father makes you give it back."

I dreaded taking it off, but I knew that this was preemptive on her part. She was smoothing things over to keep Daddy from making me give it back.

My eyes filled with tears as I slipped the ring off of my finger.

"Dry it up, Gayle. If you've forgotten your priorities so completely then I might have to re-evaluate your Thanksgiving plans."

There was no drying it up at that point. I ran from the room. I went straight to my room and threw myself across my bed.

"Now, George!" I could hear my mother as I fled. "The boy's only here for another few days. There's no need to be like this!"

"Jane, you'll do best not to question me," Daddy was stern to Mama, too.

I had never heard Mama raise her voice before. I had never even heard her say a cross word to Daddy before, so what I heard next was a first. Mama screamed at Daddy. It was so loud that I was afraid she was going to wake Millie who was sleeping in her crib in Andy's old room. It was closer to the living room than mine was.

I peeped up from my pillow as Mama really gave it to him.

"George Anderson, you stubborn ass! Your antiquated rules have already cost me one of my children. I don't know who you think you are, but I'm not about to let you cost me another! This is the happiest I have seen our daughter since Andy died. You push her, George, and she might just run off with this boy. Do you want that? To drive her into the arms of some boy like you drove Andy into the arms of that floozy?"

I wiped back my tears as I tried to listen to them. I had never heard her fight with him like that. Mama had always been so passive in the way she handled Daddy that I think the silence from him was due to shock. Like me, he probably didn't know she had it in her to yell at him.

176

"Jane..." Daddy started to say something. Even though I could hear him, he wasn't screaming back.

Mama didn't let him finish. She sounded calmer when she continued. "Gayle's a smart girl. We need to trust that we've raised her right and allow her to make good decisions before we force her to make bad ones. A class ring never hurt anyone."

"Jane," Daddy began again, "You know it's more than a class ring. You've seen how he looks at her as well as I have."

By this point I had sucked back my tears and I was tilting my head at the crack of my door so I could still hear them.

"Indeed," Mama replied. "He looks at her the way my parents used to witness you looking at me."

Daddy's voice was letting up as he continued to plead his case. "Exactly and you see where that got us."

If he was seeking understanding he didn't get it. Mama gasped. "Where it got us? Excuse me?"

"You know what I mean."

"I don't believe I do because where it got me was two beautiful children, a nice home and what I thought was a wonderful marriage. Do you mean to tell me I am mistaken?"

Daddy stuttered, "No... uh... No, but you were only seventeen when we married..."

"Exactly! The same age our daughter is right now. The only difference is I had an overbearing mother to run away from and she has an overbearing father. I speak from a double dose of experience when I tell you, George, you need to let it go."

Daddy huffed. I couldn't see him, but I'm sure he slapped his forehead. That's what he did whenever someone got the better of him and Mama had definitely gotten the better of him.

The next thing I heard were footsteps coming down the hallway. In case one of them was coming to check on me, I ran to get my night gown and threw it on. I also mussed the bed so they would think I had been laying there.

The footsteps I had heard first were Daddy's and he went to their room, but it wasn't long before I heard Mama's. Even with the covers pulled up to my ears as if I was sleeping, I could hear Mama first go into Andy's old room to check on Millie. After a couple of minutes, I heard her again followed by her lightly knocking on my bedroom door. Mama didn't wait for me to give the okay for her to enter before she gave my door a little push.

"Gayle, are you still awake?"

I wiggled under the covers and lowered them so she could see me. "Yes, ma'am."

"I think I have a chain we can put the ring on. You can wear it around your neck and inside your shift," Mama said as she took a seat on the edge of my bed. My mother was the sweetest person ever.

I sat up in bed and threw my arms around her. "I love you, Mama, and I love Daddy too, but..."

"I know, my sweet girl. This is all just a part of growing up and parents have their lessons to learn just like you children and, Gayle, there's not a one of us that's ever too old to learn something."

"Yes, ma'am." I continued to hold her and she rubbed my back.

"And, Gayle," Mama leaned back. She pressed her lips together into a straight line across her face and furrowed her brow. "Sometimes we all have to be careful that we don't learn our lessons the hard way. Be careful giving your heart so fast to this boy. Even the nicest of young men will break your heart. They might not even mean to do it, but, before we know it, it's broken all the same."

"Yes, ma'am," I nodded my head.

The next morning I awoke with Mama back at my bedside. She gave me a long gold chain and we slipped Noah's class ring onto it.

I didn't want to push my luck, but I had to ask. "Mama, Daddy wasn't serious about not letting Noah come to Thanksgiving was he?"

Mama didn't have an answer other than that we would have to wait and see. We didn't mention the subject the rest of the day. In fact, none of us mentioned Noah until he called that night. Although I could have talked on the phone with him for hours, I cut the conversation short for the sake of Daddy being in the living room, witnessing the entire call. Mama had advised me that morning that the less attention I drew to Noah, the more likely things would blow over with Daddy and my Thanksgiving plans would be safe.

Monday morning arrived and Judy sputtered into the yard in the VW wagon. I was never so glad to see her as I was at that moment. I had been dressed and ready for fifteen minutes prior to her arrival. All weekend I looked forward to seeing her. I was dying to tell her about my date. I was so excited to tell her every detail of it and of the fight with my parents.

I started spilling my guts as soon as I opened the car door and got in. I gave the lead in and quite a build-up. We were already on Highway 296 headed into Stapleton when I delivered the goods.

"You what?!!" Judy slammed the brakes in the middle of the road.

We weren't anywhere near the stop sign at the end of the road when she slammed the brakes as I told her that I confessed my love to Noah before he confessed his to me. I didn't have on a seatbelt and threw out my hands to the dash to save myself.

"What did you do that for? You nearly cracked my skull on the windshield!" I sucked in my breath as she had scared the life out of me.

Judy gripped the steering wheel with both hands and just scowled at me. "Have you learned nothing from me? Have I taught you nothing? You never say the "L" word first! Jesus, Gayle!"

While Judy went off, I ran my hands across my head and tried to smooth my hair down from being flung forward so violently when the car came to a screeching halt. I thought it was safe to take my hands back from the dash, but I was wrong. Judy hadn't down shifted and when she gave Pumpkin the gas straight from fourth gear, it lunged and jumped and tossed me forward and back again about as much as her having slammed the brakes did. It jerked to and fro and shut off right smack in the middle of the road.

"Am I destined to be the hood ornament this morning?" I huffed as I peeled myself from the dash for the second time.

"Oh quit your fussin' and tell me..."

"Whhhhhaaaaammp!"

I knew that sound, but I jerked my head around to see out of the back window of the car anyway. Judy whipped hers around as well.

"Whhhhhaaaaaaammp!" It was an eighteen wheeler, specifically, a chalk truck barreling down on us.

"Stop looking and start the car!" I screamed at Judy.

"Stop yelling at me!" She was shaking as she turned the key.

"Whhhhaaaaaaa ---Whhhhhaaaaaa!" the horn went again.

My heart raced and I checked behind us. It was closing in on us and didn't show any sign of stopping.

"Down shift! The gears, Judy, the gears!" She still hadn't taken it out of fourth gear when she tried cranking it.

"Standard H. Standard H. Standard H," Judy chanted to herself as she struggled with the stick and tried to find first gear.

"Oh, shit, there's a car coming!" I pointed in front of us.

It was Mrs. McDonald in her Cricket. She was so tiny that she sat on pillows to see over the wheel and everyone knew she was blind in one eye and I couldn't see out of the other.

Up until that moment I was confident that the truck would just go around us, but this was shaping up to be the perfect storm. The one saving grace was that Mrs. McDonald wouldn't see it coming like we were seeing.

180

"We are going to die if you don't get this thing started! I love you, but I don't want to die with you today!" I screamed at Judy again.

"You love everyone! Stop saying that word!" As Judy screamed back at me she found first gear, gave it the gas, popped the clutch and swerved to the side of the road as the eighteen wheeler and Mrs. McDonald breezed by.

My pulse was still pounding in my ears and I was out of breath. Judy was the same. We sat on the edge of the road in silence for a few minutes before she spoke again.

"Did he say it back?"

I looked away, staring out of the passenger's side window.

"Oh dear Lord. He didn't say it back." Judy was exasperated and shook her head. "Do you know how devastated I would have been if I had said that to Doug first and he did not immediately tell me the same?"

I thought for a moment before I responded. "I'm not you and Noah's not Doug. I don't want him to tell me he loves me just because I said it. I think he loves me, but I'm not so concerned with him saying it. I love him. I love spending time with him and perhaps this is about the way I feel and whether he says it or not doesn't change that."

"You gave him the upper hand."

I slipped the chain from around my neck and pulled Noah's class ring off of it. I stuck it on my finger and shoved it out in front of Judy. "I suppose I did give him the upper hand."

"Oh my! He gave you his class ring! Well, that's a start."

"He didn't have to give me anything, Judy."

"I will never understand you, Gayle Anderson." Judy shook her head and started the car with ease.

I finished the details of my weekend with Noah during the rest of our ride to school.

"Do you think your daddy is going to keep Noah from coming to Thanksgiving and you from going with him? What do you think he's going to do?" Judy pulled into a parking space in the lot next to the school gym.

"I don't know. Mama says I just have to wait and see. She says if I play my cards right, things will blow over."

Monday, Tuesday and all day Wednesday I waited to see what Daddy was going to do. I never mentioned anything. I never even let on that I was worried, but of course I was. I worried right up until we got home from church that night, until the phone call came from Noah and until I finished that call.

"Still on for tomorrow as far as I know." I cut my eyes at Daddy as I answered Noah's question. "We eat at noon. Everyone starts arriving at 10:30 and they continue to trickle in right up until we say the blessing."

Daddy was right there in the living room watching Little House on the Prairie all the while I was on the phone and he didn't say a word. He didn't interject or correct me when I confirmed our plans for Thanksgiving.

As I listened to Noah, I took my eyes off of Daddy only to glance Mama's way. She made eye contact with me and gave me a slight smile. Everything was working out just as she said it would. I had flown under the radar all week and Daddy let it blow over.

"Oh, I know," I said in a hushed tone as still not to press my luck. "I'm just as nervous about meeting all of your family, too."

"Don't worry, just be yourself and they'll love you," Noah assured me.

"I'll try." The truth was it was hard to be myself when I was around him. I wanted to be Judy, but I couldn't tell him all of that.

"Okay, well get some sleep. I'm sure your mama will have you up helping cook bright and early in the morning."

"You know us so well." And, tomorrow, after he met my whole family, he would know us even better.

"For now I'm going to say goodnight and I can't wait to see you tomorrow."

I blushed and turned my face away from Mama and Daddy so they couldn't see me. "I can't wait to see you either."

"Maybe we could steal another moment on the hood of your Daddy's T-Bird tomorrow."

I screamed with glee inside and danced around our living room in spirit and I definitely hid my face from Mama and Daddy then. I even bit my own arm to keep from squealing out loud like the school girl I was. I eased up on my arm and squeaked out the word, "Maybe," when really I meant, "Hell, yeah!"

It was a rare night that I didn't dream of Noah since the day I met him. Wednesday night leading into Thanksgiving was not one of those rare nights. I dreamed that he fit in perfectly with all of my family and I dreamed of a very long moment on the T-Bird. Unfortunately, the day that followed did not mirror my dream.

Noah was one of the first people to arrive Thanksgiving morning. He looked fresh out of the shower and smelled like Clubman, which immediately caught my attention. He smelled like Andy. That was the cologne Andy used to wear and I could not believe I hadn't noticed it before. Noah hugged me as soon as he laid eyes on me and while hugging back I could almost feel Andy. I know that was strange, hugging my boyfriend and imagining my brother for a split second, but I didn't care. Before I let go, I said a little prayer that Andy was safe in heaven and not missing me as much as I missed him. I still found it hard to be thankful any day of the week, let alone a holiday like this, without him. Every waking day was like ripping off the Band-Aid that was the reality of Andy's death.

When I let go of Noah, I noticed that he had brought flowers for Mama to put on the table and after he offered them to her, he asked if there was anything he could do to help. They took him up on his offer and I didn't see much of him again until time for the blessing. The smell of Clubman stayed in my nostrils and in my mind long after Noah left with Daddy.

Noah helped Daddy bring in extra chairs from the barn and even rode with him to get ice from the church's ice machine. While they were gone, various family members started trickling in. I introduced Noah to each and every one of them. I told him how we were related and gave him a little back story on each of them.

By the time we gathered in the dining room to hold hands and tell what each of us were thankful for, everyone from Mama's side of the family and everyone from Daddy's side of the family had arrived. The room was packed as usual and we were halfway around the circle, with my cousin Shannon Bickel reciting what she had to be thankful about.

I was related to two Shannon's and three Dawn's, so I always felt the need to clarify as to which of them I was referring in order to avoid confusion. After introducing Noah to the third Shannon, he joked, "Shannon, Shannon, Shannon," like Jan Brady used to say, "Marcia, Marcia, Marcia," on the Brady Bunch. I got the reference and punched him in the side as I snickered.

Shannon had been thankful for the new car she got for graduation that year. She had barely finished telling us that it was a white Oldsmobile Cutlass when the banging on the front door started. Every last head in the room whipped around toward the direction of the noise. With each strike the aluminum screen door made a rickety, clanking, wrapping sound that vibrated through the whole door. The room went silent and the whaling on the door rang out again and through the door, mingled with the banging was the sound of little Millie screaming her head off.

Mama, Daddy and I went running. Through the door of the dining room, through the kitchen with Mama in the lead, we ran for the door in the living room with thirty five family members hot on our heels. Noah was somewhere in the bunch, but for a moment I completely forgot about him.

Mama and Daddy had begged Rhonda to allow them to have Millie for Thanksgiving, but what was in it for her? Daddy had stopped giving her anything extra beyond what he had promised to begin with so Rhonda was holding Millie ransom. For the last few weeks we had been back to getting her only when Rhonda needed a babysitter and, even then, Daddy had to drive to Augusta to pick her up. She didn't even invite any of us to Millie's first birthday party and we weren't even sure Rhonda threw her a party. I reflected on all of this as I scowled at Rhonda through the door.

Mama threw open the door and, still screaming, Millie immediately began reaching out for Mama to take her. Millie's face was bright red and I could smell the urine in her diaper from where I stood next to the TV, about six feet from the screened door.

In quite literally the opposite fashion of Millie, Rhonda was dressed to the nines. Her skirt was about six inches too short for anyone's mother to wear. Her heels were indecent for any form of Thanksgiving celebration and her lipstick was a shade that was surely purchased from a hooker that sold Avon on the side. Her nerves appeared wracked and her hair was only slightly mussed, but other than that she was ready for a very hot night out on a corner of the lower end of Broad Street in Augusta and it was barely after noon.

Rhonda held her position on the porch. She didn't even lean to hand Millie off with care. "Just take her!" she barked at Mama.

Mama didn't respond to Rhonda beyond taking Millie. "Let's go get you something to eat and some fresh clothes, my sweet baby." Mama held Millie close to comfort her.

Millie sniffled and wiped her face as Mama turned her back on Rhonda and left her standing there.

Daddy just looked at her and I could see the veins in his head starting to show. His nostrils flared and his face went bright red. Before Daddy could say anything, I stepped in front of him.

"What sort of mother are you?" I said through gritted teeth.

"Excuse me?" Rhonda had the nerve to appear offended.

"You heard me! She looks like she's been in the same outfit for days and she reeks of urine. When's the last time you dirtied your hands to change her diaper?"

185

"What business is it of yours?" Rhonda stepped toward me.

Daddy grabbed my arm to make sure I didn't cross the threshold of the door, but I snatched away from him. Technically I was still inside the house and Rhonda was still technically on the porch, but we went nose to nose in the doorway.

"You stink of alcohol! That would be just like you to get drunk and get someone killed. What? Is Millie next on your list? Is that the next person in my family that..."

Before I could finish my sentence, Rhonda rang my jaws. She slapped me so hard that tears immediately sprang to my eyes.

Every family member in the room gasped.

It stung and took my breath at the same time, but Rhonda didn't know what hit her either. She had barely swung through than did I hit her open palmed with both hands right square in her chest as hard as I could. A hit, a push, I'm not entirely sure. It didn't matter. It had the desired effect. I knocked her clean out into the yard on her ass. Her feet were over her head when she hit the ground and the entire room busted out laughing.

I heard them laugh, but my adrenaline was so high that I paid no mind to them. Before the screen door closed I had already grabbed hold of the wooden front door and screamed at Rhonda, "Happy Thanksgiving, you bitch!" and I slammed the door shut with her still scrambling to get up.

When I turned back around I saw Noah and Daddy both standing there with their mouths wide open. I didn't even know that Noah was near me but he had managed to squeeze past the rest of the family.

The wholea room was laughing at Rhonda's predicament. Everyone in the family knew how she was and most were commenting that she got what she deserved and it was long overdue. Others were commenting that they didn't know I had it in me. They were all background noise. I was stuck in silence waiting on Noah or Daddy to speak. All of the sudden I was so embarrassed to have done that in front of Noah and Daddy. I could also feel the stinging in my cheek where Rhonda had landed her slap. Tears were coming to my eyes again and I couldn't seem to stop them.

Noah was the first to say something. "Are you alright?"

"My face hurts." I reached up and put my hand over the place where she had hit me.

As usual Daddy was a man of few words, "Her ass probably hurts."

Noah just cut his eyes at Daddy. I could tell he was trying not to laugh. There was no use in me trying. That was funny and thinking about me knocking Rhonda on her behind in front of everyone was no longer embarrassing. I laughed and it magnified the pain in my face.

"Stop. It hurts to laugh." There was a little whine in my voice. I could feel it starting to swell.

"I'll get you some ice," Aunt Dot came forward and gave me a bit of a side arm hug. "Then we will all get back to our Thanksgiving dinner."

"Yeah, let's eat before it gets cold." Daddy herded everyone back into the dining room to start making their plates.

As we all began walking back to the dining room there was a ferocious banging on the door. Apparently Rhonda was on her feet again. Five or six loud pounds on the door came before the screaming started.

"You are going to pay for this!" Rhonda continued to bang on the door.

Daddy stopped in his tracks, in the doorway to the hall that led past the kitchen and to the dining room. I was in front of him and Noah was next to me. Mama still had not emerged from changing Millie. There were at least thirty, maybe more, of our family members stuffed in our little house. They had heard the stories about Rhonda. Half of them had met her, most for the first time at Andy's funeral. Today of all days, they were getting to verify that the stories Mama, Daddy and myself told about her were not exaggerated. She was every bit of what we said she was.

I turned to find Daddy, fists clinched and counting to ten under his breath. He used to do that before he spanked me for doing something that had pushed him to his breaking point. It was a calming technique he used, like the time I threw the ball in the house and broke Mama's John Wayne collectible plate from the Franklin Mint. Both Andy and I knew what to expect when we witnessed this from Daddy.

"Daddy, let's just go and have lunch. She'll get tired and give up." I tried to get him by the hand and pull him with me.

Daddy exhaled the number ten. I didn't have a good hold of his hand and it was as if he had not heard me at all. I knew Daddy had a temper. I had seen it only a couple of times, but I knew the look on his face from those few times. I knew that counting to ten had not helped.

"Daddy," I pled, "Come with us. Don't let her make a fool of you too in front of everyone."

Daddy turned and went back to the door. He snatched it open and Rhonda was mid swing to hammer on it with her fist again.

Daddy raised his voice to the point that Mama came running. "I will not hit a woman, but lay hand on this door one more time and I will turn every woman in this family a loose on you and you will get the beating of your life. Do I make myself clear? I suggest you get your narrow ass off my property."

Rhonda screamed back. Thank goodness we didn't live in town with neighbors close by, not that the folks probably couldn't hear this all the way to Wrens.

"You can't talk to me like this!!!" She raised the roof of the porch with her yelling.

Daddy leaned out of the door and got nose to nose with her. "I just did!"

Rhonda gasped and took a step back.

188

Daddy was pouring sweat and just as red faced as any of us got when we got mad.

Rhonda fiddled with her car keys as she took a few steps back. I think she was genuinely afraid of Daddy. Tears filled her eyes.

"I've never seen her cry before," I whispered to Noah, who was standing between me and the door. "Not even at Andy's funeral."

She took two more steps back and then turned and ran as best she could in five inch heels and thick grass. Rhonda almost fell twice. One of which times was when Daddy screamed at her again, "And, next time you lay a hand on my child, I will call the law and have you arrested. I will have you arrested for the assault of mine and neglect of your own. Now I suggest you get on to where ever it was you were going before you stopped by here. Get, I told you!"

I thought Daddy was going to have a stroke, but I never suspected what would happen next. We were all so focused on Daddy and Rhonda fleeing through the yard that we hadn't paid any attention to Mama's return. Mama witnessed the entire thing.

Cousin Dawn, the one that was the best cook in the family, let out a blood curdling version of Mama's name. "Jane! Oh my God, Jane!"

Dawn was holding Millie, but managed to catch Mama as Mama clinched her left arm and headed down to her knees. Mama was white as a ghost and in that moment she appeared well beyond her years. Her face was wrinkled and twisted with pain and she didn't look much like my mama at all.

"Jane!" Daddy ran to her.

"Mama!" I called out. Noah grabbed me and held me, hugging me.

"You need to stay out of the way right now Gayle." Noah whirled me around and buried my face against him. I could feel him turn to look over his shoulder to see what was happening. I cried.

"Give me the phone! She's having a heart attack." Aunt Dot took charge and immediately called the ambulance.

"Oh God, Jane!" There was terror in Daddy's voice. I couldn't look.

Dawn's equally terrified, frantic voice followed, "Does anyone know CPR?"

The room was filling with my family and Noah passed me off to Uncle Jim. He didn't say anything as he slipped away.

"Noah?" I looked to him as he disappeared, squeezing through everyone.

I heard Noah say softly, "Let me through. I know CPR."

"So do I." I could not see, but I recognized the voice. It was my cousin Shannon.

Noah and Shannon traded off performing CPR on Mama. Uncle Jim held me close and Aunt Dot joined him with her arms around me as well. I prayed for Mama to be alright. I know Aunt Ruth took Millie and Dixon from the room.

It was a solid ten minutes before the ambulance arrived, but Noah and Shannon didn't give up. They alternated working on Mama as half of the family watched. I wasn't one of them. I couldn't look. I could not bear the thought of losing my mother, seeing her die before my eyes. I just couldn't look. I held on to Uncle Jim for dear life, my Mama's dear life.

The ambulance took Mama and Daddy rode in the back with her. Uncle Jim and Aunt Dot drove me and Noah. Before we left, the EMTs told Uncle Jim not to bother to try to keep up with them. Uncle Jim didn't listen and he stayed on the bumper of the ambulance all the way to the McDuffie County Hospital.

Highway 17, between Wrens and Thomson was where the Piedmont region of Georgia met the Plateau and it was nothing but hills and valleys.

"Jesus, Jim, slow it down! We're only hitting the tops of the hills!" Aunt Dot held on to the handle above the passenger's side door most of the way to the hospital.

Aunt Dot was right. I never knew a Delta 88 could go so fast. I always thought of the thing as a bit of a brown bomb, but Uncle Jim was letting the low side drag as we chased after the ambulance. I clutched Noah's hand tightly as we touched the tops of the hills. I clutched it for fear of a car wreck, but more so for fear that my mother was already dead in the ambulance in front of us.

Noah must have read my mind. "You know, they would slow down if there was no hope," he whispered to me.

I looked toward the window, away from him, and wiped my eyes. My cheek still hurt from where Rhonda slapped me.

For a moment, I thought about more than the loss of my mother. I thought about Noah missing Thanksgiving with his family.

"I'm sorry I am going to miss meeting your family today and spending Thanksgiving with them, but I can't leave. I won't keep you."

"Shhh, don't think about that now," Noah quieted me on the subject.

I scooted forward and leaned over the front seat. "Aunt Dot, will you and Uncle Jim please drop me at the hospital and then make sure that Noah gets back to his car. His family is expecting us for dinner tonight and..."

"Aunt Dot," Noah addressed her as well, "that won't be necessary. I'll call them from the hospital and they'll understand."

"No, no, Aunt Dot, y'all must see that he gets there. His mother will hate that he flew all the way home from Italy and she didn't get to see him on Thanksgiving."

"Noah, when we get to the hospital why don't you give them a call and let them know what's going on. You can decide then if you need for us to take you back to your car or what you need to do." Aunt Dot seemed to come up with the perfect compromise.

"Thank you, ma'am," Noah said to Aunt Dot, but immediately turned his attention back to me as I slid back in my seat. "I won't leave you no matter what's going on or what they say. I flew home to be with you. They've had me all my life. You need me today."

I tried to smile, but my mind switched back to why he thought I needed him. The tears sprang up again.

"Come here." Noah put his arm around me and held my head against his shoulder. He kissed the top of my head. "Everything's going to be alright."

As it turned out Noah was right, Mama made it to the hospital. He called his parents as soon as we got there and his mother insisted that he stay with me. Mama's doctor said that were it not for Noah and Cousin Shannon's efforts in performing CPR Mama would have never made it. They were the heroes of the day.

Once Mama was settled for the night, the last of the family members that made the trek to the hospital walked out together. Daddy stayed behind with Mama. He hadn't left her side since she first went down in our living room. Watching Daddy with Mama and pacing over her when we first reached the hospital made me know that I wanted a love like theirs. I wanted a marriage like theirs and someone who was totally devoted to me and me to them. I wanted Noah.

As much as I watched my parents that day, watching to see what was going to happen to my mother, watching how my father was mortified at losing her, I watched Noah as well. I watched how he traced the veins along the back of my hand with his thumb. It was soothing to me, but I don't think he even realized he was doing it while he held my hand and we waited for news on Mama. I watched as he offered to get all of us something from the cafeteria since none of us ate lunch that day. I watched as my father shed tears and Noah put the arm that he didn't have around me around him. Noah was my rock and I don't even know when that came to be. I wanted a love like my parents and, from every indication, I had that in Noah.

That night Noah and I rode home with Uncle Jim and Aunt Dot. It was well after dark by the time we left the hospital and I fell asleep in the backseat with Noah. His arm was around me and I drifted off to sleep before we even reached the city limits of Thomson. I could still smell the Clubman on his shirt and I was comforted by his presence as well as Andy's. I didn't wake up until the tires started across the gravel in our driveway.

"Gayle, we're going to go on inside while you say goodnight to Noah." Aunt Dot and Uncle Jim were staying at our house while they were in town for Thanksgiving.

"Yes, ma'am," I replied as I blinked my eyes a few times still trying to come to.

"I'll also get Ruth and her crowd out of here and get Millie settled down for the night because I'm sure she's still wide awake with all of them in the house."

The car rolled to a stop as I thanked Aunt Dot and assured her I would be inside in just a little while. "Oh, and, Aunt Dot, I promised Noah I would show him Daddy's T-bird so I want to make sure he sees that before he heads back to Italy."

"Alright Gayle." Aunt Dot got out of the car first and as the rest of us got out she turned to Noah. "It was nice meeting you and I'm so sorry we made you miss Thanksgiving with your parents. Please send our sincere apologies to your mother for me."

"Yes, ma'am," Noah replied. "It was great seeing you and I hope to see y'all again when I am home on leave in June."

CHAPTER 11

I finally got out of the shower with only about twenty minutes to spare. I was still on auto pilot as I dried off and got dressed. I kept my mind swirling in the past to avoid the nervousness that was trying to creep in. I had a big night planned and I didn't want to chicken out so I kept thinking about Thanksgiving and everything leading to tonight.

Back in my memories of Thanksgiving night, saying goodbye to Noah was bittersweet. Aunt Dot and Uncle Jim headed on into the house and they thought nothing of me showing Noah the Thunderbird. Daddy was always restoring one old car or another, sometimes two at a time, and they were always interesting to see. They had no idea that I had already given Noah the tour of the barn and showed off the car days before Thanksgiving so it was the perfect excuse for me to be able to have a little time alone with Noah. After all, this was more than just saying goodnight. This was saying goodbye for the foreseeable future.

I led Noah around the house by his hand, glancing back at him a couple of times as I started to realize that I needed to collect all of the images of him in my mind to sustain me for the next few months. It was cloudy out that night, no moon, but there was a night light in the yard that provided just enough light for me to see him in the dark. Each time I looked back at him, my heart was broken just a little more by the thought of having to let him go.

By the time Noah opened the barn door for me I lost it. I broke down and just cried. It had already been a trying day with it being the first major holiday without Andy, the fight with Rhonda, Mama's heart attack and the fact that she nearly died, and now having to say goodbye to Noah. This was quite possibly the worst Thanksgiving of my life.

Noah hurried and shut the barn door and pulled the cord to turn on the series of lights that strung from one end of the barn to the other. I held my face in my hands to try to hold in my sobs and to hide that I was not a pretty crier.

194

Within seconds Noah's arms were around me. "Please don't cry, Gayle. Please don't cry."

"I'm so sorry about today. I'm so sorry. I wanted things to be perfect. I wanted to meet your family. I'm so sorry. Maybe if I wouldn't have fought with Rhonda none of this would hap..."

"Gayle, none of this is your fault." Noah knew exactly what I was getting at.

"But, maybe Mama wouldn't have gotten upset and had a heart attack if I hadn't..."

"Gayle, seriously," Noah pulled back from me. "Look at me."

Noah waited for me to look up, but I wasn't as quick about it as he wanted me to be. "Look at me." He was insistent and demanding of me.

Noah peeled my hands away from my face and I looked up at him.

"There's nothing you did or could have not done that would have prevented your mother from having a heart attack. They told you at the hospital. Gayle, the doctors told y'all that it was no one's fault. These things just happen. I don't remember the exact percentage, but they said her arteries were so clogged that it was inevitable." Noah hardly blinked as he held eye contact with me and tried to assure me that it wasn't my fault.

"I could have turned the other cheek," I shrugged.

"And, that woman would have slapped you in that cheek as well. You couldn't have known..."

I turned around from Noah and wiped my eyes for the umpteenth time. I slid my hands down my face and covered my mouth. Wide eyed through tears, I glanced around the barn. There was the T-Bird, another reminder that this was not at all the day I had intended or hoped it would be. Even then, I knew I only had a few more minutes with Noah and I could not pull myself together to give him a proper send off.

I shook my head. "This isn't how I want you to remember me."

I could feel that my eyes were swollen and my face was puffy from crying for half the day. I'm sure my eyes were also the color of a blue flame with streaks of red. That's how they got when I cried. I was a mess, a real mess.

"What do you mean?" Noah eased up behind me and wrapped his arms around my waist. I could smell the hint of Clubman cologne still on him.

I rested my head against him as I spoke. "When you're back in Italy, if you think of me, I don't want you to think of me looking like this."

"Come with me," Noah whirled me around and held tight to my hand when he did. Then, he led me over to the passenger's side of the T-Bird. Noah opened the door. "Get in." He smiled.

"Thank you," I said as I got in and Noah shut the door behind me.

Noah went around to the driver's side and got in. As blood shot as my eyes were, I couldn't take them off of him.

Unlike his Camaro, the Thunderbird had a bench seat and Noah patted the space between us. "Come here."

I scooted over as he intended and he extended his arm across the back of the seat and around me.

"I forgot to show you the last time we were out here, but there's one thing about this old car that's in perfect condition." I extended my hand to the dash and turned on the radio. I had to tune the nob a little and adjust the volume, but 104.3, WBBQ out of Augusta, came in loud and clear.

Rhiannon by Fleetwood Mac played softly as I laid my head on Noah's shoulder. For a little while Noah made me forget how nothing else about the day had gone right.

196

"This is how I will remember you. The smell of your hair and how it tickles my nose every time we get close like this. I'll member the way you looked the moment I first laid eyes on you in the parking lot of the gym before the homecoming dance. You were a vision in that blue dress and I'll never forget how my heart leapt at the sight of you. In every plan I made and in every move I made that led me to you that night I wondered if I would recognize you, if you'd remember me."

Noah paused only long enough to brush my hair back and tilt his head to mine. He didn't notice, but tears rolled down my face. This time, the tears were those of being touched by his words.

"It should never be a question of 'if' I will think of you. I'll never stop thinking of you. I'll think of you standing on the front porch of our house and how the moonlight lit your face. I'll remember the way you looked when you defended your family against your former sister-in-law and how you never blinked when she slapped you. I'll always regret seeing someone treat you like that, but I'll never forget how fierce your love for your family is and one day I hope I'm a part of that family."

Noah eased back from me and I rose up to see what he was doing. I found him just looking at me.

"I will never forget one thing about you, but if you think how you look when you are emotionally spent will sway my thoughts of you one bit, you're wrong. I hate the thought of you crying like this and I would take away all of this pain if I could, but this is all a part of who you are..."

The radio played on, *Let Your Love Flow* by the Bellamy Brothers, continued in the background, but I hardly heard them. Noah might have told me that he loved me, but I could not take it anymore. I eased my leg into a semi-Indian style position under me so I could gain leverage to reach him. I caressed one of his cheeks as I pressed my forehead to his. I paused for a split second and then moved the tip of my nose around his. Slowly, gently, I pressed my top lip to his. I had to kiss him. I felt like I would die if I didn't. With the kiss, I stopped his words.

Noah didn't resist me. In fact, he pulled me deeper into the kiss. Noah had one hand with fingers spread wide in my hair on the back of my head and another gripping around my waist as I clinched fists full of the collar of his shirt, we consumed each other.

My heart raced and broke all at the same time. I had never felt such passion for him as I did then in the front seat of the car. Noah pulled me over to straddle him and the steering wheel pressed against the small of my back. My skirt was spread over him and my bare legs against his jeans and the leather seats of the car. The seat was cold due to the nip in the air that night, but the pits of my knees were beginning to sweat from the heat coming off of me. I could not imagine ending this, letting him leave, allowing him to go back to Italy for months. I could not imagine not being able to touch him like this, see him, hear his voice, feel him even if it was just to hold his hand. I didn't want this night to end.

Jimmy Buffet serenaded us with *Come Monday*. It was just about the only slow song they had played. It's funny, like the song said, I would have walked anywhere with Noah. I was sure that come Monday, I would be begging for Noah to be back by my side. Funny how things come on the radio as if the DJ knows what's going on with you at that very moment and how the song he plays will speak directly to you.

Noah's hands were under my skirt and climbing up my legs. The perspiration behind my knees was squelched with the chill bumps caused by the thrill of Noah touching me like that. No one had ever been that intimate with me even as to have a grazed my thigh so near my panties. My insides burned and I didn't make a move to stop him. I leaned back from him and bit my lower lip and Noah buried his face in the opening at the top of my blouse. I had two buttons undone and there was just the slightest of cleavage accessible and Noah slipped his tongue in. At the same time, he eased his hands from my legs to my backside and held me tight.

Noah moved gently beneath me and my legs were widened. I could feel him, there, through my panties, through his jeans. I could feel him, there. I wanted to feel him there. It didn't even matter what was on the radio anymore. For all I knew, it could have been Barry White.

"Ahhhh, haaaa," I exhaled with audible sound. A sigh, a moan, I don't know what it was. It just happened.

"Oh my God, Noah." I whispered as I leaned to his neck and planted nibbled kisses on his earlobe.

Noah continued to move gently under me for a few minutes and I began to move with him. It seemed like instinct, reminded me of when I took English riding lessons and had to learn to post. Up and down, back and forth, I used the strength in the muscles of my upper legs. Unlike on the horse, it felt better to connect with Noah.

The heat in me was replaced by a tingling sensation that was starting to build in me. My breathing became more rapid and then Noah became still.

"We need to stop." Noah said through ragged breaths.

"Why?" I was so naive.

"Because I don't want to take your virginity in a barn or in a car."

"Oh." I didn't want to stop kissing him, but this had reached kind of a fever pitch.

On one hand I didn't mind the thought of losing my virginity in the car or in the barn to him. Nothing else mattered right then, but feeling the way I did when I was with him. Of course there was a twinge of reminder that one of my aunts might come to check on us and catch us or, even worse, if Uncle Jim caught us.

On the other hand, Noah made a valid point and it had nothing to do with my virtue or the geography of the loss of such or getting caught.

Noah slipped his hands from under my skirt and I was almost disappointed. "Accidents happen every day and if such a thing happened between us, there's no way I would want you here to face that alone. People can be cruel about that kind of thing and I would never have you put through that." Noah looked sincere and concerned as he placed his hands in the same spots on my behind, but outside of my clothes.

"What do you know about accidents?" I asked him.

"I know my brother was one."

"You're kidding."

"Not one bit. My mother was from the hill section in Augusta and my dad's from Blythe. Of course they tell a more watered down version, but the long and short of it is that my mother was a bit of a wild child and my dad was the son of a farmer. They met through some friends at the lake one weekend."

"My father didn't know what hit him. When he describes meeting her, he never fails to mention that she smelled like honeysuckle and she never fails to add that she didn't even know what that was until she met him. Can you imagine being so immersed in city life that you didn't even know what honeysuckle was?"

I shook my head, "No."

"Well, that was my mother, grew up in one of the biggest houses on the hill, but thought she had it so bad. By the end of the week that they first met, she was pregnant with my brother, Nathaniel, and she soon found out what bad was. Her family disowned her and she had no place else to go. My father loved her, what he knew of her, and he married her immediately."

"Did she love your father?"

By the look on his face, I knew the answer. Noah barely moved his head and confirmed what I suspected.

"We're not them, you know."

"You're right, but I would never put you in a position to lose your family because I could not control myself."

I smiled down at Noah as I still sat straddled him. I took his face in my hands. Just looking at Noah was still capable of derailing my thoughts, but not this time. "I told you something the other night and I'm not sure you heard me so I am going to tell you again. I love you."

Noah's eyes widened. They were so blue and when he smiled they lit up any room he was in. In that moment, they were as bright as any star in the sky, dancing, almost gleeful. "I love you and I don't want to leave you."

Luckily I heard the creaking of the old wooden door when it was first touched and I slipped off of Noah.

"Shhh." I told him as I placed my finger to my lips and glanced toward the door. I scooted back into the passenger's seat and tried to look natural.

"Gayle???" It was Uncle Jim's voice.

"Yes, sir?" I answered as he came into sight, pushing the door open and standing before us.

"You're Aunt Dot sent me to see what you two were up to and if you were alright."

"Oh, yeah, we're fine. Noah just wanted to get a feel of what it would be like to be behind the wheel of a car like this."

Uncle Jim laughed as Noah added, "She said her dad never allowed anyone to drive his cars so this might be the only chance I ever got. I guess I'm busted."

"Don't worry, son. We've all done our fair share of daydreaming behind the wheel of that car, but, Gayle, it's time for you to come on in for the night. Your dad just called and he wants you to call the hospital and say goodnight to your mother."

"Yes, sir." I started to reach for my door handle.

"Wait. I'll come around and get that for you."

Uncle Jim rolled his eye. "Young love," he let slide under his breath. "Come on, you two."

Noah and I walked back to the front yard hand in hand with Uncle Jim leading the way. Uncle Jim continued into the house while Noah and I had one last kiss on the front porch.

201

"I'll see you in June. It'll be here before you know it," Noah whispered in my ear as he held me.

"I'll write to you every day," I promised.

"And, I'll call you every Wednesday and Sunday night at 8:30. Seriously, the time will fly by and I'll be back before you know it."

The lights on the porch blinked. "Oh dear Lord. I've got to go." I shook my head in disbelief. Even Uncle Jim and Aunt Dot used the light technique to kill my moment.

As I watched Noah drive away, I wasn't as devastated as I thought I was going to be. I missed him already, but my heart was not broken. It was cracked a little, but he had told me he loved me and that is what held me together.

The taillights from Noah's Camaro faded into the dark down the road and I stood there until they were completely out of sight.

"Gayle, honey," Aunt Dot stuck her head out of the door, "Your dad's on the phone."

"Yes, ma'am."

I found two things waiting on me when I arrived home from school on Monday. Mama was home from the hospital with a purse full of new medications to keep her cholesterol levels down. She had as clean of a bill of health as one who had just had a heart attack could get.

The other was a letter from Noah. It wasn't in the usual red, white and blue trimmed military issued envelope, but I knew it was from him. I recognized his handwriting immediately. I hadn't heard from him since he left on Thanksgiving night, the same night he wrote the letter. I waited by the phone from 8:15 p.m. until Daddy made me go to be at 10:00. I was little worried until the letter arrived.

November 27, 1975

Dear Gayle,

I cannot stop thinking about what you said. I'm so sorry I didn't hear you the first time you told me you loved me. I cannot believe I missed something like that. I had dreamed of that moment since the first time I saw you. I wondered what it would be like to have you feel about me the way I feel about you. I am glad I can tell you now that it feels amazing.

All of that being said and all of that's been said between us these last two weeks, I want you to know I have come to a decision about my future. I love the Air Force, but it was a patch to cover the fact that I didn't know what I wanted to do with my life. I never wanted to be a farmer and I still don't. In the Air Force, I gained direction. It's been a good fit for me and helped me realize that I want to be a pilot. The feeling I get flying is second only to the feeling I get when I stand next to you. Like you said, Augusta has an airport and I can be a pilot there just as easy as I can while in the Air Force. The difference in being a pilot at Bush Field as opposed to somewhere the Air Force sends me is that I can be with you. We can have the best of both worlds. I can have the career that I want and you can have the one that you want and we can be together.

My enlistment ends in September, 1976, but I have to make a decision about re-enlisting in May. I want you to think about this and let me know what you think. I know what you said about your father not paying for your college if you get married straight out of high school and I completely understand that. I won't try to persuade you one way or the other. I'm yours now, in six months, in four years. I'm not going anywhere, but I need to know what you think before I make things official.

I don't want to pressure you into anything. I love every minute we spend together, but I know I have more life experience than you. I don't want to keep you from anything or rob you of your dreams, but, right now, I know that you are my dream.

I hate that Thanksgiving was hard on you, but we were together and that's what I will remember about it. I hope you will do the same.

My family sends their love and prayers for your mother's recovery. I look forward to hearing from you, but please do not feel the need to answer my question right away. All I ask is that you think about it.

I love you.

Thinking of you,

Noah

When I finished reading the letter, I held it close to my heart. I knew my answer. I wanted him to come home to me right that minute so of course I was open to his suggestion that he would not renew his enlistment. There were details to be worked out, but I didn't want to think about that then. I didn't want anything to kill the feeling I had just thinking about being able to be with him all the time.

I wrote and received three letters in the two weeks it took Rhonda to show back up after Thanksgiving. I had a lot of time with Millie in those two weeks. Aunt Dot offered to stay and help Daddy and I with Millie and Mama, but Daddy insisted we could handle it. Per the doctor's orders Mama was not allowed to lift anything over ten pounds or stand for over ten minutes at a time so in the time that Rhonda was missing I took care of Millie.

Daddy took care of Mama and I took care of Millie. Taking care of Millie was nothing I could not handle, in fact, I enjoyed it. The thing I didn't enjoy was having it rubbed in my face that Noah was right.

Mama was housebound for the first week and when we ventured out the next week it was to the grocery store. While at Hadden's in Wrens I got one look after another. I was seventeen and didn't look a day older. My mother was sixty and looked every bit of her years and Millie was barely a year old. I had a baby on my hip and all the ladies that pushed their carts past us in the grocery store looked me up and down.

The ladies judged me. Of course, these were the few ladies in town that didn't know me or my family. There weren't many people in the tri-county area that didn't know us, but every last one of them showed up to Hadden's that day and helped prove Noah's point.

"I know you love that boy, so it's probably best that he's back where he belongs and you are where you belong," Mama whispered, acknowledging the looks from the women.

I didn't say anything. I felt Mama was wrong. Noah belonged with me and I belonged with him. If he belonged in Italy, then so did I, but I didn't utter a word of that.

Mama went on to caution me. "If you kept things up with this boy, you could get used to more stares like these. No one thinks good thoughts of a girl in what appears to be your current predicament. I never thought I would have to tell you this, but I'm going to put it to you like my mother put it to me. If you find yourself pregnant, you will find yourself out of my house."

"I would take a thousand of these looks per day if it meant I got to keep Millie."

Mama raised an eyebrow at me. I suppose she expected me to air my position on Noah, defend my love for him and threaten to defy her, but I didn't utter a word about him. Most mothers who'd given a warning like that would have found themselves on the end of a heated argument, but not mine. Unlike Mama, I listened when the doctors said she should be kept calm for as long as possible.

It was hardly two days later when Rhonda showed back up. She had a new car, a red, shiny Z-28, a new dress and from the looks of it, a new attitude. We saw her pull into the yard, but made her get out and come to the door. We even let her knock three times before Daddy budged from his chair.

"May I help you, Rhonda?" Daddy asked her in a no nonsense tone of voice.

"Oh, George, please call me Natalie..."

205

She sounded as if butter wouldn't melt in her mouth, but Daddy cut her off. "Isn't Rhonda the name your mama gave you?"

She passed right by the question. "I just thought I'd drop by and pick up Millie."

Rhonda peeped around Daddy who was almost fully blocking the front door. "Hey, sweetheart." She waved to Millie who was clinging to me while we rocked in the big green chair in the far back of the living room.

Rhonda acted as if she had only been gone a moment. There was no audience yet she acted as if there was some chummy relationship between our family and her. She acted as if we had done her some grand favor by watching Millie while she ran to the store or on some other errand. I'm not sure who the show was for, but she was sure putting one on.

"Gayle, please bring Millie to her mother." I'm sure Daddy loathed making the request as much as I did honoring it.

I brought Millie over, but took my sweet time doing it. I would have knocked Rhonda out into the yard again except Daddy reminded me that we were to keep Mama calm. I hadn't forgotten that detail from day her doctor told us at the hospital or two days before at the grocery store when I reminded myself.

I glared at her as she held out her hands for Millie to come to her. Millie refused and I couldn't make Millie go. I kissed her and told her I loved her, then, I gave her to Daddy and forced him to do the dirty work. I didn't even stick around for the final transfer. I ran from the room and started my next letter to Noah.

December 15, 1975

Dear Noah,

By the time this letter reaches you, it will be Christmas. I would like to go ahead and give you your Christmas present. Please forgive me that it isn't some large, heavily wrapped package, but instead something small and worthless to anyone other than you and me.

I know you said to take my time and think about your question, but I have an answer for you. I would like very much for you to come home to me and I don't just mean for the day or the week or on any sort of leave. I want you to come home to me for good.

I know what I told you the night at our house. I told you that college and being a vet was my future, but the truth is I can no longer see my future without you in it. I have given this a great deal of thought. College is still my future, but I like to think that you are, too. I love writing to you, but I love being with you more. The thing is, I will not make your decision for you. If you want to leave the Air Force, that is your decision. Please do not do it for me. Do it because it is what you want.

If there is anything I have learned from my parents' relationship it is that I will never make your decisions for you. I will always appreciate the respect that my father and mother have shown one another and the trust they have that the other is capable of making their own decisions including those that affect the both of them or the entire family. I like to think there will come a time when we will make decisions together, but I won't make your decision. So for now, my gift to you is the trust that you will make the best decision for you.

The last night we were together you refused something and that was very honorable. You mentioned that you did not want me to experience the judgment that your mother experienced when she became pregnant out of wedlock with your older brother. Mama and I went to the grocery store this week and I carried Millie through the store. I completely understand your concerns now, not that I didn't before, but I was at the receiving end of such judgment while shopping with Mama and Millie. As I told Mama, I would take a million of those judgmental looks if that meant I could keep Millie.

Rhonda was here tonight. Can you imagine she only just now showed up to get Millie after leaving her here on Thanksgiving day? She did. She showed up here as if everything was perfectly normal. Nothing about poor Millie's childhood is normal. I won't go into all of the details, but before I lost my temper with Rhonda again, I came to my room to write to you.

In writing to you about Millie, it just occurred to me to ask, do you want children? What are your thoughts on that? I suppose that's something we should know about one another. I wouldn't mind having children, but after college. My one concession to having children prior to finishing college would be if somehow I managed to adopt Millie. I don't begin to know how I would go about that or what my parents or Rhonda would think, but I would totally do that if it was at all an option.

I wish you were here so I could tell you all of this in person. Noah, I miss you dearly and I can hardly wait to see you again. I wish you could be here for Christmas, New Year's and every other day of the week.

I hope you have a Merry Christmas and that you are safe and happy.

Love always,

Gayle Anderson

Noah continued to call and we continued to write back and forth through the winter and spring of 1976. He was ecstatic about my answer and, even though he was over a thousand miles away, we grew closer with every letter and every phone call.

***

I was just about finished getting dressed for my date with Noah when my mind flashed to the last time I saw him. It was on Memorial Day weekend 1976, the weekend I graduated high school.

I was on the football field with all of my classmates. Judy was seated at the far end of the alphabet from me so she wasn't near enough to hold my hand through one of the biggest moments of my life thus far.

"Abbigayle Jane Anderson." Mine was the first name that rang out over the loud speaker. I was summoned to give the salutatorian speech.

My stomach churned. I was nervous and my knees were a little shaky as I started the walk toward the principal of Stapleton High.

I'm not sure what I was nervous about. I knew I was graduating. I knew I was salutatorian, a fact that I was still irritated about. I knew I had rehearsed my speech a million times, rehearsed it to the point that Mama and Daddy were sick to death of hearing it. I also knew this was the beginning of the rest of my life so I'm not sure what I was nervous about.

I could hear the material of my gown rub and swish against my pantyhose as I strode across the field. It was distracting and helped with the nervousness, but what was the most distracting was looking to the stands and seeing Noah. He was in his dress uniform and sitting between Mama and Aunt Dot. At Thanksgiving and in letters since then he said he would be back in May, but he never said when. I had been so distracted with graduating that the month got away from me and, although I wanted to see him desperately, I was totally surprised.

Noah tipped his hat to me and I mirrored his action by tipping my cap. I added a wink and the biggest smile I had mustered in months.

I gave the speech on autopilot. I couldn't get the grin off my face that I would surely be spending the evening with Noah. I breezed through the speech, grabbed my diploma and, as soon as we were released, I ran to find him and my parents. I made sure to hug Mama and Daddy first as not to offend them, but I looked at Noah the entire time I wrapped my arms around each of them. They meant the world to me and I would not have done as well in school without them pushing, but I saw them every day of my life.

I bit my lip and tried to contain myself, but I beamed. I couldn't wait to be in his arms. As I hugged Mama, I looked over her shoulder. I couldn't take my eyes off of Noah and he didn't take his eyes off of me.

"We couldn't be prouder!" Mama said to everyone that was gathered around.

Aunt Dot and Uncle Jim drove over from Alabama. Aunt Ruth and her clan were there, including my new cousin Dixie, who made her first public appearance at my graduation. Cousin Dixon ran circles between all of the family members as Mama and Daddy gushed over me. I tried to act humble, but I couldn't think of anything beyond Noah.

Each time I started toward Noah another family member or friend grabbed me and congratulated me. There was no way I could be rude to anyone, but I really just wanted to hug him. That was actually an understatement, I wanted to kiss him.

"Well, we should be getting on to the house. The rest of the party guests are waiting," Daddy began to corral everyone to their cars. He and Mama had planned a big graduation party for me at the house.

"Mr. Anderson, I don't want to over step, but would you mind if I gave Gayle a ride home?" Noah asked.

Daddy looked to me. "Please, Daddy?" I begged.

"I suppose," Daddy agreed.

Mama and Daddy led all of the relatives toward the parking lot and I thought I was going to get a moment with Noah, but I was mistaken. I had barely taken his hand and started to tell him how glad I was to see him when Judy grabbed me and whirled me around.

"We are high school graduates!" Judy screamed as we hugged and jumped around. This was so typically Judy. For a moment we had our own celebration and as far as she was concerned no one else was around.

After a few seconds, I finally reminded her, "You remember Noah, right?" I stepped back so Judy could notice him standing there.

"Who could forget?" she gushed over him. "You and Gayle must come by my party later. Gayle has all of the details..."

Judy was hardly finished extending the invitation when her mother called her. "Gotta go! I better see y'all later!" Judy bounced off toward her mother.

I immediately turned back to Noah. "I'm so glad you're here!"

"How glad are you?" Noah pulled me into his arms.

"Very, very glad," I beamed. His uniform was heavily starched and it was stiff against me as we hugged. I struggled to stifle everything in me as I wanted to scream with joy that Noah was there with me.

I didn't want to let him go, but as Noah pointed out, "We need to get going. You don't want to be late for your own party."

The party seemed like it was going to last forever. Noah and I were inseparable throughout the party. There were about fifty people all over the house and in the yard to celebrate my graduation. I didn't mean to seem ungrateful for their time, but I really just wanted all of them to leave so I could have time with Noah. Graduation ended at 2:00 p.m. and the party started at 2:30 and went until almost 6:00 before the last guest left. I thought they would never leave.

"Daddy, would you mind if Noah took me to Judy's party?" I asked politely as I started to help clean up from the party. Noah followed my lead and gathered the folding chairs while I asked Daddy.

"I suppose," Daddy replied. Daddy also told us to go on and that he, Mama, Aunt Dot and Uncle Jim would take care of the cleanup.

Noah and I stopped by Judy's party, but ducked out after about thirty minutes. I didn't even have to beg Judy's forgiveness for leaving the party.

"Go on, get out of here. I wouldn't want to be at your party if this was the first time I had seen Doug in six months." Judy really was the best friend I could ever hope to have.

Noah got the passenger's side door to the Camaro for me. As soon as he was behind the wheel he asked, "No one's living in our house are they?"

Noah must have read my mind. That's exactly the place I wanted to go with him.

"No," I answered.

"Good. I think I need my memory refreshed as to what it looks like at night."

When Noah wasn't shifting gears between Judy's house in Wrens and Stillwater Plantation outside of Avera, he held my hand in his. Just that little touch from him made my insides quiver. I still could not take my eyes off of him and he didn't seem to mind or even acknowledge that I was staring.

Judy lived on the side of Wrens that made taking Highway 88 to Avera a better route than going all the way back through Stapleton. We were just about to turn on Clarksmill Road when sprinkles started hitting the windshield. By the time we turned down the driveway the sprinkles were gone and a full-fledged flash flood had set in. We could hardly see the house when the Camaro rolled to a stop near the end of the driveway.

"Do you want to wait it out in the car or do you want to make a run for it?" Noah asked as he killed the engine.

Drops the size of the palm of my hand splattered across the windshield and they were coming down in sheets. They hit so hard that I flinched over a few of them. The wind was starting to pick up as well and, what I could see of the trees through the rain, wasn't good. Pines had a bad reputation for snapping in a good breeze and this was way more than a breeze.

"I'm kind of nervous about making a run for it, but I don't like the looks of those trees." I pointed out the passengers' side window. "I'd rather take my chances getting hit by a tree in a house than in a car."

Noah opened the door and the rain blew in. "I'd rather not get hit by a tree at all!" He shouted over the pounding on the roof of the car before getting out and closing the door.

For once, I didn't wait for Noah to come around and open my door. I jumped out, grabbed up my skirt to keep it from dragging in the mud and sprinted past Noah toward the porch. From the steps all the way to the front door the porch was soaked and water continued to pour across it.

As fast as I could, I stood on my toes and grabbed the key from the highest of the side light windows around the front door. I didn't even think about it, I just unlocked the door and let us in.

"They cut the power off some months ago. We may not have lights, but at least we can dry off in here." There was enough light out that we could still see clearly in the foyer.

Although I could feel that I was soaked to the bone, I looked down at my clothes to confirm my predicament. My white shirt was completely see-through thanks to the volume of water that had landed on it during the run to the house. Thank goodness I had on a good bra or there would have been nothing left to Noah's imagination. Also, thank goodness Noah and I changed out of the clothes we wore to my graduation before we left for Judy's party. We still weren't wearing anything worthy of swimming or building an ark, but it sure beat the white dress I was wearing and his uniform.

There in the foyer Noah started unbuttoning his shirt. I tried to busy myself with wringing out my skirt while attempting not to stare at him. It was obvious that Noah had on an undershirt, but with or without a shirt underneath, the act of him unbuttoning his shirt set me on fire. He still hadn't kissed me and I could not stop wondering when that would happen. The whole time we were at my party I wanted to steal a moment alone and take care of that craving, but I never got the chance now here we were and still nothing.

I could not take trying not to watch him any longer. I don't know what I was thinking, but I started up the stairs. I looked back once and Noah followed me. I was a couple of steps ahead of him, but I stopped and turned back. I took the lapel of his shirt in my hands and I eased them down to the final buttons. I looked at him and smiled. It wasn't something that I put any thought into, I just took over the unbuttoning for him. When I was done I turned and pulled him along behind me. I took the last few steps before hanging his shirt on the corner railing at the top of the stairs.

On the second floor the beating of the rain on the tin roof was more defined. All of the furniture was gone and the rooms were empty, that enhanced the volume of the rain. The only thing left in the master bedroom was an area rug and I led Noah in there.

As I sat down on the rug in the middle of the room, I mentioned, "I know it's kind of boring, but I was thinking that we could just lay here and listen to the rain."

I reached the floor and Noah didn't say anything, he just sat down beside me. I took his hand in mine and I leaned back flat on the floor. Noah followed.

For about five minutes we laid there in silence, listening to the rain, before Noah rolled over on his side to face me. I rolled over to mirror him.

"You've got chill bumps." Noah ran his index finger down my arm. It tickled as it went. I could not help but notice how smooth his hands were. They were nothing like most of the men's hands in my family. Theirs were rough and callused from years of manual labor, but not Noah's.

I bit my lip. I was a little cold, but I'm sure the chill bumps got worse and it wasn't because there was a sudden drop in temperature in the room. If anything, there was a rise in my temperature.

Noah sat up and I watched in wonder of where he was going, but he didn't go anywhere. He crossed his hands and took hold of the hem of his undershirt. Up, up, up, he pulled it revealing inch after inch of chiseled skin. His stomach tightened more and more as he lifted his shirt. I was just as star struck as I would have been if I had been watching young Elvis disrobe in front of me.

Before my eyes could completely pop out of my head Noah tossed white t-shirt to me. "Here, this is still dry. Take those wet clothes off and put this on."

I caught the shirt. "Ummm," I hesitated.

"It's barely 7:00 and I don't have to get you home until 11:00. Remember, your dad gave us an extra thirty minutes tonight?"

I nodded slowly in cautious agreement and then sat up.

"Hang your clothes up next to my shirt on the banister and they'll dry well before I have to get you home."

"Okay." I started with the top button of my shirt and noticed Noah. His eyes were fixed on me. "Are you going to turn around?"

"No." Noah paused. "Seriously, Gayle, you've got on a bra and panties so it's not like I'm going to see anything tonight, right?" There was a bit of challenge in his voice.

I rolled my eyes at him ever so slightly. I straightened my back and continued with my buttons. I was nervous and fumbled with the second and third buttons before getting the hang again of a task I mastered before kindergarten, unbuttoning buttons.

Thank goodness I did not have on one of those God-awful, pointy, cross-your heart bras that Mama bought me. Judy picked this one out and we both purchased two of them on our last shopping trip to Augusta. It was a new item at the National Hills J.B. Whites, a Wonderbra, and this was dang near fashionable compared to the usual pure functional ones. The Wonderbra was low cut and padded and it helped give the illusion that I had more going on up top than I actually did. The wonder of it was where did the twins come from when I put it on and where did they go when I took it off. Thank heavens he had already let me know I would not be expected to take it off tonight.

The buttons were finished and I opened my blouse to slip my arms through. Noah took notice of my swanky new bra. "That's modern," he observed.

How was I to respond? I didn't know what to say so I just smiled at him. I certainly wasn't going to tell him what it was called.

215

I folded my shirt and laid it down on the rug next to me. I reached over and picked up Noah's white undershirt and slipped it on. I then stood up and shimmied out of my skirt. Although my bra and panties were not a set, they were both white and matched, but Noah never caught a glimpse of my underpants due to the size of his T-shirt.

I picked up my clothes and strutted across the room and out to the banister and hung them up. Noah watched me the entire time. Walking back from the hall, I could not help but worry. Noah was bare chested and I was in his t-shirt. There would be no reason for anyone to be out at the house and I sure hoped no one else came out. Being caught like this would be really bad, but I tried not to dwell on that as Noah extended his hand to me and helped me back down on the floor.

I was no sooner seated than Noah laid back down on the floor again. He offered his shoulder for me to use as a pillow and I took him up on the offer. I could hear the rain still beating down as I thought about how badly I wanted to kiss Noah and wondered how much longer he was going to make me wait. The rain pounded on the roof like my heart pounded in my chest and the only thought I could hear was myself begging him to kiss me.

"Noah?" I said, barely above a whisper.

"Yes?"

I didn't want to be forward, but he had flown all the way from Italy so what would this matter, but to speed up what I thought was surely inevitable? I worked up my courage and asked, "May I kiss you?"

"You never have to ask that."

I rolled over and propped myself against his chest. There was still hint of cologne on his skin. I inhaled a deep breath of Clubman before pressing my lips to his. They say that the face of Helen of Troy launched a thousand ships, but if she kissed like Noah, it wasn't only her face that caused the launching of the ships.

Every inch that I could feel against me was smooth. His chest, his shoulders, his neck and his face, were all like touching

216

butter. There wasn't even a trace of stubble around his mouth to chap my face as it usually did when we kissed this passionately. I didn't mind it being chapped as there was a slight sting hours later that reminded me of being kissed by him, kissed so deeply.

The heat between Noah and I that night was something I would never forget. I was settling into my memory of him rolling me over on the floor and explaining to me that our children would be conceived in that very room one day when Mama called my name. It took a second for me to snap back to reality and as I did I could still feel Noah's jeans rubbing against me, his hands locked in mine above my head and his weight so slightly bearing down on me. I could feel the softness of his t-shirt tickling the skin on my belly while butterflies fluttered inside. I don't know how we stopped that night.

I grabbed my purse and headed down the hall as Mama called again, "Gayle, Noah's here!"

CHAPTER 12

This night had been on the horizon since I picked myself up off the ground at Andy's funeral and laid eyes on Noah. I still felt guilty about where we met, but tried to console myself by seeing Noah as one last gift from my brother.

I made my way down the hallway of our house. The paneled walls were lined with photos of Andy and me. Andy's photos hung above mine and there was one for each year of school. From kindergarten all the way to our senior pictures were all there. I hardly ever noticed them, but the photo of me from third grade caught my eye. I was missing all but my two center teeth up top and that year the kids called me "Rabbit" for a reason. I was all scabbed up from just having gotten over the chicken pox. Looking at that picture, I didn't have a clue how I got Noah.

According to Andy, I was the ugly duckling. When I fretted last year about not getting dates, Andy said to me, "You know the thing about the ugly duckling right?"

We were sitting on the front porch. Andy had just finished cutting the grass and Mama had sent me out with a glass of ice water for him. He was sweaty and tired and I was pouting. Looking at the picture, I could remember exactly how I looked that day and that Andy smelled like fresh cut grass.

I knew the story of the ugly duckling. "He became a swan," I answered off handedly.

"And, he didn't even know he was a swan," Andy explained. "It's like you don't know either. I'm your brother so I'm probably not supposed to tell you these types of things, but, Gayle, what you lack in curves, you make up for in legs. You've got legs for days and guys love that. They drool over you and you don't even notice them."

I moved on from my third grade photo to the picture of me from eleventh grade. That was about the time Andy and I had this discussion. That was one of the last conversations I had with my brother, and even to this day I still didn't completely believe Andy. I shook off the urge to tear up over him and I left my thoughts of Andy and the photos and continued to the living room where I found Noah waiting.

As soon as Noah saw me in the doorway he stood from where he was seated on the far end of the couch from Mama. His eyes lit up and I forgot about the ugly duckling on the wall. The way Noah looked at me made me feel like the prettiest girl in the world.

"You are a sight for sore eyes." The wattage in Noah's smile could have powered the entire Central Savannah River Area.

I felt the same way about him. I hadn't seen him since the weekend of my graduation and it had been a long three months of writing back and forth. In that time West Point admitted the first female cadets and Barbara Walters became the first female nightly news anchor and I still had my eye on the prize for the women in our family. I was still going to be the first woman to graduate college among us, but I came to realize that it wouldn't be worth anything if I didn't have Noah, too.

I had been thinking about him all day long, but that was nothing compared to laying eyes on him now. I wanted to, but I couldn't tell him that with Mama and Daddy sitting there. They tried to look like they weren't paying us any attention, but they were listening to every word.

I ran over and hugged Daddy and Mama goodbye and grabbed Noah's hand. "Are you ready?"

The screen door on the front of our house barely closed behind us when I reciprocated Noah's sentiment. "I'm so happy to see you!"

I could not take my eyes off of him. I watched him as he looked me up and down over and over again while we walked to his Camaro. "You look beautiful."

"Thank you." Even with what I had planned for the night, I was still bashful when he paid me compliments like that.

We continued on to his car and Noah reached to open the car door for me.

"Hold on a minute," I said, stopping him with my hand over his on the door handle. I leaned against the car door and put my arms around his neck. "Happy Birthday."

"It is now," he replied as he swallowed and licked his lips before pulling me closer. "I've lived for this moment for three months and I don't care if they're watching."

Noah's hands were firm against the small of my back and through my dress I could feel the heat coming off of the black paint on the car door. Noah pulled me closer and the kiss went deeper. I wasn't even distracted enough to pray that Mama and Daddy didn't move from their spots in the living room. I gave no thought to whether they were watching as I was consumed with Noah.

Noah finally tilted his head back. He pressed it to mine. Before he could say anything I did. "I've missed you so much." And, I nuzzled my nose against his cheek and just breathed him in.

For a moment, we just stood there. My breathing returned to normal and although I enjoyed just being in his arms, I had more in mind for the night and we needed to get going.

"Let's go. I've got something special planned." I stepped out of the way finally allowing Noah to open the door for me. "I've got a surprise for you."

I was nervous and excited all at the same time. I wondered what it would be like. Would he let me give him the ultimate birthday gift? He had been such a gentleman in the past that I wondered if he would go through with it.

Noah backed the Camaro out of the drive way and asked, "Which direction?"

"You know where I want to go."

Without taking his eyes off of mine Noah straightened the car out and stomped down on the gas. The tires made a squalling sound and laid drag behind us as we peeled out toward Stapleton.

"I love this car!" I screamed over the roar of the engine while Noah shifted through all of the gears in a matter of seconds. That car was damn sexy, and not that Noah needed any help making the hot meter move, the car helped it move for him anyway.

"You love the car? What? I'm sure I didn't hear you right?" Noah said as he pushed the pedal down further. I could feel the engine vibrate through my seat as we picked up more speed.

I laughed at the thrill of going so fast. Again I screamed over the engine, "I love you!"

Noah gave me a sideways look with a raised eyebrow. "That's more like it." It wasn't what he said; it was how he said it that made feel the need to fan myself.

It also didn't hurt that the dress I had on was shorter than anything I had ever worn before. It was so short that it rose up so far when I sat down that it barely covered what needed to be covered. Like my dress from homecoming, I was surprised I made it out of the house with it on. Mama and Daddy were definitely slipping, but nothing I would ever complain about. When Noah's right hand wasn't on the stick shifting gears, it was on my bare leg. He started off near my knee, but, with each return from the gear shift, he inched it a little higher. If he thought I was going to stop him at some point he was wrong.

Noah slowed down as we hit the city limits, but after the turn toward Avera and opened it up again. When he hit fifth gear he returned his hand to my leg, my upper inner thigh. My heart raced at the speed of the car and the nervousness that toyed with my insides.

On the Stapleton side of Avera, Noah asked, "Did you eat already?"

"Don't worry about that."

Noah looked at me curiously. The truth was that while I waited on Mama in town and then came home and got dressed, Judy delivered a picnic to "our" house. After swearing her to secrecy months ago, I told Judy about my dream to buy that house from her aunt and uncle one day and how Noah and I went there every time he was in town. She promised not to tell a soul and this time she agreed to help me with his birthday.

Noah made the turn on the other side of Avera and the next thing I knew we were flying down the tire tracks that were the driveway to Stillwater Plantation. The house had sat empty for over a year now and the driveway was starting to be overgrown. As we rolled up into the yard, I could tell that the driveway wasn't the only thing that was starting to show signs of neglect.

The car rolled to a stop and Noah shut it off. We sat there for a moment looking at the house and what it was becoming.

Noah shook his head. "I'm not complaining, but I just can't believe they haven't sold this place already."

"I know and I am complaining when I say, I can't believe anyone would let a place like this go like they are doing."

"I know, but the more they let it go the less we will have to offer when we start to buy it."

"You're still interested in buying it?" My insides leapt in anticipation of his response and my eyes danced with glee as he gathered his answer from his prior statement.

"More than ever. I'm telling you, our children will be conceived in this house."

"You seem pretty keen on us having children."

"I am. Aren't you?"

"I guess. I just don't know that I want any right away. I hate to seem selfish, but for now, I would be content to have you in this country and all to myself."

"Good answer, Gayle."

Noah got out of the car and came around to get my door. I straightened my dress as he came around. When he opened the door, he offered his hand to help me out.

"I didn't know until yesterday, but they are going to let me finish out my tour at the base in Warner Robins. I'll be back on color guard duty for the next two months and then I'm free of the Air Force."

I took his hand and stood from the car, again straightening my dress. "Are you sure you want to get out? I don't want this to be something you regret and end up resenting."

Noah took my hands in his and guided me against the car door until it closed using my behind. "What? Are you afraid I won't be as fun without the uniform, because I can be fun." He answered running a hand along my jawline and pushing my hair back to expose my neck.

I threw my head back and laughed. "I know you're fun. The thing is you make me want to be more fun."

I felt him press closer to me and I stopped laughing. Noah circled the end of my nose with his. As he did that thing with my nose, I wrapped my leg around his. The feel of his jeans tickled coupled with the thought of what was underneath, I got chill bumps. It was excruciating to be that close to him and not have his mouth on me.

"We can stay out here or we can go inside." I closed my eyes as the suggestion eased out of me.

Flip flops were all the rage and I had on a pair that matched my dress. I stood on my toes in the flip flops and could barely reach the ledge that held the key to the front door. The key was in its usual place, but it seemed I was having more trouble reaching it than I had in the past. I stretched and stretched to reach it as Noah waited behind me.

Noah was a couple of inches taller than I was and he could have offered to help me, but he was too preoccupied with the view. "Is that dress new?"

Seemed like a strange question in that moment, but I answered. "Yes."

"I like it, but I can't believe your parents let you out of the house with it on."

"Why?" "I know it's a little short, but..."

I hardly had the key and wasn't off of my toes when I was surprised by his touch and grabbed my breath.

"I can see all the way to here." Noah ran the pad of his thumb along the bottom of my left butt cheek, starting inside and moving outward toward my thigh.

I grabbed three ragged breaths and braced myself against the little windows around the door. My dress fell back into place as much as it could with Noah's hand still under it. Noah's breath blew through the tiny hairs on the back of my neck. I hadn't been sure he was going to stop, but his hand came to rest on my lower hip. The other was around my waist and there I was pinned between him and the windows around the door.

All of the sudden, Noah appeared to snap back to his gentlemanly senses. Taking his hand as he stepped back, he started apologizing. I hadn't protested, but he apologized anyway. "I'm sorry. That was probably too forward of me."

While he was speaking, I turned around to face him and his brow became furrowed. He took a few steps back. "Hold still. Let me get a look at you."

The house faced west and although the sun was on its descent, it was still beating down on the front porch. I stood there, still as I could be as Noah looked me over. My little white eyelet dress glistened in the sun as Noah's face started to turn red.

"Gayle," Noah sounded serious.

"What is it?" I really had no idea what, but something seemed to be amiss.

Noah pulled in his lips as if he was biting both of them simultaneously. Noah was speechless. He ran his hands over his face and straight up over his head, through his hair.

"Noah, are you alright?"

"Oh yeah," Noah shook his head up and down, almost shaking like. "You really don't know what's..."

"No, what?"

"Let's go inside."

"Tell me."

Noah walked over to me and took the key from my hand, unlocked the door and pulled me inside. I repeated my request, but he didn't answer until he shut the front door, not just the screen door, but the large wooden door, behind us.

"Gayle, when the sunlight hits that dress, I can see straight through it. So, I'm going to go over here for a little while and..."

Noah turned to walk away, but quickly I grabbed him. I threw my arms around him. I didn't know the exact details of my plan, but this fit into it just fine.

Leaning my forehead to his, I asked in a whisper, "Are you having a happy birthday?"

Before Noah could answer, I pressed my lips to his. I could taste him. I could smell him. I could feel his hands climb my legs and under my dress they went. With handfuls of my behind, Noah pulled at me. I eased my leg up his. There was something in me, a begging desire to wrap my legs around him.

Noah's hands were so far up my dress that his touch was distracting, in a wonderful, burning way. I had never been touched like this before.

"Gayle, I want to ask you something?" Noah laid kisses from my ear to my shoulder, stretching the neck of my dress over one of my shoulders, leaving it bare.

I couldn't respond. I just wanted him to keep going. His mouth sliding across my skin left me weak-kneed with the heat that burned between us.

"I know this isn't the ideal time to ask this, but I haven't formally asked and I have to ask."

"Noah, stop talking. Just enjoy your birthday present." I tried to catch my breath as I spoke.

"Will you marry me?"

There, he finally asked, he had beat around the bush so many times. Implied it, but this was the first time he officially asked.

I answered "Yes" as I pulled at his shirt. I wanted it off of him.

"Gayle, I'm serious." Noah took my hands and dropped to his knees.

I could hardly think, but I was clear enough to give the answer. "Yes, Noah, the answer has always been 'yes.'"

I dropped to my knees with him. I never took my eyes off of his. "I'll say vows to you now, if you like. The answer to each question is 'I do. I do , Noah, I do. I love you, and I do.'"

"Oh my God, Gayle, are you serious?" Noah fell back. I think I shocked him.

"So serious." Crawling across to him on my knees, I climbed on top of him. Straddling him as he sat propped up by the bottom step on the staircase. "Are you serious, Noah?"

Noah took my face in his hands. "I am, I do, Gayle. There's no one else for me but you."

"And you're the only one for me."

Instead of kissing me, Noah let go of my face and hung his head. "I should have asked your father first." Noah squirmed beneath me. He was suddenly uncomfortable.

226

I dropped my shoulder below his chin and lifted it enough that I nuzzled my face against his. We sat in silence for a few minutes before I spoke again. I think we both knew what would happen if Noah asked my dad for my hand in marriage now.

"Even if you ask him now, he'll tell you 'no.' His hat is hung on me going to college."

"I figured as much. I'll assure him that we will wait until after you finish college." I could feel Noah taking in the scent of my hair.

"He won't believe that you will wait four years for me and he won't agree to it."

"I would marry you now."

I gave a little giggle and leaned back to look in Noah's eyes. "In some countries the words alone would do the trick and that would mean you just did."

"Shall we seal it with a kiss?"

It's funny, I didn't want to give him his birthday present on the floor of foyer, but I missed the heat of the moment. With all of the marriage talk the conversation took a serious turn over asking my dad for his permission. To get back to where we were when we first walked in, right there, right then, would almost be forced effort and I didn't want that.

"Noah, are you hungry?"

Noah looked back at me curiously. As graceful as I could, and guarding the length of my dress, I stood up.

"I have something for you." I offered my hand to help him up.

Once he was on his feet and no longer blocking the staircase, I started up. Noah followed. At the top of the stairs, I turned into the master bedroom where I found everything laid out just as I had asked Judy.

The room was lit by the two windows on the west side of the house. The setting sun was beaming through. In the middle of the room was a patchwork quilt spread out like a large area rug. In the middle of the quilt was a picnic basket. I would do anything for Judy and she would do anything for me. She did exactly like I had asked her. How strange were we, two school girls plotting, planning and scheming, one helping the other have the most amazing experience when losing her honor.

Still missing the moment and remembering what Noah said when I stood in the sunlight on the front porch, I made sure to stand in the light of the windows when I entered the room. Picnic or not, I wanted to make sure I set Noah on fire the way he did me. After all, he had to be willing to accept the gift I was hoping to give.

Noah noticed as I hoped he would. "You may want to come away from the windows."

I smiled at Noah slyly. All bashfulness was gone and I was rising to the occasion. Instead of moving out of the light, I sat down on the quit in front of them in such a manner that either way I turned, he had a view of me. I meant to seduce him even though I really didn't know what I was doing. The dress and going without a bra was Judy's idea.

I sat with my knees tucked under me and began to dig in the picnic basket. Noah shook his head and took a seat opposite me. We ate dinner and Noah tried to keep his eyes off of me, but he struggled.

For dessert I had had Judy pack slices of a chocolate cake that I baked myself. I pulled a slice out of the picnic basket and offered it to Noah. Noah took the cake and sat it to the side.

"You don't like chocolate cake?" I should have checked with him as to what sort of cake he might like.

"That's not it." Noah stood to his knees and then slid the picnic basket out of the way. "I don't think you understand what that dress is doing to me."

"Oh." My heart raced. This was it.

Noah's eyes were blazing as he made his way across the quilt to me. They were as blue as I had ever seen them and he didn't take them off of me.

Noah's mouth was on mine with the perfect combination of force and gentleness as he searched my mouth with his tongue. He was a master at the art of kissing, skilled with his lips, his tongue and his hands.

We were both on our knees. One of Noah's hands was in my hair at the base of my skull, guiding the tilting of my head as his attention moved to my neck. The other hand was attached to the arm that was wrapped so firmly around my waist.

Noah held me so tightly that my breasts were pressed almost flat against his chest. The cotton and the eyelet pattern of the material slipped over my skin. Areas of my skin that were never the focus of anything more than an ill-fitting bra suddenly had a life of their own. My breasts were swelling and hyper-sensitive and that wasn't the only indication that I was turned on.

From the feel of him pressed to me, I wasn't the only one that was about ready to come undone. I could feel that Noah was aroused even through the material of his jeans and my dress.

As Noah nibbled at my earlobe and ran circles around my ear with his tongue, breathless from the sensation, I confessed. "I don't have to go home tonight."

"Are you sure?"

"I do." Not only an affirmation of my prior statement, but a reminder of our earlier conversation.

Noah lost focus on my neck and leaned back to get a confirming look from my face.

I took my hands from where I had them, my fingers slipped into the waistband of his pants. I unbuttoned the top two buttons of my dress, leaving the center of my chest bare to just below what would have been the bottom of my bra. I arched my back and offered myself to Noah.

Noah's grip became tighter around my waist as I leaned back. All of my weight rested on his arm around me. I could barely think at all, but I thought enough to be further turned on by the strength he had in his one arm that was supporting me.

I studied his eyes, ever nervous that he would not like what he was seeing. The material that had been secured by the top two buttons draped open more than I had expected. I was millimeters from being fully exposed. I could feel the heat of the summer sun beating through the windows and lighting up my skin.

Noah's class ring sparkled in the light as it sat perched on my sternum like a lone cupcake on a service tray. The length of the chain that held the class ring was such that it typically fell in between what cleavage I had. When I leaned back it became more and more pronounced in its isolation on my bare skin and I became more and more aware of the weight of the gold.

Noah's smooth fingers slipped down my skin, inching toward the ring, leaving a path of fire behind them. His fingers were fine, but I longed to be kissed. I longed for him to kiss me in places that he had never kissed me before. I knew nothing of being touched let alone kissed in those places, but I wanted it nonetheless.

For a moment, Noah focused on the ring. His touch tickled as he drew an outline of the ring on my skin. He circled it at least three times. Had I not squirmed, unable to squelch my skin's urge to twitch, he might have continued the torture.

"I'll get you a proper engagement ring this week," Noah commented before taking his eyes off of the ring.

Impressed by his words, I threw myself around him. "You could get me a string and..."

I was surprised and my words were stopped by his mouth's return to mine. My dress was hiked slightly and Noah's hands were around my legs. With his upper body strength and while we were still on our knees, he lifted me. As if it was instinct, I wrapped my legs around him and, in an unbelievably smooth transition; Noah laid me on my back. All the while he never took his lips from mine.

When I was safely on my back, Noah eased up and took my hands in his. He locked my fingers and raised my hands until they were pinned above my head. Again, my dress was open at the top and his class ring shone in the middle of my bare chest, a twinkling star catching what little light there was between us.

I could feel his jeans rubbing high on my thighs. I knew my dress was hiked to the point of barely covering my panties. I could feel this because my legs were spread open and Noah rested his weight between them.

I was starting to tremble, but it wasn't from nervousness. I knew that much, but Noah didn't and he could feel the shiver run from me to him as he lay pressed against me. My hands were still pinned above my head and I was straining to kiss his Adam's apple.

Noah sat up, releasing my hands. "Are you afraid?" True concern blended with the beads of sweat that were starting to form across his face.

I didn't move a muscle except to shake my head from side to side. I was so captivated by him that I couldn't even squeak out the word "no." I wasn't frightened of him or what I anticipated happening between us at all.

Noah reached down with his index finger and circled his class ring and again my skin twitched with pleasure.

"You're the bravest person I know."

Although Noah paid me a fine compliment, I saw nothing brave about it. I was simply dying for my boyfriend, or fiancé or husband, as he might have been in the eyes of God now that we had said the most important part of the marriage vows, for him to make love to me. I was eighteen, my hormones were raging, and I was desperately in love with him. There was nothing brave about it. Of course, I didn't tell him all of that. I just blushed and turned my head away for a second before turning back and smiling at him.

Noah lost interest in the class ring again and inched his fingers down to the third button on my dress. "Do you mind?"

Noah started with the button as quickly as I shook my head, my insecurities having melted away. I wanted him to see me and to like what he saw.

The third button was located midway between my naval and my breasts. He unhooked the button without breaking eye contact with me. The cloth hardly budged even though it was no longer fastened together. There were two more buttons left and Noah inched down to the fourth. Still he did not break our connection and found the fourth button by running his hand down my stomach until he caught it. I arched my belly into his touch as he was like a magician commanding his assistant to levitate.

"May I?" he asked when he reached the button.

I smiled at him, giving my consent.

My dress still had not fallen open to expose my breasts, but it was open to my belly button and the lace around the top of my panties.

There was only one button left holding the dress together and that seemed like a formality. My eyes rolled back and I sighed as he ran his hand over my panties and their satin material was the only thing that separated me from his bare hand. I tilted my hips to his touch.

I opened my eyes to meet his just as he reached the last button. I bit my lip with anticipation releasing it only to utter the words, "You needn't bother asking." And I returned my top teeth to pulling in my bottom lip. I didn't smile that time. I lifted my hips and pelvis to him for easier access to the button.

When Noah finished with my dress he untucked his shirts, the pale blue collared shirt and the white t-shirt underneath. In one swift move he jerked both shirts over his head and tossed them to the side.

I hadn't seen him shirtless but one time and that was back in the fall when he helped Daddy cut the grass. It has been a glorious memory that I had held onto all these months. Now, here he was, quite literally in the flesh.

Evidently, I wasn't the only one that enjoyed my time in the sun. Noah too had an even bronze color about his chest and arms. Unlike me there were no tan lines to be seen, no hint of a farmer's tan at all. He was tan and chiseled muscle and virtually hairless across his chest. The sunlight was fading from what was our bedroom, but there was still just enough light left for me to see how perfect he was and he was indeed perfect. His hair was a little longer than the time I had seen him last and this time its color was just a shade lighter brown. It was as if there was some correlation to its length and shade, the longer the lighter. Though he had jerked his shirts over his head with no regard for his hair, it was hardly mussed at all. He was a bronze Adonis of brown hair and blue eyes that burned for me as mine did for him.

Although I felt I was staring at him for a great deal of time, it was mere seconds between the loss of his shirt and finding him hovering over me. Noah was yet to fully uncover me and take a look as I had just done to him. The thought of wanting him to see me was fading as I knew it was on the horizon, but I did fear it may be too dark in the room by the time he tried. That thought quickly faded as well.

Noah let go of my hands and I was quick to wrap my arms around his neck. He propped on his right elbow and was so gentle not to bare his weight on me. His left hand ran all the way down, cupping my arm along the journey. At the same time, Noah moved from kissing my mouth to my neck. I wanted to reciprocate, but I could hardly move more than to tilt my head and allow him full access to my neck.

Noah's tongue licked slowly downward and across my collar bone. His hand barely kept a quicker pace. Biting at the top of my dress and using only his teeth, Noah flipped back that side of my dress. I gasped at the thrill. On one side, I was exposed from my collar bone to my panties.

Noah gave one last lick, tracing my collar bone before heading south. I let my arms fall, loosening from his neck, but leaving my fingers pilfering through his hair. I was so excited. I was about to get what I wanted.

233

Noah's hand found my breast before his mouth. The way Noah held my breast made it fuller than it had ever appeared before. I couldn't help but look. If I weren't on the receiving end of the light squeeze he was giving it, I would not have recognized it as my own.

Noah grazed his thumb across my nipple as he held firm. That act alone made my knees quake, but when his lips found it and he circled it with his tongue and grazed it with his bottom teeth, I felt my heartbeat in my groin. There was nothing between my legs, but I could feel a beat like the rhythm of a trotting horse inside of me.

At first the sensation from his teeth, I let go of the hair on the back of his head, arched my back more giving into him and grabbed fistfuls of the quilt beneath us. I groaned with what I would have assumed to be unmistakable passion, but Noah eased up from me, taking his mouth away, and asked if I was alright.

I could hardly make out what he said for the distraction of the trotting. All I knew was that he had stopped and I didn't want that.

"We can stop anytime you like..."

Suddenly, I found my words, "No, please don't stop," I pleaded with him.

Noah seemed pleased with my begging. "Come here. Let's not ruin your dress."

Noah helped me and I sat up. The dress was completely open only hanging on my shoulders. Once he had me firmly against him, Noah helped me slip my arms free of the sleeves. Still holding me, my chest pressed to his, he folded my dress behind my back and tossed it to the far corner of the quilt.

I was left there in his arms in only my panties. I loved the feel of his skin against mine so much that the trotting was still there. My heart pounded away in the space between my legs.

"It's getting dark and I have candles in my basket. If you like, I'll light them." I whispered in between the light sucks I placed on one of his ear lobes.

His face was full of skepticism as he asked, "You don't want this in the dark?"

"It wouldn't be much of a birthday present if I didn't let you see it." I didn't know where those words came from but there they were.

Skepticism was replaced with delight. Noah didn't delay in passing me the picnic basket.

I took the candles and matches from the basket. I got up and walked to the far corner of the room, opposite the door. I wanted to put them someplace that we couldn't knock them over. As I walked I looked back over my shoulder to find Noah watching me.

When I turned back after lighting the candles, my hair swirled around my neck and came to rest covering one of my breasts. I was ready for Noah to see me so I dipped my shoulder and tossed my head, slinging all of my hair down my back.

The walls of the room were white washed and the candles lit them to a pale gray color. It was a huge room that took up a fourth of the top floor of the house. There were sheer white curtains that hung around the windows, but did nothing to cover them. That was the only thing on the walls. A teardrop chandelier hung in the center of the room and the flickering light from the candles made tiny rainbows in each of the crystals drops. Directly below it, Noah waited for me and watched me approach. I could see from the change in color of his chest rising to his neck, going bright red, and in the adjustment he made to the crotch of his jeans, my actions had had the desired effect. Noah could see almost all of me by the candlelight. I had no doubt he liked what he saw and that pleased me.

Noah stood up as I approached. First he undid the button and then the zipper of his jeans. He let them fall and then stepped out of them. Now we were both in only our underwear. I had never even seen him in shorts before that moment, yet I looked away. My options were look away or stare and I didn't want to completely embarrass myself by staring at him.

Noah read my thoughts. "You can look you know. I don't mind."

So much for not being embarrassed. I gathered my face in my hands and peeped back at him through my fingers.

"Gayle, have you never seen a naked man before?"

Still peeping through my fingers and within arm's reach of him, I hung my head. "No."

Noah bent over taking his Fruit of the Looms down with him. I had nothing else to compare him to, but it was big enough that it made me start to question. My bewilderment must have shown on my face.

"It just does." Noah answered the question without me having asked it. "Trust me."

"Always." I took the remaining steps toward him.

"Turn around."

I did like Noah asked and he wrapped his arms around my belly. He moved my hair to one side, over my right shoulder, leaving the left bare. The hairs on the back of my neck stood up when he breathed his words against my skin. He eased his hands down as the wind from the words gave me goose bumps down my legs. I drew in my stomach as tight as I could as Noah's fingers entered the waist band of my panties.

"You won't be needing these for the rest of the night."

His hands were open flat with the elastic caught around his wrists when he started to pull my lace panties down. At first his hands were above my pelvic bones, but he slid them inward and down at the same time. My panties were halfway down my hips when Noah's fingers made a discovery.

"Gayle!" This time it wasn't me that was shocked.

236

Noah continued feeling downward and under. "Really? Nothing?"

I had completely shaved earlier that morning due to the prospect of wearing one of Judy's bikini's that afternoon. One thing led to another and I got a little carried away and took everything off. I was as smooth as a baby's bottom in my nether regions.

I had never been touched there before. The rhythm of my heartbeat picked up pace, the horse wasn't trotting anymore, it was running.

"Noah, you aren't disappointed are you?"

Noah pushed my panties down and spun me around. "Gayle, no, there's no way I could be disappointed. You just surprised me."

Without any shame, Noah looked down at me, down there. "You are amazing."

I blushed and pulled me into his arms. "Unless you stop me, I'm going to make love to you now."

"Okay." I liked it when he told me what he was going to do with me.

Noah guided my return to a horizontal position on my back on the quilt, our mouths connected the entire way. Noah propped himself between my legs again and there was no material of underwear, jeans or panties between us. It was just him on me.

I didn't tell him, but I wanted him to do that thing he did to my nipple again and he did. He paid particular attention to them. I raised up on my shoulder blades and gave them to him. I could feel my temperature still rising. I tried not to moan because I didn't want him to stop like he did before.

"I'm going to spread your legs a little wider, alright?"

All I could say was "okay" when I wanted to scream, "Do whatever you like with me."

Noah still balanced on one of his elbows and his legs so that he hovered above me and I did not feel on single ounce of his weight. Once my legs were wider, Noah told me what he was going to do next.

"I'm going to check to see if you are ready." I didn't know what he meant by that, but he slid the hand down my pelvic bone.

The sensation was magnificent as I anticipated what was to come.

"I can't get over how smooth you are. I love it."

I watched his hand move lower and lower. "I love you." I added as I opened my legs even wider.

Noah slid his fingers down my center and under. I gasped when he inserted them into me.

"My God, Gayle, you are so ready."

Noah moved both arms back around me and balanced evenly on both. I licked at his Adam's apple as it presented itself to me, but I nearly bit him at the first thrust inside me.

I gave a sharp exhale, "Haah! ...Haah! ...Haah!" each time he entered me. I could feel my insides tightening around him.

Each time Noah thrust in, he came nearly all the way out, but not completely. I moved with him, chasing him to keep him inside me. How long we carried on like that I wasn't sure, but I was sure that I loved him and I could spend my life doing this with him.

"I love you, Gayle."

"And I you, Noah."

Within moments Noah stilled himself inside me and as soon as he did that racing heart of mine, stopped. It pulsed and it was the absolute strangest, most unbelievable muscle spasm, I had ever experienced. I could feel my body clinch and release around Noah. Each heartbeat in my groin after that was a solid pound that came at fifteen second intervals. Noah and I lay intertwined until the pounding in me was over.

"Now I see what all the fuss is about." I smiled at him as he rolled over next to me.

"Thank you for my birthday present. It's the best I've ever received." Noah sighed as he laid one more kiss on me.

"I love you, Noah, and I would give you the moon if I could."

CHAPTER 13

Sensations swirled through me, all of them unique and different. My skin tingled and I could not describe the way I felt without using the word "elated." Beyond that I was at a loss for words.

I thought about this night for so long. The only fear I had was that I would not live up to what expectations Noah might have. So far, I could not speak for him, but being as I really hadn't known what to expect, any expectations that I had were far exceeded.

As I laid there afterward with my head resting on Noah's chest, I watched the candlelight flicker on the walls. It was hardly 9:00 p.m. and too early for me to go to sleep and I wasn't tired at all. My head rose and fell with every breath that Noah took. I could feel his heart beating beneath me as though his heart was right under my ear. Everything else was silent except for the singing of a cricket loud enough that it could have been a spectator in the room with us. I laid there with Noah, the cricket and my thoughts and remembered Judy's warning.

"Don't expect too much your first time. This is one of those things where practice makes perfect."

Thinking of her words made me wonder how many times Noah might have practiced. Not only did he know enough about what he was doing to make me feel like this, he knew enough to explain and teach me as we went. It made me think he had practiced a lot and that was nauseating. The thought of him with anyone else like this made me sick.

I rolled over so I could look at him when I asked the dreadful question. I wasn't sure I could handle the answer, but I asked anyway. His eyes were closed and he looked so relaxed, but I couldn't let things go. I swallowed hard and asked.

"Noah?" He opened his eyes and smiled lovingly at me when he heard me say his name. "May I ask you something?"

240

"Anything."

I swallowed hard once more and tried to calm my stomach before I began. "You weren't like this with her, were you?"

I think I had this need to know that he loved me more than he ever loved her, whoever she was. I don't know what was wrong with me that I asked or that I was even curious.

Noah squinted his eyes at me, clearly struck odd by my question. "No." He said calmly.

I was secretly elated by his answer. "You didn't love her?"

"No." Another one word response. He moved to sit up and I was forced off of him.

I sat up as well, becoming acutely aware that I was still naked except for his class ring which still hung on the chain around my neck. It was a night of firsts for me. I had never had a conversation with anyone, not even a doctor, while I was completely naked.

Noah was obviously put out with me and the subject matter, but he went on to explain. "I have only been with one other girl, but, unfortunately, I was with her a lot. It's not something I am proud of and I certainly take no joy in having to explain myself to you..."

"I'm sorry. I shouldn't have asked. You don't have to tell me." I was ashamed that I might have found a sore subject for him after the time we had just had. I certainly did not want to ruin anything.

"No, Gayle, I should have told you already." Noah made his way to his feet and across the room to where he had thrown his clothes. I thought he was going to get dressed, but instead he picked up his jeans and started folding them.

"I mentioned to you once before when we were here that my mother and father weren't the happiest or most well suited of matches. I told you how they met and came to be married. Well, my mother swore that none of her boys would make the same mistakes she made. She's had to eat her words with both of my older brothers, but I was her last hope. Her last ticket back into Augusta's high society. The Hill section."

The nagging feeling of nakedness ate at me as Noah spoke. I had Judy put my suitcase in the closet, so while Noah continued folding and telling his story I ventured over to the closet.

"Mama entered me in cotillion when I was in the ninth grade. She heard that one of her best friends from childhood had a daughter my age and she was going to be in it. Her name was Mary Frances Kelly and her father was the richest..."

Noah noticed me opening the suitcase and stopped mid-sentence. "You aren't getting dressed are you?"

The truth was I had forgotten to pack any pajamas, but I had thought to pack the afghan my grandmother crocheted and gave me for graduation. It was solid white and I was the last grandchild to get one before she died. I thought to bring it so we might have covers on top of the quilt. With the exception of pajamas, I had thought of everything.

To answer his question, I simply wrapped the afghan around me like a toga. "Go on."

Noah finished folding. He even put my dress on top of the stack of his clothes and then returned to sit next to me on the quilt.

"I'll tell you everything, if you will promise not to think less of me and if you will lay back down with me. I like feeling you against me." Noah went back to a horizontal position and patted the space next to him, indicating that he wanted me there.

"Okay." I paused for a moment and took the afghan from around me. I spread it over us and returned my head to his chest.

Noah picked up with where he left off. He spared me a great deal of the gory details, but my stomach still churned at the thought of him with her.

"Things worked exactly as mother wanted at first. Mary Frances was pretty, nothing compared to you of course. Anyway, she was like my mother in that she wanted to walk on the wild side. Since

I wasn't really from Augusta, I was considered an outsider among the cotillion group. Everyone knew my mother's parents, but they also knew the story of my mother so it magnified my status."

"Mary Frances was an only child and the apple of her father's eye..."

I interrupted him, "Of Kelley Enterprises that makes the knockoff Tupperware?"

"Yes, one in the same," Noah replied, confirming that my stomach had every right to churn.

I knew what she looked like; dark hair, fair skin. I would never get her out of my head now. That stupid slogan in the company commercials rang in my ears and that tap dance at the end like she was one of the Rockets. "If you care, use Kelley Rubberware! (clicketty click click click)" How could he have ever been with puppet like that?

Noah went on, "Anyway, she could do no wrong. Seriously, Gayle, she could do nothing wrong at all in his eyes and according to my mother, 'Whomever ended up married to her would be set for life."

"I had sex with her for the first time when we were fifteen. She offered and the offers kept coming. My mother thought we would get married. She was on a mission to see it happen. For the longest time I wanted to please my mother and I went along. My future was set in her opinion, but by the middle of my senior year, I felt trapped. I didn't want to be under my father's thumb farming for the rest of my life and I didn't want to be under her father's thumb as one of the managers at Kelley Enterprises. I wanted to be my own man."

Noah paused and I could feel him shift his arm from beneath his head. "Perhaps I took the coward's way out, but entering the Air Force was my chance to break things off with her. I tried to tell her weeks in advance of my leaving, but she wouldn't hear of it. She came to see me off the day I left and I put it to her flat out. Well, I sugar coated it a little. I didn't just say, 'We're done.' But, she

243

wouldn't get the picture in private, so I had to do it in front of my entire family."

"What did she say?" I was almost concerned for the puppet having been jilted in such a way.

"She slapped my face and announced to the whole lot of us that she was pregnant." Noah was so calm telling me that just like it was any other part of the story, but the thought of someone else being pregnant by him made me almost throw up.

I sat straight up, gathering the afghan tight around me. "What did you do? Where's the baby now?"

"There's no baby. Gayle, there never was." Noah sat up as well. "What I did do was call her bluff. Her face was all, 'take that' looking. My father was mortified and my mother was as giddy as a pig in slop. My brother Nathan just shook his head, but all that was okay. I got the last word."

"What did you do?"

"I said, 'Well, wait a minute, that changes everything. I'll get us one of those cute apartments on base. They have them for the married airmen. They are about six hundred square feet. Oh, you'll just love it there with all of the other wives and children. I mean, you'll have to make friends with them because we won't have any money for other means of entertainment. You can join a sewing group and make all of yours and the baby's clothes because I'm not taking a dime from your father."

"By that point Mary Frances had thrown up her hands and was storming off to her car. 'Okay, well, I'll send for you,' I called after her. My brothers, along with my dad, were dying laughing as Mary Frances turned around and screamed back, 'Go to Hell!' That was the last time I saw her, except for in the commercials. Aren't those awful?"

I didn't know what to say even though I was in complete agreement about the commercials.

Noah continued, "The last words my mother said to me for that entire year was, 'I hope you're proud of yourself. You just ran off our last chance.' To which I replied, 'I'll make my own chances.' I received my second slap of the day at that point. Right across my face. She gave it to me good..."

I covered my mouth with both hands. I couldn't believe it.

"That's how I left things with my mother the entire first year I was in the service. I got on the bus for basic training and I never looked back."

I had more questions, but I didn't dare ask them. He clearly had made peace with the situation so even though I would love to know how someone's mother could treat them like that, I didn't want to tarnish our night anymore by asking.

There was one question that I did feel compelled to ask. "Your mother wouldn't like me, would she?"

It's never good when someone answers a question with a question, but that's what Noah did. "Why do you ask?"

"Because we both know I'm not the high society type and we've been together for over a year now and you've never introduced us. I've agreed to marry you, but I've never met your family." The more I explained my question the more concerned it made me.

Noah took my fingers and played with my hands as he gave his reasoning. "We've had so little time together that I haven't wanted to share you. Plus, you were supposed to meet them at Thanksgiving, but with everything that happened..."

I looked down at our hands. "I know, Thanksgiving was awful."

No longer content to play with my fingers, Noah pulled me into his arms and kissed my forehead. "There's nothing to be worried about. Why don't you come for lunch on Sunday and you can meet all of them. It will be after church and they'll all be on their best behavior."

"Okay," I agreed. "Let's lay back down."

Noah and I laid there quietly for a few minutes. He stroked my hair and I relished just being there with him.

"Noah, I planned all of this, so no one's going to worry when I don't come home, but do you need to go? I don't want your family to worry." I didn't want him to leave, but I would have understood.

Noah laughed, "You silly girl, today I turned twenty-two and they haven't waited up for me since I don't know when."

We continued to talk until the last of the candles burned down. Even there on the hard floor and his chest for a pillow, I knew this was the way I wanted to fall asleep for the rest of my life. The last words I remembered Noah saying to me before I drifted off were, "This has been the best birthday ever. I've never felt more loved."

I couldn't help feeling sad for him. I grew up knowing that both of my parents loved me. My brother loved me and all of my extended family adored me. There was never a time when I didn't feel loved, but I had a sinking feeling that Noah had experienced times when he didn't feel loved. I knew it wasn't necessarily my job or my place, but I vowed I would spend the rest of my life making sure he felt loved.

Recalling how his mother tried to use him, I just couldn't imagine a mother doing that until Millie popped into my head. Her very existence was Rhonda using her to trap my brother. I knew Rhonda had gotten pregnant by my brother simply so she could be a doctor's wife. That elevated her status just by having the title of "doctor's wife" so in a sense she used Millie. I knew this about Rhonda, but I hated to think of Noah's mother as villainous like her. I really hoped that wasn't the case.

Sometime during the night I rolled over onto my side and Noah followed. I could feel every breath he took as his chest heaved against my back. His arm was wrapped around me and one of his legs as across mine. We were intertwined. I would have never noticed to this extent had I not been woken up by a heavy clap of thunder followed quickly by a flash that lit the entire room to the equivalent of broad daylight. It scared me so badly that I jumped and I clutched Noah's arm tight around my waist. Not three seconds passed and another round of thunder clapped with a simultaneous flash of lightening.

The house shook as the thunder rumbled around it. It was a violent storm and the last strike hit a tree. No sooner did the sound of thunder cease than did the struck tree come crashing down near the house.

By the third boom that rattled the windows I knew I couldn't go back to sleep. I laid there with Noah wrapped all around me. I couldn't believe he was sleeping through all of the noise. The longer I laid there the more I reflected on our evening. I pondered the concept of having lost my virginity and couldn't grasp the use of the term "lost." I didn't feel like I had lost anything. The more I thought about it, the more I replayed it in my mind, the more I wanted to lose it again.

"Noah," I whispered as the room was lit up with another flash.

He didn't respond so I persisted. "Noah," I whispered his name once more and rolled over beneath this arm.

Noah started to stir, but he still wasn't awake. It was the middle of the night and who could blame him for wanting to sleep?

For the third time, I whispered his name. I let my hand glide over his skin, as light as a feather, from his shoulder all the way down to where the afghan covered him at his waist. I paused when my fingers hit the yarn. I was so aroused that I was aching to have him awake.

I inched my hand under the blanket to find his bare hip. I also pulled myself closer to him and when I did his arm that had been limply lying over me became firm. He pulled me closer still. I was so pressed to him that I had to drape my leg over him so I could continue to balance comfortably on my side.

Within seconds Noah was on me, in me and making me pant for him. The storm raged on, but the thunder and lightning only added to the thrill.

As I did earlier in the night before, I followed directions given by Noah. Before, he held me under my waist and guided me to him while I was on my back. This time without saying a word he rolled on to his back and took me with him. He was so strong, controlled and gentle all at the same time as he sat me on top of him. His hands were below my hips guiding me as he liked.

The lightning flashed and lit up the room in three consecutive strikes. For intervals of a split second I could see how Noah's eyes lit up as he watched me. It was what I imagined making love under the strobe light at the skating rink would be like.

When Noah was spent and after I had had that crazy muscle spasm thing that made me scream this time, all I could think about was how I hoped he felt like I did. I wanted to wake up in the middle of the night with him and come morning I wanted to feed the new addiction to him again.

Our hearts were racing. I could hear his beating in his chest as well as I could hear my own. Noah broke the silence, "You can wake me up like that anytime you want."

Noah ran his fingers up and down my spine, caressing my skin which remained hyper-sensitive.

The storm had passed and the only sound left from it was the rain dripping off of the roof. I just laid there listening to it and to Noah's heart as the beating started to slow to a normal pace. I was almost asleep when he spoke again.

"I've been thinking, when my service is up in October, I'm going to find a house to rent in Washington, Georgia. One of my CO's has pulled some strings and I've been offered a job at Daniel Field. I wanted Bush Field since it's the big airport in Augusta, but this is a good start. I will be a flight instructor and I will get to build my flight hours."

My heart leapt at the thought of him renting a house just so he could be near me. I was also happy for him about the job. I sat up with excitement pulling the afghan to cover my breasts. I still wasn't used to having conversations while topless. "That's wonderful! I'm so happy for you!"

"Really, Gayle? It's a little late to keep me from seeing you." Noah gave the afghan a little tug. My face turned bright red as it fell.

"Anyway," he continued, "I was thinking that Washington is centrally located to Augusta and to Athens. I know better than to ask you to live with me, but I want to be with you. I don't want this night to be a onetime thing?"

The truth was I was already wondering when the next time I could be with him like this would be. I was scheduled to move to the dorms at UGA and start college in two weeks and he was scheduled to be discharged in October. Until his discharge, he was stationed in Warner Robins and that was half the state away from Athens. Seeing Noah regularly would be near impossible, but seeing him as the husband and wife we had pledged to be would be even more impossible.

"My parents would die if they thought I was living with you, but I can't imagine being without you." My eyes filled with tears at the thought. I wasn't able to wipe them away before Noah noticed.

Noah pulled me back to his chest. He tried to make light of the situation. "Everything will be alright." He patted my head as it lay on my new found pillow. "You'll get to college and some football player will turn your head and you'll forget all about me."

"You're wrong. There will never be anyone else." I knew that as well as I knew my own name.

Noah tried comforting me, but it didn't stop me from missing him and he wasn't even gone yet. We drifted back to sleep in each other's arms.

The light through the window woke me. Noah was clearly a deep sleeper. Again, it took me three times saying his name and kissing him before he woke. I knew it was nearly 7:00 a.m.

"The water is from a well and although they cut the power to the house, I bet they still have it running to the pump. I bet they never cut it off in the winter so they could keep the pipes from freezing." I started getting to my feet.

249

"It will be a cold one, but we can get a shower." I held out my hand to help him up. "We will have to be quick. We have to meet Judy at Walden's Church. Since I was supposed to be spending the night with her, she's got to be the one that drops me at the feed store for work this morning."

My morning started off with a whole new set of firsts. It was my first time waking up with Noah, my first time showering with anyone, but it was my third time experiencing Noah. In the shower was great, but not my preference.

We scrambled to clean up the room and pack everything back in my suitcase. We ate the last of the cake from the picnic for breakfast before we made one last sweep around the house to make sure nothing would give us away. I locked the door while Noah carried my suitcase and the picnic basket to the car.

I hadn't lost my mind, but something compelled me to say something. As I turned the key in the lock, I found myself thanking the house. "Thank you for helping make last night the most wonderful night of my life. I love you and one day you will be mine."

I took the key out, put it back on the window ledge and ran to jump in the car. We were almost to Walden's church. "I know this is a strange request, but would you mind taking the long way home? It's just that no one else has a car like yours and if my parents happen to be out and see you on the highway then…"

"I don't know any other way home," Noah said disappointingly.

I quickly gave him directions by way of a series of back roads around Stapleton and Wrens to Stellaville and all the way around Campground Road until it met up with Highway 1, just before the Richmond County line. It was so far out of the way of my house that there would be no way anyone that would recognize his car would see it. It had been such a wonderful night that I certainly didn't want it ruined by Mama and Daddy finding out that I had lied about staying at Judy's.

"Okay, I can get home from there."

We pulled into the parking lot at the church and Judy and her orange VW station wagon were nowhere in sight. The fact that she was perpetually late worked to my advantage this morning. It gave Noah and me a chance to say our goodbyes and get in a couple of last kisses.

"Tonight Judy, Doug and some friends are going to the rock quarry in Sparta. They've invited us to come long. Would you like to go? Everyone goes there to go swimming."

Before he could give me an answer, Judy pulled up. One day she would surely learn how to drive that car without all of the sputtering and shutting off prematurely.

Noah gave me one last kiss before I jumped out of the car. "I'll see you tonight at 6:00. We'll go to dinner and then wherever you want. We could even go back to our house if you like. And, Sunday, I will expect you to come with me to lunch and meet my parents."

I smiled bigger than I ever had. "Thank you! Thank you for everything!"

I swung open the car door and stood. I hadn't forgotten, I was just being dramatic. I turned and ducked my head back inside. "I love you," I said with a reassuring nod of my head.

"I love you, too, and this really was my best birthday ever!" Noah beamed from ear to ear.

I didn't know how I was going to get through the day without him, but I tried to be brave. I bounced toward Judy's car. Halfway there, I turned back. Noah was watching as I blew him a kiss.

During the ten minutes it took Judy to drive me to work, I told her almost everything.

"You know what you said about practice makes perfect and how I shouldn't expect much on the first attempt?" I asked her as I brushed my hair again and tried to look normal, not high on being deflowered, before arriving at work.

"Oh, no." Judy took her eyes off the road and looked at me with total sympathy.

"Eyes on the road!" I pointed at the road, the other side of it where we were headed.

Judy jerked the steering wheel and snatched us back to the right side of the road.

"Anyway, you don't need to pitty me. You were wrong and you know that girl who tap dances at all of the Kelley Rubberware commercials?" I rolled up my nose like I smelled a dead animal.

"Yeah?"

"That's who Noah practiced with and they practiced a lot." I put my pouty face on, on top of my road kill smelling face.

"Really? The Rubberware girl? Dang, I will never be able to look at him again without thinking of Rubberware girl." I wasn't the only one that smelled the road kill that was Mary Frances Kelley now.

"I know. Well, she trained him well. So well, maybe I should put her on the Christmas card list."

"And what would that card say?"

"Yeah, not my best idea. All I know is thank goodness the stations out of Augusta aren't the ones at UGA and I won't have to see her face again until I'm home for Christmas."

Judy laughed and we continued to careen down the road toward Stapleton. Like Noah, we took the back road since Judy's car was as recognizable as Noah's. It was the only orange VW around.

We were about two miles outside of Stapleton when I looked over at Judy. I don't know what I did to deserve her. "Judy, thank you so much for helping me with all of this. It was the most wonderful night of my life and Noah said it was his best birthday ever. You know, he told me he had never felt more loved. Can you imagine? Anyway, I couldn't have done it without your help."

"Aww, Gayle, you don't have to thank me. That's what friends are for." Judy reached over the gear shift and patted my leg.

"Still, you're the best friend I could ever have."

Judy then cracked that sly smile of hers. "Seriously, all I did was tell you to lose the bra, wear white and stand in the direct sunlight."

We both let out a howl of laughter because we both knew her trick worked. "It's as effective as lingerie." I took her word for it as I was barely eighteen and knew nothing of lingerie.

"Judy Wren, if you were a man you would be a real scoundrel!"

Judy took the back driveway into the feed and seed store on two wheels. In normal form, she didn't down shift while applying the brakes and Pumpkin all but hiccupped to a stop. There was no escaping notice now. Mr. Smith, the owner, was standing there on the loading dock with three of Daddy's friends. I was five minutes late and every last one of them would die before they kept that information to themselves.

"Noah and I were planning to get some dinner and then met y'all at the rock quarry. Would you and Doug like to join us? I thought we'd go to Raley's." That was mine and Noah's go to place.

"Sure."

"Good. We'll see you there at 6:15."

I told Judy fifteen minutes earlier than I knew she would arrive. If only I would have thought to tell her that this morning then maybe I wouldn't have to sprint up the ramp by the dock now. The old men had no idea what I had been up to, thank goodness, but the judging looks were flying my way all the same.

"Good morning," I said as sweetly as possible while huffing to run up the ramp past them. I also turned and waived bye to Judy before finishing my run into the back door of the store to clock in.

253

By 9:30 I was well into stocking shelves when Mrs. Smith yelled for me. "Gayle, telephone. It's your father."

Of course he was calling to give me a good what for about being late to work. Like I knew they would, one of the old roosters ran right home and called him. They were as bad as the hens in these parts.

For three minutes Daddy went on about me getting my priorities straight and my responsibilities. Most of my responses were, "Yes, sir," and "No, sir," and an "I know, sir," thrown in for good measure. I finally had enough. It was the first time I had ever been late to work before and he was going overboard. The whole time my supervisor, Mrs. Smith, was sitting there, listening to me on what was a personal phone call.

"Daddy, I have already apologized to Mrs. Smith for being late this morning and she accepted my apology, but I can't imagine that she's real keen on me being late and then getting a personal phone call so I'm going to have to let you go now."

In all honesty, Mrs. Smith didn't give a hoot that I was late and if she did it was because she was dying to have someone under the age of seventy to talk to. In fact, she gave me the thumbs up for the way I handled Daddy.

I kind of coasted through the rest of my day on auto pilot. Mrs. Smith tried to get details out of me regarding the permanent grin that was plastered across my face and the spring in my step. I knew better than to breathe a word to her or anyone. I liked Mrs. Smith, but Judy was the only person in the world I would trust with any information about last night. Poor Mrs. Smith, by the time 2:00 p.m. rolled around and I still hadn't confided in her, I could tell her feelings were hurt. I hated that.

2:00 came and went. Mr. and Mrs. Smith locked up and she offered to wait with me until Daddy came to pick me up, but I wouldn't hear of it. I took a seat on the step at the sidewalk out front and waited.

I knew what was up and I dare not involve anyone else. My father was never late a day in his life, but 2:15 came and went and I sat there. When he did arrive at 2:30, he didn't say anything. He didn't have to. I knew he was still making his point about my punctuality.

As we approached the house, I could see Noah's car parked in the yard. I checked for Daddy's facial expression and he wasn't happy.

"This boy's getting to be a bit much," he griped, not noticing that half of the yard was freshly cut.

I didn't say a word. Again, I didn't have to. Daddy turned the wheel of the truck just as Noah came riding around the house on the mover. I tried not to laugh as Daddy ate his words. I also tried not to get hot and bothered at the sight of Noah, shirtless and glistening in the sun.

CHAPTER 14

March 27, 1997

Dear Judy,

I hope this letter finds you in as good of spirits as one can expect under the circumstances. I know you must be wondering why you are hearing from me after all of these years. This morning I picked up the Augusta Chronicle and saw your father's name among the obituaries. My heart broke for you and I was compelled to write.

I have so very much to apologize to you for, so very, very much. I am so unbelievably sorry that I have been an awful friend when you were never anything but kind to me. I'm sorry that I wasn't there to hold your hand through your mother's battle with cancer and your loss. I'm sorry I blamed you for what happened to Noah, but most of all I'm sorry it took me over twenty years to tell you.

There hasn't been a day that passed since we last spoke that I haven't thought of you. I miss our friendship dearly and I was a fool. I remember the exact day and time that I last spoke to you. I remember the bitter words I said to you and they will haunt me all of my days.

I know you are thinking that I have fine timing writing this letter now, but I saw your father's name and I couldn't let another moment pass without reaching out to you. Although I wish I could erase all of the distance between us, I am not asking you to forgive me. I am simply writing to apologize and convey my sympathy for your father.

Your father was the greatest of great men and I have so many fond memories of him from the time I spent at your house while growing up. He always made time to ask how we were doing and he always did it with a smile, always. If there was ever one ounce of trouble in his life, he never showed it. It was your father who set the perfect example of how a husband should treat his wife. My parents had a fine marriage, but your parents' was such a loving marriage. I only saw moments of true affection between my parents as a result of my brother's death, when Mother had her heart attack and when she died. No one ever had to guess about how much your father loved your mother. He loved your mother dearly and no one doubted it. I know it devastated your father when she died. Folks around town say he was never the same, but, if there is any comfort to be had on this day, it is in knowing that they are together in Heaven with our Lord and Savior.

Anyway, I'm not sure if it matters to you, but I just wanted you to know that I was thinking of you. I hope you have had a wonderful life as you deserve nothing less.

Sincerely,

Gayle Anderson

There was a perfectly good mailbox out by the road, but today's mail had already run and I didn't want Judy to have to wait one more day for my apology and to know that I was thinking about her. I got in the T-bird and drove the letter to town.

Two days later, I was in the barn checking on the new foal when I hear the noise the gravel made when someone started down the driveway. At first I thought it was just someone turning around as I wasn't expecting Thomas until later in the evening. The noise of the gravel was getting louder as the car kept coming. I finally got down from my perch atop the stall door and went to have a look.

Through the trees I spotted bits of orange making its way down the driveway. Not in a million years would I have expected to see what emerged from the tree line. I shook my head in disbelief. It was Pumpkin and Judy Wren. She had finally learned to drive a stick shift. Just the sight of that car brought back so many memories and it looked exactly like it did when I was a teenager. For the first time in my life, I saw Judy bring the car to a stop without shutting it off.

At first I was thrilled, but in the few seconds between the engine cutting off and the opening of the car door, I suffered a moment of panic. What if she got my letter and came straight out here to slap my face over my timing?

Daddy had once accused me of making everything about me. He made that accusation in front of Judy when I was fifteen. As soon as Daddy was out of earshot, I asked Judy if I did that, made everything about me? She replied by giving me that scrunched smile that people give when they don't want to hurt your feelings so, yes, apparently she thought I did that, too.

From that day on, I had been paranoid that I made everything about me. It was a character flaw that I tried to work on, but I couldn't help but wonder if I had done that now. Had she received my letter and gotten offended that I had made her father's death about me?

I stood there quaking in my stall mucking boots as Judy emerged. I couldn't see her face right off as she bent over to straighten her skirt. When she stood up, she was smiling. I was so relieved.

Judy didn't see me right off. Her gaze went full circle around the yard, sizing up everything, before she found me frozen in front of the barn door.

Judy looked like a movie star. I looked like I had been mucking stalls because that's what I had been doing before I looked in on the new baby. Lord, if she hated me, and who could blame her, this would be a thrill for her to see me like this. I looked like Hell, still had blood on me from birthing a calf that morning.

Judy teeter-tottered toward me in her black stilettos. She was still grinning from ear to ear. I just stood there. I was finding it a bit hard to believe she was there. Halfway to me, Judy threw up her hand to her forehead to block the sun and get a better look at me. "Gayle Anderson, is that really you?"

Although she didn't look like Rizzo from Grease anymore, her voice hadn't changed a bit. I reckon no amount of west coast living could get that twang out of her.

I slipped off my work gloves, threw them back inside the barn door and started toward her. What did I have to lose?

I yelled back across the yard, "Yep, it's me." I tried to sound friendly and not shocked or terrified to see her. Never once when I wrote the letter to her two days ago, did I expect her to show up almost on my doorstep.

The closer I came to her the more intimidated by her looks I became and the more self-conscious about my own. I could even smell myself. My God, she was going to think that I bathed in horse manure, cow blood and the sweat of a ditch digger. I reeked and there was no saving me from the humiliation that I deserved.

"Jesus, I hate you!" Judy announced and I could feel my eyes instantly fill with tears. "You haven't aged a day!"

"What?" I choked out while wiping my eyes and sucking through my nose. I had gone zero to sixty in cry mode in seconds.

"You look exactly the way I remember you." Judy took my hands and held them out, moving them so she could take in the full sight of me. "Tell me that is not your natural hair color!"

For a second I thought about checking behind me to see if Millie was standing there. Millie, that's who looked like me from twenty years ago. Millie looked like young Gayle and I looked every bit like forty year old Gayle.

I didn't know what to make of this, but I sucked back my tears once more and replied cautiously, "It's still my own color."

Judy stepped back and looked me over again. "I just can't believe it's you." She shook her head for a moment then up on her toes in those high heel shoes she went, threw her arms around me and she held on tight.

I stiffened immediately. It's not that I minded her hugging me, I just didn't want to get her dirty. It was only 1:00 p.m. so the funeral for her father hadn't started and I didn't want her black dress covered in the remnants of all of my days' work.

"Judy, you may not want to hug me. I birthed a calf this morning and just finished..."

Without budging, Judy sighed, "You don't think I couldn't smell that from ten feet back? I don't care if you rolled in a septic tank. You are my best friend and I've missed you!"

At that point I threw my arms around her and cried, "I'm so sorry." I repeated that phrase a dozen times through my tears and Judy did the same.

I don't know how long it was that we stood there before she let go of me. "How do you feel about going to a funeral?"

"If I can have fifteen minutes to shower..."

"You've got ten!" She grabbed my hand and almost sprinted toward the porch. She moved like a pro across the grass in those shoes.

Inside the front door I pointed to the rooms on each side. "You can make yourself at home in the living room or the library." Then I darted up the stairs.

Judy yelled up after me, "Mind if I have a look around and see what you've done with the place?"

From the top of the stairs I yelled back, "Not at all. Mi casa es su casa." That's about the only phrase I knew in Spanish."

I bathed and washed my hair as quickly as I could. I dried off and threw on the one black dress I owned, the one I wore to Daddy's funeral almost two years ago. Once the dress was in place I grabbed my heels, makeup bag and brush and ran bare footed down the stairs.

I found Judy in the dining room admiring the photograph above the buffet. The pictures on the buffet were a hodge-podge of photos of the rest of us, but the gilded framed, eighteen inch by twenty four inch photograph hanging on the wall was of my brother, Andy. It was his portrait from the air force and Judy was staring at it.

"You mind if we ride with the windows down?" I asked and startled her.

Judy jumped, but didn't take her eyes from where they were fixed on the wall. "That has to be his finest moment, trapped in time." She paused for a moment. "You know, I had the biggest crush on him. He was married and so much older than us, but I was broken-hearted all the same. I actually lost my virginity to Doug Matthews the night I found out he died. I was a stupid girl. I remember thinking, might as well, it's not like I'd be giving it to anyone special then."

I couldn't see her face, but she shook her head as if she was disappointed with herself.

"I had no idea." I really didn't remember her ever mentioning anything about Andy or noticing anything.

I finally moved from the doorway and stood next to her. We both looked at Andy's picture for a moment.

"Yeah, well, can't change anything now, but I love this picture. He looks exactly as I remember him." She cut her eyes up at me and nudged me, bumping me with her hip.

"I love and hate that picture. No matter where you stand in this room, he is looking at you. The eyes, they follow you."

She turned her sights to the Andy again. "Really?"

"Try it."

Judy accepted the challenge. She left the spot in front of the buffet and walked around the table to the window farthest away. No sooner did she stop to look than did she go running from the room, hands flailing about and screaming. "Oh that's creepy!"

I went chasing after her. "I know. I love him, but that picture gives me the heebie-jeebies."

According to the newspaper, the funeral was scheduled for 3:00 p.m. Usually the family arrived about an hour to thirty minutes before that. Judy was an only child so it wasn't like they would start without her. That's the reason she gave when we passed the Wrens city limits sign at 2:15. I was fretting about making her late, but she didn't have a care.

"It's not like Daddy's gonna know," she assured me. She hadn't changed a bit. She'd surely be late to her own funeral one day.

Judy pulled into the parking lot of the Wrens funeral home and was waived around back to park behind the hearse. One of the men from the funeral home opened the driver's side door to help Judy out about the same time as another opened mine. The man on her side nearly lost his hand when Judy snatched the door back shut.

The man on my side offered his hand to help me from the car, but the slam of Judy's door startled him and he snatched his hand back as fast as his partner did. I knew these men and they knew me. The speaking looks flew between all of us until I glanced to Judy. Her head was hung against the steering wheel and she was sobbing.

261

"Would y'all mind giving us a moment?" I pulled my door shut for privacy.

"I'm a horrible daughter," she cried. "Just horrible. I'm late and I drove this thing to his funeral."

Judy slammed her fists on the wheel beside her head. I sat quietly.

She finally raised her head and through broken words, Judy said, "Do you know the last thing people are going to remember about my Daddy?"

I shook my head, "No."

"That a clown car followed him to the grave. An old orange clown car!" She dabbed at the tears on her cheeks.

Judy continued, "And they'll remember that his snooty California grandkids couldn't be bothered to come."

"Oh, don't be silly. People won't say that." I told her that knowing full well that folks might not say anything about the car, but they'd definitely be talking about her and her children not visiting for years and then the children not even attending his funeral.

"It's true, Gayle! You know why my children aren't here? I told people it's because we couldn't afford to fly the whole family out, but that's a lie. I'm a big fat liar. We've got more money than I could ever spend. They aren't here because I am an asshole."

I gasped. I'd never heard someone call herself an asshole before.

"I am an asshole! I truly am! I was never cut out for small town life and I got the hell out as fast as I could. When the thing..." Judy paused and tried to start again, "Well, when Noah..."

Judy turned her head and looked out of the window on her side. I waited silently. I knew what she was getting at, but now was not the time or the place to get into all of that.

Judy cleared her throat, "Well, if I didn't have you any more then there wasn't anything keeping me here. Unfortunately, I never stopped my children from thinking this was the most backward place on Earth and now here I am alone. They refused to come. Can you imagine?"

I reached over and took her hand. "I'm here now."

Judy turned back to me at the touch of my hand.

"Judy, you don't know these people anymore and they don't know you. Sure, some are going to talk, but what do you care? You don't live here anymore and you never have to see them again after today. Plus, most of them are good people. They're just happy to see you and want to tell you how sad they are about your dad. They don't care what sort of car you drive and some of them probably don't even know you have children."

Judy wiped her eyes. "I could really use a drink."

"Well that would be the surefire way to get them to talk about you, if you got drunk in the car behind the hearse while the funeral started."

"Sweet Jesus, wouldn't it?" Judy started to laugh.

"Come on, let's get in there..."

"And get it over with," she added. Judy did her best to smooth out her makeup to cover the tear stains before opening the car door.

"Here take these." I handed her my big giant, black, Jackie Onassis sunglasses from my purse. "Put these on."

The gentlemen from the funeral home saw us open the car doors and returned to help us out. After putting on the sunglasses and pressing out her skirt, Judy apologized to the gentleman who opened her door.

As my escort took me around to meet up with Judy, I whispered to him, "You see that black Cadillac parked three spaces out?"

He nodded. Of course he knew the car. Everyone knew everyone in the tri-county area and what they drove.

"That's my Aunt Dot's car. Will you go and ask her if I may borrow it? She'll give you the keys and when she does I want you to move her car to where the orange car is. Give me a minute and I'll get the keys for the wagon for you. You'll need to give those keys to my aunt once you've swapped them and do tell my aunt I said, 'Thank you.'"

When I met up with Judy on the other side of Pumpkin, the men opened the doors for us and I offered to take her keys and purse and put them away. Judy gladly passed me her things and, discretely, I passed the keys along and the gentleman was on his way as I had asked.

As the one gentleman slipped away, the other one told us that the rest of the family was already in the parlor room so, "Y'all go on in."

"Thank you, sir," I replied as we passed him.

On our walk between the front door and the parlor, Judy asked me if I would mind singing. "You always did such a beautiful rendition of "Amazing Grace", would you mind?"

"I guess not, but don't you already have someone lined up?"

"Yes, but you know how my daddy loved to hear you sing. Come on, Gayle, this would thrill him to pieces. You were the closest thing he had to a second daughter."

Judy was right, he was just about a second father to me during my teenage years and her mother was a second mother to me in those years as well.

"Plus, the only person I've got lined up, as you put it, is Aunt Pauline and she's gonna cry the whole way through. She'll be relieved to know she's off the hook."

I agreed after I made her promise her Aunt Pauline's feelings wouldn't be hurt.

"Oh, and could you do it a cappella?" Judy added to her request.

"You don't want much, do you?" I joked.

Judy stopped in her tracks, lowered the shades and looked me directly in the eye. "I want my daddy back. I want more time to

264

be a better daughter. I want my children and my husband here with me, but, since I can't have that, this will have to do."

"A cappella it is," I replied as one would who had been put in their place.

"I'm sorry," Judy immediately apologized. "I'm just ready for this to be over."

I really should have known better than to joke with her. I was feeling like we had fallen right back into our old selves, as if we had only been apart for five minutes, but that simply wasn't the case. Judy snapping at me was a perfect reminder of that fact.

When it came time during the sermon, I sang "Amazing Grace" just as Judy requested. I could tell it was the highlight of the funeral for her until we stepped back outside. As soon as she spotted Aunt Dot's Cadillac Deville and when she was handed the keys one would have thought she had died and gone to heaven.

"You made this happen?" Her voice was so full of gratitude that I knew without a doubt whatever favor I might owe Aunt Dot in return for loaning her car was well worth it.

"You're welcome."

Standing in the open driver's side door before getting in, Judy told me again, "You really are the best friend I ever had. I'm sorry I paid you any attention that night when you told me never to speak to you again."

I leaned over across the hood of the car, "And I'm so sorry I ever said that to you. Can you ever forgive me?"

"There's nothing to forgive."

As was the custom in the area, the church of which the deceased was a member hosted a meal for the family after the graveside service. On the short ride between the Wrens city cemetery and the United Methodist Church, Judy commented on how this was quite possibly the longest day of her life. To me this was only a blip, but I could understand her sentiment. The day of my father's funeral was one of the longest days of my life, too.

"I swear, it is never ending. Oh, and if I have to hear one more person tell me 'I didn't know Mr. Wren had a daughter,' I am going to scream." Judy put on the blinker to turn at the intersection with Estelle Street and never took her eyes off of the road.

Most folks hadn't forgotten her. Most everyone knew her, after all; she was related to half the county in some way or another. What she failed to realize is that occasionally new people moved to the area. Even the new people in town came to know her father. He was the man to see about land clearing. If anything was being built, then it needed land clearing. It also didn't hurt that he was the man selling most of the land that needed clearing.

I didn't have a chance to explain all of that to her before Judy started up again. "Seriously, I've got some paper cuts if they wanna put some lemon juice in those, too!"

"Well, it will all be over soon."

I barely finished my sentence when Judy sighed, "No, it won't. I have to go back to the house tonight. I swear Daddy never threw out a single thing after Mama died. The place has the most God awful mildew and old newspaper smell I've ever endured.

My mouth fell open as I could not believe her father was living like that.

"I can hardly stand the thought of spending another night there."

We made the turn into the church parking lot and I found myself offering to let her stay with me. Judy was quick to accept my offer. My first thought was that it would be like old times, spending the night with one another, a sleepover. Although she was in the car right next to me, it was still hard to see Judy as a grown woman. I most assuredly knew my own age, but all afternoon I had struggled not to think of us as teenage girls again. For so long I only pictured Judy eighteen, wearing her cap and gown and hanging all over Doug Mathis. I also knew how old Doug was since I still saw him around town once or twice a month. Despite all of that, I thought of her as I did Andy, frozen in time, but Judy hadn't died. She was now a forty year old woman just like me.

After getting over the nostalgia of having a slumber party, the reality of what our evening together would hold set in. We were bound to have to talk about what happened to Noah. It's not that I had forgotten him; it just wasn't a subject that I ever talked about to anyone. Plus, it had been so long, that I was a little fuzzy on what

266

actually happened and what I dreamed. It also didn't help that when the subject was approached it was as if I owed an explanation as to why I could never let go and move on. I never felt I owed anyone anything other than Noah.

Maybe I had worried for nothing. When Judy and I returned home from the funeral we found Robert's Porsche 911 parked in front of the house.

"Who's that?" Judy's eyes lit up at the sight of the brand new automobile.

It was as white as the columns on my house and I was blinded by the sun reflecting off of it. I held my hand up to block the sun.

"That's Robert," I answered.

On one hand I was happy to see him. He would make a nice buffer between Judy and me. Just his presence would keep us off of the subject of Noah. On the other hand, I was never excited to see him anymore.

For the last six months I lived under the constant dread that he was going to pop the question. Millie felt it coming as surely as I did. She was thrilled and had told me as much, but marriage was not in the cards for me.

Robert was sitting on the steps of the front porch and he became visible to us as we rolled past his car and parked. It was hot for March and by the obvious sweat rings on his linen shirt he had been there a while. His hair was rusty blonde and the little bit of gray that he had was sparkling in the sunlight.

"Tell me that's your boyfriend and I'll be envious forever." Judy sounded proud of me and surprised at the same time. "He's not from around here is he?"

"No. He's from Atlanta."

Everything about Robert gave him away. Men in these parts were either farmers or chalk mine workers. There wasn't a whole lot of in between or beyond. His look screamed executive, from his haircut to his attire. Robert's jeans looked better than most folk's Sunday best, including mine.

Robert didn't recognize the orange Volkswagen and he didn't recognize me in it either. He had a look of concern, furrowed brow and squinting eyes, to make out who was in the car. If we hadn't swapped back cars with Aunt Dot he would have realized it was me well before I threw up my hand and waived.

Judy parked the car on the barn side of Robert's, but couldn't take her eyes off of him as she did. "My, my, Gayle, he's fun to look at."

I just looked at her and shook my head. Again, she reminded me of the girl I used to know.

Robert stood from the porch and made his way over to greet us. My first words to him were, "I didn't expect you until late this evening or I would have called."

I could feel Judy's eyes on us. I figured she expected Robert to receive a warmer reception. I immediately introduced the two of them. She was Judy, my friend from high school and he was Robert Graham. I stumbled over what to call him and blurted out that he worked for UPS. My inner monolog was that of screaming at myself for essentially introducing him as my UPS man as if he drove a truck and delivered packages.

Normally I would have allowed Robert to hug me or at the very least hold my hand on the walk to the house, but not today. I slinked back forcing Judy and Robert to walk beside one another. We looked like moving points on a triangle while I facilitated small talk.

Yes, she lived in California and he lived in the Buckhead section of Atlanta. She had two children and he had none. Judy had been married twice and Robert never found anyone suitable until...I changed the subject abruptly.

"Did it rain on you on the way down?" I asked him.

He answered and Judy commented on the weather. I didn't really hear them. I felt nauseous. What was wrong with me? The same thing that was always wrong with me. I had a twenty year old broken heart and that sinking feeling that I was betraying Noah was back. It was magnified by Judy and Robert being together, my past and present colliding. I thought I might one day get past it, but I was wrong.

Once inside the house I showed Judy to the guest room. Just opening the door to that room was like entering an episode of the Twilight Zone for me.

"Wasn't this the master bedroom?" Judy looked puzzled. I looked like I was seeing a ghost.

"It was the master bedroom when your aunt and uncle owned it."

"Then why aren't you using it?"

I waited for Robert to pass us in the hall and close the door behind him as he went into my room before I started my explanation. Waiting on him to be out of earshot also gave me a chance to formulate a response. I didn't want to tell her that I could see Noah sitting on the area rug in the middle of the room with nothing, but my grandmother's afghan wrapped around him. I could see him there better than I could see the bedroom suit that occupied the room now.

"Since I wanted to buy the house on my own and Daddy usurped it from me, we compromised that neither of us would take the master bedroom." It was as truthful of an explanation as it would have been if I had told her what I lost in that room.

"He usurped it from you?" She cut her eyes back to me as she carried her suitcase in and put it on the bed.

I just stayed in the door jam and tried not to look inside. "I don't know how much you heard about us, but we ended up getting custody of Millie. Mama died a couple of years before that was official, but she was never in the greatest health after the heart attack she had at Thanksgiving that year."

I didn't budge from the doorway. "Anyway, it left Daddy and me to raise Millie. I was about the only real mother she ever knew, but I always dreamed of buying this place. I had dreamed of it since I was a little girl and when your aunt put the sign out I called about it straight away. I was going to take Millie and raise her here. I told Daddy about my plans and he refused to allow Millie to come with me."

"Daddy and I had a huge fight. You remember how controlling he was? Well, that got worse after N... and after Mama died. Mostly I think he just wanted to protect Millie and me, but it was suffocating and I wanted out. I guess he figured the only way he could keep us together was if he moved with me. While I was getting the financing to buy the place, he called your aunt and made her a cash offer. So, he usurped me. I would say he stole my house, but there was never any real doubt that he considered it mine and he acted a bit like a guest in it. Strange right? Well, that was my daddy, pig headed and a little strange, but I loved him."

Judy shook her head in disbelief.

"Daddy didn't like the stairs so the room that's now the library, across from the living room, that was his room. Millie's room is down there across from mine and this one has always been the guest room."

"You also don't use this room because of Noah? Am I right?" Judy was very observant.

I hung my head. She had me.

"I remember setting up this room for you for his birthday the night before we all went to the rock quarry. You can't stand to come in here, can you?"

Robert had such great timing. He happened back along and asked what we were having for dinner before I had a chance to respond to her.

CHAPTER 15

"I noticed four horses in the pasture next to the barn when I drove up. I couldn't tell you the last time I've ridden a horse," Judy commented in between bites. "In fact, I couldn't tell you the last time I had cucumber and tomato salad either. This is delicious."

Since we had only just eaten at the church, I made a light dinner for the three of us. I put the salad on the table and we settled into the dining room to eat. I sat at the head of the table. Robert sat to my right in front of the buffet and Judy sat across from him.

Almost every room in my house held some memory that made me uncomfortable. Each room held a detail that required me to adjust to it. The dining room reminded me that the chair at the head of the table was only mine because my father died. I hated sitting in that chair, but I could no more sit comfortably in it than I could allow Robert to sit in that spot.

"I was thinking of turning in early, but you girls should go for a ride. Take the horses out." Robert turned his attention directly toward Judy. "Gayle loves to show off the property. I don't know how I'm ever going to get her away from this place."

Luckily his eyes were on her because it was my instinct to roll mine at the mention of leaving my home. Judy caught me and cocked her head in a curious manner. She quickly straightened her face to a smile so Robert wouldn't notice.

"Are you sure you won't mind me stealing her away?" Judy patted his arm in a flirting fashion.

"Oh, no, not at all. Y'all go have fun catching up. I'll even do the dishes."

I chimed in, "Perhaps we should wait and ride tomorrow morning. By the time I get the horses saddled it'll be dark."

I didn't mean to sound bitter, but it was already well after 5:00 p.m. and it would be dark by 6:15.

"Tomorrow's fine." Judy looked toward the window where one could easily see the sun descending behind the trees at the edge of the side yard.

The three of us sat silently for a few minutes each concentrating on the food on our plates. I noticed Judy staring over Robert's head to Andy's portrait again. I thought of what she told me earlier, that she had been in love with my brother. I thought I knew all there was to know about her back then, but I never knew that. As I pushed the last few tomatoes around my plate, I wondered if Andy ever knew.

"Did you mention earlier that you raised Andy's daughter?" Judy looked to me from the picture of Andy.

"Daddy and I did." I responded.

"How did that come about? I mean, what happened to what's-her-name, Andy's wife?" Judy continued with the questions.

Robert put down his fork. "I'd like to know that story, too." He glanced at Judy. "This one's like a vault. She never breathes a word of anything. I think I'm going to have to torture her just to find out her middle name."

Judy and I answered in unison, "It's Jane," my voice a little sharper than Judy's.

Before either of them could react to my tone, I softened my voice. "Would either of you care for coffee?" I asked as I cleared the plates from the table.

Each agreed politely that coffee would be nice. I put on a pot as I started the story about how we came to have Millie.

"It was always apparent to everyone in our in our family that Millie had never been more than a means to an end for Rhonda. Rhonda never wanted a baby let alone a toddler or a growing child of any sort. She only wanted a pregnancy that would trap herself a doctor. Lord, what my brother had in book smarts he completely lacked in common sense and he got her pregnant. And if she hadn't looked so much like Andy, we'd have sworn she wasn't his."

"Anyway, not long after Andy died, Rhonda started..."

Judy interrupted with a snicker. "Didn't she try to pass herself off as someone named Natalie?"

"Yeah." I rolled my eyes again.

"What?" Robert was completely sucked into the story, leaning in with elbows propped on the table and his face propped in his hands.

Judy giggled and flirtatiously slapped at Robert. "As I recall she was nothing but poor trash who tried to ditch her roots."

"That she was," I agreed.

"Boy, we used to hate her ass!" Judy laughed.

"Still do," I smiled as the words slid from my lips like venom.

Robert didn't know what to make of this. "Wow! The only other person I've ever heard Gayle speak ill of is Gabe's ex-girlfriend."

I was quick to clue Judy in, "Gabe is Millie's husband and his ex would give Rhonda a run for the worst mother ever trophy. Joan Crawford had nothing on these two."

"Rhonda must really be something if she's in the same league with Gabe's ex." Robert continued to try to keep up with the conversation.

"As you might recall," I said to Judy, "Rhonda would leave Millie with us for weeks on end. She'd just drop her off and we'd never know if or when she was coming back. Then just about the time we would give up on her returning for Millie, she'd show up and take her away."

I shifted in my chair and kept going with the trip down memory lane. "Mama died a week after I graduated college..."

Judy interrupted once more, "So your mother lived to see you graduate from college?"

"Yes."

"That's so wonderful!" This time I was on the receiving end of Judy's patting hand. "I remember how much it meant to your

273

mother that you were the first female in the family to graduate from college. There were times when I thought that was more her goal than yours. I'm sure she was so proud of you."

Robert was speechless. Aside of the stories that the rest of the family told at holidays these were the most details he had been given about my past. He knew I could sing, play the piano, what I did for a living and that I was pretty. It was always easy to keep him distracted with those qualities and never have to have a real conversation with him.

"Well, I was already planning to open up a veterinary practice in the area and Mama's death solidified those plans. I knew there was no way Daddy could care for Millie for weeks at a time by himself. Plus, Mama had been the closest thing to a caring mother Millie had had and someone had to fill her shoes. On top of all of that, there was no way I was going to allow Daddy to lose Millie on top of having lost Mama and Andy."

"I moved home right after college and took over as Millie's part-time mother. When she was eight Rhonda remarried and moved Millie to Florida to live with her and her new doctor-husband. This cut down on Millie living with us. Daddy and I were devastated. Millie was devastated, too."

"At first Rhonda allowed Millie to call us every day, but within weeks the calls stopped. Rhonda told Daddy that Millie needed to adjust and we needed to stop interfering. I was floored at her use of the word interfering. She clearly didn't know the definition, but she soon learned it."

I stopped only long enough to get up from my seat and get the coffee pot to serve Judy and Robert a refill. "Millie had barely turned nine and it had been about three months since they moved, when I got a call one afternoon from Millie's school."

"Apparently Robert was riveted and demanded, "What did they say?"

"Yes, do tell," Judy insisted. She too was leaned in, propped up with her face in her hands.

"Millie had begged the school counselor to call Daddy. He wasn't home, but I was. The woman said, "Ma'am, I need you to talk some sense into your niece. She's accusing her step-father of trying to molest her and is insisting that we call her grandfather to come

274

and get her. She's hysterical and I cannot locate her mother or father this afternoon. These are serious accusations and these sorts of things happen with new students and new parents and them lashing out. She says her parents are starving her,' the woman tried to explain, but I was appalled. She wanted me to explain to Millie that lying was bad and there would be consequences if she kept it up."

Judy moved from propped up on her hands to covering her mouth with her hands. She was equally shocked at what the counselor had said to me.

"She warned me that Millie's lies could ruin her stepfather if this got out. I finally stopped the woman and asked her to put Millie on the phone, which she did promptly. I then asked Millie two questions. The first question was, "Has your mother and step-dad hurt you?' and Millie replied, 'Yes, ma'am.' The second question was, 'Would you like to come live with me and Granddaddy forever?" and again Millie answered, 'Yes, ma'am.'"

"I got off of the phone with Millie and the counselor and I was on my way to get her within fifteen minutes." Robert raised the question, "You didn't take your father with you?"

"Lord, no!"

Before I could add any explanation Judy took over. "Her father would have killed Rhonda and her new husband."

"Yeah, if I would have told Daddy then that Rhonda's husband had tried that sort of thing on Millie, he really would have killed them both. I mean, it took all of my self-restraint not to kill them."

Robert covered his mouth with both hands. I had always been so demure around him. I suppose this story did shed me in a different light to him giving credit to the fact that he hardly knew me even though we had been seeing each other for quite some time. From between his fingers he asked, "What did you do?"

"I grabbed a change of clothes and the file I kept on her and then I left a note for Daddy. By 1:45 I was on my way to Florida."

"You kept a file on her? What kind of file?" For a smart, well-educated man, Robert was having trouble following.

"The kind that documents child abuse and lays the foundation for..."

Judy finished my sentence, "Blackmail."

"You two are making this up!" Robert laughed.

I shook my head at Robert. "You really don't know me at all."

Judy cut her eyes to him and tilted her head sympathetically. She tried to soften the blow for him while the both of us could see he was pondering my statement. "Robert, Gayle would do anything to protect those she loves. She's one of those people who have no boundaries when it comes to someone hurting the ones she cares about. She's always been this way." I could hear in Judy's voice that she was speaking from experience. She had been on the receiving end of my love and my wrath before.

"What did the file have in it and did you blackmail Millie's mother?" Robert still needed clarification.

"The file contained four years of notes, audiotapes and photographs of Millie. Photos of the bruises on her little arms, legs, back and even one of a hand print around the back of her neck. It looked like someone had tried to choke her from behind. I took that picture of her when she was just four."

Judy had tears in her eyes over my description of the photos.

"I recorded her telling me how she got the bruises. The one on the back of her neck was when she refused to eat corn and Rhonda held her face in her plate until she ate the corn. What kid doesn't like corn? Millie said it gave her a stomachache and Rhonda accused her of lying, thought she was just being difficult. Rhonda made her eat the entire bowl of corn and it almost killed her. As it turns out Millie has an allergy to corn. It really does give her stomachaches. And it really could have killed her."

"Daddy and Mama had met with Attorney Bell about getting custody of Millie, but the bruise on the back of her neck and the corn incident was the first time I went. He promptly told me that all mothers experience times where their children make them snap. All mothers learn the hard way what their children are allergic to and Rhonda would be seen no different from ordinary mothers by the court. He also explained that I was only twenty-two, unmarried,

276

living with my parents and stood no chance of getting custody of Millie."

"So, I gathered information, kept a file on Millie like I did the animals I treated and I built what I thought was a good case. Every six months or so I would go back to Attorney Bell's office and he would tell me just about the same thing, 'Keep working on it.'"

"You waited four years?" Judy was disgusted.

"He kept telling me I didn't have enough for a court to pick me over the child's mother. And, as for the blackmail, was I supposed to wait until after she was molested by some pervert her mother was mixed up with? Was I supposed to do that and then let my father kill them and end up in jail? It would have been too late. Killing them wouldn't have brought back her innocence or her security or faith in people. What was I supposed to do?"

Robert couldn't make heads or tails of this. I guess I wasn't the Jane Austen character he thought I was. Judy, on the other hand, cheered for me.

"Yes, I blackmailed Rhonda. As soon as I saw the school bus pulled away with Millie on it, I rang the doorbell at her big mansion. That house was three times the size of this one, swimming pool, palm trees, she had arrived. It was all she ever wanted and I banked on that when I threw that file in her face the moment she answered the door."

"Literally, I threw it at her and it hit her. She threatened to call the police and I said, 'I wish you would,' and then I started pointing to the photos of Millie that landed face up on the floor of the foyer and the front stoop. 'I'm sure the police will be real interested to know how you and your husband are treating your child. For that matter, let's go ahead and call the local TV news and the local paper. They love stories about prominent doctors getting arrested. And, rest assured, while I have their attention, I'm going to make sure the whole country knows that Dr. Allen tried to molest a nine year old little girl. So, please call the police, I dare you.'"

"'That little liar, I'm gonna...' Rhonda started about Millie, threatening her, and I hauled off and slapped her. I had wanted to do that for so long."

"'Why don't you try picking on someone your own size?' I asked her. I was actually bigger than she was , but she got my meaning."

"Still grabbing her face she asked me, 'What do you want?' And I told her I wanted Millie and for her to never show her face in Jefferson County again. I told her if she liked her big house and her hoity-toity life, then she would give me Millie."

"Can you believe she had the audacity to ask me, 'Or what?' So, I slapped her again and told her that I would use the file I kept on Millie to ruin her and her husband and if she thought I was playing then to test me. I would make sure her husband was never allowed to practice medicine again and by the time I was done with him he wouldn't even be able to give a dog a Band-Aid."

"Daddy said she either believed me or she didn't give two shits about Millie. I think it was both, but I didn't care what her motive was. She called Millie's school and instructed them to release Millie to me. By 9:45 a.m., Millie, the file and me were on our way home and Millie has been with us ever since."

Today was already filled with memories of Noah courtesy of just seeing Judy. Most days he was never far from my mind, but today he might as well have been seated at the table with us. As I finished telling about bringing Millie to live with us something he said to me rang in my ears. It was as if he was there and whispering to me the reminder.

"It's kind of funny, someone once cautioned me on getting knocked up as a teenager and having to endure judgmental looks from people. I'm just sixteen years older than Millie. People have always assumed I was her mother and, yeah, I've received more than my fair share of looks, but I would have taken a thousand times as many as I received if I could have been her real mother. I think about the things that have gone wrong in my own life and those things pale in comparison with hers, yet she's the kindest person I know. I have never heard her complain about any of it. I've never even heard her feel sorry for herself."

Judy got up and hugged me. "That's a credit to how you raised her, Gayle. I wish I could say the same about my children. Complaining's a full contact sport for those two."

The most Robert could add to the conversation was how amazing Millie was and he agreed with Judy.

278

More small talk went on between us. Judy told about her life in California. Robert told about the time he went for training in L.A. They both amused each other with stories about how everyone asked them to repeat themselves all the time.

Judy put on a heavier drawl than was her norm. "They are fascinated with my accent, like I'm from some foreign country."

"Do you still scream 'shit-fire!' when someone scares you?" I directed toward her.

"Of course and, I swear, my friends sneak up on me just so they can get a laugh. Even my gardener does it and he's from China." Then Judy did her impersonation of him, "Sheet-fiah – Waahaahaa!"

Robert told his own story about not being able to find sweet tea anywhere west of the Mississippi. "And as you know, you can't just add sugar to unsweetened tea. Oh, they didn't carry it, but every place I went paraded out no less than three servers and two managers so they could hear me ask for it."

I was envious of their travels. The farthest away from home I had ever been was the trip to pick up Millie in Tampa that time. That was as far south as I had been and Chimney Rock, North Carolina was as far north. The truth was that I never really felt the need to go too far from Daddy or Millie. Aunt Dot and I took Millie to the beach at Tybee every other year, but Daddy refused to leave the tri-county area and the older he got the more that area closed in. Also, the older he got the more difficult it became to leave him alone.

It was nearly 8:00 when we finally got our fill of conversation and left the dinner table. Robert held to his word and turned in early. Judy excused herself to borrow the phone and call her husband and children. When the two of them left the room I found it nice to have time alone while I cleaned up the dishes.

I was putting the last plate in the dishwasher when Judy popped her head in the kitchen door. "I'm still on California time, but if you want to turn in, I completely understand." Judy winked at me.

I knew what she was getting at, but that was the farthest thing from my mind. There was no way I could have sex with Robert with my head so full of the past.

279

"Oh, gosh no. That's not happening." I all but shrieked as if the thought was offensive to my ears.

Judy was taken aback and stuttered through her question, "Well, you have... I mean, you do with him...right? Lord knows I would. He looks more like John F. Kennedy, Jr. than John F. Kennedy, Jr. does. He's about a dead ringer for the president."

"We have, but..."

"But what? You aren't holding back because I'm here, are you?"

"That's not it."

"Then what is it?" Judy circled me as I wiped off the countertops. "You must tell me."

"Not here," I was abrupt as I tossed the dishrag into the sink.

"What do you mean 'not here'?"

"Not in this house." I glanced around the room and shook my head back and forth.

I could see the light bulb flash on in Judy's head. I left the room and she followed. I went all the way to the front porch.

"Have a seat." I gestured to the first rocking chair, offering it to her.

Judy wiped the dust out of the seat and sat down. "It's been twenty years and you're still hung up on that boy?"

"It's not that simple." I flopped down in the second rocking chair. I had never told anyone that Noah and I said vows to one another the night we first made love. In that moment I married him and there was nothing that ever undid that moment. My heart was stuck on him.

"You are!" Judy was amazed. "You never got over him. Gayle, I'm so sorry." She genuinely felt sorry for me.

"I remember everything as if it was yesterday."

"That whole night still confuses me. I remember joking around with him and you saying something to me. I didn't hear what you said, Noah was telling me not to push him and we were horsing around. Doug ran past and jumped off the cliff. We were all laughing and playing and then I pushed Noah..."

I put my feet up against the column in front of me and used it to push and rock. "You remember us laughing and I remember screaming at you. I told you that he couldn't swim that well and both of us were asking you to stop. He only came with to the rock quarry because I wanted to go. Then when we all went to the top...It happened so fast. I remember screaming at you not to push him in and you pushed him and he went over."

It was interesting that Judy remembered the night like she was in a fog, but I remembered it with crystal clarity. I suppose that was to be suspected since it was the defining moment in my life, not hers. She only lost a friend that night, but I lost my entire future.

"On the ride to Sparta that night Noah warned me, 'I'm not the greatest swimmer. I know it sounds weird,' he told me, 'but, I'm more of a rivers and streams kind of guy.' He added that he was only doing this because I wanted him to get to know y'all better. I had never had any interest in going out there before."

"We both asked you to stop," I redirected my topic from the past to the present. I tried not to sound as accusatory to Judy as I did the night it happened, but I almost couldn't help myself.

Looking out across the front yard as we talked and rocking in the rocking chairs, I didn't see the grass or trees or the barn across by the pasture. I saw the rock quarry as it was that night. It had been so many years, but I could see it. The shear walls of what looked like marble on one side and a big square hole full of water. Also a big shed with walls of tin roofing and a cable run crane of some sort. In the building there was and old flat head Ford V8 motor that powered it. Doug gave us the tour when we first got there. I remember the rock walls seemed to have a pinkish color to them. You could see where they had drilled into the rock to split off slabs of it.

"I know you blame me. There was no mistaking that the night it happened, but I never meant to hurt Noah and I would have never done anything on purpose to hurt you, Gayle. I cannot tell you enough how sorry I am. I promise it was an accident. I would totally understand if you still wanted to scream at me. If you think it would make you feel better, go ahead and scream at me. Get it out." Judy pleaded with me, repeating herself. "Just go ahead and scream. I understand more now that I deserve it."

"Oh please," I nearly laughed at her. "I screamed at you so much the first ten years that I'm surprised your ears didn't burn off of your head. The last ten years I grew up and tried to stop blaming you. We were teenagers, who's to say I would have listened any more than you did? I think I always knew it was an accident. I just needed someone to take out my frustrations on. I'm sorry too, you know."

We continued to rock on the porch and for a few minutes the only sound was that of the thumping rhythm of the rockers as they went back and forth on the wood beneath them. There was a tree frog croaking, calling out to the rain that we could smell on the horizon. Once I could see past the video of the night I lost Noah replaying in the yard, I could see a few stars peeping through the clouds. It was a nice night, not too cloudy, not too breezy. It was just right for sitting outside, I thought.

"May I ask you something?" Judy stopped rocking.

"Sure." What did I have to hide at this point?

"What's going on with him?" By "him" I knew she meant Robert. "I mean, I've seen you in love and this ain't it. Plus, I think we've clearly established your heart may always belong to Noah."

"I don't know. When I first met him it hadn't been too long after my dad died. I was lonely. He was nice."

"And good looking," Judy added while fanning her face with her hand.

"Yes, and that. I told Millie that I dated while she was growing up, but that was a lie. I went out a time or two, but never twice with the same guy."

"Anyway, Robert was interested and interesting. He was fun and I really liked him. He was a lifelong bachelor so I thought I was safe. He would just be someone to have fun with. After all, he'd never been that serious about anyone else so why would I have ever thought there would be anything special about me? I thought he would get bored eventually, but it would be fun while it lasted."

"Now, the more he comes around the more I feel as though I have completely betrayed Noah. I hate myself for that and I am starting to, well, I don't mean to, but..."

Judy sat quietly, listening, until she reached over and stopped me. "Sometimes things just don't work out, but you owe it to Robert to tell him."

I knew she was right and I nodded in agreement.

As I started to drift off into my thoughts Judy chose to lighten the mood. "Lord knows, if I would have just told my first husband that he kissed like a coon dog all slobbery and all over the place before we got married, I could have saved myself the expense of the wedding and the divorce."

The image of her being kissed by a coon dog sent me into a hysterical fit of laughter. I laughed until I cried and my sides hurt and Judy laughed right along with me.

"I'm not kidding. After each make-out session, I had to blow my nose like I had a sinus infection!"

"That's awful!" I giggled. "What was the appeal there?"

"Oh Honey, he was so good looking he made my clothes fall off just by smiling at me. But, he couldn't kiss worth a damn." Judy fanned herself the entire time she talked about her first husband. "Tall, blond hair, blue eyes, reminded me of your brother. Don't think I didn't try to train him. I did."

"So what happened?"

Judy rolled her eyes. "He decided to get training elsewhere."

"No!"

"Oh yeah, I caught him and the hussy next door in my closet with nothing but my best jewels and my favorite pumps on. I beat the cold livin' shit out of the both of them."

What else could I do but laugh? Judy and I were both doubled over giggling like school girls when the screen door to the house flung open. It was such a racket that both of us jumped to attention. There stood Robert with his luggage in hand.

"What's going on? It was nearly ten and he appeared to be leaving.

"I'm just going to go on and head back to Atlanta so you don't have to worry about me." Clearly he felt slighted and I didn't understand why.

"At this time of night?" Judy asked him.

Robert extended his hand to Judy and she and I stood up at the same time.

"It really was nice meeting you," Robert told her as she shook his hand.

I was still confused by all of this. It wasn't like him to leave like this. Even though he hugged me goodbye and gave me a kiss, I knew something was wrong. I asked him that much while I walked him to his car.

He remained silent on the matter until after he loaded his bag into the front seat of the Porsche. "Just a clue for you, Gayle: next time you take a trip down memory lane with your long lost best friend, make sure all of the windows to the house are closed."

My eyes grew wider with every word he spoke and I gasped. My bedroom, where he had turned in early, overlooked the front porch, the side of the front porch where Judy and I had been sitting. Robert had heard everything.

"I'm so sorry," I began to apologized, but he was not receptive.

"There seems to be more than enough of that here tonight."

"Robert, I am sorry I really didn't mean to hurt you."

"It's alright, Gayle, after all I'm a lifelong bachelor and there really is nothing special about you." With those words Robert got in his car.

I stood there and watched while he cranked the car. He meant to hurt my feelings, but mostly I just felt ashamed of myself for him having heard all of that. Judy walked out and stood with me at the edge of the yard. She put her arm around me and we watched until his taillights faded into the darkness down the driveway.

"Are you okay?" Judy glanced up at me though her lashes.

"I feel bad that I hurt him." I always felt terrible after I hurt someone and, in that moment, I felt especially terrible about having hurt Robert.

"But you feel relieved too, huh?" Judy was right. Relief was what kept me from crying.

I wiped my face and shook off any notion of tears. "Why put off 'til tomorrow what you can do today, that's what Daddy always said. That really was overdue, but not the way I intended things to end."

I let out a big exhausted huff, "The rain's coming and I need to check on the new foal then we better get inside."

The rest of the night I felt both relieved and guilty about Robert leaving. I knew I would miss him, but not the way I missed Noah and still missed him.

Before going to bed, I went to the room Judy was using. I knocked and was immediately welcomed in. I found Judy in her nightgown and reading The National Enquirer by the light of the bedside lamp.

I stood in the doorway and spoke to her. "I just wanted to make sure you had everything you need and to tell you again how sorry I am about your father. I hate that this evening caused us to lose focus of why you were really here."

Judy patted the edge of the bed and insisted that I come sit with her. "Gayle, please don't apologize to me anymore. I regret the way our friendship ended so many years ago, but, if there was anything good to come out of Daddy's death, it is that he brought you and me back together." Judy got a little teary eyed.

"Still, this wasn't supposed to be about me today, but I swear when you drove up you might as well have had the ghost of Noah Walden in the car with you. I think of him all the time, but today was different."

"I think you needed to get some of this out of your system and I'm glad I could help. It's the least I could do and I am so glad that Michael called me as soon as he got your letter out of our mailbox. He's such a good husband to me. He knew I would want to know about the letter so he read it over the phone to me and I rushed right over here as soon as I hung up with him. I'm sorry I robbed you of having a man like him."

CHAPTER 16

It was 4:00 a.m. and there was no reason for me to be awake. There was no storm, no sweet-gumballs or pecans hitting the tin roof and no creaking or settling of the old house. The only noise was the sound of my own frantic breathing. There was no reason other than my own mind playing tricks on me that awakened me.

For every good dream I had about the night I gave myself to Noah, I had the nightmare a dozen times more. It was the nightmare that forced me to relive the night I lost him. It was a torturous thing that left me relieved that it was only a dream, but reality of the actual event was not that much better.

Like most nightmares, the sheer terror of it woke me. I sat straight up in bed, trembling and trying not to scream as I regained my bearings. It was pitch black in my bedroom and I couldn't see my hand in front of my face let alone the rest of the room. It took me a moment to realize it was indeed a dream. The same bad dream I had been having for so long.

The dream went the way most dreams do, like chopped up scenes from a movie. It jumped from one random image to the next. The first flash I got was of Noah in the car driving us to Raley's for dinner. His teeth were so white. He had the prettiest teeth of any man I had ever seen in person. His eye teeth were perfectly proportioned to the length of his other front top teeth and just enough of a point to give a hint of a likeness to Dracula.

The dream jumped to the next scene. We were eating dinner. The image was that of his hands. He had long smooth fingers and he held his fork so delicately. The years of cotillion had served him well despite his experience with Mary Frances Kelley.

The dream jumped again and the scenes kept coming in split second flashes. The third was of the four of us hiking up to the highest peak at the rock quarry. Doug was in the lead, then Judy and me. I stopped to hold out my hand to Noah who was bringing up the rear. He barely had the words, "Are you sure about this?" out of his mouth before the dream jumped again.

A flash of him falling was next. His eyes were so blue and bright. The setting sun caught in them. There was surprise and helplessness in them as I watched him go over. I watched him go over. I could hear my own voice ringing in my ears as I screamed his name.

The dream picked up pace. It went from me leaping from the top of the cliff to jump in and try to save him to Doug and me pulling his limp body through the water. There was so much blood. There was another flash of Doug driving us all to the hospital with Noah's head in my lap. His head, arms and back were bleeding. It was bad and we were all scared. Judy was throwing up out of the car window and crying. I was too scared to cry. I didn't know whether he was dead or dying, but I prayed anyway.

Blue lights of the Warren County Sheriff's department rotated through the car again and again. Doug was speeding and subsequently pulled over as we flew through Warrenton. Doug kept his foot on the pedal. They gave chase, but Doug didn't stop. At one point there was a hint that Noah might be alright. The lights from the sheriff's car threw blue shadows over my face and Noah's as I cradled his head in my arms. The dream gave me a glimpse of his eyes, helpless and confused as they were.

"I love you," I whispered to him. "You're going to be fine. I promise."

I don't know who I was trying to convince more, me or him. I hadn't the faintest idea of whether he would be alright or not. For all I knew, it could have been a muscle spasm or something that caused his eyes to open.

The dream then jumped to the waiting room at the hospital. There was the flash of my first encounter with Noah's mother. She was a pale woman with jet black hair and eyes so blue that they almost lacked pigment. It was 11:30 p.m. by the time they made it to the hospital, but she was in full makeup and Noah's father looked like he had just come in from the field. Noah's oldest brother and his wife trailed behind them.

I was still in my bathing suit, but the hospital had given me a blanket to wrap around myself. They had done the same for Judy. Doug was still in his swim trunks, but my Daddy gave him his top shirt to cover up.

Even though I had never met her she knew me by Noah's class ring that was hanging on the chain around my neck. The ring was so obvious since the blanket and bathing suit didn't hide it.

I stood to greet her and give her what update I could on Noah's condition. Before I could get the words out, Mrs. Walden screamed at me, "You did this!" and she snatched the chain from around my neck by grabbing the ring in her balled up fist.

The chain sliced at the back of my neck and broke as she yanked it. I dared not complain or even flinch as who was I to say anything not knowing what condition her son was in. I withdrew from her. I could feel the trickle of blood run down the back of my neck. It hurt and tears rolled down my face without my consent.

Whenever I would get in trouble and Daddy would punish me, if I cried he would say to me, "Why are you crying? If anyone has a right to cry, it's me. You've embarrassed me and yourself so don't you dare cry." In saying that he always threatened me that I better dry it up. If ever I understood that I didn't have a right to cry, I understood that then. I understood that Noah was the one who had the right to cry in this moment. I understood that his mother had a right to cry, after all, he was her child and for all any of us knew, he had died and they were only waiting on her and the family to arrive to tell us all. I did not mean to cry and I felt guilty for not being able to stop.

The dream jumped again and again and again and with each scene came more blame from Mrs. Walden. There was more screaming from her and accusations and more stoking of her fire by Noah's sister-in-law. With each frantic beat of my heart, with each way I rolled in my bed, with every gasp for air I took came another flash of those two women in my face.

Finally, I jerked free of the dream. I sat up in my bed and was completely disoriented. Was it 1976 or 1997? I couldn't get my bearings. I could still feel the sting on the back of my neck from the chain and I could feel the indentions in my arms above my elbows from where Mrs. Walden had grabbed me and shook me just before Daddy stepped in. I rubbed at my neck and there was no blood, I had had *that* dream again and, as usual, I was so relieved to wake up. My heart was racing and my head was pounding, but I was so glad to be back in 1997.

If ever there was a woman that scared me, it was Mrs. Walden. I had had tons of teachers in school that I thought were mean, but they had a reason to be mean. They were on their last nerve from thirty years of unruly children. Mrs. Walden was mean for the sake of being mean and I knew that within moments of meeting her. To this moment I wondered how she gave birth to Noah. He was so sweet and considerate and mild mannered. I couldn't imagine there was a hateful bone in his body.

I trembled as I sat there in the darkness, still haunted by the image of Noah falling, calling back memories that weren't shown in my dream, and picturing his mother. I tried to shake off the lasting effects of the dream, but I dared not turn on the bedside lamp for fear of seeing Mrs. Walden's face in front of me.

In the days that I went to the hospital after the accident, trying to see Noah, she told me more than once, "I'll get you for this." She got me when she had the restraining order taken out against me, forbidding me to come near him, but I always suspected that that was not enough for her.

There was no chance of me going back to sleep right then. In fact, I didn't want to go back to sleep. There had been a few times over the years when I had had the nightmare and then rolled over and went back to sleep only to find myself right back in the clutches of Mrs. Walden. Even though I was nowhere near having a full night's sleep, what sleep I had managed to get was enough.

I twisted in my bed and set my feet to the cool wood of the floor, missing the rug altogether. A chill ran through me and I was reminded that I never closed the window before going to bed. I gathered up the extra blanket that was folded across the end of the bed and wrapped it around me

I cuddled my arms around me and held the blanket tight as I sat there on the edge of the bed, working up the courage to make the trip to the bathroom. My mind would not let go of the dream. It always jumped around from one point to the next. It gave just enough of the glimpse to shock my mind and put me in each and every pivotal moment. It was so fast that when I awoke from it I suffered some adrenalin pumping, breathlessness that one being chased might suffer.

The reality of that night was not like the dream. There was nothing fast paced about it and there was certainly nothing I had forgotten about that night.

I remembered every detail from the pink tint of the marble rocks on the jagged wall of the quarry to the clarity of the water. There was no telling how deep it was just by looking at it. Two feet, ten feet or fifty feet, it looked the same and you could see all the way to the bottom. When I first saw it, I was fascinated. I had never seen water so clear in something akin to a lake before.

Near the head of the path to the tallest jumping off point, Noah passed me. It seemed like no big deal at the time. I stopped to scratch my leg. I had a mosquito bite and it itched. I hated mosquitos and I could never just ignore the urge to scratch. If I hadn't bent over, if only I would have been able to resist, Noah wouldn't have passed me. I must have scratched for three minutes, long enough to make a whelp on the side of my leg the size of a quarter.

I could hear Judy and Noah laughing and messing around. I can't remember exactly what they were saying, but I heard as clear as a bell, Noah became serious. I glanced up as I continued at my leg, wishing I had a Brillo pad, and I saw Noah and Judy.

"No, don't push me. That's not funny," he said to her. He wasn't panicked or loud, but he was serious.

Judy ignored him. She was laughing so hard and so loud that she probably didn't even hear him. I could see it unfolding like a train wreck. I scrambled to get up, to run to them. I just knew something bad was going to happen. I could feel it in my stomach just like I could feel the stinging twitch in my leg.

I spun in the dirt when I tried to run. The whole time I was trying to get to them, I yelled for Judy to stop. "Don't push him!"

Everything was in slow motion. Her hands were on his chest. She was smaller than he was. His back was to the edge. Doug ran past and lept off the cliff. Noah turned his head at Doug's passing. I was scrambling to get to them to grab him, to grab Judy. To stop what was unfolding. There was loose dirt near the drop off and, just as I had done when I first tried to get to them, Noah lost his footing. Judy drew back her hands and Noah went over. Never once did Judy consider that a running start was required to make the jump.

I remembered the sound of Noah's voice. There was nothing unmanly about the way he called for me as he went over. It was the last time I heard him say my name and it settled in my ears, repeatedly waking me up during the night for weeks, months. Even the thought of it now was as effective as being in the moment. I could still hear him.

I reached out for him, but by the time I made it to the top, I was too late. Not only did I see Noah hit the quarry wall on the way down, but I heard it to. It was a thud that echoed off the opposite ridge. Judy gasped. Nothing was funny then. Her hands immediately covered her mouth. I knew this without seeing it as I never took my eyes off of Noah.

Noah bounced off of the side and tumbled end over end the rest of the way down. Forty feet up I stood, frozen, I heard the slap of Noah's entire body hit the water. It was so loud as if it had been a blow to my own face.

I heard it all, but the worst was not hearing Noah. The silence that followed was mortifying. Judy was standing on the edge of the cliff with me. She began to scream, "Oh my God!" she repeated time and again. I could feel the vibrations of her screams, but the silence from Noah was deafening.

There was no splashing as one would expect when someone popped up out of the water because Noah didn't pop up. He landed some fifteen feet from Doug who was swimming vigorously to get to him. I snapped out of my shock and came to my senses enough to

292

back up for the running start what was needed to safely make the jump to the water.

My fall was over in a split second where watching Noah's felt like ten minutes. Nose pinched, arms folded tightly across my chest, feet locked together at my ankles and toes pointed down, I hit the water like a bullet. Noah hit like he was doing a horizontal jumping jack. I sprang up, a cork on a line snapped by an elusive fish. Noah sank like a weight on the line.

Doug had just pulled Noah up when I was able to see through the running mascara and water draining from my eyes. He was battling to keep Noah afloat. Noah wasn't moving. He wasn't speaking, moaning or crying out in pain. Not a sound was coming from him, but that spoke volumes.

I managed to get to them and help Doug. We pulled Noah to the shore. I remember the fleeting feeling of relief that came over me when Doug told me, "He's still breathing."

We loaded Noah into the folded down back of Judy's Volkswagen. There was no question that Noah's Camaro would out run the station wagon any day of the week, but Doug insisted that we lay Noah down as flat as possible. Doug drove and he ran though the gears of the wagon as if it was getting the jump off the start line at a Nascar race. I sat in the back with Noah, scared to take my eyes off of him. I was under the illusion that as long as I was watching him, he would keep breathing. I also held his wrist, my thumb pressed firmly to his pulse, feeling his every heartbeat all the way from Sparta to the nearest hospital any of us could think of, McDuffie County Memorial Hospital in Thomson.

My bladder reminded me of what my intentions were when I took the spot on the edge of the bed. I was called back to the present and reminded that I needed to go to the bathroom. That reminder came just in time to keep me from reliving the blow by blow that Noah's mother dealt me.

I tiptoed across the floor, mindful that footsteps on the hardwoods made them creak and in the quiet of the night they rang out like beating a wooden drum. As always, the toes of my left foot were like a divining rod for the side chair that sat in the path to the bathroom door. The collision made a God awful racket that made the creaking of the floors pale in comparison.

No matter how far I scooted that chair back toward the wall, it was never far enough. And, as per usual, I whacked the two toes on the end of my foot to the point that I was left nearly hobbled and stupefied by the pain. I momentarily forgot about the dream and any attempts to be quiet.

First the chair had made a crashing noise against the wall and that sound was promptly followed by the giant thud of me falling to the floor to grab my foot. I was so much in my own world that I didn't hear Judy coming down the hall. She was the farthest thing from my mind as I rubbed and rubbed my foot and my toes. The throbbing in my two toes made me forget about the headache, but I was reminded of that when Judy cut the overhead light on as she opened the door to my bedroom.

"Are you alright?" She was white as a ghost and clearly the noise had startled her.

I was still sitting in a heap on the floor when she burst in. I looked up at her while still writhing in pain. "I think I broke a couple of toes, but other than that I'm fine."

Judy walked on over to where I was. "Here, let me help you." She leaned over and got me under my arm and helped me up.

I struggled to stand on my remaining good foot. "Sorry about the noise. I didn't mean to wake you."

"Oh, please, I've still got mommy ears and two teenagers that I'm bound and determined to catch if they ever try sneaking out. I heard you the time your feet hit the floor."

"It sounds like you are a great mom."

"I try, but I'm guessing you weren't sneaking out so what has you up at this time of night?"

"No, but I do feel a little like a child waking up in a panic from a bad dream." Judy helped me to the bed and I sat back down and held my foot up to keep the blood from rushing down and increasing the throbbing.

"Bad dream?" Judy sat down beside me. "The night of Noah's accident?"

"Yeah, how did you know?"

"I dream about that from time to time."

We sat there in silence for a while. Each of us was trapped in thoughts of that night, but neither of us wanted to rehash the details of it.

"You were so mad with me that night and I was so hurt by all of it. I didn't think you would ever forgive me. I was a coward and I ran away." Judy nudged me. "I could not bear finding out that he died or that I killed him so I ran away."

"You didn't kill him." I felt sorry for her, that she had lived with that all those years.

"What happened to him? I just assumed since you weren't..."

I didn't let her finished. "The story around town is that he died in my arms and that's why I never married. When Millie was about fifteen she wanted to date the boy from the next farm over. I didn't think it was such a good idea. She had the nerve to say to me, 'What do you know? The only boy you ever loved died in your arms and now you can't love anyone and you'll never understand.'"

"What did you say to her then?" Judy gasped.

"That was the only time I ever slapped Millie and I felt horrible for doing it. I immediately apologized and asked her where she got her information. She told me from Mrs. Tenley. Can you imagine? I almost slapped her again."

"Oh, no! Everyone knows she's the biggest gossip around and the queen of misinformation. Surely you had warned her about talking to that woman."

"The remainder of the conversation started with, 'How many times do I have to tell you not to talk to that woman?' I sounded just like my mother. 'I thought you were smarter than that!' I remembered telling her."

Judy just shook her head.

"He didn't die. I don't really know what happened because his mother was so hateful to me that she took out a restraining order to keep me away from him. I tried to get information on him. I went to the hospital every day that I knew he was there. I knew one of the nurses that worked at the hospital. She was a distant cousin on Daddy's side of the family. She snuck me in after visiting hours and let me sit with him."

"Judy, he was so pitiful. I just sat there and begged him to come back to me. One night I arrived at the hospital for her to sneak me in and she told me that his family had him moved. She didn't know where, but it was to a rehab facility. I didn't know where they took him. I asked around. My mother even helped me and she called some of the Walden's that she knew in Matthews, but they didn't know anything. No one knew a thing."

"He just disappeared?"

"Just disappeared."

"I am so sorry, Gayle. I know you were devastated."

"I kept thinking he would come find me. I just knew he would come find me. I mean, if he was alive, then he would get better and he would come for me. He wouldn't let them keep us apart." Tears fell down my cheeks as I thought about how he never came for me. "I wonder if I knew what actually happened to him would I be able to get over him. I never saw an obituary for him in the paper. I still look almost every day."

"So you never saw him again?"

"No. My parents insisted that I set my mind to college and try to get over him. I remember Mama asking me about my options, 'What choice do you have, but to focus on your studies?'"

Judy picked at the lace on her night gown and tried not to look at me. I could tell she was disappointed. "You could have tried to find him." She sounded almost offended that I gave up on Noah or didn't fight for him.

"The only place I had to start was knocking on his parents' front door and asking what they did with him and, trust me, nothing says welcome like a restraining order."

Judy looked at me in awe. "I still can't believe they did that to you."

"Really? We all did and said some pretty horrible things in the name of blame back then. They blamed me like I blamed you."

Judy got up and started to pace around the room. My toes were still throbbing so I just sat there. "I just cannot believe you never found out what happened to him. You've dreamed about him and pined away for him and you don't even know what became of him." She rung her hands and rolled her eyes.

"You know, sometimes I was as disappointed in myself as you are in me now. What kept me from finding him? It was something my father said to me early on. He put his arm around me and said, 'If he loves you, he'll find you. You should never have to chase a man, Gayle. If they're interested, trust me, they'll come to you.'"

"Hogwash! Sometimes you have to take matters into your own hands. There is such a thing as making your own luck."

My toes were starting to turn purple and the only thing I was going to be making was a puddle if I didn't finish my attempt to get to the bathroom. I stood on my good foot and hopped a couple of steps before Judy caught hold of me and helped me to the bathroom. This was enough to distract her from the subject of Noah.

"I don't remember this being a bathroom," Judy observed before I closed the door.

I continued to talk to her through the door. "It was a pass through between this room and the one you're in."

"I thought so. I used to hide in there when we played hide-and-go-seek when we were kids."

"I remember. When it was my turn to count I was always petrified to look in there and without fail you always jumped out at me when I finally worked up the courage to open the door."

I could hear Judy laugh. "It was always so fun to mess with you."

"Yes, you always were a prankster."

Her laughing stopped. Judy knew as well as I did that it was her prank of pushing Noah that called a halt to our friendship.

Judy's voice cracked as she spoke, "What seemed funny then doesn't seem so funny now." She finished her statement and I heard her footsteps. When I limped out of the bathroom I found her gone.

I thought about going after her. Before I could make the effort, I was distracted by the open window again. A breeze floated in and, despite Mama's old patchwork quilt that I had wrapped around me, it chilled me to the bone. I tightened the quilt and went and shut the window. While pulling it shut and even though it was still pitch black out, I could clearly see the rocking chairs below on the front porch. The embarrassment of Robert having heard us returned and it magnified the shiver that ran over me.

I crawled back into bed. It was still the middle of the night and I figured everything with Judy would keep until morning. It had been an unusually long day for both of us.

I tried to go back to sleep, but all I managed was a few cat naps. I tossed and turned, trying to get comfortable. Each time I closed my eyes, I saw Noah's face. Judy's disbelief in me not knowing what happened to him stirred about in my brain. I wondered if he was all right. I wondered what he might look like now. I wondered if I would know him if I saw him.

Until today, both Noah and Judy were forever the same in my mind as they had been in 1976. I now knew what she looked like, but I couldn't help but wonder about Noah. Had his life been as fortunate as Judy's appeared to be? I rolled over and over, winding myself up in the covers, as I tried to shake the urge to find him.

I drifted off between 6:30 and 7:00 a.m. into the longest of the cat naps. It was somewhere between dreaming and wishful thinking. I normally didn't think of Noah this much and I had never seen him as a forty year old man before, but in this dream he was. It was just getting good when I was awakened by the smell of bacon wafting through the house.

My first thought at the smell brought the question, "Daddy?" to my lips. Reality set in quick enough, but I was blessed enough to have a glimpse of the memory of Daddy in the kitchen cooking a hot breakfast for Millie before I drove her to school. I always found it interesting that he took up cooking after Mama died. It was just another of the tasks that he voiced his opinion about.

"If you want it done right, you gotta do it yourself," he always said. I laid there in my bed with the covers up to my ears with a smile on my face over the thought of him.

Before going downstairs, I got dressed and tried to make myself presentable. Not that I needed to compete, but seeing Judy yesterday made me want to put forth a little more effort. She looked like a million bucks and I looked like a buck-fifty. She was the definition of sophistication and I was a country vet.

Even though my thoughts were still on Daddy as I brushed my teeth and put on my lipstick, I knew it had to be Judy in the kitchen. We were the only people in the house, so who else could it be? I knew it was her, but it didn't keep me from wishing with all of my heart that I would find him in the kitchen wearing one of Mama's old aprons and sampling the bacon when I got down there.

From one thought to the next, I was in another world and missed the last step on the staircase. I went stumbling across the foyer toward the front door as I tried to regain my footing. Thank goodness the door was shut or I would have flailed about and ended up in the yard. As it was, I caught myself when I crashed into the door.

Just before the "Holy crap!" moment of nearly breaking my neck, I was contemplating how much time I spent wishing to see those I loved that were no longer around. My life had been flashing before my eyes ever since Judy pulled up yesterday and I only hoped all of this would stop once she left. I didn't particularly want her to rush off, but I wanted to get back to my normal self, the version that didn't wallow in self-pity and in the past like this. Of course I thought about Noah a lot and I thought about Daddy, but I wasn't so stuck that I couldn't think of anything else.

Of course it was Judy I found in the kitchen and bacon wasn't the only thing she had conjured up.

"Good morning, Sunshine," Judy announced as she spotted me coming through the doorway. "I hope you don't mind. I tend to cook when I can't sleep."

"How long have you been up?" I asked as I took in the view of the spread on the kitchen table. I really didn't know I had that much food in the house.

"Since 5:00 a.m." I couldn't believe she made all of this in two hours. I also couldn't believe I hadn't heard her. She must have washed the dishes as she went because I also couldn't imagine that I had enough pots and pans to have cooked all of this.

"Is that spaghetti?" I pointed to the far end of the table. Most everything else laid out was breakfast foods except the large platter at the end which was definitely red sauce and noodles.

"Oh, yeah, I figured you could eat that during the week. I also put some fried pork chops in the refrigerator for you." With one hand she gestured to the refrigerator and with the other she poured the bacon drippings into the grease container by the stove.

One would have thought Judy was a Waffle House short order cook at some point during her life by the way she slung the hash browns on the tray, golden crusty side up. After the hash browns were squeezed onto the table, Judy lifted the apron she had borrowed and wiped the sweat from her brow. From the way she looked when she first drove up yesterday, I would never have thought she would dirty her hands to cook anything let alone the type and volume of food that was laid out.

"I dare say, this table only sees this big of a spread at Christmas," I observed.

Judy transferred the contents of the last pot on the stove to a serving bowl and set it on the table, grits. I don't know when I have had grits and hash browns in the same sitting, but everything looked wonderful. I was certain that I was gaining weight just by looking at it all.

Judy tossed the dirty pot with the remnants of grits in it into the sink. "Well, dig in before it all gets cold." Judy emphasized the word "cold". Taking her seat, she advised, "I never mastered the art of getting everything done and on the table all at once."

Judy offered me the plate of country ham and, as I helped myself to a slice, I asked, "Do you cook like this out in California?"

"As much as I can, I mean, it's hard to find some things out there." She laughed as she finished, "Try finding grits in Southern California."

"I bet that is a task." I gave a little chuckle as well.

"It's funny, my children are California surfer kids with Southern stomachs."

I nearly snorted my sip of coffee through my nose over the thought of the stereotypical surfer kid sitting down to a plate of fatback and collard greens.

Judy and I continued to laugh as we finished making our plates. She went on telling stories about her cooking out there. "Growing up, my mother put fatback in everything and that's who taught me to cook. So naturally, I put it in everything as well. My kids have grown up with it in all of their vegetables. They know to pick around it and that we don't eat it, but they think nothing of it."

Judy paused long enough to say the blessing before we started eating and then she picked up where she left off. "My daughter,

Abbey, had a friend over one weekend and I made a big dinner; fried chicken, biscuits, butter beans, fresh creamed corn, mashed potatoes and gravy, stewed apples and a ten layer Coca Cola cake for dessert. I cooked all afternoon to impress this twelve year old little girl."

I shook my head as I swallowed a fork full of the cheese and eggs. I listened knowing she wouldn't be telling this story if there wasn't a punchline at the end.

In between bites of her own, Judy finished the story. "After we all sat down at the table for dinner was when my daughter chose to tell me that her friend was a vegan."

I nearly choked laughing at the situation.

"I know!" Judy gave a slight eye roll. "Abbey had the nerve to give me attitude as if I was the biggest moron in the world for not knowing that the girl was a vegan."

"Well, I had worked all afternoon and, by God, this child was not going to go unfed at my house! Not thinking about the fatback in all of the vegetables, I served the girl helpings of the corn, the mashed potatoes, the apples and the butter beans. I was right proud of myself. I handled the situation and I was not the village idiot to my daughter anymore...Until..."

"No..."

"Yes." Judy threw her fork down imitating the child, "'It's a worm! A worm in the beans! A worm!' Needless to say, the girl was traumatized especially when my son explained to her that it wasn't a worm. It was pig fat for seasoning. I thought the girl was going to fall out. I really did, just faint, dead away at my dinner table."

Somewhere between the story about the vegan and the fatback, my fifth piece of bacon and third cup of coffee, the subject turned to Noah again. I promised myself that I wasn't going to dredge that up again and I didn't. I didn't want to put her in the frame of mind that sent her fleeing my room in the middle of the night. I wanted to talk about other stuff. Surely there were other shenanigans that went on in California that she would like to share. I tried to steer her toward such stories, but I failed. Judy brought up the subject of Noah and wouldn't let it go. She kept on about why I hadn't looked for him harder.

CHAPTER 17

The wind was blowing and my hair was whipping around my face. I could hardly see as I made my way back to the house. I had been to the barn and I could hear the thunder rolling in the distance. A storm was coming and it sounded like a bad one.

The horses were in their stalls and I was tempted to turn them out. I didn't want them tearing down the stall doors trying to get out if the weather got worse, but I knew how much time I had. The scanner was going off in the office in the barn and I could hear it as I put up the last mare.

"A tornado's been spotted near Baston Mill Road and Highway 102, headed southeast." There was crackling and three different voices, but that was the gist of what they had to say.

I knew the area. Batson Mill Road intersected Highway 102 just outside of Gibson. From the sound of it, my house was in the direction the tornado was headed. Uncle Jim and Aunt Dot lived almost directly across Hadden Pond Road from me, but luckily they had gone to visit friends in Birmingham so I didn't have to worry about making sure they were safe. I was a bit relieved that I only had myself to see about, but as I started from the barn I heard the gravel of the drive way start to stir from the onset of tires.

The tops of the pines were already starting to bend and there was a whistling and rumbling that wasn't being made by whatever was coming down my driveway. I stopped for a moment to smooth back my hair from my eyes so I could see who it was. I also looked around for Tanner, my yellow lab. He was a traveling man. He roamed the property and it wasn't unlike him to take up down at the Wilkes' farm about a mile down the road or over at Aunt Dot's. After a few days, he always found his way back home. I didn't see Tanner anywhere in the yard. I called for him, but he didn't come. I prayed he was just out visiting and he would be alright.

After scanning the yard, I looked back to the driveway as I continued across toward the house. It had hardly been a month since I waved goodbye to Judy as she boarded the plane at Bush Field in Augusta, but there came Pumpkin speeding from the opening in the woods with Judy at the wheel. Since she left, we spoke on the phone every Sunday night, but never once did she let on that she was coming back anytime soon. I was about as surprised to see her as I was to see the storm coming. Both seemed to have sprung up out of nowhere.

Judy ran the car almost right up to me before slamming the brakes and jumping out. "You don't happen to have a storm cellar, do you?" Judy screamed while the car jerked and shut off. That was the driving I was used to from her.

I waited for her with my hand outstretched to her. "No, but we can get in the crawl space under the house. Come on!"

"I've never seen anything like it! It's headed this way!" Judy trembled as she took my hand and we ran together.

Around the house we went. Judy had on a skirt, a blazer and black boots with four inch heels, but she ran as well as I did in my jeans and stall mucking work boots. Any other time, I would have been impressed that she nearly out ran me in those shoes, but I didn't have time to think of any of that.

By the back steps was a small wooden door with a latch that led to the underside of the house. I snatched up the bolt on the latch, threw open the door and, as I did, I could feel the ground begin to shake beneath my feet. I held the door open for Judy and she crouched down and crawled inside. I went in after her and pulled the door shut. This was the first time I had ever had to go under the house like this. Luckily Daddy had installed a latch on the inside of the door as well.

"I don't know if this will hold if we get a direct hit," I said as I fastened the hook and eye together. "Oh, who am I kidding? If we get a direct hit we'll more likely have to deal with the whole house falling on our heads than the stupid latch!"

Judy and I crawled to the center of the house near one of the brick supports and sat there. We prayed for the people that were in the path of the storm, the people that had already been hit, those that would be hit and ourselves. We prayed for the storm to spare us and miss us all together.

It seemed like an eternity that we sat there, but it was more like five minutes and the shaking of the ground under us became more and more violent. We sat with our backs propped up against the pillar under the house and the tops of our head barely touched the cross beams under the floor. Judy and I both were scared out of our wits.

Judy clutched my hand so tightly that I could feel my bones rubbing together.

"I saw it in the distance and I didn't think I was going to make it here. I didn't slow down when I made the turn into your driveway and I almost flipped the car." She glanced up at me. "Are we going to be alright?"

"This house has stood for over a hundred years. She's a tough old girl. We'll be fine."

No sooner had I said the words than did the whole house start to shake. The vibration of the brick pillar reverberated through my back and I leaned forward pulling Judy with me. I hunched over her and covered her head with my body and my head with my hands.

The children's book The Little Engine that Could came to mind and in my head I chanted, "I think I can. I think I can." I think I can survive. If I thought it hard enough it would be so. Judy and I would survive. My home where Daddy took his last breath, where I had my first kiss, where all of my good memories of Noah were housed and where I raised Millie, would survive.

There was the classic sound of the tornado, a train with no whistle, just locomotion and vibration. Through that noise it sounded like a twenty-one gun salute as the windows in the house blew out. The boards above our heads rattled together, but they were holding.

There was a slamming, crashing sound of a something hitting the back side of the house that jarred the ground.

Judy screamed so loudly I could hear her above all of the violence of the storm, "Please tell my children I love them!"

I held on to her tighter and she cried until it was over. I could feel the tears running down my face as well. They were involuntary as I tried to believe that we would survive. I didn't want to give into the fear. If I let it in, if I lost faith, well, I just couldn't do that.

In my head, I kept chanting, "I think I can. I think I can." I kept thinking of Millie. Even though she was married with a family of her own, she still needed me. I was not ready to leave her. I was not ready to leave her babies. Gabby was so pretty, a little china doll, with brown hair, curly lashes and the sweetest disposition. She had just started to walk last time I saw her. And, George Anne, looked just like Millie, just like my brother Andy. Sure, she had Gabe's hands, long fingers and the blue of his eyes, but she was Millie made over. I loved holding her because I could easily mistake her for Millie when she was that age and it made me feel young again.

I kept chanting, but my thoughts were completely with Millie. I didn't like to worry her. I wonder if she had heard the weather report for down here? How could she? She was supposed to be in class. I would definitely call her as soon as this was over and then I would call Aunt Dot. Aunt Dot would be worried, too. I was going to survive this and I would call them both.

If measured in heartbeats, that whole experience lasted at least a decade. Measured in real time, it lasted only about a minute, but it was the longest minute of my entire life.

There was an eerie quiet when it was all over. Neither Judy nor I made a sound. We just sat there still holding on to each other. I think we were both afraid to move. I was definitely afraid to move. I was afraid of what I would find when I crawled out from under my house. Would there be anything more than the floorboards that were covering our heads left standing?

As the worry was about to get the better of me, Judy breathed out the words, "I found Noah. That's why I'm here. I found him and I thought we were going to die just now. I came all this way and we almost died. After all these years, I just wanted you to know."

307

Judy took back her arms and hands and covered her face and just sobbed. "I've never been so scared in all my life."

I was speechless. The chanting was gone, replaced by the question, "You found Noah?" I didn't say it out loud, but it played like a record with a skip in it, over and over in my head. "You found him?"

Judy continued through huffs and sniffles, "I know where he is and I thought we were going to die before I could tell you and before I could really make things right for you, but I couldn't think of that then. All I could think about was that I would never see my children again."

Under ordinary circumstances, I would have had a million questions, but now it didn't register. Normally, I would have jumped up and ran to find him. I would have asked him all of those questions. Where had he been? Why hadn't he come to find me? I wouldn't have stopped there, but today was not that day.

I stood up without thinking and didn't make it far. I racked my skull good on the beams that supported the floor. Judy gasped as I fell back down. I don't know what I was thinking. The hair on the top of my head was already touching the bottom of the boards so whatever made me think I could stand up, I did not know.

I rubbed my head and started to laugh. This was definitely one of those moments where laughter replaced crying due to the pain.

Judy wiped her face before leaning over to check on me. "Are you alright? Let me have a look?"

"Whew, this smarts!" I continued to rub.

"You really knocked it good!"

"We have to get out from under here!" I started to pant.

I had never been claustrophobic a day in my life, but one would not know that by the way I was feeling right then. I just wanted out of there. It was too small, too tight, and it was closing in. My heart was racing, more than when the tornado was coming, and I was starting to sweat. All the typical signs of claustrophobia, I had them, but the blow to my head distracted me a little.

"What is it?" Judy begged as she dried up her crying. She was finding it hard not to laugh at what I had done to myself.

"I always wondered about him. I thought he died or something and I just didn't know it. I knew if he was alive somewhere, he would have come for me. You just told me...Well, you said you know where he is, but I guess you didn't really say he was alive. Is he alive?"

Before she could answer my thoughts jumped to Millie. "This isn't the time for all of that. I've got to get out of here and call Millie. I have to let her know that I'm alright. I have to go check on Aunt Dot and Uncle Jim's place and call them. I have to check on the horses. My house. Oh, God, all the work Millie's done at Seven Springs."

The subject matter of my thinking took another turn. "No, this isn't the time for that! I can't imagine why he would not have come for me. We said vows! I can't think of this right now!"

"Gayle, he is alive and you can't think like that. You don't know what happened to him. You don't know what they might have told him. You don't know..."

I interrupted her and repeated to Judy what Daddy had said about boys, "If they are interested, they'll come for you."

"Oh, bullshit!" Judy nearly spit.

I shook off her words, still trying to keep the walls from closing in. "Well, there's no sense worrying about that now. We have bigger fish to fry."

I crawled toward the back of the house to the latch, which by some miracle had held. Judy crawled behind me and waited as I unlocked the door and gave it a shove. The door barely opened, but not anywhere near wide enough for either of us to squeeze through.

I rubbed my hand over my face and huffed. "That's just great! We're stuck."

309

Whatever had hit the back side of the house was jammed up against the door to the crawl space. Whatever it was, was heavy and, although I put all of my weight behind me, it didn't budge.

"You're going to have to help me." I looked to Judy as I scooted to the side.

"Are we really trapped?" Her face fell at the thought and the tears came back to her eyes. My thoughts were switching gears from her to Millie to Noah and all around the country side to places and animals I needed to check on and Judy's only concern was about seeing her children again.

"Stop crying and just help me! Maybe if we push together."

I don't know what came over me. All I could think was how dare Judy continue to cry. It was highly likely that all of my horses were dead, my cars were flattened or worse, twisted among the pines, and my house was a pile of splinters with only a floor left and I wasn't crying. I could understand the need she had to see her children, but crying really wasn't going to change anything.

Judy blinked back the tears and helped me. We pushed together. We gave it three tries, but nothing happened. We even turned over on our backs, laid down in the dirt and pushed with our feet and all the strength we had in our legs and our backs. On the second try we were able to get the door to budge and both of us popped up. We took turns trying to peep out to see what was blocking the door, but neither of us could get our heads through. Judy came closer than I did, but just couldn't quite get it.

"If we can get two more inches, I could probably squeeze through." Judy scooted over so we could get a straight shot at the door again.

"Maybe if we try kicking as opposed to just pushing," I suggested.

"Alright on the count of three," Judy added and then gave the count.

We struck the door at the same time and it moved just about three more inches. We screamed with pure excitement. Judy was closest to the opening so she went first. She squirmed around and managed to get her head through and looked around.

I scooted up next to the door so I could hear any description she gave. I was dying to know if I had lost everything.

"Oh, no!" Judy shrieked.

"What is it?!!" Every worst case scenario ran through my mind, but Judy didn't immediately confirm or deny any of my suspicions.

Judy slithered about until she slipped her arms and shoulders through. Using her upper body strength and, while lying on her side, she pulled herself through the opening.

"Please tell me what you see!" I begged and tried to get my own head through the opening for a look. I just couldn't seem to get turned in the right direction to see what was blocking the door, but I could see to the left side of the back yard. The trees were still standing and that side of the yard looked untouched.

I ducked my head back inside the crawl space and whatever was against the door slipped and slammed the door back shut. I screamed for Judy and I could hear her come running back.

"Oh my God." Judy squatted in front of the door and tried to pull at it as I pushed.

The door budged open about two inches. I was more trapped than before. Judy was afraid I was going to freak out and she tried to calm me by starting to tell me what she was seeing out there. "The good news is, from back here, the house doesn't look so bad. The windows are busted out and there are a few boards missing, but nothing major."

Although we were only able to talk now through the small crack in the door, I was relieved at what she was telling me. I still could not help but ask, "What's the bad news?"

"My car that was parked in the front yard, that's what's blocking this door."

"NO!" I covered my mouth with my hand nearly slapping myself in the process.

Judy brushed the hair back from her face and sighed, "Pumpkin's upside down and it ain't going nowhere. It's gonna take more than me and you to move it. It's missing a wheel, but one that is still on is wedged against here. We managed to turn it a little earlier, but I think it's stuck this time."

I tried not to dwell on the fact that I was trapped and asked her to check on the rest of the place and my animals. "Can you make your way toward the barn and then come tell me what it's like?" I was still terrified for my animals. This entire time I had regretted not turning them out. At least if I had done that, then they would have had a fighting chance. I felt so guilty.

"I'll be back in a minute." Judy stood up and then disappeared from in front of the opening. The entire time she was gone I feared what she was going to tell me when she got back. There was no sense in chanting "I think I can" any more at that time. What was done was done. All I could do was wait for her to return.

I leaned my head up against the side of the door so I could see her when she came around the corner. I was alone with my thoughts and they still swirled about in my head jumping from one thing to the next. Each time the thought of Noah being alive popped into my head I shook it off. For years, I wondered about him. I always had the fantasy that one day he would knock on my front door. In the fantasy he always came for me. Today, I survived a tornado, but it felt like the fantasy of Noah coming for me died. It felt like I lost him all over again. I knew it was silly, but that plagued me more than the thought of the damage to the house. Oh, I knew I would be devastated if I lost the house, but I could rebuild it. I couldn't rebuild the dream that Noah would one day come for me.

I was just about to cry over Noah when I heard Judy's footsteps and eased my head up for a better look. She squatted down in front of the door.

"How bad is it?" I asked.

Before I could fire off one question after another Judy gave me a summary of the damage. "The barn wasn't hit at all. Your horses and your dog are fine. I mean, they're all shook up, but they're fine. Your daddy's T-Bird is fine in the back of the barn and your truck that was by the barn didn't get a scratch on it."

"The house is in pretty good shape. The roof is mostly still on. There's some tin pulled back, but nothing that can't be fixed. It's weird, but I think most of the damage to the house was done when the tornado picked up Pumpkin. One of the columns on the front of the house is missing a chunk, but it wasn't cut in half or anything. There's orange paint on the white of the column and I think it's safe to say the paint came from the car. Luckily, the column that was hit was one of the center columns so the weight of the roof is still supported by the other three columns, so I don't think we have to worry about structural damage from that."

"There's also some more paint from the car on the side of the house by the upstairs windows, but it looks like it was only drug past. There's no hole in the wall from an impact. It just looks like the car got whipped around the house."

Judy went on to describe that there was debris everywhere around the house, but the driveway seemed to be a cutoff point. "It was as if the thing just jumped the barn. I can't tell where it might have landed next. As far as I can see toward the woods, it looks like the thing might have vanished."

I was so relieved, but not as relieved as I would be when I was able to assess the damage for myself.

Judy continued, "There are trees across the driveway. I didn't walk all the way to where the woods start, but as best I can tell there are a couple of pines and at least one big oak laying across it. Your truck is sitting over there untouched, but..."

"Millie's four wheeler is in the back of the barn. She keeps the keys in it. Do you know how to drive one?"

Judy slammed her head against the door. "Of course not."

"Jesus!" I screamed. Nothing was going right. I took a couple of deep breaths and tried to think. "Take one of the

313

horses. The one in the third stall on the right is one I'm housing for one of the hunt club members from Thomson. It's used to jumping so it can clear whatever's blocking the driveway. There's a saddle in the tack room. Saddle, no saddle, do whatever you want, just please go get someone to get me out of here."

"Okay, I'm going. I'll be back. I promise. I'll be right back, Gayle!"

"Wait!" Judy started to run, but I stopped her. I started at the laces of my boots. "You won't get anywhere in those shoes. Switch with me."

Judy didn't even question it. She sat back down and slipped hers off while I stuffed my boots through the tight opening. Mine were a little big on her and I just sat hers to the side. There was no need in me even trying to put on shoes at all in this situation let alone heels. As soon as she finished tying them, Judy jumped up and ran. Everything was so quiet that I could hear a pin drop a mile away so of course I could hear as Judy took the first jump and galloped away on the horse to get help.

It was around 4:30 p.m. when the tornado hit and I had lost track of time since then. Now, it was getting darker where I sat under the house. The sun was setting and what light there was coming through the small opening in the door was fading. It wouldn't be long until I was left there in the dark.

I leaned up against the foundation wall next to the door and waited. I had nothing but time and nothing to do but think and pray. At first I thought this might have been the longest prayer of my life, but I was wrong. The most time I ever spent praying was the night I found out Millie had been injured in the bombing and I prayed just about as long the night that Noah was injured at the rock quarry. This prayer paled in comparison because I was praying for myself. I never prayed for myself, but today I begged God to send someone to get me out from under my house. I prayed for him to let the three columns on the front of the house to be able to carry the weight until I could get someone out to fix it. I prayed that my house really was only as bad as Judy said it was, but mostly I prayed to thank him for letting me survive and for saving all of my possessions, the things that held my memories.

I thanked God for saving the barn that held my horses and Daddy's Thunderbird that was parked in there. Daddy spared no expense when he restored that car, but I would have loved it even if it was still up on blocks like it was the night I sat on the hood and wrapped my legs around Noah or the night we listened to the radio.

My prayer to thank God for saving the car faded to the many memories the Thunderbird held for me. Even before it was restored and before we moved out here, whenever I was home from college, I spent a great deal of time sitting in the car listening to the radio. Whenever life was getting the better of me, whenever I felt anything less than myself, I sought refuge in that car. I sat in the passenger's seat and leaned my head over on the headrest of the driver's side. I closed my eyes and imagined Noah's arm around me and the headrest was his shoulder. I could feel him, smell him and if I let myself I could taste his kiss on my lips. I lost myself in that car to thoughts of him. I could have lived and died right there in that car with the memory of him.

Even though Daddy technically bought this house, it was mine. It had always been my house, mine and Noah's. I built a shrine of memories to him in this house. Just like I sat in the car in the barn at our old house, I often snuck away to that bedroom upstairs where I gave myself to Noah. I laid there on the floor and remembered how it felt to be with him. I wouldn't even let Robert touch me in this house and I never even let Robert in that room. It was the master bedroom in the house and I as much as boarded it up so that no one could ruin it for me.

When Mama died of a heart attack, I was devastated. As devastated as I was, I was relieved that she felt no pain and it happened fast and that we didn't have to take her to the hospital in Thomson. That hospital was where I last saw Noah. It was tainted.

Noah was everywhere. As much as I knew he was gone, he was with me. Riding in the car one day the song "Both Sides Now" by Joni Mitchell came on. I was headed to pick up dinner for me, Daddy and Millie one night from Raley's. I was about three miles from there when the song came on. I have never been able to listen to that song again. By the time I got to Raley's dinner was cold and the manager had called Daddy to see if something had happened that we didn't pick up our order. Nothing had happened, I just had a

315

mental breakdown on the side of the road where I parked and cried all the way through the song. Millie was a senior in high school when that happened. I listened to the song and searched the clouds to see if I could see Noah in the form of an angel looking down at me. Of course I saw nothing. I cried so hard that day over the words of the song that it took my breath.

I cried like that so many times. I cried myself to sleep more times than I could count. I lived my life missing him and I never let anyone else in because he was already there. There were no vacancies in my heart because Noah was always there.

So, today, to find out that Noah had been out there all along and not come to find me was heartbreaking. I just could not imagine why he would have never come. I loved him all of my life and I could not imagine why that would not have been enough to draw him back to me. What had I ever done to deserve a life spent pining for a memory? I always thought that I would give anything just to have one more hour with him, but now what?

I don't remember when I started to cry, but I cried until my eyes hurt and I couldn't catch my breath. I sat there in the dark and I cried. I wished she hadn't told me he was alive. I could have gone on living, complacently, my version of happy, with his memory. Now, I felt like it was all a lie. I never felt sorry for myself, but for once in my life I did. I saw myself the way others saw me, as a fool.

Sitting there alone with nothing but the lightening bugs to illuminate the space around me, I wallowed in self-pity. I should have been happy to know Noah was alive and somewhere out there and deep down I was. I was glad for him, but I couldn't help feeling as shattered as the windows that were in my house.

It was still cool out so there weren't many lightening bugs and only a few had ventured under the house. I could see them flicker here and there. To preoccupy myself, I tried counting them. As best I could figure, there were only four and they flashed sporadically near the opening. One danced through the opening, in and out, as if he was taunting me. He could flitter away at any moment and I was good and stuck. I swatted at that silly bug. What did he know? I was no stranger to being stuck. I had been stuck for twenty years.

The one that teased me flew away with the others when they heard the same sounds I did. Two new sounds started to fill the silence. One sound was that of a galloping horse approaching the house. The other sound was a buzzing, winding up and down sound, and it was more of a background noise. It was the distinct sound of a chain saw. Judy was back and she had brought help.

As soon as I heard the noises I rolled over on all fours and gave the crawl space door a push. It opened as far as it could and I anxiously peered through that two inch space to see Judy when she came around the corner. First I saw the hooves of the horse. It only took a few steps around the house before Judy gave the "Whoa!" command for it to stop. She jumped down and ran the rest of the way.

Judy stuck her hand out to me as soon as she dropped to her knees in front of the door. "Help's on the way," she assured me.

I took her hand, "Thank you so much."

There was no hiding that I had been crying and now I felt bad that I had told Judy to suck it up earlier. She was crying for fear of dying without seeing her children and I was crying over a twenty year old broken heart. Knowing I was the one that needed to suck it up, I took back my hand and used both to pat my face dry. It was useless. I could feel how puffy I was, a few tear stains on top wouldn't make a difference.

"Please don't cry, Gayle. We're going to get you out soon." Judy reached through and brushed her hand against my cheek. "It's going to be okay. We'll get you out of there, get this placed fixed as good as new and then we're going to go find Noah. We're going to find out why he never came back."

"But..." I was going to tell her that I didn't want to go find him. I had had enough of him, but it was as if she read my mind.

"No buts. We'll worry about those later. For now, we're going to focus on getting you out of here."

Judy smiled at me with an assuring nod. I smiled back through my tears and agreed.

"Listen," she said, "They're getting closer with the chain saw. It won't be long now."

Judy continued to hold my hand through the space in the door until we heard the buzzing whine of the chain saw stop.

"They've got a truck with a wench. They'll be able to pull Pumpkin off of the back here. I'll go show them around here."

Judy left to go check the status of my rescuers. It wasn't too terribly long before the ground started to rumble beneath me again. This time it was nothing like the shaking of the tornado. There was a distinct difference and now I knew it. This was nothing more than a Dooley truck coming my way. I had never been so excited to hear a truck in my whole life. I thought it was the most beautiful sound in the world right then.

As it turned out there wasn't just one Dooley truck that showed up in my yard then, there were three in all. Judy had ridden Blueberry, the horse from the fox hunting club, all the way to the store in Avera and along the way she found that the town had been completely spared. Of course everyone in the county had heard the warnings on their scanners and taken cover, but past my driveway there wasn't a single tree or limb down from the storm.

At the store Judy found the usual group of old men trickling in. They were later than normal, but they still ventured down to the store to get their afternoon visit and the latest gossip. Boy, did Judy have some gossip for them. Not only were the store squatters the type of old men that loved a bit of gossip, they were the type that still loved to be useful and prided themselves on how helpful they could be. Some had little more duty in their lives than holding down the porch, but others were still in charge of their own cotton fields. Every one of them was approaching eighty, but by no means did they think of themselves as out to pasture.

There wasn't a soul in the store when Judy got there that hadn't known me since childhood. In fact, Daddy was a regular at the store as much as any one of them before he got sick. Like the good friends of Daddy's they were, they sprang into action as soon as Judy caught her breath enough to tell them what had happened.

Unfortunately, Judy had grossly understated the damage around the house. After a few minutes Judy returned with about four men. They couldn't get the truck past all of the downed trees in the yard, but the five of them worked together and manually pushed that old Volkswagen out of the way just enough for me to climb out.

Once free, I was immediately handed a flashlight. Around the house I went and, even in the dark, what I found was the five men that Judy brought from Poole's store rallied the troops and everyone capable of holding a saw or moving a limb was converging on my lawn. There was hardly enough light for anyone to see, but all of Avera was lending a hand. They brought trucks, chainsaws, rakes, shovels, hammers and nails. Someone even brought a ladder and boards to put across the windows to keep critters out until we could have them replaced. Every spare hand in the town came to my aid.

Not only did I find all of my friends and neighbors, I found what could be considered a pulpwood company's dream. I shined the light around to see a path of splintered off trees, many cut some thirty foot off in the air, their tops lopped off and left to stand like giant pikes. The missing tops from the trees were staked and strewn around my yard.

The shrubbery that lined the walkway from the front steps to the driveway were buried and crushed under the trees. I dropped the flashlight and covered my face. It was hard to digest the sight of things and know that my house had held its own and protected me and Judy. It terrified me to think how close all of this was and how close we came to being just like the shrubbery.

There were people talking to me and all around me, but I didn't hear them. In the distance I heard a deep bark. I slid my hands down and peeped above my fingers toward the direction from which the bark came. It was Tanner and he was running toward me. My house, me, Judy, the barn, the horses and Tanner, my dog, we had all survived and for this I thanked the Lord. The thought of Noah crept in and I thanked the Lord he had survived as well. I was still hurt, but I thanked the Lord.

CHAPTER 18

The light drifted through the window. It was so bright no amount of curtains could keep it out. For a split second I forgot where I was. I forgot that across the road and through the woods, my house was in shambles. I forgot everything about yesterday including the news about Noah.

I rubbed the sleep from my eyes and rolled to check the alarm clock on the side table. I barely had a view of the numbers. It was after 8:00 a.m. and I could hardly hold my head up. I was bone tired, exhausted. My joints ached and I was reminded of my age. I just wanted to bury my head under the covers and go back to sleep. Memories of the day before started coming back and I knew I couldn't do that. Even though I could hardly see, my hearing was just fine. I could hear my own voice coming from the television in the living room.

The reporter from Channel 6 introduced me. "I'm standing here in what's left of the yard of Jefferson County veterinarian, Gayle Anderson. Ms. Anderson, I've been told that your home took a direct hit from this afternoon's storm. Would you like to tell us about your house? I hear it has a name."

I know I looked like death warmed over and the light of the camera they held in my face was so blinding that I blinked rapidly like a crazy person.

"Well," I turned from the camera and looked back at the ragged column on the front porch and the blown out windows behind me, "I would have rather told you about it before it was beaten to Hell and back."

I tried to joke about the situation. The reporter, who could have been The Fonz from Happy Days' twin, gave me a look that let me know there was no need in me trying to be funny. It was hard to talk to him seriously. He had been in my house every night for the past ten years. He didn't know it, but we were friends, and I expected him to laugh at my snarky little remark about the house. I expected him to understand that if I didn't joke about it, I would cry and I had cried enough for one day already.

"Yeah, looks like it suffered some damage. Can you tell us what the storm was like?" He tried to get the questioning back on track and held the microphone as close to my mouth as he could get it without shoving it right in.

I took a step back and put my hand on the reporter's shoulder, stopping him from coming back into my personal space with the microphone. "It was just like everyone says it is; like a freight train coming through. Everything shook and vibrated and it sounded like every dish in my kitchen hit the floor and shattered. As for your earlier question, my house is called Stillwater Plantation and she's stood a hundred years and it looks like it will take more than a tornado to do her in." I smiled politely and refrained from making any more sideways comments.

"I understand you hid in the crawl space while the storm passed over."

"I did. I hid with my friend, Judy." I extended my hand to Judy pulling her into the interview with me.

"What did you ladies think while you were trapped? Were you scared?" The reporter asked us, waiving the microphone between us.

"We prayed for others to be spared and we prayed to see our loved ones again and for their safety," I replied and Judy nodded in agreement.

"It appears your prayers worked. Despite the EF-3 status of the storm, there have only been reports of a few homes destroyed, but not one single report of injury."

I was probably being over sensitive, but I was a little offended by him making light of property damage. I managed to remain calm while the camera was on.

The reporter signed off, gave his name and then reiterated, "Reporting from storm ravaged Avera, Georgia."

I heard the end of the interview from my spot in the bed in one of Aunt Dot's guest bedrooms. There had been more to it than what I heard from the television, but I guess it had been edited to fit the time allotted on the show.

I laid there in bed and recalled what happened after the interview. As soon as the bright light from the camera was out of my face and I could see and think at the same time again. I quickly corrected him about property damage. He was walking back toward the news van. I followed him. "You know, this isn't the first tornado to hit Jefferson County. I've seen trailers, people's homes, after the tornado when all that was left was wrapped in treetops like ribbons and I've seen their faces when they realized all they had worked for was no more."

I was disappointed. This wasn't what I expected from my friend that I invited into my house every evening.

It was nearly 9:00 p.m. and people were still swarming all over my yard. A few were still working, sawing trees and picking up limbs. A few men were putting the final boards across the windows. I could hear the hammering the entire time the news reporter was interviewing me. A few people had stopped, put down their tools and were watching me and the reporter. They were still watching when he turned back to me.

"I apologize if you thought I was being insensitive but you may recall that you were the first to make light of the condition of your own home."

My face went hot and I could have spit nails. Before I could comment it was brought to my attention that he only stopped long enough to take a breath.

He continued his apology, "I didn't mean to seem cold, but, Ms. Anderson, you have had a long day and you need to get some rest. I wish you the best and I hope you are able to repair your home. It really looks like it was a lovely place. Now, if you will forgive me, I need to get this back to the station so we can make the 11:00 p.m. news."

I didn't know what else to say. "Of course. I'm sorry for the misunderstanding. Thank you so much for coming out tonight."

I knew I had to get out of bed, but I couldn't seem to find the energy to make it happen until I thought about all of the people who showed up to help me last night. They had no incentive at all, other than being helpful, and they showed up. Thinking of them and all of their kindness was the motivation I needed.

As tired as I was, I rolled out of bed, threw on some clothes and went to find everyone else in the house that was already up. Aunt Dot and Uncle Jim came in from Birmingham in the middle of the night and I found them nursing cups of coffee with Judy at the kitchen table.

Millie was on the phone at the far end of the room with her back to me. She was discussing how her daughters were doing without her. I listened as she finished her conversation. "I'll be home as soon as we get Aunt Gayle sorted out. ...No, I'm going over there in just a few minutes. ...Oh, I know, I'm sure someone would have already reported back if there was damage to Seven Springs."

I turned my attention from Millie to the other conversation in the room.

"Just a few shingles missing, not even worthy of a new roof." I lingered at the door way to the kitchen, listening to Uncle Jim, answer Judy's question as to the damage to their house.

"That's good," Judy replied.

From the corner of her eye, Aunt Dot noticed me. "Good morning, sunshine. I hope we didn't wake you."

"No," I started to the table, "you didn't wake me. I needed to get up. I have to get over to the house and get to work. Time's a wastin'."

I channeled Daddy with that last statement, "Time's a wastin'." I said it just the way he would. He was such an up and at 'em fella that he would have been over there at the break of dawn this morning. He wouldn't have waited for daylight to wake him. There was a moment when I felt him with me under the house

323

yesterday. There were also times under the house yesterday when I thought I was about to meet him again.

Aunt Dot handed me a cup and I helped myself to the pot of coffee that was sitting on the table.

"I've got a whole 'nother pot over there if you need more." Aunt Dot tilted her head in the direction of the kitchen counter where the other pot of coffee was still percolating.

I filled my cup three fourths of the way. "This should be enough for me, but would you mind if I took that pot with me so we could have it on hand this morning? I don't know who all might show up, but it would be nice to have something there."

"I was thinking the same thing. I don't mind at all. I've even got some Styrofoam cups you can carry with you." Aunt Dot left the table to scour the kitchen for the cups.

Uncle Jim redirected the conversation to the condition of the property. "I walked over there just a little while ago. You've sure got a lot of work to do."

"Way to state the obvious," Judy said in jest.

Uncle Jim gave Judy a sly look. "I've seen shacks with better kept yards. I'm just sayin'."

"I'm glad you two think this is funny." Aunt Dot scolded them when she returned with the cups.

I couldn't help but to think of the interview. "Oh, it's alright, if we didn't laugh we'd cry." That seemed to be the theme for this whole ordeal.

Millie joined the conversation. "I'm going to run over to Seven Springs and check on things, but I'll be back in a few minutes. I'll meet y'all over at your house," she told me.

"That's fine. I'll see you there."

Millie hugged me and turned to leave. She didn't make it as far as the carport door before she turned back. "I meant to tell you that I called the contractor for Seven Springs and he's already over at your house shoring up the roof and assessing what to do about that busted column. I hope you don't mind."

Judy added to Millie's topic, "And the folks from Jay's Hardware in Wrens have already been out to take measurements on the windows."

"Wow! I guess everyone's been up and at 'em but me this morning." I felt guilty for sleeping in, but I wouldn't have if I could have gotten the alarm clock to work last night. It was well after midnight when I crawled in bed.

Aunt Dot got up from the table and put the coffee in a thermos for me. From there I left on foot headed back to my place with coffee to share and cups in hand. I stepped out of Aunt Dot's front door and the heat hit me like a ton of bricks. It was humid like middle Georgia was famous for being after a storm. Between the heat and humidity it was as if I was wearing a hot, wet blanket.

I knew it wasn't a day for looking pretty, but that knowledge didn't stop me from fretting about my hair as I crossed the yard headed for my driveway. My hair and humidity were not friends. It was a day for working and getting dirty so what did it matter? Work gloves, construction boots and flat hair was my fashion statement of the day.

I continued on foot down Hadden Pond Road to my driveway. I was already counting the cars parked along the side of the ditch all the way from Aunt Dot's to mine. I counted a dozen just along this stretch of the road. I recognized some cars and some I didn't.

I was so much in my own world that I hadn't noticed Aunt Dot and Uncle Jim trailing behind me. I knew Judy stayed behind to call her family in California so I thought I was alone.

"Lord have mercy, Gayle, you must be livin' right. There's Edmond Carpenter's old station wagon."

When Aunt Dot spoke it startled me. It was the first indication I had that she was behind me and I jumped. I jumped and snatched my head around to find Uncle Jim giving her a playful, but corrective smack on the arm.

"Dorothy, shhh!" he gave her a light hearted chastising. "You should be ashamed."

Aunt Dot all but rolled her eyes. "Oh, shhh, yourself. Everyone around knows that his name is synonymous with the word 'peculiar.'"

"I think he's nice," I said as I picked up my pace again.

"I think he's weird!"

"Dorothy!" Uncle Jim exhaled with exasperation.

I had a million things on my mind, but they were hard to ignore as they tagged along.

"Seriously, do you know where he lives?" Aunt Dot asked Uncle Jim. "Do you?"

"No." I didn't turn back, but I could just see Uncle Jim shaking his head at her. The ease with which Aunt Dot embarrassed Uncle Jim was stammering.

"Does anyone know where he lives? He just drives around that old station wagon with that dog of his."

They continued to discuss Mr. Carpenter. I knew he was a bit of a social outcast. Until I got to know him, he kind of frightened me. Aunt Dot was right, he did just drive around that old yellow and wood paneled station wagon. The sad thing was he did live in it with that big old German Shepherd dog of his.

Mr. Carpenter was a Vietnam vet and he had some lingering ill effects from the war. Not everyone knew that. They only knew what they saw, a scruffy middle aged man that hardly bathed.

One afternoon Mr. Carpenter found the dog while he was rummaging for aluminum cans at a dumpster. Someone had abandoned it as a puppy, just left it there by the dumpster. The poor thing was eat up with mange and sick with Parvo. He hardly had enough to feed himself, but he rescued the pup and shared what he had with it.

Mr. Carpenter named the pup Bess, after his childhood sweetheart, and tried nursing it back to health, but he just didn't have the resources. The pup got sicker and sicker and that's how I came to know him. One of the ladies from the church always put out leftovers for him. He didn't typically knock on her door, but he needed help with Bess and the lady sent him my way.

The reason people didn't know where he lived was because in the summer he lived in a tent on some hunting land along Briar Creek, but in the winter he lived in the station wagon. It was February when he found the pup and he took it in to live with him in the back of the station wagon. He didn't have a home and he didn't have any money to pay for vet services, but he insisted on paying me. Miraculously, I saved the pup and in payment he made me the most beautiful cutting board shaped like the state of Georgia. I kept up with when Bess needed her shots and when it was time again, I tracked him down and told him I needed another one of the cutting boards. I had one of almost every state in the South. Bess was five now and I even paid him a few times to make them so I could give them as gifts. I gave Gabe one last year for Christmas. Before that I gave Aunt Dot one of Alabama. He even used a wood burner and marked several of the key cities on it, Birmingham, Mobile and Montgomery.

I kept walking along the side of the road, next to the cars. As I passed Mr. Carpenter's car, I looked inside hoping I didn't see Bess. I had warned him about leaving her in the car in the heat and how detrimental it could be. It appeared he was heeding my warning because the back of the car was empty except for some pillows.

I kept walking and passed by the car parked in front of Mr. Carpenter's. It was my brother's Corvette. It belonged to Millie now, but it sat in the barn for so long and we referred to it as Andy's for so many years, that it would always be his car to me. I had the thermos by the handle and shifted the cups into that same hand, freeing my right hand. I gazed at the car as I slid my hand along from tail fin all the way along past the window and over that hump on the front end above the tire to the headlight. Millie kept the car in showroom condition just as Daddy taught her and the paint job reflected it. It was freshly waxed. It was still slick and my hand just glided along so smoothly. I loved that car as much as any car of mine.

Seeing the Corvette there made me remember, Millie had driven down in the car Gabe had bought her after giving birth to George-Anne. The Corvette being there meant Gabe was here. He typically worked all day on Saturdays so I was touched that he took the day off to come down and help. Despite the fact that he had one crazy ex-girlfriend, I couldn't have picked a better match for Millie. The way they loved one another always reminded me of the love I thought I had with Noah. Secretly, I envied them.

I continued on past Andy's Corvette and past a couple of cars I didn't recognize before making the turn down my driveway. More cars filled the driveway and when it opened up into the yard, I could see in the daylight just how much damage there was.

I stopped in my tracks. I was in awe of what I saw before me. Aunt Dot and Uncle Jim continued on past me, but I stayed put. They each picked a spot and went to work. Aunt Dot picked up limbs and Uncle Jim joined in cutting branches into more manageable pieces.

In the light of day, I could see what looked like the aftermath of a bomb set off in the forest. To the right back corner of the yard was a path of splintered off trees that ran through the woods for as far as the eye could see. They looked like giant spikes waiting for Vlad the Impaler to put heads on.

Regardless of the heat and humidity of that April morning, the air was alive with the smell of fresh cut wood. Some of the trees, like the pines on that new path through the woods, were snapped off by the tornado and the others, like the two hundred year old oak that used to be the focal point of my yard, was just pushed over by the storm. There were half a dozen men manning chain saws around the yard, four alone were on the old oak. Mixed with the scent of pine and oak was a world of sawdust that floated on what little breeze there was.

I used to love to go with Daddy to the timber tracts when he sold the chords for harvesting. He would always drive out there to get the logging crew started and then he would drive out again to check on them about midway through and then back again when they finished. When I was younger I insisted on going with him. He would point out the different tracts and tell me that was his retirement fund. Daddy saw money in the trees and Millie was just like him. He had trained her well, but I saw nature. I loved the smell of it, standing or cut. Most of the time, the smell of fresh cut wood was among my top five favorite smells, but I wasn't sure that would hold true after today.

There was a washing machine in the middle of everything and it didn't come from my house. There was no telling where it came from, but I was certain it was not mine since my appliances were still in their places. It was propped upright, lid open just waiting there in the middle of a triangle of three fallen pines for someone to toss a load in.

I didn't just see devastation. I saw friends, neighbors and strangers working tirelessly to get my house and my land back in order. The scaffolding that Millie mentioned was in place supporting the roof and the column. I saw how bad the column was and I didn't know how that could ever be fixed. Just the worry of it made my stomach churn and I felt nauseous.

"Ms. Gayle," one of the men manning a saw on the oak yelled to me. He had to call my name twice before I snapped out of my assessment of the downed trees. "Ms. Gayle, do you mind if I have the trunk of this tree?"

I took me a moment to register what he was asking and I'm sure it showed on my face. He seemed to notice my bewilderment and repeated himself, clarifying what exactly it was that he wanted. "May I have the trunk of the tree to take to the mill?"

As he waited for me to answer, he took out a red handkerchief and wiped his brow. He owned a saw mill and I didn't. What would I do with the tree? Nothing. So I might as well give it to someone who could put it to use.

"Sure," I replied. There was no need in my tree dying in vain. Nonetheless, giving the tree away did not make it any less painful to see it go. I always planned to hang a swing from one of the branches, but never got around to it. My nausea turned to sadness as

I thought about how much I was going to miss that tree. I just couldn't imagine what my yard was going to look like without it.

"Gayle," another voice from close to the porch steps beckoned me.

I recognized the voice, but I turned to look for who was calling me all the same. It was Gabe and he was headed my way. As soon as he was within arms' reach, he wrapped them around me.

"I'm so sorry about all of this," Gabe said as he hugged me.

"Oh, these things happen sometimes," I shrugged.

From the volume of sweat I could feel on Gabe, he had been out there working for a while before I showed up. I felt guilty about that. I felt guilty that everyone had showed up well before me and I still hadn't made the first contribution. There was so much to be done. I really didn't know where to begin.

"You always have the best attitude about things." Gabe released me and one after another almost every person in the yard expressed the same sentiment.

Once all of the hugging and condolences were over, I joined Aunt Dot in shaking dirt loose from the root ball of the oak tree and shoveling it into the hole that was made when the tree was pushed over. The hole was about ten feet across and six feet deep. We shoveled for at least an hour before one of the church deacons arrived with a tractor and pushed the dirt in.

The day passed and each time I set my hand to doing something I was pulled away by someone else. I was required to make one decision after another.

"Do you want us to pull of all of the shrubbery so you can start fresh with all the same size and type?" asked one gentleman.

"Do you want us to go ahead and start burning the piles of limbs that we've stacked up or do you want to have them hauled off?" asked another.

There were so many more questions than that. Even Aunt Dot had a question, "Do you want me to go to town and pick up barbeque to feed everyone lunch?"

Of all of the questions that was the easiest to answer. "Yes, please, and let me know how much you spend and I will pay you back."

It was approaching lunchtime and there were at least thirty people still working in the yard. The coffee was gone and, beyond ice water, I had nothing to offer them. I had to do something. Feeding them lunch was the least I could do.

When Aunt Dot returned, she and Judy set up a small buffet line of barbeque sandwiches, potato chips, fried peach pies and sweet tea on the tail gate of the truck I inherited from Daddy. People sat here, there and everywhere around the yard to eat their sandwiches. Aunt Dot, Uncle Jim, Judy and I found spots on the front porch.

"Aren't you afraid of the roof falling on your heads?" Millie asked us as we sat down with our plates.

"I figure if it was coming down it would have done it already," I answered her.

Millie didn't have as much faith in my house as I did. She and Gabe found clear spots a few feet out in front of the porch and sat in some of what was left of the grass in the yard.

A few men sat on the trunk of the old oak tree. It was a good fifteen yards from the porch. From where I was sitting I recognized three of the men. The forth looked slightly familiar, but I just couldn't place him.

As I leaned over to pick up my tea from a spot next to my foot I felt someone watching me. When I looked up, I caught the man looking at me. There was a curious look on his face as if he was trying to figure something out. The look puzzled me. No sooner did my eyes meet his did he look away.

I took a couple of swallows of my tea and returned it to the spot on the porch step next to my right foot. When I leaned back up,

I found the man studying me again. I had no idea who he was and the way he looked at me made me a little uncomfortable. Was I a fish in a bowl? I already felt like that with everyone continuing to fuss over me, asking what they could do to help, but this was different. I felt a little embarrassed by the way I kept catching him looking at me.

I ate a couple more bites of my sandwich before I casually asked Aunt Dot, "The guy in the white Old Navy t-shirt, sitting on the far end of the oak tree," I directed her. "Do you know who he is?"

Aunt Dot was chewing a mouthful of her own sandwich so she nodded, letting me know that she had no idea who he was either.

I glanced back and he looked back to his own plate quickly. I didn't get a creepy feeling from him looking at me, but I definitely had a feeling that I knew him from somewhere.

Everyone hurriedly finished their lunches and got back to the business of clearing my yard. All afternoon I continued to catch glances from the guy and it continued to bug me that I couldn't figure out who he was.

At one point I caught Millie while she was getting a drink of water from the cooler that Uncle Jim had brought over. I asked her the same question I had asked Aunt Dot at lunch.

Millie swallowed and then answered, "I don't know, but he's quite attractive. Since Mr. Graham isn't in the picture anymore..."

I interrupted her, "That's not why I was asking."

"I'm just saying. He looks about your age and he's hot."

"Amelia Jane!"

Millie rolled her eyes, knowing when I used her full name it was as good as a scolding. I would give Millie credit, but, of course I would not use the word, "hot". I couldn't figure out how old he was, but he looked to be about my age and the years appeared to have been kind to him.

He didn't catch me looking, but I got a look at him once when he removed his Braves ball cap to wipe the sweat from his forehead. His hair was brown and had what appeared to be natural curls. The sunlight caught only a couple of grays hairs near his temples. I had already noticed that his hair was longer than most men our age wore theirs because of the way it hung from under his cap in the back.

He had a tan, but not enough of one to make me think he was a farmer and worked in the fields. He was broad shouldered and sure of himself when wielding the chainsaw. I was never close enough to him to get a good look at his eyes or tell exactly how tall he was. I could tell he was at least as tall as I was and I could tell from the distance I was at that he had more than good hair going for him.

I continued to rack my brain as to how I knew him and he continued to sneak looks at me when he thought I wasn't looking. Had I treated his pet? Was he a member of the church, but not a regularly attending member? Was he someone from the chalk plant that Daddy had introduced me to at some point? It bugged me that I couldn't think of where I knew him, but it didn't bother me that he kept sneaking looks at me. I'm not sure why it didn't give me the creeps, but it didn't.

It was nearing 4:00 p.m. and the crowd that had been working in the yard all afternoon had dwindled to a handful of us. The yard was shaping up, but it didn't look like my yard at all. It looked like a blank slate of a yard. It still amazed me that the house was still standing and standing as well as it was. It amazed me that Judy and I survived and it amazed me the yard that took me so long to build was destroyed in a matter of seconds.

I stood at the busted up walkway at the edge of the driveway looking toward the house. Again, I found myself with hands on hips, taking in the situation. The limbs were almost all gone, the trunk of the old oak tree was gone, my shrubs were gone and what was left of the grass would surely die. I wondered what I was going to do.

The wind had picked up and the temperature was dropping. A cold front was pushing in. I brushed back the hair from my face as the wind whipped at it. I stood there with my attention fading from what I needed to do in the future to reminiscing about it. The place looked a lot like it did when Daddy first bought it. In the years between Noah and I coming here and Daddy buying it, it fell into disarray. No one took care of it at all.

When we first moved in the yard was dead, the roof was shot, there was a tree lying through the kitchen and for one reason or another every window needed to be replaced. Daddy supervised the structural work and left me to the cosmetics. He let me have my way with almost everything. It took three months of work to get the house to where we could move in. There was so much to do that I felt that I really just hit the high points to get it livable. So much money was spent to get the house in order that we just moved all of the furniture in from the old house and made do.

We didn't start on the yard until after we were living there. We started with fresh gravel for the driveway and followed with planting grass. Daddy didn't believe in hiring anyone to do something we could do ourselves. A professional landscaper would have laid sod, but we weren't professionals and, Daddy was thrifty to say the least, so we started the grass with seeds and straw. It took us almost two years to get the grass to fill in and, by that time, where it didn't fill in, I created beds of pine straw. Daddy, Millie and I worked tirelessly and I saw that same kind of work in my immediate future as I looked at the house and the yard.

I was starting to wallow in the dread of what lie ahead of me until I was distracted by sound of one of the horses rolling air out of its lips. I turned to the barn, which I still amazed me. I couldn't believe it was completely unscathed by the storm. I found the mystery guy propped against the fence scratching the ears of the new colt. This was the first person that skittish animal had let get near it since it was born. I couldn't take it anymore. I had to know how I knew him. I turned to start toward him, but Millie caught me.

"I hope you don't mind, but Gabriel and I are going to go ahead and get on the road. I think you're in pretty good shape so..."

I stopped her with a hug. "I know you're anxious to get home to the girls."

Millie smiled. "Last night was the first night I've ever spent away from them."

"And you miss them. It's okay."

Gabe approached and I let go of Millie to hug him. "Thank you both for coming and helping out today. I really appreciate everything y'all have done."

I had never wanted to rush Millie and Gabe off before, but I glanced back to make sure he hadn't left. I had thanked everyone who had been in my yard that day helping and I wanted to make sure I thanked him, whoever he was, just as I had thanked everyone else.

Gabe gave me a good squeeze. "You don't have to thank us. We're family and this is what we do. Y'all taught me that."

Millie joined back in with an arm around me and another around Gabe. "We love you and I'll be back to check on you in a couple of days."

"You don't have to check on me."

"I know I don't have to, but I'm going to anyway." There was no arguing with that girl. Millie was always one to do what she said. Once she set her mind to something there was no changing it.

Gabe eased back from us. "If you need anything, all you have to do is call."

I sighed, "I'll call if I need you. I promise."

"Alright then." Millie kissed me on my cheek and then she and Gabe headed off down the driveway hand in hand. I watched them until they were out of sight.

I looked back around and Aunt Dot was sweeping off the porch. One of the porch rockers had been lost to the storm, but the other was in pretty good shape. Judy was moving it back in place and Uncle Jim was still holding down a seat on the step. Mr. Familiar was still playing with the colt at the fence.

I walked back over to the porch. "Did any of you figure out who the man over at the fence was?" I asked as I laid down my work gloves.

335

Judy shrugged. Aunt Dot shook her head and Uncle Jim said, "Why don't you go ask him?"

"I think I will." I poured a cup of water from the cooler and took it with me. I figured I would offer it to him. It seemed the least I could do for all of his hard work.

For the first half of the walk across the yard I wondered what I would say. For the second half I wondered why I was wondering what to say. He heard the shuffling of my boots as I tripped over one of the stray limbs that had yet to be picked up. The cup of ice water flew all over him, but he was kind enough to ignore that and catch me anyway. Thank goodness he grabbed me. I very nearly fell flat on my face. He caught me by the waist and I braced myself hands flat against his chest. The cup of water was lost in my near fall.

"I'm so sorry!" I gasped. All of the worry on the walk over and it came down to that. I was embarrassed to the point of mortification. I threw water on him. I tripped all over myself and, oh my God, I could feel my cheeks become red and flushed.

"That's perfectly fine. Are you okay?" He asked, but still hadn't let go of me.

His voice was familiar as well. It was deep, but soft at the same time and concerned. I squinted as I studied his face still trying to figure out how I knew him and why I couldn't think of his name. I was good at remembering names and faces.

"I just wanted to come around and thank you for coming out to help today," I explained as I took a step back, removing myself from the almost embrace I was in with him. I looked back to the Styrofoam cup lying in a puddle of what was left of the water. "I was going to offer you a glass of ice water, but that didn't work out so well."

"You're welcome and you didn't have to bring me anything." He bowed his head and kicked at the dirt, in an "awe shucks" manner.

"I hope you will forgive me, but I have to ask. We've met before, right?" I bit my lip and tried not to embarrass myself further by having to confess to this man who had worked so tirelessly at my house all day that I did not know who he was. I suppose some people would have just thanked him and sent him on his way, but the fact that I couldn't place him ate at me.

"I was hoping you could tell me," he responded and this time it was he who studied my face.

My face reflected more bewilderment in that exchange of looks than it had in any others all day.

He continued, "I got a call last night that told me to watch the 11:00 p.m. news on Channel 6."

He slipped off his ball cap and ran a hand through his hair. The way his fingers slipped through gave evidence of a long scar. One could have easily mistaken it for a part, but as near as I was to him, I could see it was a scar. Still, things were not clicking for me.

"I don't typically get calls late at night from strange women with instructions. I shrugged it off as a prank, but come 11:00 I was still up and the news was on and there you were. I know this sounds weird, but I felt compelled to come. I don't know why and I was hoping you could tell me. I know you've got enough to worry with, but I just thought..."

The whole time he spoke, I thought about when Millie was injured in the Olympic Park bombing last year and how Gabe's ex-girlfriend saw Millie on the news. I thought about how that turned out. This should have been giving me a weird vibe, but unlike Beth, Gabe's former girlfriend, this seemed harmless. He seemed sweet and he had the prettiest blue eyes I had seen since...

I didn't let myself finish that thought. I cocked my head to the side and really looked at him. "What did you say your name was?"

"Noah Walden."

CHAPTER 19

My mouth fell open. My jaw hit the ground. My knees shook and my heart raced. I could not believe my ears or my eyes.

"Excuse me?" I needed to hear it again because clearly I had misunderstood.

"My name is Noah."

I looked back. Aunt Dot and Uncle Jim were watching from the porch. I looked at the big picture, my house and all of them watching. Judy was holding the broom where she had been sweeping on the porch and getting up the glass from the shattered windows. She was watching, too, and from one look to her she could tell what was going on. Judy dropped the broom and went running inside the house.

I could feel the blood draining from my face. After all these years, was this really him? If so, this is not how I thought I would react. I had played out every scenario in the last twenty years, but this wasn't one that I had envisioned.

"Ma'am, are you alright?" he asked me. He reached to steady me, but I stepped back out of his reach.

"Your name is Noah, Noah Walden?" I asked, repeating what he had said.

He seemed confused as to why I was asking. "Yes." There was caution in his voice.

Judy came running, carrying something tucked under her arm. She got between us and stuck out her hand for an introduction. "Hi, I'm Judy St. James. I'm sorry about the late phone call last night."

He took her hand and started to say his name again, but I interrupted.

"This isn't funny! It's not one bit funny!" I didn't say it out loud, but I couldn't believe he didn't know who I was. I couldn't believe he didn't recognize the house. If he was Noah, my Noah, then he would recognize everything. I turned and stormed toward the house.

"Wait, Gayle!" Judy reached and caught me by the wrist. I could not get free of her. "Mr. Walden, I know this all seems strange, but would you mind showing us your driver's license."

He looked skeptically at Judy, but didn't move. He looked at her like she had three heads.

"Please?" She pleaded.

The look on his face didn't change, but he looked to me. Just when I thought I couldn't embarrass myself more, tears were starting to pool in my eyes. They were bound to find their way down my cheeks. I wasn't one to cry all the time, but the tornado, the damage to the house, the loss of all the work we had put into the yard over the years, and I was on my last nerve. I needed a good cry, but this wasn't when I wanted to fulfill that need. I turned my head when he looked at me. Even though I had a world of mixed emotions, I didn't want him to see me cry.

He took out his wallet and, from it, pulled out his driver's license. He placed it in Judy's outstretched hand.

"Mr. Walden, do you know my friend here?" Judy asked him as she let go of my wrist and started to look over his license.

From the corners of my eyes, I glanced back for his answer. He shook his head, "Yes and no."

Judy handed the license to me. "I told you he was alive."

After looking over his license, I cut my eyes to her and handed it back to him.

Judy flashed a smile at me before she turned her attention back to Noah. I wiped my eyes and continued to look away.

Judy handed Noah the frame that she brought with her when she came running from the house. "Do you know this girl?"

I was curious as to what she handed him. It was my graduation portrait in my cap and gown.

He studied the photograph and looked from it to me repeatedly. I hadn't changed so much over the years that one couldn't look at the photograph and know it was me.

"Why did you say to her, 'I told you he was alive'?" His brow furrowed and I was no longer the only one uncomfortable with how this was going.

Judy answered his question with a question. "Were you in an accident when you were in your early twenties?"

"How do you know that?" This time, it was Noah that backed up from us.

"Because we were there when it happened..." Judy started to tell him, but I stopped her.

I stepped between them. I focused my attention on Judy first. "Thank you for finding him for me. Thank you for trying to help, but I'll take it from here."

"But..." Judy started.

"Thank you," I repeated.

Judy took the cue, the photo of me back from Noah and then excused herself.

I tried not to be distracted by the second crash of all of my hopes and dreams in the last two days as I looked into his eyes. They were the same eyes that I fell in love with so many years ago and I tried not to let that distract me either. The more I looked at him the more I could see the boy I knew in the man before me. The years had been kind and he was as attractive as ever, but I didn't want to make any further of a fool of myself than I already had. The cold hard truth was, at this point in our lives, we were strangers.

"It's been a long day and I really appreciate you coming today and working so hard. I really do, but I don't want to do this." I motioned at the both of us filling in the gaps with my hands.

I tilted my head, indicating toward the house. "As you can see, I really have a lot on my plate. You said you were curious as to why you felt compelled to come today and I don't know the answer to that because I can't understand why it took twenty years passing before you were compelled."

Noah's face fell with a blend of questions and understanding. "I see."

I stood there by the fence. The colt scattered away into the field as soon as soon as Noah stepped away. I watched him head down the driveway. I didn't know if I would see him again and maybe that didn't matter. Judy was right, Noah was alive. Maybe that was enough.

I picked my way through dinner, but hardly ate. I made polite conversation, but each time it turned to the subject of Noah, I turned it another direction. Everyone had questions.

That night as I laid my head on the pillow I knew it wasn't enough to just know he was alive. I tossed and turned all over the guest bed at Aunt Dot's, trying to shake off feelings of regret. I should have asked him flat out why he hadn't come before now. I should have asked him why he didn't recognize me, not even in my graduation picture. I should have asked him so many questions, but I didn't.

I flopped onto my back and watched the ceiling fan. It was set on low and the light of the moon through the curtains was enough for me to see the blades spin round and round. I counted the rotations like some folks count sheep. It didn't help. By midnight, I was no closer to sleep than I had been when I turned in at 10:00 p.m.

It was going to be the longest night of my life. When I got bored with watching the ceiling fan, I turned my attention to the alarm clock. I watched the red numbers turn from one to the next as the minutes drug by. Neither the fan nor the clock could distract me from thoughts of Noah.

It finally occurred to me that the clock was a clock radio. I fiddled with it until I managed to get the radio off of snooze and to the on position. "Holding on to Nothin' But the Wheel" by Patty Loveless was just starting when I cut the radio on. It must have been broken hearts night on WTHO because they played one sad lost love song after another. I made it through four of them before Stephanie Bentley's "Once I Was the Light of Your Life" came on. Even though I didn't have any more tears to cry, I turned the dial anyway.

I found a station out of Augusta. It came in with a ton of static, but I could make out the song. The first one to play was "Let's Go to Vegas". I thought I had gotten lucky, but the very next song on that station was another sad love song. I finally just leaned over and cut the radio off.

I think the last time I looked at the clock was sometime after 2:00 a.m. When I finally fell asleep, I had one dream after another of Noah. The last dream I had before I read the clock at 6:00 a.m. was of kissing the man that had been before me the afternoon before. It was one of those Praying Mantis, eat him alive, can't get enough, type of kisses.

Under the covers, I stretched to the four corners of the bed. Daybreak wasn't here yet and there was no light in the room, but my eyes were adjusting. I wasn't ready to wake up. I wanted to fall back into the dream and pick up where it left off. It was so potent of a dream that I could still smell his aftershave on my skin and taste him on my lips. I brushed my hand gently against my cheek and leaned into my own touch. I imagined it was my cheek against his.

Again, sleep didn't come and I just laid there thinking about Noah. I laid there and wondered if he was thinking about me. I wondered if he dreamed about me. I ran my fingers through my hair and shook out the tangles that had accumulated during the night. I wondered what he thought of me. Had I aged as well in his eyes as he had in mine?

The question popped back into my head and I knew the answer. No, knowing he was alive wasn't enough, but what would I do about that now? I decided I would do nothing until after I got my house in order. Plus, there was no excuse. He knew where to find me if he wanted to talk to me.

I laid there. I tried to go back to sleep. It was no use. I managed to make it all the way to 7:15 before I rolled out of bed. I laid there that long just to keep from waking the rest of the house. I passed the time by making mental notes of what plants I would need to get to restart the shrubbery around the front porch and what type of tree I wanted to replace the oak. On one hand I wanted something that grew fast that I would be able to enjoy in my lifetime, but on the other hand I wanted something that would be there for generations to come.

I quietly eased from under the patchwork quilt that my grandmother made and that covered the guest bed. One wouldn't think a quilt would be needed in Georgia in April, but Uncle Jim was a big fan of A/C and he kept it cold enough to hang meat in the house from March to October. The rug was cool, but manageable. The hardwood floors were another matter. They were as cold as a marble slab and I covered my mouth to stifle my squeal. I didn't normally put on socks first, but I quickly got dressed starting with my socks. I would have put on shoes second if I thought I could have got my jeans on over them.

It was Sunday morning and everyone else would be getting up and getting ready for church soon. I'm sure they expected me to go too, but I just wanted to go home. As soon as I was dressed, I tip-toed down the hall, left a note explaining where I had disappeared to and then I crept out the back door.

I walked the same path as I did the morning before, but this time I didn't have anything following me, but my own thoughts. There were no cars lining the road. There were no work trucks clogging the driveway.

I continued my trek down my driveway. The smell of spring flowers should have filled the air, but they didn't. The smell of sawdust still lingered instead. A hint of cedar mixed with the pine. It wasn't roses, but it was pleasing to my nose.

The driveway was almost a tenth of a mile in length from Hadden Pond Road to where it opened up into my yard. When I reached the point where it opened up, the sight was so much better than the morning before. I was certainly glad to see everyone yesterday morning, but this morning it was nice to see that most of the debris had been cleared except for the stray cotton bales. They had been carried in by the storm and there was no telling how far they had been blown before landing here like snow.

The cotton wasn't the only thing I found in the yard. I also found what appeared to be a fairly new double cab Ford F-150. It was black with silver trim and the windows were tinted so dark that I couldn't tell if anyone was in it or not. The truck blocked the most direct path to the house. All of those things combined with the fact that I didn't recognize it, made me nervous.

All sorts of possibilities ran through my head. Was someone there looting my house? Everyone around knew I was staying at Aunt Dot's. What if I surprised them? I wasn't armed and all of my guns, Daddy's guns really, were in the house.

I headed around the truck and toward the barn until I could see around it. All of my worry about someone robbing me was for nothing. Sitting on the top step of the porch was Noah. I was relieved for more reasons than one and I couldn't hide the smile on my face.

As soon as he spotted me, Noah stood. He seemed taller than I remembered, taller even than yesterday. The ball cap was gone. The Old Navy t-shirt was replaced by a baby blue buttoned down with rolled up sleeves and a pair of darker jeans. I think it was the darker jeans that gave the illusion that he was taller. Like the rest of us, Noah had put on a little weight over the years. He wasn't overweight, but filled out, nicely filled out. My heart skipped a beat at the sight of him.

I walked closer. Looking at Noah now, I couldn't believe I didn't recognize him straight away yesterday. He smiled at me and I restrained myself from running to him.

"Hi," Noah said cautiously.

"Hi." My lips trembled and I clinched them together. I didn't want to give myself away. Feelings of nervousness and joy filled my stomach and for the first time in what seemed like forever, I had butterflies.

"Can we talk?" He blinked rapidly. He was as nervous as I was.

"Of course." I took a seat on the step and Noah returned to where he had been when I first noticed him.

I gripped the edge of the porch step next to my knees. Noah did the same and sat there just like me, leaning forward and staring out into the open air in front of us. I didn't know what else to do with my hands. I was so close to him, I could smell his cologne. Clubman, I never forgot the smell, but then again, how could I forget it? I purchased a bottle every time I saw it in a store. Occasionally, I spritzed it in my bathroom just so I could conjure up memories of him. I cut my eyes to Noah. With all of the new colognes on the market, I couldn't believe he still wore that. Some things hadn't changed at all.

We sat there in silence for I don't know how long. Noah appeared to be working up the courage to say something, but he was having trouble putting together the words. I finally took the lead.

"I'm sorry about yesterday." I squinted with my cheeks puffed up near my eyes and with a look I asked him to forgive me.

"It's okay. You don't owe me an apology. If anyone needs to say 'Sorry', it's me. I didn't have the best timing. I believe you pointed that out." Noah leaned over and nudged me.

I couldn't help but let my head rest against his shoulder for a moment and smile up at him. I was seventeen again and as good as back on the porch of Briar Creek Baptist Church right after Andy's funeral. The butterflies swarmed in my stomach as much today as they did then.

"Look," he continued, "I think we already established that we used to know one another, but I would like for you to tell me about that if you would."

"Before I go into all of that, may I ask you something?"

"Sure."

"What happened to you that you don't know how we know one another?" Of course I knew about the accident, but was that the answer?

"My mother told me that I was out with what she called 'some so called friends' and I fell while diving at a rock quarry." Just the mention of that woman and I scooted away from him. I would rather take a snake bite than ever deal with that woman again.

"What happened to the friends?" What I meant was: What did she tell you happened to us? I tried to mask my face from giving away my opinion of his mother.

"I was in a coma for days and when I woke up Mama explained that they didn't come to see about me and they were nowhere to be found."

My face flew red hot and you could have lit a match off of my skin. I had to look away from Noah. It was all I could do not to spit fire and scream out, "That lying bitch!"

I refrained, bit my tongue and asked, "Who were the friends?"

"I really don't remember. The truth is I don't know; what's a real memory from that time in my life and what I dreamed over the years."

"Did you have amnesia?" That would be just fitting for a Danielle Steele novel, but not in real life.

"No. The doctors described it as a traumatic brain injury. It affected my short term memory and wiped out some time around the accident, but it's not like I forgot my name or anything."

That wasn't true. He did forget something. He forgot my name and where to find me. Before I knew it, I pointed that out. "You forgot me. And, your mother reinforced that fact by taking out a restraining order against me. I was eighteen. I will never get over that, a restraining order." I shook my head and there was no mistaking the bitterness in my tone.

I went on, "Those 'so called friends,' that was me and Judy and her boyfriend at the time. We came to see you. I came every single day and I waited for word about you. Then, one day when I arrived at the hospital, you were gone. Before I could even put good effort into finding you, a sheriff's deputy showed up at the feed and seed store where I worked and served me a restraining order in front of half the town of Stapleton."

"On top of that, I had faith in you that you would never do that. I had faith that you would not stand for me to be treated like that. I knew you would have died before you let anyone mistreat me so, eventually, when you never came, I thought you were dead. I called home every day that I was away at college and my mother checked the Augusta Chronicle for me to see if your name was in the obituaries. When I came home after college, I checked them myself..."

Finally, Noah stopped me. "I'm so sorry. I admit I could not remember your name, but I never forgot your face. I asked both of my parents about you. At first, I just remembered your eyes and blue lights flashing across your face. I remember the song 'Have You Ever Seen the Rain,' Creedence Clearwater Revival was playing."

"I thought I remembered everything about that night, but I don't remember what song was playing. I remember the blue lights were when we were in the car on the way to the hospital with you that night. I thought you were dead then. Your eyes were open, but, well, I can't believe you remember that."

"I asked both of my parents about you. I did. Eventually, I described that picture your friend gave me yesterday. I described it to a T. They told me it was a dream. I described this house. They always told me that I dreamed it all up while I was in a coma."

"As you see, I'm not a dream. I am a real person!" I lifted the hair off of the back of my neck.

"See this right here?" I pointed to the scar on the back of my neck. "Your mother gave me this when she snatched the chain that held your class ring from around my neck at the hospital the night of your accident. If both of my parents weren't deceased I'd march them out here to tell you how she treated me."

As much as I ranted about his mother, Noah never bothered to challenge me. He never even looked offended or surprised. He looked at the scar and ran his finger over it. It was a two inch raised mark right across my spine. If I hadn't been in the midst of a tantrum about his mother, his touch would have given me the chills. As it was, I hardly felt him at all.

"Why would they tell you that?" I demanded at the end of my rant.

"They told me that because they wanted to keep control of the money the Air Force paid. I got a substantial disability check for being injured while I was still enlisted."

"They did all of that for money? Look around here. I've never wanted anything that I didn't work for. I never had anything handed to me and I've never taken anything from anyone. They didn't know me and it was for money?"

I let go of my hair and returned my hands to where they had been earlier, gripping the overhang of the step we were sitting on.

Noah inched closer to me. "I'm so sorry, Gayle. I want you to know I never really believed them. I knew you were real, you had to be real. I didn't believe that my wounded brain just made you up."

He finally twisted around so that he sat facing me, one leg bent and propped over the other.

"Look at me," he asked as he took my hand and gently pulled me around to face him.

"It's like I have a whole bunch of pieces to a puzzle up here." Noah tapped the side of his head and it sent a little wave through is hair.

The wave was just enough to give a little peak at his scar. We all had scars from that night and the one on my neck was nothing compared to his.

"I cannot seem to make them fit, not even enough so I can figure out what or which pieces are missing."

348

The whole time he spoke, he kept hold of my hand. My hand in his was the natural fit that it was so long ago.

"I don't want to scare you, but I would like for you to help me with the puzzle. I want to know why I have dreamed of you almost every night for the last twenty years."

My heart leapt at that statement. "He dreamed of me," I repeated inside my head.

I thought about what he said and then it came to me. "Wait here," I said to him as I stood up. "I'll be right back.

I got up and ran inside the house. Up the stairs to my bedroom and into the closet I went. I reached to the back of the top shelf and pulled down a shoe box. In the box was every letter he ever wrote to me. I returned to the porch with the box and handed it to him.

"These are the letters you wrote to me. I am only loaning them to you."

I had them arranged by date, oldest to newest. Noah opened the box and started to pull one out.

"Please don't read them now. Take them with you and then bring them back to me when you're done. You know where to find me."

Noah returned the lid to the box and sat it to the side. "Do you want me to leave now?"

"No." I sat back down on the porch next to him.

"It doesn't scare you that some guy from your past has suddenly showed up out of the blue?"

"No." It didn't even occur to me to be scared. I had wanted this, to know what happened to him for so long. I couldn't stop looking at him. I still had that Praying Mantis urge to kiss him.

"It scares the Hell out of me." Noah ran a hand through his hair.

349

"I thought you died in my arms when I was a teenager, still a baby, and when someone goes through something like that and the tornado the day before yesterday, this doesn't compare."

"Would you mind if I called you sometime?" Noah shifted his posture.

"I would like that very much."

Noah and I continued to talk about the small stuff, but we agreed that he would read the letters before we spoke much more about our past.

"I think you might get a better understanding from your letters than you would from me telling you," I explained and he didn't put up an argument. "I wish I had the letters that I wrote to you, but..."

"I found them once. I almost forgot about that, but it was right after I got out of the rehab center..."

"The rehab center?" Of course I jumped to the wrong conclusion, but when the word rehab is used it typically means drug abuse.

"I had to relearn some things after the accident so I was sent to a rehab hospital at a base in Texas. I was there about six months before they sent me home."

"Anyway, I managed to read one of the letters before my mother caught me."

"You did?"

"Yes, I was almost done reading it when she snatched it away. While I was in Texas, the Air Force shipped my belongings home. I found them one day and started going through everything. The letters were among my things. My mother caught me in the living room in front of the fire reading. She snatched letter from my hand and threw it and the entire box in the fireplace."

"Did she give you a reason for doing that?"

"I scrambled to try to get them, but she said, 'Why do you want some letters from some foreign girl that dumped you?' I had more lies told to me than the Bible's got Psalms. When she wasn't watching me she had my sister-in-law watching me. I was a grown man, I couldn't live like that."

"What did you do?"

"I had some savings so I convinced my mother to agree to allow me to move out as long as I didn't take the disability check with me. She actually thought they were going to save the farm with that money, but that was hopeless."

"Even with the disability check?"

"Oh, yeah, five hundred dollars a month was nothing considering how much they needed."

"Really?" I huffed and rolled my eyes. "Five hundred dollars?" I just shook my head. I was absolutely disgusted.

I couldn't believe that's what our future was worth to his mother back then. Put into another perspective, that was the price of my honor. I thought I would wait for marriage and that I was giving myself to my husband the night before the accident. Little did I know, it was going to be a twenty year-long one-night-stand.

I know that was a lot of money to some people. There had been times when it was a lot of money to me, but I would have never sold Millie's happiness for any amount of money, let alone five hundred dollars. Noah's mother rivaled Millie's for the worst mother award in my book.

"I moved out. I wasn't one hundred percent so I was discharged from the Air Force. I remembered how to fly, but, with my medical records, no one in their right mind would allow me in a cockpit, so I got a job."

Noah went on to tell me that the farm had been doing well for a number of years, but when his older brother joined the family business he insisted on doing things his way. His father stepped back from the day to day running of things and by the time his second brother came home from the service, it was almost too late.

"Nate came up with a plan to develop some of the land into a subdivision, sell it off in lots and use the money to pay off what was left. Nicolas, my older brother refused to sell anything. Daddy put them both in charge and nothing could be done without the both of them signing off on it. All of the loans were in my father's name so it left my father on the hook for everything. On the eve of the foreclosure, my father killed himself. Nate found him hanging in the hay barn."

"Oh my God!" I covered my mouth with both hands. "He killed himself? I am so sorry. I had no idea."

"It was years ago. I think he spent a lifetime of being a failure in my mother's eyes and he just couldn't take it anymore. Losing the farm was the last straw for him. At first I wondered if I had went into farming with them, could I have changed anything? I don't think I could have."

"What happened to your mother and your brothers?"

"Mother remarried. Nick got divorced and Nate lives in Washington, D.C. He got as far away as possible. It's funny, I only got as far away as Washington, Georgia and Mom got back to the hill section of Augusta."

I was no longer interested in what became of his hateful mother. I wanted to know what led him to move to Washington. "You went to work at Daniel Field and you moved to Washington? Why did you move to Washington?"

Noah dropped his head to his hands and rubbed his face before he answered. "If you haven't already decided that I'm crazy, you will if I tell you why I moved to Washington."

"Try me," I prodded him softly.

"I had a dream. In the dream the blonde girl, you, and I discussed that she would go to college at UGA and I would rent a house in Washington and we would be together every weekend. I know. It's crazy. A dream of a girl, whose name I couldn't remember, told me to move and I did."

"It's not crazy and it wasn't a dream, it was a memory," I told him. "I had been planning to go to school at the University of Georgia since before I met you. Then we met and I got accepted and we made that plan together. You'll see when you read the letters. It wasn't so much of a dream for you as it was a memory."

I didn't think he was crazy and this wasn't getting scary for me, but I did think we should tone it down with the trip down memory lane. I wanted him to kiss me. I wanted things to pick up where they left off before his accident, but despite all of this talk we were strangers to each other.

Usually, it was Daddy's words that sprang to mind, but this time it was Mama's. "You don't want to seem too available," I remembered her cautioning me.

Someone once said, "Love begins with a smile, grows with a kiss and ends with a teardrop." I sat there next to Noah on the porch and wondered if the tears I had cried all those years were the end.

Noah's eyes were so blue, mesmerizingly blue to the point of near transparent. Through those eyes, I could see the young man I knew all those years ago. His collar draped open and I could see the faintest amount of chest hair peeking up his neck where there had been none when he was twenty-one. There was the slightest trace of grays at each of his temples. He was distinguished looking, that's what Aunt Dot said about a man like that. She was right. Age hadn't hurt Noah a bit and I couldn't stop stealing looks at him.

Sideways glances, smiles, twisting my hair in my fingers, I couldn't help myself. I was flirting. I tried to stop. I repeated, "Don't be too available," in my head over and over again. That chant fell on deaf ears even inside my head.

I remembered every detail of him. After all, he was the first man I had ever seen naked. He told me of his dreams of me and I was convinced those dreams were memories, but I wanted to know for sure. I didn't dare ask and I didn't dare share all of my memories of him.

I took comfort in the fact that Noah was here, that he had come back after yesterday. Surely, that said something. Coupled with what he was telling me of the dreams, the letter that his mother burned and the questions he was asking, he wanted to remember me.

CHAPTER 20

Noah and I were well on our way to talking all Sunday morning. We were as long winded as any preacher at any pulpit in the CSRA. All of that was cut short when the phone started ringing in the barn. We could hear it from the office I kept in the tack room all the way across the yard.

"Even if I ran, I wouldn't get there before the machine picked up, but I should see who that is." I could not hide the disappointment in my voice that we had been interrupted.

"It's alright," Noah ran his hand through his hair. It seemed like a fidgeting habit and each time he did it I noticed the scar along the part of his hair. "I should be getting back anyway."

It puzzled me. Suddenly, I was afraid of him having a girlfriend or a family of his own. For him to have waited to live in his dreams during the night as I had done most of the time was very unrealistic. He must have had someone to go home to. I had to know, but I asked with guarded caution, "Get back to where?"

"I have lunch with my land lady every Sunday. She's like the mother I should have had," Noah laughed and I was relieved.

Noah stood and pressed down his jeans and dusted them off. When he was finished he offered me his hand to help me up.

I placed my hand in his. "You were always such a gentleman."

"It's not fair that you can say things like that about me and everything I can think to say to you, every compliment I could pay you, would just come out weird."

"Try me." I blushed.

"Okay, but I warned you." Noah paused for a second to get his words in order. "I just always thought you were my guardian angel... It's just surreal."

I held my arm out to him. "Do you need to pinch me to make sure I'm real?"

"Tempting, but no."

Since his big Black Beauty version of a truck was parked between the house and the barn, I walked Noah back to it. We said our goodbyes along the way, but when he got to the truck he opened the door, loaded the shoe box of letters that I had given him into the seat before turning back to me. There was this awkwardness between us. The question on both of our minds was: What as appropriate; a hug or a handshake or what?

I look the initiative and hugged him, forgetting again what Mama said about availability. Perhaps that only applied to teenage girls. I was forty and nothing, if not available to him. I had been available to him for twenty years so why put on airs now?

I held him tight. For a second I laid my head on his shoulder and lingered a little too long in his scent. I lingered so long that I could make out the distinct smells of Clubman, Bounce fabric softener and Head and Shoulders shampoo. I made another memory of him just by breathing him in.

The shirt Noah was wearing was a pillow of cotton under my head. I would have given every dime in my bank account to have that shirt. Left to my own devices, I would have put it on right then and never taken it off. I would have turned up the collar to hug around my neck and reach up as close to my nose as I could get it. I would wear that shirt and nothing else. I would imagine it was him draped around me.

I breathed him in once more and brushed my cheek across the material over his shoulder before pulling back. I opened my eyes to see my reflection shining in the paint over the back quarter panel. I liked that truck, but not nearly as much as I liked the Camaro he used to have. I made a mental note to ask him what happened to the Camaro next time we talked. I was certain we would talk again.

As soon as Noah's truck was out of sight, I ran to check the machine in the tack room. No sooner did I lay eyes on the phone next to the answering machine, I realized I didn't give Noah my phone number.

"Dang it!" I slapped my forehead.

I still had no idea where he lived. He said he moved to Washington after he got out of the service and moved out of his parents' house, but he didn't say he still lived here. There was no need dwelling on it now. The light on the machine was blinking and indicating that I had more messages than I could count on both hands.

One after another the messages played. Each was a frantic call about an animal either hurt or scared out of its wits due to the tornado. The electricity and the phone line had been ripped away by the storm so some of the callers were beside themselves as they had been calling repeatedly since Friday night. I began returning calls immediately and setting up times for me to call on the owners and tend to their pets and livestock.

I worked well past night fall and by the time I crawled into the tub at Aunt Dot and Uncle Jim's that night I had birthed two horses, a litter of English Bulldogs, euthanized a squirrel and a hog, and stitched a spot on a horse's leg that was as long as my forearm. For the calves, I received cash. I got a check for the hog and the horse and as payment for birthing the pups, I now have the promise of an English Bulldog puppy. As payment for the squirrel, I received a bushel of peaches.

Multitasking was one of my specialties. I tended to make my calls on the cordless phone while in the tub. Most everyone I typically called was in the other room except Millie. I dialed her number and it was snatched up on the first ring.

"Hello?" Millie answered in a frantic whisper.

"I'm sorry for calling so late," I began. In all honesty, I should have known better than to call so late. Plus, I also knew that Sunday nights were about the only nights that Millie and Gabe got to spend with the girls.

"It's okay," Millie replied to me, but followed with a question to Gabe. "Can you take her?"

"I'm fine. How about you?"

"Oh, Bossy Pants, won't go to sleep tonight. I just handed her off to Gabriel. She's such a daddy's girl anyway. He'll probably just whisper the words, 'Go to sleep,' and she'll be out like a light. Can I get her to do that? No."

One would think that Gabby would be the one that gave Millie more of a fit with having the biological mother she has, but after Gabby got past the colic she took it easy on both Millie and Gabe. George-Anne was another story. George-Anne was hardly five months old and she already exerted her own free will at every opportunity.

"Millie, she's the perfect combination of you and Gabe. Both of you are strong willed and the poor girl got a double dose."

"She's so sweet most of the time, but, dang, if she doesn't let us know it when she's not getting her way. And another thing, I think she hates my singing."

"Hates your singing?"

"Oh, yes, Gabby loves my singing. It calms her right down. I have sung to Gabby since the first moment I got her. Not Bossy Pants, I let go of one note and she starts screaming. I love her and all, but I will be glad when she learns to talk so she can just tell me what's the matter."

"And once she starts talking, you'll wish she would stop."

"No, I'm serious. Anything beats the screaming. I'm telling you, I was trying to give her a bottle tonight and she looked at me and I could have sworn she screamed the words, 'Stop it!' I was almost glad because I could understand that. She likes to be held and walked around. We get along like a house on fire when I am standing and walking around with her."

"What? Do you have to constantly give her a tour of the apartment?" I laughed and found all of this ridiculous.

"Yes!"

"Have you tried feeding her something other than a bottle yet?"

"No. The doctor said we shouldn't feed her anything just yet. I mean, we mix rice cereal in there, but nothing other than that."

"Millie, I'd be willing to bet the poor thing's starving and not getting enough to fill up on with just the bottle. Go and get some baby food tomorrow, vegetables and fruits to start. You really liked carrots when you were a baby."

Millie took a different tone, a softer somber one. I could hear in the cracking of her voice that she was holding back tears. "I don't know what I would have done if something would have happened to you the other day."

"Nothing happened to me. I'm fine and the house is going to be fine. Everything's going to be like it was."

"I'm serious. You're the closest thing I've got to a mother so I can't have anything happening to you. Who would tell me how to raise these babies?"

"I'm sure you would do just fine without my interference."

"Interference? Are you kidding me? You have never been one to interfere!"

"Well, thank goodness Daddy isn't alive to hear you say that or he would know I'm not doing my job as your, what did you call it? Closest thing to a mother?" I joked with her.

"You know what I mean!" Millie playfully snapped back.

Millie had attempted to call me "Mother" a time or two in the past, but it never stuck. I was fine with her calling me Gayle or Aunt Gayle.

"Anyway, I received word that the window folks are coming on Wednesday and then I will be able to move back to the big house."

"Good because I hated seeing what you'd done with the place. That sort of redecorating is just awful. I mean, honestly, if

359

you wanted the yard redone you didn't have to nearly tear the house down to do it."

It felt good to be able to laugh with Millie about the situation. "If I didn't laugh, I'd break down and cry, right?"

"That's what Granddaddy always told me."

"Well, it's getting late so I guess I'll let you go." Millie was no stranger to our conversations from the bathtub. She was used to the sloshing water so I felt no shame when I told her, "Plus, I'm starting to prune up. I need to get out of the tub. Kiss the girls for me and tell them that GeeGee loves them."

"They love you too and we'll see you soon."

"Remember, get George-Anne some food tomorrow."

"I'll send Gabriel to the store now." I still would never get used to her calling him Gabriel and the rest of us calling him Gabe. Each time she said it, I had to remind myself who she was talking about.

Everyone else was in bed by the time I got out of the bath. I snuck into Judy's room. It was pitch black in the room, but I found my way to the bed. Even though she was no child, I sat on the edge of her bed and told her goodnight. I thought she was asleep and arranged the covers around her.

"Gayle, are you tucking me in?" I was surprised to say the least when her voice came from the darkness.

"Uhhh..." It seemed odd when put like that and I didn't know what to say.

"That's sweet, but go to bed," Judy yawned.

I yawned back. It was contagious. "I just wanted to say goodnight."

"Goodnight." Judy rolled over to face me as I stood to leave. She reached out to me. "I should probably say goodbye now too."

"Goodbye?" I was confused, but took the hand that she offered.

Judy held my hand while she explained, "News of the tornado and our near death has scared the life out of my husband and he has insisted that I return home tomorrow. Plus, you've found Noah."

"More like you found him and he found me. I really haven't done anything."

"Tisk-task, details. The point is that my work here is done. I'm taking a flight out of Augusta tomorrow morning. Your Aunt Dot's already offered to drive me."

I hated that Judy had to go, but I could understand her family wanting her home and to see that she was okay. I know how worrying worked from when Millie was involved in the hospital last year. I didn't believe she was alright until I laid eyes on her. I'm sure Judy's husband felt the same way so I didn't give her any grief about leaving so soon.

"I'll take you to the airport tomorrow. It's the least I can do since your car got destroyed at my house." I felt about as bad about Pumpkin being totaled as I did the damage to my own house.

"I never thought I would say this," Judy shifted under the covers, "but, I'm going to miss that car."

"It held a lot of memories," I agreed.

I thought for a moment about Daddy. If he were here he might be able to restore Pumpkin. Judy recognized the look on my face and knew what I was thinking. "Don't even think about it."

"What?" I shrugged.

"Not all the kings horses or all the kings men could put that car back together again so don't you even try. I know how you Andersons are about cars and memories. I've seen what you drive and what Millie drives."

I did not even try to pretend that I didn't know what she was taking about. She was right. A person's car represented them. After

361

all, I would have paid any amount of money to buy Noah's old Camaro if I had known where to find it.

Before I hugged Judy and told her good night, I asked, "What time is your flight?"

"9:00 a.m. I know you've got house calls to make in the morning so don't worry about me."

"I'll get those sorted out first thing and I'll take you to the airport."

We argued for a moment and then Judy reminded me that the landscaper was coming tomorrow at 7:30 in the morning and it was too late at night to cancel. I apologized profusely, but had to let her go with Aunt Dot. The chief horticulturist from Dudley's in Thomson had agreed to come out as a favor to one of my good clients from the hunt club and I had to be there.

After we came to the conclusion that I could not take her to the airport, we had a very lengthy discussion about my morning with Noah. Judy could tell I was practically salivating over him.

"I know I got this ball rolling, but I think you should keep in mind that you don't really know him." Judy paused, knowing that the wheels inside my head were turning with the reminder of how long I had known Noah. "I know, I know, but you don't know the man he is now."

"I don't think he's an ax murderer or anything."

"No, I'm sure he's not, but what I'm sayin' is don't get your heartbroken."

I slapped my hand over my mouth to keep from laughing outloud and waking the whole house. "Getting my heartbroken?" I laughed as quietly as I could. Judy knew as well as I did why I laughed; my heart had been broken for more years than any of us cared to count.

"You know what I mean!"

I did know what she meant, but it didn't change the facts.

362

I crawled over in the bed next to her and we rehashed and analyzed every aspect of my morning with Noah until the wee hours of the night. It was just like we were teenagers again. Finally, Judy rustled her covers on the bed and stretched and yawned.

"I am so tired. While you were out healing every pet in town, I swept up and picked up and threw out every shard of glass that flew in the house from the tornado. I did the outside yesterday and the inside today. I'm exhausted. I know you're exhausted too so would you mind if I just called you tomorrow night." Judy yawned again.

Yawning was contagious and I spoke through one of mine. "Well, you better call me tomorrow night and let me know you got home safely."

"Lord, you sound like my mama," Judy snuggled into the covers and closed her eyes.

"Goodnight. I'm going to bed." Instead of getting up, I rolled over and clutched the pillow on that side of the bed.

There's an old wives tale about putting a slice of wedding cake under your pillow and it will make you dream of the man you would marry. I'd been to a minimum of three weddings a year since that night at the rock quarry. Needless to say, I swiped a piece of cake from every single one of them and every single time I dreamed of my wedding, but never once did I see the face of the man that was waiting at the end of the aisle for me.

Not being able to get a glimpse of him was so frustrating. I could see the yard at the house with all of the white chairs lined up in rows. I could see my family members seated in those chairs and their heads followed me as I passed them. I could see the flowers, white lilies and yellow roses were everywhere. I could see every detail as I walked toward the alter that was at the top of the steps on the front porch of my house, but the closest I ever got to seeing the man I would marry was a pair of patent leather tuxedo shoes. I think the only reason I saw those was because I had noticed how shiny the ones the groom was wearing at the wedding I had been to that day. It was just a detail that got lodged in my psyche, but meant nothing.

I didn't sleep on a piece of wedding cake in a Ziploc bag under my pillow that night, but for the first time I saw the face of the man waiting at the end of the aisle. Despite the warnings from Judy, I dreamed of Noah that night.

It was all the same as usual. I could smell the blend of lilies and roses in the air mixed with the fresh cut grass of my lawn. The rows of chairs were full on my side with familiar faces and the rows on the groom's side were full, but I didn't recognize a one of them, not even his sorry mama. None of that mattered because for once, I could see Noah waiting for me. He wasn't wearing shoes that I could see my reflection in, but that didn't matter either. All that mattered was that he was there and I could finally see him.

Somewhere during the night I figured out it wasn't real. It was just a dream, but it was the best dream I had had in years. There were times when I coasted through my days and lived in the dreams I had at night. Then, there were the times when I had the nightmare and my life during the day wasn't nearly as bad as that. This time, I wasn't frustrated or disappointed or terrified when I woke up. The best description of how I felt was guarded hopefulness. I had hope for my own future. It was a good feeling and it carried me through the next week.

Things took longer at the house than I had anticipated. Sunday morning was the first morning that I didn't have any appointments scheduled from one corner of the county to the next. The only appointment I had was to be at the house when the contractors arrived to install the new windows. The column was repaired on Friday and all that was left before I could move back in was the installation of the new windows, which was scheduled for Monday. It wasn't completely necessary for me to be there, but I was excited about the work being completed. I was excited about moving home and anxious about when I might hear from Noah.

After breakfast with Aunt Dot and Uncle Jim Monday, I left and headed to my house, but this time I took the truck. I pulled across Hadden Pond Road along beside my mailbox and rolled down the window. In all of my rushing about for work and to three different hardware stores to pick out just the right shade of white to repaint the house, I had forgotten to check the mail yesterday. I opened the lid to the box. Along with the slew of sale papers and

364

bills, was a box wrapped like a brown paper sack and addressed to me. I wasn't expecting any shipments, but it appeared I had one.

I pulled the package from the box and left the truck running while I opened it. There was a letter under the wrapping, taped to the top of the box. I pulled the letter off and unfolded the paper.

April 20, 1997

Dear Gayle,

I hope this letter finds you well. Please see that I have returned the box of letters as you requested.

I thought about calling you and realized I did not have your phone number. I thought about dialing the operator and getting the number, but in looking back on the letters you gave me, I decided to write instead.

I enjoyed reading the letters and thank you for sharing them with me. I feel as though I know myself a little better now or at least I know who I once was. I will always be grateful to you for giving that back to me.

Thank you for your kindness.

Sincerely,

Noah Walden

When I finished reading I slung the whole lot of mail in the passenger's seat, the letter, the box and all. Some of the envelopes and papers slid into the floorboard, but I didn't care. My mind was stuck on, "What was that supposed to mean?"

I had been dying to hear from Noah again, but that letter was less personal than the junk mail from Publisher's Clearinghouse. I was completely dumbfounded, so much so, that I didn't even know if my heart was broken over whether it was a final kiss off or not.

Even though no one was behind me and the distance between my driveway and the mailbox was microscopic, I put on the blinker for the turn anyway. The rest of my day went just like that. I was absentminded to the point of being useless. I just could not reconcile that bizarre, cold letter with the warm, kind man I had chatted so freely on my porch last Sunday. It made no sense, so of course I dwelled on it all day.

That afternoon the roof was secure and the scaffolding was down. Everything was coming together and I thought for sure I would be moving home that night, but I was wrong. Only the top floor of the new windows was complete by the time the contractor and his crew called it quits for the day.

Staying at Aunt Dot's wasn't horrible, but it wasn't my home either. Uncle Jim played the television entirely too loud. It was so loud that there was no place in the house that was safe from the volume. I swear there had been times during the fall, right after he got the new television and the surround sound, when my windows were up in the house, that I could hear it all the way across the road and through the woods. I wasn't sure if he liked it that loud or if he was completely deaf and I had never noticed before.

Needless to say, I liked a little less noise and I wanted to move home as soon as the windows were in, but there was no way I was moving back as long as the ground floor windows were still missing. I had been lucky not to have been robbed thus far, but there was no need to tempt fate. I played it safe and risked wearing out my welcome and my hearing by staying with Uncle Jim and Aunt Dot another night.

The next afternoon, I checked the mail on my way in and found another letter. The hand writing matched that of the one that had come with the return of my letters. There was no return address, but it was postmarked two days earlier in Washington, Georgia. I hadn't noticed the postmark on the first letter, but recalled Noah said he moved to Washington when he left his mother's house. If he still lived in Washington then that meant we had only been forty-five miles apart all of this time.

Just like the day before, with the window still rolled down, the truck still running and the door of the mailbox still open, I tore into the letter right then. The air conditioning was escaping out of the open window, but I didn't notice. The only thing I did that amounted to good sense was to keep my foot firmly on the brake while I read.

April 22, 1997

Dear Gayle,

Again, I am writing to you knowing that calling would be probably be quicker. Some might feel this form of communication is antiquated, but I have a feeling you are not one of those people.

To be honest, since I read the letters you gave me, the thought of writing to you has become a distraction to me, so much a distraction that I gave it a shot with my first letter. It's in part because of that letter that I am writing now. I must apologize for it as it was my first attempt. Things I should have said I could not put to paper, yet I cannot fathom saying them to you directly either. You must forgive me as I lacked the courage in yesterday's letter to tell you that the mere fact that you kept my letters all these years moved me and scared me at the same time.

I fear you will realize that I am a coward and I am certain you question the ambiguity of my last letter. Perhaps you think I am a coward now for not saying these things in person. I am. I am terrified to tell you that I have loved the dream I have of you all my life and now I fear the loss of the dream as I will surely fail in reality. I have failed at every relationship I have ever tried to have. I fear I will not live up to the boy that wrote those letters to you.

I fear all of this, but I would love nothing better than to see you. I mentioned before I only write to you, in part, for the sake of getting the words out. I guess I'm using this like a diary. The second reason I write to you is because I haven't the time to drive to Avera and risk telling you all of this in person.

I'm not sure if you watch the news, but there was a plane lost off of the coast of Georgia. If you have seen or heard about it, you may know it was chartered out of Athens. What the news has yet to report is that it was one of my planes. I rented it to one of my friends, John Weatherby, an attorney from Athens. John's been licensed for about three years. I was the one that taught him to fly. He likes to fly his wife and two children to St. Simon's for vacations. He has rented the same plane from me a few times and he has tons of flight time. I don't know what's going on, but I am leaving for Savannah to join the search as soon as I mail this letter. I ask that you pray for them. I'm trying to have faith, but I fear the worst.

It is one thing to write all of this to you, but it would be another for you to hear it in my voice. I can call myself a coward, but I would never want you to think of me as one. I can tell you that I am scared, but I want you to think of me as brave. I write so that I my keep the image you have of me as that young adventurous airman intact.

I hope you don't mind me writing to you. I will do my best to write again soon, but I do not know what awaits me in Savannah. I pray we find John and his family and they are safe. I ask you do the same. I pray this is all some mix up with his flight plan and they are on a beach somewhere relaxing in the sun with the girls. I'm glad you cannot see me as I worry about those children. They are six and eight, two girls, and I was just playing with them the afternoon that they took off. I held their hands as they boarded.

Please know that I think of you often and not just as the young girl that visited me in my dreams. I think of you now, the way you are, and I am proud to have had the chance to meet you again.

-Noah

I watched every channel to find out the latest in the search for the "Lost Plane Off the Georgia Coast," that's what the stations were referring to it as. I searched for a glimpse of Noah in all of those that were interviewed in conjunction with the plane, but I never saw him. I was scared for the family that I never met and I was scared for Noah. I could tell they were more than clients and my heart broke for him. Noah's letter raised so many new questions about his life, but none of that mattered. It only mattered that those people were found and hopefully found safe soon.

The next day I rushed to check the mailbox for word from Noah. I knew it was unrealistic to expect a letter from him every day, but that didn't mean I wasn't disappointed. I flipped through all of the sale papers, searching for a letter that might have gotten stuck between their pages, but there was nothing. There was no letter, but the windows were in the first floor of my house. As much disappointment as I had in not finding a letter from Noah in the box, I was giddy about being able to move back to my own house and to sleep in my own bed and to have peace and quiet.

Being home was wonderful. I could walk from my bathroom to my bedroom naked if I wanted without fear of anyone seeing me. I could even walk downstairs naked if I wanted to. I guess walking naked in my own house was my version of freedom. Everyone had their own definition of that word and this was mine.

I didn't prance around the house in the nude all the time, but when I forgot to replace the towels in my bathroom, it was no big deal. If I happened to want something to drink while I was going for the towel, then I went downstairs to the kitchen and got one. That was no big deal either. I was the only one home so who cared?

That night, I forgot to put out new towels and didn't notice until I was just about to step into the shower. I left the bathroom and headed toward the linen closet down the hall. On my way to get a towel, I thought about how nice a Coke would be and continued on to the kitchen to get one. Earlier, I thought about turning on my music, but decided against it. I liked the quiet. It was just me and my thoughts and that quiet made the knocking at the door all that much louder.

Normally, I heard every rumble of every piece of gravel when a car came down the driveway, but not that night. I didn't hear a thing until the three bangs on the front door rang out. I was halfway down the stairs and it startled me so bad that I nearly missed a step. There was no time for me to run as I noticed Uncle Jim's face pressed against the little window around the front door. From the look on his face, he was as embarrassed as I was. I whipped around and dashed back up two steps at a time.

I threw on a robe and tried not to laugh at the entire situation. Heading back down the stairs, I could see that Uncle Jim had shied away from looking through the windows and had his back turned altogether. I tried harder to squelch the urge to laugh.

I opened the door and Uncle Jim could hardly make eye contact with me.

"I guess the mailman figured you moved in with us," Uncle Jim said, offering me an envelope. "Maybe that's why this was in our box. Sorry I forgot to give it to you earlier."

I thanked Uncle Jim and without ever looking at me he scurried off of the porch. I couldn't contain it any longer. Uncle Jim had seen me naked and there was no way I could un-ring that bell no matter how badly I wanted to. While opening the letter I laughed until my sides hurt.

CHAPTER 21

Still laughing, I slumped against the back of the door as soon as I pushed it shut and tore into the envelope. The first thing I noticed was that it was on the courtesy stationery from The River Street Inn in Savannah. It had beautiful letters of gold and navy. Below the fancy embossed logo was Noah's handwriting.

April 23, 1997

Dear Gayle,

I am at it again. I hope you don't mind me using you as my confidant.

This evening I write to keep my mind off of what is going on here. It hasn't hit the news yet, but the plane has been found. There are no survivors. That keeps bouncing around in my skull. I can hear the little voices of the girls saying it to me, "no survivors."

I've never had to deal with anything like this before. I remember volunteering for the color guard and all of the funerals, but I didn't know those people. I remember my father's death, but it was so fresh after my accident that it did not really resonate with me. I didn't feel it like I am feeling this now. Is it because I was so close with them and this involves the loss of two children? I don't know.

It was my plane they were in, my plane that is at the bottom of the ocean. I can't help but think that this is somehow my fault. I've replayed everything over and over in my head. I checked everything personally. I checked the gauges, the gas and I replaced the parachutes two weeks ago.

There's going to be an investigation and no one has mentioned any reason for the crash yet. They haven't brought the plane up, but they said the cabin is intact. I just don't know what could have gone wrong. I don't know when they are going to bring

371

it up, but I've been asked by John's mother to stay until... They want me to identify... Jesus, Gayle

I can't write the words, but I have to do it. John had a son from a previous marriage. The boy is only twenty and I can't imagine having to do that at his age.

All of this has been a reminder of how short and how precious life is. I wish I was sitting on your porch steps telling you this in person. I think of you constantly and that's what gets me through this. I've been so careful these last few days for fear of scaring you off and because I've scared myself. I know I sound crazy. I can't explain it, other than to say I've lived a life of missing you and I've only just now realized it. I don't want to miss you anymore. I know it is selfish, but I hope you have missed me, too.

When I get back, I'll ask you out on a proper date. I'll do all of the things the letters said I did and more. I just want the chance to win you back. Thinking of the possibilities with you is what keeps me going down here.

With love,

Noah

I don't know when I put my hand across my mouth. I don't know when tears started down my cheeks. I don't know when I slid down the door and to the floor where I sat while I read. All I know is that I found myself like that when I finished reading.

I folded the letter and put it back in the envelope. For a few minutes I just sat there. I felt so sorry for a family that I didn't even know. I felt so sorry for Noah, so sorry that I couldn't even think too much about the last half of his letter. In the first half I could tell how devastated he was and I wanted so badly to comfort him. I closed my eyes and leaned my head back against the door and cried for him. Uncontrollable sobs came from me, the kind that take your breath away.

The vision of Millie as a little girl came to mind and him holding her hand as she climbed the tiny staircase into plane. I pictured the little girls as her and there was no stopping the tears. I wiped my face and tried to think of other things, but I was stuck, crying on the floor of the foyer for a good ten to fifteen minutes.

The thing that stopped me from crying was the idea that I knew where Noah was and the phone number for the Inn was right there on the stationery. I went to the kitchen and picked up the phone. Of course there was the voice in my head, my mother's saying, "Girls don't call boys." It's a good thing I was no longer a girl. I was a grown woman and I would call whomever I wanted to call.

I found the phone and dialed the number to The River Street Inn in Savannah. I held my breath with nervousness as the phone rang on the other end of the line.

"May I have Mr. Noah Walden's room, please?" I asked the receptionist as I realized the letter I had just read was two days old and he might not even be in Savannah anymore.

She didn't tell me he was no longer a guest there she simply said, "Hold, please."

It rang twice and then I was rewarded with Noah's voice, "Hello?"

"Hi." I kept it simple while mentally shushing my mother's reminder.

"Gayle?" Noah was hesitant to believe it was me. I was a little amazed he recognized my voice at all.

"Yes," I matched his quiet tone. "Are you okay?"

There was silence on the line, at least thirty seconds worth of silence before he answered. "Not really."

"Did you have to..."

Noah didn't let me finish my question. I could tell he still wasn't comfortable with the words or the act. "Yeah," he exhaled.

"Oh Noah, I'm so, so sorry." I didn't know what else to say.

"They pulled the plane up yesterday and I, well, today..." Noah paused and another bout of silence passed through the line. When he spoke again, his voice cracked out the words, "It was hard. It was really hard."

"I've got ten planes; the ones in Augusta, Thomson, the one in Washington and this one. This is the first time. I mean it, nothing even remotely... Remotely close has ever gone wrong before. I just... I just cannot wrap my mind around..."

Noah seemed to stream along with pauses and fragments until I stopped him. "Noah, do you have anyone there with you?"

"No?" It sounded more like a question of why I was asking than a one word answer.

"I'm on my way." I hadn't really thought it through when I answered, but I didn't stutter or falter in the gesture.

"You don't have to..."

My mind was made up. As soon as the idea first left my brain and fell out of my lips, I raced up stairs carrying the phone to pack.

"I'm coming. You shouldn't be alone with this." I grabbed Daddy's old leather duffle bag from the closet.

"But, Gayle..." I only half heard Noah for the sound of the rustling of my clothes as I threw them in the bag.

"I'll be there in about two hours. It's almost 7:00 p.m. now so I'll see you around 9:00." I started to hang up but assured him one last time, "I'm on my way."

That was the fastest I had ever packed in my entire life. I'm not even sure what all I threw in there, but I grabbed it, my makeup case, my toothbrush and the keys to the T-bird. I was almost out the door when I realized I was still wearing the robe and that I hadn't showered. I threw everything down by the door and ran back upstairs, showered, threw on some jeans, tank top and some sneakers.

374

My hair was still wet when I ran out of the house. Driving with the window down took care of that. The towns clicked by like the miles on the odometer and my hair was dry by Swainsboro. I was lost in thought most of the drive and by the time I reached the Metter exit on I-16, I realized I forgot to pack socks. I wasn't real sure I had packed underwear either, but then I remembered I had.

The sun set as I drove. I kept it to sixty miles per hour the whole way. I sang along to the only station that came in clearly, WZNY, Sunny 105 out of Augusta. It wasn't my usual station, but it didn't fade out until almost all the way to the city limits of Savannah. I was more of a country music girl than rock, but on this particular night they were playing a flashback to the eighties. I knew the songs of the eighties so I sang along to *I Drove All Night* by Cindi Lauper. I was definitely open to the possibilities that the song suggested. I got chills thinking about driving to a hotel in Savannah to meet Noah.

I had never driven the T-bird farther than Louisville, but it still drove like a floating dream. Luckily The River Street Inn had a parking deck because I didn't think about having to park on the street when I left home in it, but I sure did when I drove down Bay Street, looking for the hotel. I saw all the cars parked at meters along the street and worried about leaving the T-Bird among them.

I parked the car and went to find the lobby. The first thing I saw when I entered the lobby of the Inn was Noah. From that distance, he looked taller. He still hadn't shaved in a day or so, but he didn't look scruffy. He looked manly, rugged, but not unkempt.

Of course it was new to me, seeing him at this age. The jeans and shirt he had on reminded me of the outfit he wore after the homecoming dance. The blue of the shirt made his eyes bluer than they appeared in the plaid he had worn the last time I saw him. I could have watched him for hours. Now that I had found him again I felt the need to take mental pictures of him as if I was preparing for an interrogation by a police sketch artist. I knew that wasn't the case, but it was still such a relief just to lay eyes on him.

The longer I stood there watching, the more I started to really take in the whole picture. He looked panicked. He was pacing frantically and as soon as he spotted me he nearly ran to me.

"You said two hours." He threw his arms around me and hugged me. "I was about to call the police."

I was caught off guard by the gesture and it took me a couple of seconds to reciprocate. I wrapped my arms around him.

"It took a little longer to get here than I thought it would." Counting my shower, it was more like three hours from Avera to Savannah.

"I was worried sick." He looked it, too. Up close Noah looked like an overly exhausted version of himself.

"There was no need to worry," I whispered as I rested my head against his, taking in his scent. I could have melted in that moment; just melted into him.

"Come with me." Noah slid his hands down my arms. In one hand he took the handles of the duffle and for a second we both held on to it. "Let me get this for you."

Noah's eyes were as blue as ever, even with the red veins ripping through them from his exhaustion. There was a control about them that possessed me and I don't even think he knew it. I glanced away for fear that I would give myself away. I wanted him and maybe that's the real reason I had driven all that way to be with him, to really be with him.

Noah held tight to my hand and led me quickly across the lobby to the elevator. He pressed the button with the same hand that held my bag and never let go of my other hand. We stood there side by side.

I looked at my hand still not quite believing he was holding it. Past our clasped hands I noticed Noah tapping his foot anxiously as we waited. He had on brown, square toed cowboy boots. They were well worn and reminded me of a pair that I had had since high school. I cut my eyes up at him, thinking some things you just love forever no matter how old or worn or damaged they get.

He must have felt me looking at him. Noah glanced around at me and I quickly looked away, back at my own feet. I had on flat Keds tennis shoes. They were so flat that it magnified that Noah was a couple of inches taller than me. I hadn't noticed that before. I also hadn't noticed the crook in the bridge of his nose. I thought back and I could remember his twenty-one year old face with crystal clarity and that little hump was not there back then. Somewhere along the way, Noah had had his nose broken. I was curious about how he got that and made a mental note to remember to ask him about it.

The ding of the bell indicating the elevator's arrival snapped me back from thoughts of his nose.

"After you," Noah gestured as the elevator doors opened.

"Thank you." I smiled back at him and walked ahead, pulling him with me.

I turned around to face the doors like everyone does when they get in an elevator, but Noah didn't. He dropped my duffle bag. It made a solid thud when it hit the floor. Noah reached behind him and pressed the button for the second floor. It happened so fast. Instead of turning around to face the doors with me he pulled me toward him. He never let go of my hand, but his free hand went around my neck. I could feel each one of his fingers distinctly. His grip was firm.

"I've wanted to do this since the first time I laid eyes on you last week." Noah caressed my nose with his and I went weak in the knees.

My chest was pressed to his, my legs to his. I could feel his lashes against my cheekbones as he leaned in closer, head cocked to the side and his nose still slipping across the end of mine. His hold around my neck eased to direct me to tilt my head and I did. I tilted my head so his lips could finally touch mine. Just the first brush against mine sent a shiver down my spine.

Who knew that's what heaven was like? An elevator in Savannah, Georgia, that was it? I was kissing Noah and I was in heaven. It was everything I thought it would be, everything I dreamed it would be. It was soft and slow and deep. I was lost in him. I would have driven a thousand miles for this.

I let go of his hand so I could wrap my arms around him. That free hand of his went to the small of my back and pulled me tighter. The elevator door opened and we were interrupted by the sound of an elderly woman clearing her throat. Noah jerked around, rejoining his hand to mine as he went. Who knows what would have happened if the woman hadn't been there or if the building was taller and we had farther to go than just the one floor.

"Excuse us," he said to the lady. He grabbed my bag and started out of the elevator.

The look on her face conveyed that we had clearly offended the "Queen of the Blue Hairs." I giggled as Noah pulled me past her. I couldn't believe I had just been caught in a public display of affection in an elevator. "PDA" is what Millie called it when Gabe kissed her in front of the family. She never seemed to mind and neither did I. Normally I was easily embarrassed, but not this time. After all, I would never see that lady again so what did I care?

Noah was walking briskly down the hall and I followed. I struggled to keep up, but he kept hold of my hand and pulled me along. One door, two doors, there were five in all that we passed before Noah came to a stop.

"Just so happened the room next to mine was available. I hope you don't mind." Noah gestured to the next door down the hall.

"No, that's fine. I hadn't even thought about... I don't know what I was thinking." I hadn't thought about where I would stay when I was on the phone with him earlier and told him I was on my way. Even then, my mind was stuck on kissing him.

Noah stuck the key in the lock and opened the door for me. I peeked around him to see the prettiest hotel room I'd ever seen. It was a large room with a huge four poster, canopy mahogany bed in the center.

"Wow! That's a big bed." All of a sudden I was a school girl spitting out my observations without regard to any implications. I stepped around him to get a better look, completely in awe of the room.

"Yes. It is a very big bed." Noah raised an eyebrow at me.

"It kind of makes my bed at home look small."

Noah sat my rugged looking excuse for luggage in the chair next to the door. "I've never seen your bed at home so I guess I'll have to take your word for it."

When I looked back to Noah, laughing from realizing how silly I sounded, like I had never left home before, I found him waiting, just waiting there. The door was still open and I could not tell whether he was anticipating me releasing him to leave like a bellhop or if he was waiting for me to invite him in. Nothing about this night had stood on ceremony thus far, so I was confused by his just standing there.

Of course I didn't want him to leave me. "Come in," I insisted.

I whirled around and noticed the doors to the balcony. Immediately I went to Noah and took his hand. "I bet you haven't looked at the view the whole time you've been here."

"I really hadn't thought much about it," Noah drug along behind me.

I threw open the doors and pulled him out with me. The night air had a breeze that carried the scent of magnolias and the salt from the ocean. "Do you smell that?"

"What?"

"The smell of Savannah." I leaned over the balcony and sucked it in. I rested my arms on the railing and propped myself up as I took it all in.

Noah took the same stance as me and so close that I could feel his arm against mine from elbow all the way to my shoulder. From the corner of my eye I could see he wasn't taking in smell or the sight of the headlights flickering across the Eugene Talmadge, Jr. Memorial Bridge up the river from us like I was. They flickered like fire flies on and off as they passed the rails along the bridge. The bridge was huge, almost two miles long and I knew this because I took a wrong turn and ended up on it. I had to drive that far just to turn around.

I watched mesmerized at how dark the city was despite all of the headlights, street lights, and the lights from the buildings. People walked along River Street below the balcony. From bar to bar they went, but they were quiet as mice and I didn't hear a peep from them. A cargo ship floated up river and there was a flood of lights on it. I could see all the colors of the cargo containers, but Noah saw nothing. It was after 10:00 and despite all of the amazing surroundings and sights to see, this time it was him looking at me. I wondered if he noticed every detail about me as I had of him.

I finally turned my attention back to Noah. I wondered if he wanted to finish what he started in the elevator, but I dared not ask out right. I figured it was as good a time as any to get back to the business that brought me there.

From my shoulder to his, I nudged Noah. "Are you alright?" I asked sincerely.

"I'm better now that you're here."

I blushed and looked away slightly embarrassed. Noah nudged me as I had him before and I turned back.

"I would like to kiss you again. Would you mind terribly?"

I shook my head, giving my consent.

"You don't mind?"

"No." Again, I shook my head.

Noah leaned toward me, took my chin in his first two fingers and guided my face to his. His kisses were sweet and soft, touching nothing but his lips to mine. I wanted the depth that we were headed for in the elevator. The longer we kissed the closer I inched myself to Noah. Finally he took hold of me, wrapped me in his arms and I wrapped mine around his neck.

I ran my fingers through his hair and Noah ran one of his under the strap of my tank top near my right shoulder blade. That touch alone send chill bumps down my legs. It tickled and I squirmed and the strap fell over my shoulder.

Although he still held me in his embrace, Noah pulled back and apologized. "Sorry about that. I didn't mean to get so carried away."

I could feel my chest heave against his. "There's no need to apologize," I whispered as I buried my face in his neck, planting kisses all the way up to his ear.

"Oh my God, Gayle." Noah shook off whatever sensation was coming over him. He backed up from me and headed back into the room.

"Is something wrong?" I followed him.

In the middle of the room he turned back. "Nothing's wrong except I don't want to rush you."

"Oh." That's exactly what I wanted to hear, but I laughed anyway. "Rush me? Are you kidding?"

Noah looked surprised that I would mock the situation.

I stepped closer to Noah. "I've waited for you for so long. It's funny that you would think you're rushing me."

"Are you hungry?" Noah changed the subject.

Now it was me that looked surprised.

"There's a café just down River Street from here."

"Sure," I agreed and Noah held out his hand to me and we left the room.

"We might better take the stairs," Noah gestured to the elevator as we passed it.

On River Street we found not just any café, but River Street Sweets. That was my favorite stop on my one prior trip to the city. It's where I was first introduced to pralines. Even at that late hour there was a fresh batch on the marble slab in the window. Noah opened the door for me and the heavenly smell of brown sugar and pecans flooded my senses. I squeezed his hand without even knowing it.

"It's the little things sometimes, right?"

"Yeah," I nodded and smiled as big as I ever had.

At the counter Noah ordered, "We'll take a pound of pralines, two Cokes..."

"The ones in the bottle," I specified.

Noah repeated, "The ones in the bottles and two Moon Pies." It was an afterthought, but he asked, "Do you like Moon Pies?"

"Yes, but not as much as I like pralines and Coke in a glass bottle." I could not get the giant grin off of my face. I was beginning to feel self-conscious of it, but I couldn't seem to stop.

Noah handed me the first half of everything the shop girl gave him. I quickly found the opener for the Cokes. Noah handed me his to open as well.

"I can't believe we are eating Moon Pies and pralines at nearly 11:00 at night," I commented as I popped the caps.

"And drinking Cokes."

"Oh, Honey, I could drink Coke all day and all night. They say it kills brain cells, but I disagree."

Noah threw his head back and laughed whole heartedly, as I described my love of Coca-Cola. "It won't keep you up all night?"

"No. I'm one of those rare folks that could fall asleep almost anywhere and wake up fine the next day."

We headed back onto the cobblestone street outside. We found a bench close by and Noah dusted it off so we could sit down. We were seated no more than a second before Noah raised his bottle.

"Here's to our first date," and he gave me a wink.

Noah knew as well as I did that it wasn't our real first date, but I didn't correct him. I clinked my bottle to his and took a sip.

I opened the bag of pralines and offered them to Noah.

"I'm good with the Moon Pie. Thanks." He opened the package and took a bite.

"You don't know what you're missing."

"Oh, but I do. I ate a whole pound of them by myself over the course of the last two days."

"They are the best I've ever had." With those words my mind went to the gutter.

I'd only been with two men. I'm sure Robert had way more experience than Noah, but still Noah was better. I could not believe I was having those thoughts. I began to question whether I had just inflated the memory of our night together and finally I could feel my cheeks becoming red with embarrassment and I had to look away.

"What is it?" Noah noticed the change in me.

"Nothing."

"Seriously, what is it?"

I wasn't one for lying, but there was no way I was telling him what I was thinking. I tried to redirect him. A piece of his Moon Pie broke off and fell on his collar on his last bite. "Here let me get that for you."

I reached over and picked it off his shirt. Very unexpectedly, Noah grabbed my wrist pulled my hand to his lips and ate the crumble of Moon-Pie from my fingers. He stared me down while he did it. I had to withstand the urge to fan myself yet again. I held my breath trying to keep the stupid smile from returning, but I was not successful.

Noah released my hand. "Tell me more about us."

"What do you want to know?"

"The letters referred to someplace we called 'our house'. Tell me about that."

"You remember my friend Judy?"

Noah agreed that he did.

"Judy's aunt and uncle owned a house outside of Avera. Her uncle's job got transferred and her aunt refused to sell the house. It sat vacant for a while and then one night you showed up just when I needed a date for homecoming. I wasn't allowed to date, but my parents made an exception for you." I shook my head gently, remembering that even my parents realized he was special.

I continued, "They agreed to let me go out with you after homecoming. You've seen the area. There's not much of anywhere to go. I didn't just want to sit in your car with you on some dirt road somewhere so I gave you directions to Judy's aunt and uncle's house. I knew no one would be there."

Noah listened intently and did not interrupt me. He finished his Coke and Moon Pie. I finished mine as I went on with the story.

I contemplated not telling him what became of the house, but I went ahead and told him. "We called it our house because we went there several times to be alone. We planned on buying the house and making that our home."

A curious look came over Noah's face. "You bought the house anyway didn't you? That's your house now?" He took my hand and clasped it in both of his as he posed the questions.

"I had to have it." I sought his understanding with the shrug of my shoulders and demure smile and a few bats of my lashes. "Most every memory of you is intertwined with that house for me. It took me years to save up the money and by the time I did the house was in shambles. There was a tree through the kitchen window and a pack of rats the size of house cats living in it, but I didn't care. That house was the backdrop for most every single one of our dates. I had my first kiss on the steps of that house and I lost my..."

384

I couldn't finish the sentence. I bit my lip and covered my mouth with my free hand. I looked away sheepishly. As old as I was and I still wasn't real comfortable talking with anyone about the loss my virginity.

Noah caught on and he didn't have a problem with the word at all. "You lost your virginity to me in..."

I looked back up at him. "Yes," I jokingly rolled my eyes, "in our house."

"So we've?"

"You're really going to make me say it?"

"No, I'm not." Noah nudged me and then he stood up. "It's getting late. We should probably head back."

Noah offered his hand and helped me and what was left of the bag of pralines up. All the while I had talked, I nibbled on one after another. Coke might not keep me up, but the quantity of sugar in those might.

Along the walk back to the hotel I asked him what he remembered of the night of the accident or the night before.

"What I remember comes in dreams and there's no time line."

"I sure wish you remembered."

"Me, too."

We walked for a while in silence before Noah broke. "You're welcome to tell me about it."

Noah opened one door after another for me as we proceeded back through the River Street Inn. Our conversation continued about what he remembered. When we finally arrived at my door he asked the big question.

"I know this might sound odd, but did we get married? Are we married?"

My eyes became wide with wonder. If he didn't remember, why would he ask such a thing?

He went on to explain why he asked. "One of the reoccurring dreams that I have of you involves us saying vows to one another. It's so strange, I never see a church, but we were definitely saying the words. Lately I've been thinking that the dreams that I've had over and over again are the ones that are actually memories manifesting themselves as dreams. I had this particular dream countless times, probably more than any other."

"I wanted to tell you about that, but I didn't want to scare you off."

Noah used the key and opened the door to my room. Once more he waited for an invitation to come in.

"Really? Get in here!" I snapped at him playfully. Our conversation had taken such a serious turn that it needed something to lighten the mood.

I walked through the room and kicked off my shoes. "We had a plan, you know. We were young and foolish and in love and we had a plan."

I crawled up on the bed and all the while I felt Noah's eyes on me. I sat up cross legged on the right hand side of the bed. "Take your shoes off. Come on over here and make yourself comfortable. I know you're exhausted so we'll just sit here and talk."

Noah obliged with the only hesitation being the bed. He looked to the wing back chair in the sitting area. He looked back at me, trying to make his decision and I gave him an "are you kidding me" look. I patted the spot on the bed where I intended him to sit and he came over.

"The night I lost my..."

Noah filled in the blank with a snicker, "Virginity."

"Yes," I emphasized with exasperation, "that."

Noah adjusted his posture and I went on. "We made a plan that I would continue on to college. You would get out of the Air Force and get a job at Daniel Field in Augusta. I believe I recall you saying that you did do both of those things. Anyway, your ultimate goal was to get a job as a pilot for Delta at Bush Field. You were going to get a house in Washington, since it was close to both Athens, where I would be at school, and close enough for you to drive to Augusta for work. We didn't legally get married then because my father wouldn't have paid for my college and we weren't financially ready for that yet. Regardless, we said the vows and they were pretty official to you and me for about twenty-four hours. Longer for me, but definitely twenty-four hours for you."

"What do you mean, 'twenty-four hours for' me?"

"Your accident happened the very next night."

"Ah." Noah looked at me with concern. "I never knew."

"That's because I never told anyone other than Judy the day of the tornado and you just now."

"No, I'm serious, you never told my family that…"

"That we what? We were two stupid kids who said marriage vows so that we would feel more comfortable having sex? Or, that 'I'm sorry, I don't have any paperwork, but your son and I are married and I'm entitled to his military benefits? Oh, and, my parents, what was I supposed to tell them? No, I never told a soul. Plus, there really wasn't time between your mother being utterly hateful to my face and then stealing you away in the night."

Noah shook his head, but didn't challenge me about his mother this time either. Most folks would have. They would have been cross with me for speaking ill of their mothers, but I had a feeling he knew her for what she was.

I rubbed my eyes. I was getting tired too. "In all honesty, I had a twenty-year one night stand that only I knew about."

I fell back onto the pillows of the bed. There were four or five on my side of the bed alone. They were so fluffy I sank into them. I wondered what he would do now that I had told him we were married.

Noah chuckled at the notion of a twenty-year one night stand. After a couple of seconds he eased into a lying position on the pillows on his side of the bed. We were both flat of our backs and we just laid there, each with our own thoughts. There was four or more inches between us, but the back of my hand brushed against the back of his. I didn't move at all. A few minutes passed and Noah intertwined his fingers in mine. We continued to lay there.

CHAPTER 22

The door to the balcony was still open. The lights were still on. My clothes were still on and I was on top of the covers on the bed. It was 4:00 a.m. and it wasn't a noise from outside that woke me. It was the thrashing about of Noah, the heavy breathing and the sudden scream that got me.

"Noah!" I leaned over and shook him with the push of my hand and he sat straight up in bed. He barely missed racking my skull with his own when he came up.

Noah struggled to catch his breath. I spoke his name again and the only response I got was his panting.

Finally the phrase, "Oh my God!" came from under his breath as if he had just finished a race and was amazed he had won.

Noah had had a nightmare and it reminded me of the ones Millie had when she first came to live with us. I did the same to Noah as I had done to Millie way back then. Of course, he wasn't a child, like Millie, but I prayed it would work. I hated seeing him like that.

I put my arm around him and leaned him into me. "Shhhh," I told him. "I'm here. I'm here. You're not alone."

When Noah came to his senses, he realized we had fallen asleep in my bed. "I'm sorry. I'll go to my room."

I found myself more stunned by his apology and leaving the bed than I did being awakened by his nightmare.

"Don't you want to talk about it?" I scooted across the bed after him. I got to my feet, but Noah was really on the move.

"No. You should get some sleep. I'll see you in the morning." Noah grabbed his shoes and took off out of the door. He didn't even look back.

I went over to Daddy's leather duffle bag that I never moved from the chair near the door. I unzipped it and began looking for my nightgown. I found a fresh pair of underwear and I was relieved I packed those. I still didn't find any socks and I didn't find a nightgown either. I could have just slept in my bra and panties.

Noah mentioned earlier that he was the next door down. I opened my door and peeped out. The hallway was as bright as it was earlier, but that was all I had noticed then. My eyes were on Noah, not the décor or the people in the hallway. Now, it was empty as I scurried quietly about fifteen feet down the hall and tapped lightly on the door.

There was no way I was going to give the door a full knock, but what I was doing wasn't working. I didn't worry that Noah couldn't hear me. I worried that for whatever reason, whatever he had experienced in the dream, that's what made him want to be alone. That was what kept him from coming to the door. I gave up and I was almost back to my door when Noah stuck his head out.

"Gayle," he gave in a voice just above a whisper, as mindful as I was about the other sleeping guests on the floor.

"I'm sorry to bother you, but I need to borrow something," I explained as I walked back to him.

I was spitting out the words, "I forgot something to sleep in," when Noah snatched me into his arms.

It was elevator time again, but without the elevator. My arms were instinctively around his neck and he held me so tight, so tight the only inch of us above our clothes that wasn't touching were our lips. There was a split second before he kissed me that my nose was pressed to his and I was able to grab a big breath. In that same moment he whirled me inside the door and kicked it shut behind him.

"So much for not waking the neighbors."

The room looks just like mine, but everything that was red is blue in this room. That was about all I noticed. All of my attention was on Noah. I could hardly wait for his lips to touch mine and, when they did, it sent a shockwave of relief to my core.

My heart was beating so hard that I'm surprised Noah didn't feel it pounding through my chest and against his. By the way I wanted him, one would have thought I had never been kissed before, but it wasn't that at all. I had ached for him for so many years and there was nothing to fill the void, but him. Nothing compared.

His dark hair curled around my fingers as I clinched them in it. It was soft and not enough of the gray had taken over the dark brown to give it that wiry feel that grays often did. I loved it. I loved his hair in my grasp, his lips on mine and the way he said my name for me to come back to him just moments before. I love him and I had never stopped loving him.

Noah might have been pushing forty-three years old now, but there wasn't a thing about the way he picked me up and carried me to the bed that suggested he was any less than he was when he was twenty-one. He caught me under my thighs and lifted me. With my legs wrapped around his waist is how we went and once there he laid me down gently.

"I want my life back," Noah begged as he buried his head in my chest.

For only a moment he rested there and I continued to run my fingers through his hair. It was an indulgence for me to touch him like that. On the third time through, Noah stood up.

"I can wait if you want." His eyes were blistering and my blood boiled for him.

"Wait for what?" We weren't teenagers anymore and there was no one but ourselves to be accountable to so what reason was there to wait.

"For you to know..."

I reached for the belt in his jeans and unbuckled it. "I know you just fine and I've loved you the better part of my life, but if you want to wait..."

The furrowed brow that he had moments before melted away to a look of pure pleasure. He was relieved and beautiful and I couldn't stop looking at him.

"I missed you." I licked my lips and bit at my bottom one, pained by the thought of how badly I really had missed him. I slipped his belt free as I added, "There's not a day that passed that I didn't think of you. I never forgot you and I never stopped wanting you back. I just missed you."

Noah took my wrists and pulled me from the bed and into his arms again. "It's strange, but I know I've missed you, too."

I steadied myself with one hand on his shoulder and, this time it was me that took his face in my other hand. I stood on my toes to make up the two inch difference in our height. Before I pressed my lips to his, I breathed the words, "I don't want to miss you anymore."

I could taste the lasting hint of toothpaste on his tongue as mine explored his. He hadn't come to the door earlier when I knocked because he had been brushing his teeth. None of that mattered. I left his mouth and, traveled to his neck, leaving a trail of kisses as I went and he let me.

Noah's hands moved down my back to the hem of my tank top. As I twirled my tongue around his Adam's apple, he inched my shirt up until I had no recourse but to raise my arms. I had worn a thin lace bra. It had underwire, but little else in the way of support. The tank top had a built in lining that had shielded Noah and the world from seeing my arousal all night. The tank top was gone and I was virtually bare up top. If Noah noticed then, he didn't let on.

I reciprocated the gesture and slowly unbuttoned the buttons on his shirt. When I was done with them, I slid my hands slowly up his chest over his undershirt and then under the collar and down his arms, freeing them from the sleeves. Even through his t-shirt I could feel that he had kept himself in good shape. The taut pecks indicated he had not let himself go.

I pulled back from him and took a fist full of his undershirt, "I'm going to need this to sleep in."

"No. You're not," Noah said in a challenge that sent the goose bumps down my leg.

"Well, I'm going to take it now anyway." I was defiant.

Letting go of the grasp I had on the cotton shirt, I reached for the part of it that puffed up from where it was tucked in his jeans and pulled it loose. Short of blinking and pulling it over his head, I never broke eye contact with Noah as I pulled the shirt up. Not a hair on his head was mussed by the shirt, but he shook his head and ran a hand through it anyway. Without meaning to I found myself just watching him, my head cocked to the side, biting my bottom lip and thinking about how amazing it was just to see him do simple things like shake out his hair.

I was right, he was in shape and I could tell this as I lifted the shirt to expose his abs. I didn't look, I could just feel them. I could also feel that he had more hair on his chest now. He had the chest of a man.

"You are the most beautiful woman I've ever seen." Noah pulled me in closer.

One of his hands was in my hair around my neck and the other was inching down from the small of my bare back. I tilted my head and my cheek rested on his neck. My eyes rolled back at the release of joy and delight and relief all mixed together just by being held in his arms. Such an overwhelming since of relief came over me that I felt tears coming to my eyes. Lord knows, I didn't want to cry then. That would definitely ruin the moment.

The tears were as good as forgotten as soon as Noah's hand traveled around the waistband of my jeans to the button in the front. With that one hand he unbuttoned and unzipped my jeans. They fell and Noah loosened his hold on me for me to step out of them.

Before I realized I was without pajamas, I took off my socks in my own room. When I tip-toed to his room, I did it barefoot. Now, I stood in front of him in nothing my thin underwear. Perhaps I should have been self-conscious, but I wasn't.

"Black. I like." Noah observed as he took my hands and turned us around.

I hardly ever wore matching bra and panties, but this was one of those rare occasions. In all honesty, the set was an afterthought when I was getting dressed. When I left home in a mad dash to Savannah, it had not occurred to me that this might be where the night would head. The fact that I had on Victoria's Secret's finest was just dumb luck on my part, but in that very moment I sure was proud and thankful for it.

Noah took a seat on the bed and with a grip around my buttocks, he pulled me to a position straddling him. I took his face in my hands and kissed him.

"I could kiss you forever," I breathed while he moved from my lips down to my cleavage.

My arms draped over his back and my head fell back in ecstasy. I could feel him through his jeans and through my panties. I rolled my hips. I couldn't help it, it just happened. I could practically feel him inside me. Would that and the touch of his finger inside the top of my bra be enough to make me lose control? I worried as I became more and more aroused.

I squirmed again. There wasn't a bone in my body that didn't ache for Noah. There wasn't an inch of my skin that didn't beg to be explored by his hands and his lips and most every other party of him. It wasn't all about receiving for me, but that part was definitely fun and rewarding. By the time he unbuttoned his pants every part of my body had been reintroduced to him.

The last time I squirmed, Noah wrapped his arms tightly around me and flipped me on my back. I squealed at the surprise of it. I sunk back into the bed and watched.

As badly as I wanted Noah, suddenly I was flooded with emotions. Seeing him standing before me, ready to fulfill most every desire I had had for the last two decades gave me a pang of hesitation. For a split second the question, "What if this is an epic let down?" flashed through my mind.

The question was wiped away by the devil and angel on my shoulders. The angel was sitting upright, crossed legged and pursed lips. "Don't give yourself away so easily," she insisted.

The devil was sprawled back over the other shoulder. I was her chase lounge in an invisible French boudoir. Knees in the air, legs spread and dressed like a high-end hooker, she fanned herself. "Don't be a cock tease," she hissed.

I was astounded. I couldn't say "virginity" out loud earlier, but my conscious easily threw out the phrase "cock tease."

I scoffed internally at the idea of giving myself too easily. How many offers had I had over the years? So many that the men around the county still used my high school nickname, Ice Princess.

I shrugged off those questions and my mind flowed back to how badly I wanted this. Noah was the exception to the rule. I wasn't just doing this for him. I was giving myself because I wanted to and because I really couldn't give something that had always been his.

I was laying crossways of the bed and had hardly moved a muscle since he stood up. I had stayed still with my thoughts as he dropped his pants and tossed them over the back of a nearby chair. My clothes lay crumpled on the floor with his shirts, but his pants were nice and neat, waiting to be worn again.

Noah stood at the side of the bed, taking in the sight of me. "You're amazing." His voice was sweet and low and he touched the inside of my ankle with the pad of his thumb as he spoke.

Chills ran up my leg as using just that one finger, Noah inched up the inside of my leg. Along with the touch came the direction for me to open up and I did.

Noah licked his lips. "So smooth," he smiled slyly and I tilted my pelvis toward him.

By the time he reached my knee, he took away that one finger and with his whole hand he grabbed me behind my knee. He grabbed me behind the other knee as well and pulled me toward him.

I let out one peep of a giggle at being jerked toward him. I shook my head and tried to keep from full on laughing. I was amused by him taking charge of me. I liked it.

"What?" Noah wondered what I was laughing about.

"Nothing." I smiled and held back more laughs.

I couldn't bring myself to tell him I liked him tossing me around, but I did. I certainly couldn't tell him that the only down side to him pulling me across the bed like that was that the panties that I was so proud of were now so far up my arse that I wished they were thongs.

I must have given some indication as to the status of my panties or maybe it was just that time because Noah glanced at them. "Do you mind?" he asked as he slid hand hands up from my knees to the waistband.

The bed was a four poster, just like the one in the room he had booked for me. It was a king and the mattresses were about as thick as they were wide. It was high off the floor. It was so high off the floor that it almost needed steps for me to get up on it. And, it was so high that with Noah standing flat footed on the floor, he didn't need to squat any. Noah was tall and so was the bed. He barely leaned when he made his way to my underpants.

I sucked in a deep breath and let it out like a quiver, a reflex from Noah circling my belly button with his tongue as my panties fell away. I raised my head to see the top of Noah's head. In the line of view was just how erect my breasts were through my bra. I let go of my fists full of the bed comforter and reached down for his face. I just wanted to kiss him and kiss him and kiss him until the cows came home.

Noah didn't immediately come to my calling. I coaxed his face toward mine, but he took detours along the way. While he crawled onto the bed and over me he drug his nose and his tongue from my navel to one breast and then the next. Outside of the lace and then inside of it, not too hard and not too soft, he grazed his teeth over my nipple on one side while he rolled the other about with his thumb. Never had I felt the sensation of both at the same time before. As if I wasn't panting and ready for him before, Noah knew exactly what a woman's breast were made for and what he did to them nearly sent me into a climax and he hadn't even penetrated me.

Foreplay with Noah was better than any main course I ever had with Robert Graham. Robert and I had not parted on the best of terms and it wasn't that that colored my experience with him. All along it was me that tainted that relationship. It never stood a chance because Noah was always in my heart and always on my mind. To this day, everything with Robert felt like I was cheating on Noah. This, with Noah, didn't feel like cheating at all. It felt like my favorite version of everything in the world wrapped altogether.

Finally, I was near begging when Noah lowered himself to me and I rose to meet his lips. I had never wanted anything more than I wanted him. I was so distracted by the exploration of his tongue that I didn't realize he had taken hold of my hands. The first I knew of my fingers being entwined with his was when he entered me. The thrust of his pelvis and the grip of my hand were simultaneous. The pressure in the clasp of our palms came and went with thrust and retraction. It was a glorious multitude pleasure. With each thrust he slid his chest over mine and that just added to the sensation, the hairs of his chest tickling over me.

"Jesus Christ, Noah," I moaned as I could feel myself drifting toward a fever pitch.

"Not yet." His voice was controlled and low as he gave the direction.

This was more than I ever expected, more than I ever hoped for and I struggled to stop myself. "I can't."

Noah slowed to a stop, but didn't leave me. "Wait." The word was soft and begging.

I could hardly stay still. I didn't want to come down, but, at the same time, I wanted to please him.

With our eyes locked, Noah released my hand and brushed the sprigs of hair out of my face. "I don't want it to be over so soon with you."

Noah was so serious and his tone was that of fear or insecurity, like I might suddenly disappear. Tears began to make their way to my eyes and I bit them back. "You don't know by now? It will never be over with me."

I took his face in my hands. "Come here and let me kiss you."

Within moments Noah brought me to a climax. It was the explosion of every cell in my body, like something I really had been waiting forever to arrive and it was finally here. It was the Christmas of all Christmases. Only a moment more and Noah joined me. I was barely over my own and yet I could feel the pulse of him and the tightening of his arms around me.

We laid there still tangled in one another, still on top of the bed covers and with all of the lights on. We didn't move. We just breathed and rested. My face was pressed to his and his was buried in my hair.

"I love you, Gayle. I love you and I've never said that to anyone." Noah whispered and again I was reminded just how little he truly remembered of us because he had indeed said that to me before. He said it to me well before throws of passion.

We finally fell asleep around 4:30 in the morning. I slept the rest of the night in Noah's bed and in his arms. What I didn't sleep in was a borrowed t-shirt. I slept in nothing and that was a first. At 6:00 a.m. I rolled over and was awakened to the reminder that I was naked and so was Noah.

My head was on his shoulder and one of my legs was draped over one of his. Feeling his leg against my pubic area aroused me. I tried to ignore the feeling. I rubbed my eyes and looked for the source of the light in the room. It was so bright and I knew we hadn't left a light on and it was too early to be the sun.

I lifted my head and looked over toward the balcony doors. Unlike the ones in my room, they were closed, but the curtains were wide open. The light was from a passing cargo ship and it flickered through the panes of the doors as it floated up the Savannah River. Lights and multicolored freight containers, it was lit up like a Christmas tree. It was an amazing sight and despite it, I couldn't ignore the burning ache I had for Noah.

"Noah," I whispered and he barely stirred.

I inched my leg up his and my hand across his chest. I whispered again, "Noah, would you..."

I didn't even have to complete the question. Noah pulled me on top of him and this time was every bit as toe curling as the first time.

Who knows when I would have woken up had housekeeping not burst in the door? It was after 10:00 a.m. when I heard the key in the lock. There was hardly time for me to pull the sheet up to cover myself before I was staring down a three hundred pound lady in a maid's uniform. At least I think it was a lady. I had little more than the fact that the uniform was a dress to go on.

"Excuse me, Miss. Beggin' ya pardon. I didn't think no ones was in heah." Her hair was cropped short to her scalp and her voice was deep.

Noah was nowhere to be found and neither was the comforter. All I had over me was that paper thin white sheet. My clothes were still strewn about the room where Noah had tossed them. Oh, his were nice and neatly placed over the couch as he removed them, but mine were thrown to the four corners of the room, spoils of a conquest.

Her name tag said Percy and Percy didn't bat an eye. Mine on the other hand grew bigger by the second. She was unphased and started to tidy the room as I clutched the sheet and inched further and further to the back of the headboard. I'm sure she had seen it all and heard it all, but she hadn't seen or heard all of mine and I preferred to keep it that way.

"How you know, Mr. Walden?" Her wide nose twitched up and she cut her eyes at me as she dusted the television. She thought I was a hooker.

I answered as if it was any of her business. "We were high school sweethearts."

"Umm hum." She grunted, nodded her head and looked altogether like she smelled something rotten. "You don't look like no high school girl."

399

Thank heavens for the sound of the key in the door again. This time it was Noah and he had coffee and doughnuts in hand.

"Ah, I see the two of you have met." He seemed pleased that we had made some grand acquaintance. "Ms. Percy has been taking such good care of me during these last few days that I've threatened to steal her away from The River Street Inn."

Noah moved around the room, sitting down the breakfast items. The box of doughnuts was placed on the end of the bed and the coffees on the nightstand before he walked over to her and took out his wallet. "Oh if only she was interested in moving to Washington. Gayle, tell her it's beautiful."

Did no one else in the room gather that I was completely naked were it not for that sheet? Was I the only one there that was the least bit uncomfortable? If I had completely lost my mind, I would have gotten out of that bed and strutted to the bathroom just to prove the point. I had not lost my mind and there was no point worth proving that badly. I comforted myself with the thought that this had to end soon. Noah would tip her and she would be on her way.

I was wrong. Noah offered her doughnuts and they carried on a conversation about how lovely Washington was.

"You know, it was one of the few cities that survived Sherman's march to the sea," he went on as he started to pick up my clothes and sit them out of her way. "Everyone likes to talk about Madison and how it survived, but there's more to the Antebellum South than Madison."

"I've got people from up around Madison, but I haven't been there in years," Percy kept up her end of the conversation while she dusted.

Neither of them took the hint by the look on my face that I was mortified and I feared she was going to start stripping the bed with me still in it. Finally, I couldn't take it anymore.

"Noah, would you mind getting me a robe?"

"Jesus, I'm sorry, Gayle." He immediately apologized to both me and Percy. "Ms. Percy, this is just fine. The room is fine. It's been great visiting with you again."

Noah tipped her ten dollars and sent her on her way. She was all smiles and thank yous to him, but didn't say to words two me, not kiss my foot or nothing. As soon as the door shut behind her Noah went about getting the robe for me.

"I don't need the thing now!" I got out of bed and marched to the bathroom.

Noah found the situation comical and laughed as I made my grand exit.

"She thought I was a hooker!" I yelled from the toilet.

"No!" He choked out through his chuckling.

"Yes!" I paused to finish and wash my hands and put on the courtesy robe that had been hanging behind the door. I threw open the door to the bathroom. "Oh my God, yes, she did. She thought I was a hooker! I could just die!"

Noah stopped laughing. His tone changed and he came to me and took my hand. "I'm sorry, Gayle. I'll tell her. I'm so sorry. Don't be mad."

"I'm not mad. I'm embarrassed. In all of my years, I have never been mistaken for a whore before." I could feel that my face was still every shade of red and I could do nothing but join in laughing at the situation.

"I love to hear you laugh. If candy made noise, your laughter would be what it sounded like."

Noah whirled me around and into his arms. I melted. What man says stuff like that? Had he spent the last twenty years reading women's romance novels? Was he about to make love to me again? I wouldn't object.

Noah had a way of gripping the hair at the base of my skull that sent my mind spinning. It was that force that let me know he meant to kiss me and kiss me good. It let me know who was in control and it wasn't me. Strangely enough, I liked it when he let me know he was in control.

When Noah finally slipped his lips free, he cradled my head over his shoulder and held me. "What would you like to do today?" He asked as he caressed my cheek with his. He still hadn't shaved and the stubble tickled.

I remembered that he was down there on business and, although I didn't want to pour salt in his wounds, I was concerned that I didn't keep him from anything.

"Do you need to do anything else regarding the plane?" I didn't want to say the family or the crash. I tried to be as considerate as possible with my question.

"I made all of the arrangements yesterday for..." Noah let go of me and walked to the bed.

It was still a sensitive subject for him. He picked up the box of doughnuts and took one out. "Would you like one?"

He still didn't turn around, but I could tell Noah wiped his eyes. I went to him and draped myself around him, tucking my arms under his and laid my head over his shoulder. He let the half eaten doughnut drop to the bed and wrapped his arms around mine.

"You don't have to turn around." I was certain he didn't want me to see him shed tears and I didn't want to press him.

Finally, he did turn around. "I want to tell you something that I've never told anyone."

Noah took my hand and led me to the couch. He gestured for me to sit and I did. He followed. "I am begging you not to judge me."

Noah leaned over and propped his elbows on his knees. The entire time he spoke he held my right hand in both of his and focused on tracing the veins in the top of it over and over again.

"I dated John's wife before they got married. John's mother is my land lord and he was probably the first friend I made when I moved to Washington. We were friends way before I met Julie. It wasn't anything serious between us. I've never been able to have anything serious with anyone. Anyway, Julie and I broke up and after a few months and me assuring John that I didn't have any problems with him asking her out, they started dating."

Noah glanced up at me. "Gayle, this wasn't my finest moment and, if I could change it I would." He shook his head in that manner that people do when they are seeking understanding.

I was starting to gather where this might be going, but I didn't say anything other than, "Noah, you can tell me anything."

I rubbed his back with my free hand and hunched over with him.

Noah started again. "I don't know how it happened. They were engaged and the wedding was only weeks away and she showed up at my place one night. They had a fight and I was drunk. That's no excuse, but I haven't drunk anything stronger than a Coke since. Gayle, I don't know why I did it. Of course she swore me to secrecy and I loved John like a brother. I know that sounds hard to believe after what I've just said I did."

Noah didn't say what he did, but I understood. I knew he had slept with her. It made my blood curdle at the thought of him with someone else.

"They weren't married three weeks before Julie announced she was pregnant. Honeymoon baby is what everyone thought."

I snatched back my hands and covered my face. I slid them down until only my gaped open mouth was still covered. Noah's eyes were on me, studying my reaction.

"I kept the promise I made Julie. I never told anyone until this very moment. Oh, God, Gayle, that child was mine. I'm certain of it. Any fool could look at her and tell. Even yesterday. Oh God, even yesterday, I could tell."

Noah's eyes swelled with tears and he dropped to his knees and hid his face in my lap. I rubbed my fingers through his hair and held him as he cried. "What kind of person am I? She died and she never knew. Short of you, she's the only other person on this Earth that I have ever truly loved."

I let him have his cry. I let him get it out of his system. I let him mourn his daughter. I could not imagine what he must have been going through these last few days. My heart shattered at the thought of him having to identify her little body. Tears streamed down my face as well, but I didn't dare take my hands off of him to wipe my face.

After about ten minutes, I lifted Noah's face to look at me. His eyes were like looking into blue flames, their usual tint and bloodshot from crying.

"We all make mistakes. It's how we rise above them that defines us." I did my best to comfort him, but how could one be comforted in a situation like this?

"I'm a horrible person. I'm a horrible person and you should probably run as far away from me as you can."

"I'm not going anywhere. Noah, you did the right thing. Yeah, it started out all wrong, but you rose above. By honoring your word not to tell, you allowed her to have a stable loving family. What sort of life would she have had if you had told? You put her needs above your own. You gave her a family."

"But I didn't acknowledge her as mine?" Noah whimpered.

"What good would have confessing have done? Eased your conscious a little? That's not love. That's selfishness. You were in her life as much as possible, right?"

"Of course."

"I have a feeling she knew you loved her and even though it wasn't the love of a father that she knew from you, she knew you loved her and that's what matters."

"You don't think I'm a coward?"

404

"Not at all. I think you made the best of a bad situation." I wiped the tears from his cheeks. "I cannot tell you how sorry I am for your loss. I'm so sorry, Noah, and I will never tell a soul anything that you just told me and you can always talk to me about her."

"I cannot believe you aren't disappointed in me."

I smiled at him. "You're not getting rid of me that easily."

CHAPTER 23

After sitting with his head in my lap for the better part of an hour, Noah finally pulled himself together.

"Let's get you dressed and go do some touristy things," Noah suggested.

I didn't dare say no to him. I felt so sorry for him that there's nothing I would have denied him. I was sure if I was in his situation I would have needed to do something to take my mind off of things as well.

Noah stood and helped me up.

"Thanks." I smiled at him and caressed his cheek. "My things are still in my room. I'm gonna scoot down there and shower and change, okay?" I pulled my robe tight and started toward my clothes that Noah had piled up while Ms. Percy was in the room.

That's when Noah put me to the test about denying him and he didn't even know it. "What do you say we let that room go and you stay in here with me?"

I had just laid hands on my dirty clothes from last night when he asked. For a split second, I thought about the night before and what all had transpired between us. What was the harm in staying in his room at this point? Plus, I would do anything to make things easier on him right now.

I looked over my shoulder and tried to reply before he thought I was having to consider it. "Are you sure?"

"I am," he nodded. "I want you here with me."

"Alright, but how long are we staying? I need to call home and let Aunt Dot know where I am." I rolled my eyes remembering that I hadn't told a soul I was going anywhere. "If she's figured out that I'm not there, I'm already in trouble."

Noah opened the door to the room for me. "We don't want that."

He didn't say anything as we walked the few feet down the hall, but I could tell he was thinking about something. After unlocking my door for me, Noah finally let me in on what he was wondering.

"How do you feel about staying through Saturday? They're doing..." He cleared his throat and forced the words out, "autopsies on the..."

"Right, I understand." I knew what he was getting at so I didn't make him go any further.

"Yeah, I planned on driving back behind them when they're transported home. I was told they'd be sent back on Saturday. Can you be away from work that long?"

I went on in and sat my dirty clothes next to my duffle bag. I turned around to find Noah taking a seat on the couch. This time I didn't have to invite him in. He followed me in and the conversation continued.

I didn't even have to think about my answer. "Sure, I can stay."

Noah waited in my room while I showered. I took the cordless phone from beside the bed into the bathroom with me. I called Aunt Dot as I got undressed. She was stunned at the news, but elated for me. Gleefully, she agreed to take care of my animals for me and field any calls from my customers. I wasn't gone often, but when I was, she knew to refer my clients to Dr. Bob. I promised Aunt Dot I would tell her every single detail as soon as I got home and reluctantly she agreed not to press me further at that moment.

The rest of the time I was in there all I could think about was that I could never understand what he must be feeling. I lost track of time and had my own good cry while the warm water flowed over me. I didn't want to keep him waiting, but I couldn't control myself. I held my face in my hands to muffle the sounds of my sobs. I didn't want Noah to hear me. I certainly didn't want him to worry about me in all of this.

They say there's nothing more devastating to a parent than having to bury a child. I didn't always buy into what "they say," but I believed this. It's against the laws of nature for a child to go first. I witnessed it first hand with my parents when my brother died. My mother and father were never the same.

I knew the heartbreak of losing my high school sweetheart, my parents and my brother, but that paled in comparison to what I suspected Noah was feeling. I couldn't fathom the loss of a child. I never had a child of my own. Millie was the closest I had ever come. I raised her and even though I nearly died last year when she was injured in the Olympic Park Bombing, did I think that came close to what Noah was going through? No, I didn't.

It wasn't the same at all. There was one fundamental difference. Millie lived and Noah's daughter didn't. If there was anything left to be said or fixed about my relationship with Millie I still had the chance to make that happen. Short of not sleeping with his best friend's girl in the first place, there was nothing I thought Noah should have done different with the child. Regardless of what I thought, there were no more chances for him to fix anything or do better by her. He would have to find a way to live with that regret. That was the price he would have to pay.

I finally collected myself and got out of the shower. As I looked at myself in the mirror while I dried my hair, I thought about Millie again. She was shattered when she first found out about Gabe's ex-girlfriend's pregnancy, utterly beside herself that another woman was having a child by Gabe. The fact that Noah admitted to me that he had a child by someone else had not phased me at all. I didn't care. I could think of a dozen women who would feel the same way Millie felt if they found out the man they loved had a child by someone else, but I wasn't one of them. I loved Noah and it didn't matter to me. I knew in my heart that had the child lived, I would have loved her for Noah's sake.

My makeup covered most of the signs that I had been crying, but like all of the women in my family it still showed in my eyes. I wasn't puffy and I didn't have dark circles around them. After each time I cried they turned this wild color of turquois.

When I finally emerged from the bathroom, I counted myself lucky that Noah was so glad to see me that he didn't notice my eyes or anything else that would have given away the fact that I had been crying. If he did notice, he was kind enough not to say a word.

"I was beginning to wonder if you fell in," Noah said in observance of how long I had taken to get ready.

"If you were so concerned, you could have come in and joined me." As soon as I finished the sentence I regretted saying it. After this morning's revelations, I wasn't sure if it was appropriate to tease him about sex. Last night was light and today was dark. I wanted things to be light again, but I certainly didn't want to infringe on his time of mourning or usurp his daughter's memory.

While I dwelled on what I said, I hardly heard Noah's response. "I didn't realize that was an option."

I was relieved I had not offended him and it was only an option in our banter. If he had come in, he would have caught me crying and that would have ruined the moment anyway.

I changed the subject, "Let's get out of here. I'll take my things to the other room while you call the front desk and release the room. Please tell them I'll be down the settle up in just a little while."

Noah walked over to the bedside table, took out his wallet and laid down a twenty dollar bill. "Don't worry about the room. I've already taken care of it."

Twenty dollars as a tip for the maid on the room that was hardly slept in was a bit much. The fact that he had already covered the charge on the room for me seemed a bit much as well.

"You shouldn't have done that, but thank you."

I resolved myself not to tell him how to spend his money, but I still wondered how he could afford it. I didn't care how much he had. That didn't matter. I could provide for the both of us with little to no effort at this point in my life. Of course, both of my parents would have spun in their graves at the notion that I would support a man, but I didn't care because this wasn't just any man. It was Noah, the love of my life. I would have gladly lived in a dirt hut on the sands of Egypt with him. It appeared I didn't have to worry about any of that, but I was still curious as to how he made his money.

Over lunch at Mrs. Wilkes Boarding House, which I insisted on being my treat, I worked the conversation around to the point of being able to satisfy my curiosity. "So, you know I'm a veterinarian and you've told me you have several planes, but what do you do for a living?"

At Mrs. Wilkes' the guests sat together like old friends and family. Despite that, Noah and I kept our conversation to ourselves. The waitress had just brought the food to the table and while passing the fried okra to the lady next to him, Noah began to explain to me what he did and how he came to do it.

"When I first got out of the service I was still recuperating from the accident. They told me there was little chance of me flying a plane again."

"I'm sorry," I shook my head. Every time he mentioned that he couldn't fly anymore, it broke my heart for him. "I'm sure you were devastated."

"I was, but clearly life was going to go on. I had to do something and farming was never my thing..."

"Plus, they were losing the farm," I added.

"Right, so two strikes against farming and the third strike was my need to be independent and away from my mother. My CO from the Air Force kept in touch with me. I couldn't have asked for a better mentor. Anyway, I couldn't fly, but there were other things that I could do related to planes. He used his connections and helped me get a job as a fueler at Daniel Field. For about six months all I did was drive a little tanker out and gas up the planes."

"Did you hate it?"

"What?"

"I don't know how you could be around a plane and not be able to fly. If I had to be around sick or hurt animals now and I

410

couldn't help them, it would kill me. So, as much as you loved flying, I don't know how you did it."

"I guess I just did what I had to do to survive. I had to feed myself somehow and I didn't' know much else. I guess I just figured being a pump jockey at an airport was better than being one at Jiffy Mart."

"I suppose you're right. You seem to have had such a great attitude about the accident and the aftermath."

"It wasn't always like that. I had my dark days after the accident too."

Noah continued eating and telling me his story while trying not to talk with his mouth full.

"After a while, I started taking classes at Augusta Tech and as soon as there was a spot open I went to work as a mechanic on the planes. All the while I saved my money and learned all that anyone was willing to teach me. I was a sponge. It didn't take long and I was the best mechanic there. It had been five years since the accident and one weekend the guy that ran the flight academy got killed. It was a real bad situation. Everybody loved the guy. One thing led to another and ultimately I moved into that spot. I couldn't get up in the air, but I could manage the program and all of the ground training."

I hung on Noah's every word as I ate bite after bite. "One afternoon, I was talking with one of the flight students, a banker from what was The Georgia Railroad Bank, and we were discussing how I needed to start investing my money instead of just letting it accumulate in a savings account. During the conversation, he mentioned he only took the flight lessons as something unique to put on his resume, but now that he had taken the classes he wished there was some way he could continue flying. He couldn't afford to buy a plane, but he could afford to rent one occasionally. Unfortunately, the only ones around for rent were the same ones for the flight school and they were constantly in use. On a whim, I decided that would be my investment. I bought my first plane in 1988 and by spring of 1992 I had five."

"In the spring of 1992, early June to be exact, I watched Millie graduate from high school," I interjected making a comparison between what both our lives were like back then.

"You had family and I had a business."

"Oh, don't be fooled. I had a business and I'm sure you had family, too."

"Not family like you had."

I was reaching for my tea, but changed directions and took Noah's hand. "Sometimes, family is where you make it and I have a feeling that you have a family. It just might not be the same as mine, but..."

Noah squeezed my hand. "I guess you're right, bu..."

Before Noah could finish the word, I cut him off much as he had just done to me. The difference was that I anticipated the dark place that line of conversation was about to take and I redirected the conversation.

"Is that John Cusack?" I discretely pointed across and two tables over.

My diversion worked. Noah glanced in the direction and responded. "Oh, yeah. He's filming a movie down here with Bridgett Fonda. I met her a couple days ago with Clint Eastwood."

"You met Clint Eastwood?" I nearly snorted the creamed corn that was in my mouth through my nose.

"He was taller than I expected and so was she." Noah paused and looked at me cross. "So you're more impressed with Clint Eastwood than John Cusack? Isn't he a little old for you?"

"Get your mind out of the gutter." I smacked Noah on the arm. "Daddy loved the Dirty Harry movies and those were the first movies we got on tape when we got a VCR. We watched those things over and over and over. When Millie wasn't watching Gone With the Wind, Daddy was watching Dirty Harry."

"I so envy you." Noah shook his head as he took another bite.

"Whatever for?"

"I would have killed for a family like yours."

We were back there again. What did I say now? I looked around the room for another celebrity to point out, but I didn't see anyone. The best I could come up with was, "It's not too late, you know."

"Not too late for what?" Noah didn't understand my meaning.

"For you to have a family like mine."

A few more minutes and dessert was served. We muddled through the rest of lunch in virtual silence. I hoped I had just given him something to think about and not upset him. As I cleaned my bowl of peach cobbler, I secretly said a prayer that I hadn't forced him to reflect on the loss of his daughter.

After lunch we walked around the squares of Savannah until we found a bench under the Spanish moss. The only time Noah let go of my hand was to wipe off the bench for me to sit down. The bench faced the fountain at Forsythe Park and we sat there for the remainder of the afternoon talking about everything under the sun. There was a breeze on the air and I could smell the salt of the ocean.

Part of the afternoon I spent with my head on Noah's shoulder and the other I spend sitting, facing him. I'm not sure which position I liked better, the feel of his shoulder under my cheek or watching the light dance in his eyes as he told me about being medically cleared to fly again.

"Last year I got my wings back."

I just assumed from everything he said so far that he never been allowed to fly again, but I was mistaken. Hearing that was the highlight of the afternoon. Tears of joy filled my eyes when he told me.

"Are you crying?" he asked as he reached and gently wiped a tear from my cheek.

I stuttered through the words, "I always blamed myself for taking that from you."

"Why? It wasn't your fault."

"It was. If I hadn't insisted we go to the rock quarry that night none of this would have ever happened to you or to us."

"No, Gayle, it was an accident. You didn't do this to me."

"Honestly, you told me on the way there that you weren't the greatest swimmer and I" I paused to sniffle. "Well, if we hadn't gone things would have been so different for us. You would have had the family you deserved. You would have had me and my family and I would have had you."

Noah pulled me into his arms and held me tight. "No, Gayle. It wasn't your fault and we have each other now. Things are going to work out the way they are supposed to. I could never blame you and you shouldn't blame yourself."

"But..."

"No buts. We're together now and I'm never going to let you go. If I had known where to find you sooner, I would have come for you. None of this is your fault." The entire time Noah whispered in my ear, he stroked my hair.

I finally regained control of myself and Noah and I went back to talking about things that were not life shattering. I learned what he did other than buying and renting out planes. He had his own business working on small aircraft engines as well. He also did a little crop dusting and aerial photography.

Noah and I continued to talk and the hours passed in a flash and before we knew it the street lights were starting to kick on. Noah finally stood and offered me his hand.

"I guess we should start back."

414

"I suppose." I was reluctant to leave. I just wanted to stay in that moment with Noah for as long as possible.

On the walk back, Noah mentioned dinner. "I'll take you wherever you want to go. What would you like tonight?"

The answer was that I wanted him, but I couldn't bring myself to say it. I covered my real answer and asked, "Why don't we just order in?"

"Room service?"

"Sure. I've never had room service before."

"Then there's no time like the present."

The rest of the walk back, we weren't just holding hands. We were entwined with one another in our every step. Our hands were clasped and arms wrapped to the point that there was friction from my shoulder to my elbow with every move.

Inside the River Street Inn we came to the elevator and Noah suggested, "Let's take the stairs."

"I'd rather not." I winked at him and pressed the button to call the elevator car.

Noah looked surprised, but not as surprised as we both did when the door of the elevator opened and the same blue haired lady that had busted us the night before started out. Her nose was as high in the air as it had been the night before and Noah cut his eyes at me and tried not to snicker. She didn't remember us, but we remembered her. I don't know what came over me, but I grabbed Noah and kissed him. With my arms around his neck and a leg wrapped all around him, I really put it on him. I had been saving that for the elevator, but I went for it there in front of the old snob and forced her to notice us.

"Excuse me!" She drew out the words to emphasize how offended she was by our display.

I pulled back from Noah just enough to utter the words, "No, excuse us," and I drew out the words as well.

415

Noah pulled me into the elevator and what started out as a game to irritate the grand dame of the super snobs, was no longer a game. We made out like teenagers from the time he pinned me to the back wall of the elevator car all the way to the room. I don't know how Noah managed to unlock the door. He might as well have been blindfolded with me draped all over him and already starting to unbutton his shirt.

This time was different. I hadn't just driven two and a half hours. It wasn't the middle of the night. I was rested.

Noah kicked the door shut as soon as we were inside and pulled me tighter to him. I bit his bottom lip gently as he eased his hands up under the hem of my shirt. Every inch of me seemed to stand on end as his hands inched up my bare back, floating over my skin. It tickled and titillated at the same time.

I feared earlier that he might be too distraught to touch me again the way he had the night before. I wasn't insensitive to what he lost, but I had just found him after all these years and I wanted him. In this moment, I was relieved that he still wanted me.

I clinched to Noah, my chest pressed to his. We moved in sync as we breathed in and out in a rhythm together. I raised my hands signaling Noah to keep inching his hands up, taking my shirt with them.

"I still cannot get over how beautiful you are," Noah sighed as he planted kisses over my shoulder along my bra strap.

I shrugged my shoulder and let the strap fall. Millie explained once that every time Gabe touched her it was like sending a little lightning bolt through her. Noah's lips sliding over my shoulder, his fingers just inside the waist of my pants as he felt his way around to unbutton them sent a vibration straight to my core. I didn't understand what Millie meant before, but I understood now.

Everywhere he went those tiny little hairs that covered my body stood on end. They followed him, bending like branches in the wind as his touch went from one to the next. It was an electric sensation and he was the only power source.

I forgot about ordering dinner as I devoured him and he devoured me. I was near my wits end with pleasure and I could not hold it in. I screamed and covered my mouth, mindful that the walls of most hotels were paper thin. I wasn't sure if that was the case at the River Street Inn, but I certainly didn't want anyone else to hear.

"I've never had that effect on anyone before," Noah laughed and held me down. He toyed with me, intent on making me scream again.

I squirmed as his touch sent the sensation through me for a second time. Twenty minutes later and he gave it to me for a third time.

I don't remember what time it was when I fell asleep, I remember it was in Noah's arms and, despite the shower, I could still smell the hint of Clubman on him. If I died in my sleep, it would be with a smile on my face.

I didn't die in my sleep. The red letters of the alarm clock that was on the bedside table faced me. Aside of the little bit of light shining through the curtains to the balcony, the light from the alarm clock was all there was in the room. It was 4:13 a.m. and I was still so tired that I couldn't decide if I was really hearing Noah's voice or if I was just dreaming.

The covers were pulled up to my shoulder and that was all that we had on. I was lying on my side. Noah's arm was around me and his hand rested against my belly. My knees were bent and I could feel his tucked in behind me and his chest was pressed to my back. I could feel him breathe in and out in rhythm with me. My hair was up over the pillow and my face and neck were bare. There was a chill in the room from the air conditioning, but, under the covers, Noah was a heater next to me.

With his every word a vibration floated over my neck. It tickled, but I didn't move. I'm not sure how long he had been talking to me, but I could tell he didn't think I was awake. I consciously started to hear him in the middle of a sentence.

"...how much I love you? So much that it surprises me and I don't understand it. Have I been in love with you all this time? I

417

never thought I was the marrying kind, but you told me we were married when you were just a teenager. We were just silly kids."

Noah moved his hand and ran from my belly down my hip. "My God, who could resist you?"

I was flattered as he seemed to be admiring me and I became aroused from his touch. I could tell he counted on me being asleep and, although he asked questions, he had no intention of me answering them. I stayed as still as I possibly could and listened.

"I've never thought of myself as the marrying kind. Maybe I was the marrying kind, but deep down somewhere in me I always knew I was married to you? No, that's stupid. I can't stand cheaters and that would mean I was a cheater."

I nearly gasped. The thought of Robert Graham popped into my head and I just wanted to die. I cheated.

Noah went on, "No, I'm not the marrying kind. We weren't married. I didn't cheat. None of that counts."

He paused. I'm not sure what he could see, but I was certain he was looking at me. It was so dark I couldn't see a thing, but what was glowing red sitting near the clock. It was as if he was trying to convince himself. He was making me nervous.

Noah took a deep breath and finally spoke again. He repeated himself. "I'm not the marrying kind, but, now that I've found you, it's all I think about. Every day with you is better than the day before. I don't know what's come over me, but I hang on your every word."

It was funny that he said that because I was holding my breath and hanging on his every word at that very moment. My heart was racing and, as much as I wanted to hear his thoughts, and he was putting those out there in spades right then, I wanted to roll over to him. I couldn't get enough of him.

"Madelyn would have loved you. I wish you could have known her."

It took me a moment to realize who Madelyn was, but that was his daughter.

"Of course you couldn't have known Madelyn without knowing Zoe. Zoe looked like Julie, but Maddie looked like me. Luckily Julie and I had the same coloring so everyone just assumed Maddie looked like Julie's side of the family. I knew better. She looked like photos of my mother when she was a child, right down to the curls in her hair. She was sweet and tenderhearted. I could never see my mother as either of those things."

"Zoe was one of those children that if you turned her one way, she looked just like her mother, but a second later and another look at her and she looked just like her father. She looked like John and his side of the family. Zoe wore glasses from the time she was two years old and she was shy compared to Maddie."

"You would have loved both of them, but they wouldn't have liked you right away. They never liked the women I brought around. No one was ever good enough, but they would have warmed up to you. I know they would have."

"I still can't believe they're gone..."

Noah pulled his hands from me and rolled over to the other side of the bed. He didn't say anything else, but I could hear him sniff back. He had done well not to dwell on it all day and he had amazed me in that regard. I could tell he was losing it now and I couldn't take it. I couldn't just lay there and pretend to be asleep anymore. I rolled over and wrapped myself around him.

"Noah, I'm so sorry. It's going to take some getting used to the idea of them being gone."

"Zoe didn't have her glasses yesterday. I've got to find her glasses for her. Julie gets mad with her when she loses her glasses."

"Noah," I said patiently. "I'm so sorry."

"And Maddie can't sleep without Mr. Fuzz. She takes him everywhere. I've got to find him. That stuffed rabbit looks like

419

science project on germs, but she's had it since she was born. I've got to find it."

I held tighter to Noah and he cried. I cried too as I explained to him, "They're with Jesus now and Zoe won't need glasses in Heaven and Mr. Fuzz is already there and he's a real bunny, like in the book, <u>The Velveteen Rabbit</u>. They've all got their wings in Heaven and Zoe will never be in trouble about glasses again and Maddie will never be without Mr. Fuzz."

"Gayle?"

"Yes, Noah," I sniffed to clear my nose.

"Do you think in Heaven John knows what I did? Do you think he knows about Maddie? Am I going to Hell, Gayle?"

"That doesn't matter in Heaven. All is forgiven there."

"How do you know?"

"Because there's no such thing as grudges and regrets there. Everyone's so thankful to be there and they're too busy meeting the Lord and loved ones that have gone before us to even worry with things like that. Do you think that when I get to Heaven I will think once on your mother and how she wronged us? I won't. I'll be too starry eyed over my parents and my brother waiting at Heaven's gate to welcome me."

"You're certain you are going to Heaven. I wish I was certain."

"I'm not certain. I am hopeful. I want to see my family again and I would give anything for that. Up until recently, I thought you were already there so I was looking forward to seeing you there, too."

"I'm not sure I'm going there."

"I don't understand why you think you wouldn't go to Heaven, but even so, it's not too late to change that."

Noah only elaborated to say that he didn't think he would get to heaven because of what he had done to John and the fact that he

420

lived a lie for so long. I assured him that he more than made up for it by never telling.

"I don't condone lying, but what was the lesser of the evils? I asked you earlier this morning, would you have had Maddie grow up without a father and a shamed mother so you could have cleared your conscious? Would you feel better now if you had confessed and John had left Julie and the baby all so you could have been a part-time father? If all of this is about what would make you feel better, then, yeah, you're probably going to Hell."

I eased out of the bed. I had to use the restroom and on my way across the room I explained to him again. "What you did by not speaking up was selfless. I am proud of you having made the best of a bad situation and at a personal cost to you. You did what was right for your child despite how it affected you and even if no one other than me and you knows about it, that's something to be admired about you." I shut the door behind me.

When I came out and returned to the bed, I found Noah sitting up. Noah reached over and pushed back the covers for me to climb back into bed. "I think you're the only person who's ever told me they were proud of me."

"I'm proud of you and I'm heartbroken for you over losing them, but now's not the time to second guess your decision. I just hate all of this for you."

Noah pulled me close to him and pressed his forehead to mine. "I love you, Gayle, and I don't know what I did to deserve these last few days with you. I don't know how I'd survive this without you."

Our conversation faded and we went back to sleep, spooning again.

The next morning we awoke to the ringing phone. Noah remembered to put out the do not disturb sign so it wasn't housekeeping that rose me that morning. It took a couple of rings, but the phone got the job done that Ms. Percy had done the morning before.

Unlike the morning before, I found Noah still there in the bed with me. It was 10:00 a.m. and I had slept like a baby. I couldn't recall the last time I had slept that late two mornings in a row.

On the third ring, Noah answered the phone. I sat up in the bed and listened. I could tell from his end of the conversation that the morgue was finished with the bodies and they were releasing them.

"So 1:00 p.m.?"

I didn't hear their answer, but Noah assured them we would be there, wherever "there" was and we would be "there" by 1:00.

As soon as he hung up, Noah filled in the gaps of the conversation. "I know I said we would stay through Saturday, but they're being sent home to Washington today and I..."

"It's okay. I understand."

Noah leaned over and kissed me. "Thank you," he said as he stroked my cheek. The sincerity oozed from him eyes.

It was kind of like cutting short my honeymoon and I was a little disappointed, but I would never let him know that.

We hurriedly got dressed and packed and checked out. We took one last walk down River Street after loading our bags in our respective cars and found a café.

Yesterday had been so sunny that I was blinded each time I took my sunglasses off. Today was the opposite. It was damp and overcast. Outside of the River Street Inn we strolled along among the other images in what appeared to be a black and white movie.

We had breakfast and still had an hour and a half before Noah had to meet the van that would be transporting the bodies. To kill time we walked in a few shops along the street.

In one of the shops Noah found a case containing vintage baseball cards. As Noah perused the cards, I wandered around the shop. I found a case that held jewelry, in particular a ring that caught my eye. For a moment, I thought it was my mothers. I was so convinced that it was her ring, which I knew was not possible as she had been buried with it on her hand, that I called the shop owner to pull it out for me.

As soon as the frail lady pulled it from under the glass, I could easily tell it wasn't mothers. The center stone was the clearest diamond I'd ever seen and when she put it in my hand, it was the largest I'd ever held. I should have easily noticed how much bigger it was than my mother's, but I hadn't seen hers in close to fifteen years. This was just an example of how the details of my mother were beginning to fade from my mind. Before I could feel too guilty about my slipping memory, Noah called my name. I immediately handed the ring back to the shop keeper.

"Gayle, you've got to see this," Noah insisted.

I wandered over to where he was hunched over the case of cards. "Look," he pointed, "Francisco Cabrera."

I looked, but short of Babe Ruth, Mickey Mantle, Hank Aaron or a couple of the current Braves players, I had no idea who anyone was.

Noah's excitement was lost on me. "Remember in 1992 when the Braves went to the World Series?"

I shrugged my shoulders.

"In 1992 the Braves won the National League Series, the playoff games that sent them to the World Series. In the last game of the playoffs, Sid Bream slid into home and that was the winning run that sent the Braves to the series. Everyone remembers the slide, but this guy, Francisco Cabrera, is the guy that hit the ball that allowed Sid to take home. It was a two out pinch hit over the shortstop's head to left field. It brought in David Justice and behind Justice was Sid Bream. Barry Bonds, of the Pirates, recovered the ball and threw it home, but Sid slid and the Braves took the pennant. I'm buying this card."

Noah proceeded to settle up for the card and, while the clerk made his change, he asked me if I found anything.

"No, not really," I replied.

"I thought I saw her take something out for you." Noah put his change back in his wallet, but kept it out as if he wasn't really done shopping.

"It was nothing." I wasn't about to tell him I was looking at rings.

"Alright then." Noah put his wallet in his pocket and we wandered back out on to River Street.

We were only about five paces away from the door when Noah stopped. "Do you mind if I run back inside and use the restroom? I'll only be a moment." Then he took out his wallet again and while handing me a ten dollar bill asked, "River Street Sweets is just right down there. Would you mind getting a pound of pralines for us to carry home? I've been craving those since I had a bite of yours the other night. I promise I'll share with you."

I thought nothing of his request. I agreed and took the money. He kissed me and we went our separate ways.

CHAPTER 24

Two days later we were on the front row at the graveside service. It was hotter than blue blazes. It was weather fit only for swimsuits and bare feet, not panty hose and heels.

The April sun was beating down and the chairs under the tent couldn't hold everyone one. Neither Noah nor I felt right about taking a place reserved for family. Both of us tried offering our seats to elderly ladies, but Mrs. Weatherby, who insisted we take the seats to begin with, refused to let go of Noah's hand and he refused to let go of mine. Mr. Nelson, Julie's father, sat at the end of the row followed by her mother and then John's mother, Mrs. Weatherby. Noah sat next to Mrs. Weatherby and I sat next to him. Julie's pregnant cousin sat on the end of the aisle next to me. Sitting on the front row wasn't the only thing that Mrs. Weatherby insisted upon.

Although they lived in Athens, the family plot was in Washington and that's where the service took place. There was no church service so Noah and I agreed to meet at the graveside and he was waiting for me when I turned into the beaten down grassy area reserved for parking.

Noah opened the car door for me and immediately began to apologize for what he was about to ask. "I am supposed to play "Taps" for John today and one of Julie's cousin's was supposed to sing. She's not going to be able to do it. She's understandably overcome with grief. I told John's mother that you would do it. Would you mind terribly?"

Noah seemed to be holding it together just fine so what was I supposed to say? Naturally, I would do it. "What would you like for me to sing?"

"Can you sing 'How Great Thou Art'? It was her favorite hymn."

Of course I agreed. There wasn't anything I would not have done to make this easier for Noah or any of the folks there to pay their respects.

As the sermon drug on I became concerned that I was going to be overcome with grief if the minister didn't hurry up and break for me to sing. He went on and on about the potential the girls had and how their lights had been snuffed out far too early. He described them almost exactly as Noah had, Zoe with her glasses and Maddie dragging Mr. Fuzz by the ear everywhere she went. I was thankful that the caskets were all closed, but I wondered if Noah had managed to get Mr. Fuzz from the wreckage and put him in the casket with the poor thing.

Whether anyone else knew why or how much, he loved that child and would have gone to gates of Hell for her. Although I was certain Noah found Mr. Fuzz, the preacher drug on and I couldn't help, but worry if that child had her bunny. I thought of Millie as a little girl and Nick, the brown Teddy Bear Mama bought her with green stamps. He was a reward for her being a brave girl at the hospital when she had her tonsils removed. Millie carried that bear everywhere until she was almost fourteen years old.

I could feel the tears starting to build in my eyes as I compared Millie and Maddie. If I cried there was no way I would get through the song. I looked around the graveyard for things to distract me. The thing I found to focus on was a statue of little a cherub looking angel. It was concrete covered in moss, but it still looked just like Gabby. Focusing on the little statue, picturing Gabby worked and before I knew it the preacher introduced me.

I made it through the song with not one crack of my voice and not one note off key. I had a lot of practice with that song. It was one of Daddy's favorite and at every opportunity he had me sing it at church.

When I finished we were all asked to bow our heads for prayer. We did and that's when Noah took his place among the headstones in the distance. The first three notes rang out and I was transported back in time. I closed my eyes and I could see him standing among the headstones the day Andy was buried. The angle of his elbow when he held the bugle, the prestige of his uniform and the pride with which he stood so stiffly as he played, was the moment I first fell in love with Noah Walden.

The notes rang out through the stillness of the heat. That he made it through the song was amazing. Although almost every person approached me at the end of the funeral to tell me how beautiful my song was, I scarcely heard them. I thanked them of course, but all I wanted to do was get to Noah and tell him how well I thought he did.

I could see him and there were twenty people milling around between us. I started to make my way to him when someone grabbed me by my wrist.

"I would recognize you anywhere. I might have known you would one day be back in the picture."

I didn't have to turn around to recognize the voice. The scar on the back of my neck from the night of Noah's accident, the night she snatched the chain from around my neck, caught fire as if she had taken a match to it. There was a snake that still lived in her throat that hissed venom when she spoke. It was Noah's mother and even though it had been twenty years coming this wasn't the time or place to deal with her.

I didn't dignify her with a response. I didn't even turn around. I yanked away from her and picked up the pace toward Noah.

"I don't know who you think you are. How dare you walk away from me!" She followed me and I refused to turn.

I was almost to Noah when Mrs. Weatherby noticed who was behind me and caught me by the arm. I was whirled around to face Noah's mother. This was the first time I had seen her since the hospital. Some folks age like a fine wine, but not Mrs. Walden. She aged like milk.

"Well, Nancy Walden, as I live and breathe." Mrs. Weatherby announced. "I thought you said you'd never set foot in Washington, Georgia again. Oh forgive me, where are my manners? Have you met Noah's friend Ms. Anderson? She did such a lovely rendition of How Great Thou Art, don't you agree?"

Mrs. Walden, or whatever her name was now, rolled her eyes. It appeared Mrs. Weatherby had her number.

Mrs. Walden wasn't taller than me or Mrs. Weatherby, but she had a way of looking down her nose at us regardless of that fact. She was a small wicked woman that wore bitterness so thick on her face that no amount of Estee Lauder could cover it. I wasn't sure if she wore all black as that was proper funeral attire or if that color just exuded out from the lump of coal that occupied the spot where her heart should have been.

Despite Mrs. Weatherby's attempt to intervene, Mrs. Walden had her sights set on picking a fight with me.

"Didn't you do enough damage to my boy all those years ago?"

I was wide-eyed, blinking back tears. My feelings weren't hurt over her accusation. Feeling as though I had caused Noah's accident was nothing new to me, but the notion of tolerating abuse of any kind from that woman was. The tears were simply frustration rising from me in liquid form.

I pursed my lips and flared my nostrils and took a deep breath. I did my best not to be sucked back to 1976 when I should have slapped her face to begin with.

It was a funeral and no good Southern funeral went without a fender bender, a congealed salad laced with food poisoning, a kiss on the lips of the corpse by a former love or licks being passed. As I stood there taking what Noah's mother was dishing, knowing the life she stole from Noah and I, I felt my palm twitch with the urge to ring her jaw. Noah saved me from being one of those people that made for a good funeral once before and just as I was about satisfy the urge to slap his mama, Noah saved me again.

Noah didn't say a word to her as he grabbed her above the elbow and drug her away from us. He simply said, "You'll have to excuse my mother."

Noah marched her away and she protested as they went, but it appeared he only tightened his grip and clinched his jaw harder.

"Some people just don't know when to shut-up!" Mrs. Weatherby said in a voice loud enough to taunt Mrs. Walden.

Mrs. Walden whipped her head around and glared at us. I smiled sweetly back at her. Mrs. Weatherby turned up her nose and gave Mrs. Walden an eat shit and die look. It was priceless.

"How dare she come to my son's funeral and show her ass like that!" She patted my hand. "You come on and distract me before I lose what's left of my mind and give all these folks a piece of my mind."

Mrs. Weatherby led me around to the church fellowship hall where the ladies had prepared a meal. Before we turned the corner, I looked back to check on Noah. I spotted him across the cemetery and on the far side of the parking area. He was standing next to a black Cadillac and he appeared to be giving his mother a good what for. I know it wasn't right for a man to ever strike a woman, but I can't say I didn't wish he would shake the shit out of her.

"I don't know half these folks," Mrs. Weatherby said when I turned back her way. "Most of them are Julie's people from over in South Carolina and the rest are John's business associates and a couple of friends. When you get to be my age, your friends that aren't dead are on lockdown at the nursing home."

"You're sure taking all this pretty well," I observed as I held the door for Mrs. Weatherby to go enter the hall.

"That's 'cause I've been eating Valium like it's M&Ms."

I was shocked at the matter of fact way she confessed. I almost laughed out loud.

We fell in to the buffet line and there wasn't a soul in the room that didn't stop Mrs. Weatherby along the way and pay their condolences once more. She was so sweet to each of them, but in between them she gave me a commentary. Comments ranged from, "Associate at the firm" and "Some relative of Julie's," and my personal favorite, "I don't have the faintest idea." Not once did she point out a relative of her and her son's.

At the end of the line we picked up a red solo cup of sweet tea and there was a brief break in people approaching her. I took that opportunity to ask her about her family or lack thereof.

"My husband was an only child and so was I. We had another son, Jimmy, but he died when John was a baby. John was by all accounts an only child until Noah came along. Even though they were in their twenties when they met, it was as if they were long lost brothers. Noah became the closest thing to family we had around these parts."

"So you all aren't originally from Washington?"

"No. My husband was an insurance agent by trade, but in his spare time he fancied himself a Civil War buff. He moved us down here from Ashville to search for the lost Confederate gold. I would have followed that man anywhere and anywhere just happened to be Washington, Georgia."

I knew I just met her, but I confided in her anyway, "I know what you mean. I'd live in a two room shack just to be with Noah."

Mrs. Weatherby smiled at me and gave me a little wink. "You'll never have to worry about living in a shack as long as you're with Noah."

I don't think what she said had anything to do with her being his land lord.

We found our seats and I asked if we should wait on Noah and she advised against it. "He hasn't seen that thing that calls herself his mother in I can't remember how many years so they might be a moment." Mrs. Weatherby shook her head, "That tart's always had fine timing."

Mrs. Weatherby and I continued to make conversation. I still couldn't get over how at ease she was. My mother was not at all like this when Andy died. I really did hope it was just the valium that had her so detached.

We were almost done eating when Noah walked through the door.

The funeral had been heart wrenching for me. There were four people lost, two of which were little more than babies, a whole family lost. I didn't know them and I didn't know Mrs. Weatherby, but I did know that she and Noah were coping so much better than I would in their situation. I couldn't imagine having lost my entire family all at once and that's what Mrs. Weatherby had been telling me. Regardless of the Valium and despite the choice words he might have had with his mother, I admired Mrs. Weatherby and Noah for the poise they carried themselves with today. Those were the things that came to mind when I laid eyes on Noah standing in the doorway of the fellowship hall looking for us.

After apologizing for taking so long, Noah told me, "You won't have to worry about her ever again."

"Don't worry about it. Mrs. Weatherby was kind enough to keep me company." I didn't know exactly what that meant and I dared not ask. Had he disowned her or just told her to leave me alone? It didn't matter then.

Noah could see through my words. By the look on my face, the stiff, forced smile and nodding of my head, Noah could tell I was curious about what had gone on between them in the parking lot. I was determined not to ask him, but no less relieved when between sips of tea, he leaned over and whispered to me, "I'll tell you later."

I smiled politely and we all continued with our lunch over stories of the family.

"Noah here's the only one I've got left." Mrs. Weatherby reached across the table and took his hand before she looked toward me and added, "Gayle, he's made his mistakes like the rest of us, but he's paid for those mistakes eight times over. He's one of the finest men I know."

Something she said made me think she might have known about his biggest mistake. She said he paid for them eight times over. Maddie was eight. Was she really talking to me or was she giving Noah the hint that she knew and telling him it was time to forgive himself? I had no idea, but it sure made me think. It made me think to the point that I realized I was sitting there with my mouth dropped open while they went on with the conversation.

We finished our lunches and Noah walked me to my car. He opened the door for me and questioned, "I should remember this car shouldn't I?"

"I had it in Savannah," I countered skeptically.

"No, from before," he clarified as I took my seat behind the wheel and he shut the door of the T-Bird.

The top as well as the windows were down and I looked up at him. "You should, but..."

"It didn't always look like this." Noah glanced from one end to the other, bumper to bumper, and back to me. "I sat right there where you are sitting. My arm was around you and your head was on my shoulder. The only thing that worked in the car then was the radio and we listened to it while the car was up on blocks in your daddy's barn one night."

"That's right." I couldn't conceal the surprise in my voice.

"I didn't dream that."

"So you remember?"

"Only a few things, but this has always been one of them. Long ago my mother did her very best to make me forget you and she came close to succeeding. In a way, she stole you from me and I told her I would never forgive her for that. She won't be bothering you ever again, Gayle, because I told her she was dead to me as dead as she tried to make me to you."

Noah leaned in the car and kissed me. "I've got some things to tend to around here, but I just wanted you to know that before you left."

I thought seeing his mother was the cherry on top a rotten day, but, driving home, not knowing when I would see him next was the real cherry on top.

Noah called me every night that week like clockwork. By Tuesday night when the phone rang at 9:00 p.m., I was already in my pajamas, in my bed with the cordless phone in hand waiting on

432

it. My stomach did flips each time I answered and heard his voice. We talked about everything imaginable. The few weeks since the tornado hit and he found me had been a crash course in getting to know each other again.

On Wednesday Noah asked me out on a proper date for Saturday night. I was disappointed that he was putting me off until then, but I didn't complain.

On Thursday, a letter arrived. I recognized the handwriting on the envelope. It was Noah's. I skipped over the date and the salutation and went right to the body of the letter.

My first few letters were written because I lacked the courage to tell you how I felt in person. It was too soon. It's probably too soon even now, but I'm not writing because I can't say the words to you in person. I'm putting this in writing so you can put these words in your box of keepsakes with the other letters that I wrote to you long ago. You can take this out years from now, hold it in your hand and allow me to tell you what you mean to me all over again.

If I made a list of things I would like to remember about you it would begin with what it was like to kiss you for the first time. I imagine standing on the porch of your house and taking your face in my hands and pressing my lips to yours. I'm certain it was the thrill of my young life. As I close my eyes tonight, I can picture you and feel your lips against mine. I would love to be able to remember the moment you told me about after your homecoming dance.

The second thing on the list wouldn't be taking your virginity; it would be waking up with you the morning after. It was such a joy to wake up next to you in Savannah that I can hardly comprehend the pleasure it would have been to have woke up next to you all this time. I would give anything to be twenty-one again and have my whole life to live over with you. I know I would have never let you go. Even now it's hard for me not to jump in the car and drive to wherever you are. It's near impossible to think of anything else.

There are so many other moments that you have told me about in the last few weeks that I wish I could remember and so many memories that we didn't have a chance to make. I feel as though I have been robbed.

Like I mentioned to you at the funeral; thank you so very much for never forgetting me. Thank you so much for never ceasing to love me. Thank you for being you because now I love more than I knew I was capable of loving.

I skipped over his signature and hugged the letter to my chest. Tears poured down my cheeks and I couldn't wait for his call that night. Like Tuesday night, I was snuggly in bed waiting his call. When it finally came through, I hit the receiver on the first ring and answered, "Hello?"

"I can't talk long tonight. I have an early morning meeting tomorrow, but I wanted to call and hear your voice."

I was a little disappointed that he had to cut it short tonight, but I didn't let it show. He said he wanted to hear my voice and I had an idea. "Do you have about five minutes?"

"Yes."

I got out of bed and took the phone with me downstairs. "You said you wanted to hear my voice so here comes. I'm going to put you on speaker phone, okay?"

Curiosity seeped through the phone. "Okay."

I sat the phone on the end table in the living room across from the piano and took a seat. I opened the cover from the keys and flipped to the page in my new book of music. I had heard the song tons of times, sang it to near perfection in the shower on multiple occasions, but I wasn't as gifted as Millie. I could sing it and match the melody, key and pitch, but she could hear a song once and recreate it on almost any instrument. I needed the sheet music to play along.

I turned to the page and laid my fingers on the keys required for the instrumental and began to play. I sang along with the piano and performed "Like We've Never Had a Broken Heart" by Trisha Yearwood. There were soft parts in which the piano nearly drowned out my voice, but there were other parts that flexed my vocal cords and reverberated off the walls of the living room.

I didn't really think about the words of the song when I chose it. I just thought about how Noah complimented me on my singing at the funeral. I wanted to show off for him and this was the first song that came to mind that would allow me to wow him with my talent. Part of the words applied, when I was with him it was easy to pretend, or forget even, that I had had a broken heart over him, but I never had to picture anyone else. Those things dawned on me as I sang, but it was too late to stop.

When I was finished I heard nothing but silence from the phone.

"Noah, are you still there?" I asked as I got up from the piano bench and started toward the phone.

"Yes, Gayle, I'm still here. That was amazing and now I'm going to have to either drive over to see you or go and take a cold shower."

I laughed and picked up the phone and released it from the speaker setting. "I'll leave the light on for you."

"Thanks and I wish I could come down tonight." That's when he said exactly what I was thinking, "I don't have to pretend you're someone else, but I've had to pretend they were you."

My hand went to my face. A nervous tick of mine when I was nervous was to either cover my mouth or just rub my hand over my forehead. I didn't know what to say.

"I have to go. I've got to run to Augusta early in the morning. I love you and I'll talk to you tomorrow night, okay?"

"Okay." I paused and worked up the courage to tell him. "There's only been one other than you and I tried to pretend he was you, but it just didn't work. They say there's nothing like the real thing."

I bit my lip and smiled with embarrassment. He couldn't see me, but I blushed over confessing that I had been with someone and now was giving him the slightest bit of information about that encounter.

"Let's agree not to talk about other experiences, alright."

"Fine by me!" I was eager to agree with that rule.

Friday came and I had Aunt Dot help me pick out the perfect outfit for Saturday night.

"Lord, girl, one would think you were sixteen again," she said as I pulled one hanger after another out of my closet and threw them across my bed.

We finished going through my whole wardrobe and I still couldn't settle on anything she put together. To solve the problem we decided to go shopping at the mall as soon as the car would get us there the following morning.

Unlike the prior nights of the week, I cleaned house for four hours while I talked on the phone with Noah. I managed to get out of him that he planned on taking me to Raley's in Mitchell. Raley's didn't warrant a new outfit, but he did.

I finished cleaning and the house was as close to being able to eat off of the floors as it had ever been. It was nearly midnight and I carried that trusty cordless phone right into the bath with me. Noah was still on the line. We didn't hang up until well after 1:00 a.m. That call ended like all others had since we returned from Savannah. He told me he loved me and I reciprocated the sentiment. The only difference was on Friday night there was something extra.

"Gayle," Noah said just as I was about to hang up, "I'm sorry I missed the last twenty years of being with you and I'm so thankful you never forgot me." He repeated what was in the letter from yesterday.

436

"I could never forget you." He was the love of my life. How could I forget him?

Saturday afternoon I straightened the pillows on the couch as I waited for Noah. I straightened the magazines and books on the coffee table and the frames hanging on the wall of the living room too. Noah said he would pick me up at 6:00 p.m., but I had been ready and fidgeting since 5:30.

The house was spotless, new sheets were on my bed, just in case. Along with a new outfit, I bought a new bed set while we were at J.B. Whites in Augusta. Aunt Dot joked that my new shirt and jeans were just like twenty others that I had hanging in my closet, but I didn't care. I liked what I liked, but to show her I wasn't afraid of leaving my comfort zone, I bought strappy black high heeled sandals instead of a new pair of cowboy boots. The sandals went perfect with my same old jeans and white shirt, but new cowboy boots would have gone just fine, too.

As I was tweaking the position of one of the accent chairs at the end of the couch, I heard the rumble of a car engine coming down the driveway. In one stride I was at the window, peeping from the crack between the curtain and the wall. My heart leapt at the sight. I felt lightheaded and my knees trembled. I steadied myself with a hand against the window frame and couldn't believe my eyes. It was midnight on wheels and the paint twinkled a thousand stars in the sunlight. It was Noah in his Camaro, the one he had when I was in high school.

As excited as I was to see that car a rush of relief washed over me. I always wondered what happened to that car. I worried about it because the last time I saw it, it was parked along the lower cliffs at the rock quarry the night of Noah's accident. I was so relieved he still had it. I had wanted to ask him what happened to it, but one thing always led to another and that was a subject we hadn't gotten around to yet.

The proper thing would have been for me to wait for him to park the car and come to the door, but we were past what was proper. I dashed from the window breezing back the curtain as I went. Through the living room, the foyer, out the front door and down the steps, I ran. Noah was barely out of the car and on his feet when I threw my arms around him.

"Gayle?" The unspoken question of "Are you alright?" was cloaked in just his mention of my name.

I let go of him and stepped back to admire the car, but Noah kept hold of my hand. "I'm so happy to see this car! I worried all this time about what happened to it."

I glanced back to catch him. Noah rolled his eyes, shook his head and twisted his mouth in a manner letting me know he was amused. "I still find it amazing how much you remember about me."

My face turned red with a hint of embarrassment. I guess I sounded a little obsessed. I let go of his hand and laid mine on the car. The paint was as slick with wax as I remember it being back then. I could see my reflection.

Noah followed as I walked along, looking at every inch of the car. I slid my hand along as I went.

"My mother sold the car before I was even out of the hospital."

I gasped. "No!"

"There was a time there when they really didn't expect me to pull through and she had the heir and the spare and then me so..."

"But you were her ticket back into the Augusta elite? You were supposed to marry the queen of fake Tupperware. I thought that's why she got rid of me. With your memory of me virtually erased, I thought getting you back together with, what's her name, would be a forgone conclusion."

"You really don't forget a thing do you?"

I cut my eyes back to him as I made the turn to go around the taillight on the driver's side corner. "Millie calls it the 'Magic Memory,' it runs in the family and always kept her from getting away with anything."

Snickers from Noah followed me. "Seriously, Gayle, Mama did try getting me back together with Mary Frances Kelly."

"Figures." I snarled my nose like I smelled something dead.

"It didn't work out."

"I can't imagine why."

"Really? You can't?"

Noah was as sarcastic as I was and I liked it, but I didn't want to continue with stories of what other nastiness his mother inflicted on him. The thought of that woman, and Mary Frances Kelly, made my stomach churn so I changed the subject.

"Looks like you bought the car back."

"I did." The guy that bought it stuck it in a barn to save for his kid. Rats ate the entire interior and it took me years to get it back to what you see here."

"That's awful, but it looks exactly the way I remember it." I rounded the next taillight and continued dragging my hand along the trunk as I went. I loved the feel of it.

I didn't look back, but I knew Noah stopped at the fender. I turned my gaze to the cab of the car ahead of me.

"I love cars," I started. "I'm a car person. There's something about them that are just extensions of a person to me. For a long time we had Andy's Corvette in the barn, even though he never drove it. It arrived on order from the factory after he died." I clarified as I stopped at the passenger's side door.

"Before Daddy gave the car to Millie, whenever I started to forget Andy or whenever I would have a situation that I wanted to discuss with him, I would go and sit in the Corvette. Millie never knew him, but she said on more than one occasion that she could feel her father in that car with her. I felt the same way. My mother would visit his grave and talk to him, but not me. I was never closer to him since he left us than when I was sitting in the passenger's seat, imaging taking a ride with him."

I continued, "My Thunderbird; it was Daddy's before it was mine. Even though he lived in the house with me, I never feel closer to him since he passed than I do when I drive that car. If I go too fast, I can almost hear him telling me," and I did the voice mimicking Daddy's, "'Slow it down, Gayle.'"

"As much as I love Andy's Corvette or my Thunderbird, there's never been a car that I wanted more than I wanted this one."

When I turned my head to Noah, I found him listening to me go on. His hands in his pockets and a smile on his face, but he didn't say a word. He just let me go on.

"I would have killed for a piece of you." I bit my lip, turned my back and confessed toward the car. "I dreamed of you and me in the back seat."

"Did we?" was Noah's only interruption to my rambling.

I looked over my shoulder, with my eyes following from his shoes up to his eyes, "Not yet."

Noah whirled me around and pinned me to the passenger door. "In broad daylight?"

My chest heaved and I exhaled, "Uh-ha."

Noah slipped his hand down my side to my hip and around me behind me. I was half way teasing, but for a moment I thought he was actually going to take me there. To my surprise, I heard the clicking sound of the door latch as Noah lifted the handle of the passenger door.

"Well, not now." Noah kissed me on the cheek and guided me out of the way of the opening door. "Let's go to dinner."

"I need to lock up first."

"Then go lock up and come on."

It wasn't as easy to run across the newly sodded yard in those strappy sandals as it would have been in the boots I really wanted, but I managed. It wasn't real graceful and I hoped Noah didn't watch, but I did it. I ran in those shoes. I was thirty-eight years old and I ran for him like I did when I was a teenager while he waited by the car door.

The vibration of the engine through the seat was something I had never forgotten. I rolled my window down so I could feel the wind through my hair as Noah gave it the gas and we sped down the driveway.

I giggled as he really womped down on the gas. "Fishtail it onto the road!" I couldn't believe I had said that. "If you don't mind."

"Seatbelt." Noah instructed as he shifted and did it.

When we got to the end of the driveway, Noah threw caution to the wind and whipped the wheel and the backend slung around onto Hadden Pond Road. I screamed so loud with excitement that I can't imagine that Aunt Dot and Uncle Jim didn't hear me.

Noah took his hand off of the gear shift and put it on my thigh. Between longing for him all week, the excitement of the car and the way he looked that night, I would have given into him in broad daylight in the yard of my house. His hair was tossed by the wind sweeping through the car and the blue of his shirt brought out the color of his eyes. I wanted him and, if he could read my mind, he would have pulled off onto a logging road between my house and Raley's Seafood. I never thought I would be one of those girls or women that gave it up in the backseat of a car, but there was something about him, something about that car, something that made me want him any place, any time, all the time and doing it in that car was not beneath me.

Noah couldn't read my mind. We carried on from one country road to another until we pulled into the restaurant. Hardly a thing had changed in the years since Noah was last there. The table clothes were still the red picnic checked ones. The light brown, wooden, ladder back chairs were the same. They weren't the most comfortable, but they were durable. The view, it was the same too except for a little less water in the pond due to the drought, a few pine saplings springing up and newer cars parked along the driveway circling the building and along the dam of the pond.

Dinner was as fine as it ever was, fried everything and a baked potato, but the entire time Noah seemed preoccupied. He was pleasant, holding my hand between ordering and the arrival of our plates and again between that and the slice of pecan pie that we were going to share. A dozen or more people interrupted us to say hello and Noah smiled when I introduced him. I knew all of the servers, the owner and most all of the patrons. If I didn't know them from living in the area all my life, I knew them from being the closest vet to Gibson, Mitchell and Edge Hill. At one time or another I had treated most everyone's animal.

When dessert arrived, Noah pushed it away and took a big gulp and finished off his sweet tea. "Do you mind if we have them box this up?"

"No, I don't mind." I wasn't sure what was going on with him, but his body language definitely said something was up.

Noah raised his hand and gestured politely for our server, a girl with whom I had attended high school. She came over straight away.

"Is everything alright?" She asked and I was wondering the same thing.

"Oh, yes. I'm just stuffed. Would you mind if we got the check and a to-go box?"

"Sure," she replied and then trotted off only to return with check and no box.

"Jesus," Noah said under his breath as she returned to the kitchen for the box.

"Are you okay?" I leaned across and whispered to him.

"I'm fine."

The check was paid and we were on our way. Although Noah held my hand, there wasn't a word spoken all the way home except for the "Holy shit!" he shouted when we swerved and narrowly missed Bambi and his mother who were standing smack in the middle of the road.

We pulled down the driveway and I halfway expected him to roll to a stop and tell me he had to be getting home. I was wrong.

Noah pulled up in front of the house and shut the car off. He got out and came around for my door. "I don't suppose I could persuade you to give me a tour?"

"Of course."

I hadn't brought my purse and, were it not for the hide a key that I had to replace after the tornado, we would have been locked out. The key that was blown away in the tornado was the same one that Noah and I used to let ourselves in back when we called it "our house." I stood on my toes and stretched to reach the key on the ledge of the transom window by the front door.

"Here, let me." Noah reached the key with not nearly the effort it was taking me. It was as if he knew right where it was.

Noah proceeded to unlock the door and hold it open for me. Upon sight of the foyer, he commented on the photos. "I love that picture of your dad and that's Millie?"

We stood in front of the black and white photo that hung by the entrance to the room to the right of the front door.

"Yeah, she was five in that photo and he was teaching her to pluck the petals off of daises. You know, 'He loves me. He loves me not.'"

Noah's attention moved on to the library. He went in and I waited by the door.

"You've got quite the collection in here." Except for the front wall, the others were completely covered in shelf after shelf of books.

"They were mostly Daddy's. Well, except for my college text books."

"You didn't sell them back?"

"No, he insisted that I keep them. 'Never know when you might need them,' he would say." I pointed to the bottom shelf on the far wall. "Oh, and those are Andy's and the overflow of Mama's cookbooks, but the rest are definitely Daddy's."

"Ah, this one is definitely not one of your dad's." Noah pulled out my senior year book and started flipping through it. "Oh, my God, this is us?"

Noah turned the book toward me. It was a picture of us on the football field at homecoming. "You were my escort for homecoming." I proceeded to tell him the story of how he just showed up and saved me after my cousin Billy abandoned me.

After a few minutes we moved on to the rest of the rooms downstairs. "You've followed me into every room, but I get the feeling that you don't go in the library. Why is that?"

We started up the stairs and I explained my aversion to the library. "In the last stages, we had to turn that room into a bedroom for Daddy. He died in that room. I haven't been in there since."

At the top of the stairs I passed by the first door we came too and Noah noticed. "What's in that room?"

"I was saving that one for last."

"It isn't another room in the house you don't go in is it. No one died in there, right?"

It seemed a little insensitive and brought back to mind the weird way he had been acting at the restaurant. I turned back and opened the door. A rug that covered the floor was about the only thing that was in the room and I pointed to the center of it.

"I lost something right there one night about twenty years ago." I was a little short with my comment on that room.

Noah understood what I was saying. "Oh." He hung his head and pulled me into the room. "I'm sorry. I'm sorry about most everything tonight, but I've been working up the courage to ask you something."

In the middle of the room, Noah reached in his pocket and dropped to his knee. I didn't realize what was going on and I thought he tripped or something. When he reached for my hand I thought he wanted me to help him up, but that wasn't it.

Noah looked up at me and held eye contact for a moment before he started to speak. "There hasn't been a moment in the last few weeks that I haven't thought of you. As I told you, I don't know how it is or exactly why, but I miss you. I can't explain what happened to me all those years ago, or what happened to that part of my brain or my heart or any part of me that would let me forget a second with you. What was damaged in me that made it so easy for me to be sold on the idea that you were just a dream? I don't know. I haven't been certain of a whole lot in my life, but I'm certain of this, despite everything, I've loved you forever. I'm certain I don't want to spend another day without you."

Noah's hand trembled in mine until he let go of my hand long enough to open the tiny box that he had pulled from his pocket moments before. The entire time he spoke my eyes were wide and my jaw was steadily headed toward the floor. I now knew why he was acting so strangely all night. He was nervous. I had wanted this for as long as I could remember, but I found myself nervous as well.

Inside the box was the ring that I mistook for my mother's, the ring from the antique shop in Savannah. It sparkled everywhere, but hardly distracted me from what Noah went on to say.

"I know it's sudden, but I can't stop thinking about it. I want the life that the boy in the yearbook photo had ahead of him. I want my life back. I want my wife back and if you're agreeable and if it's not too late, I want there to be pictures on the walls here of a child of ours with those of Millie. I want everything that was stolen from us. I want you to marry me."

Noah paused to catch his breath and I was just about to answer when he finally asked, "Gayle Anderson, will you do me the honor of making it official this time? Will you marry me...again?"

I forgot about what I considered my indiscretion with Robert Graham and answered Noah, "There has never been a time when I haven't been married to you. Of course I will marry you. Again. Officially, this time."

445

As I reached for the top of the window frame to let it down for the night, the light reflecting from my wedding set caught my eye. For a moment I rested my hand there on the ledge and admired the diamond. Past its sparkle I could see through the window to the flickering candles that hadn't yet burned out in the mason jars that lined the aisle.

I was only supposed to let down the window in my old bedroom on the front of the house and then return to the room I shared with Noah, but I became enchanted by the leftovers of my wedding day. From the empty rows of white wooden folding chairs set out like church pews, I could still picture the crowd from earlier in the day.

Aunt Dot and Uncle Jim were on the front row watching as Noah and I got married on the front porch of our house. She was crying as she does at every wedding and he was sneezing as he does over most any flower. Like yawning, crying was contagious and I remembered Mrs. Weatherby dabbing her eyes. I remembered all of our family and friends, Judy, Aunt Ruth, Uncle Bud, their kids, a number of my clients, some of our church family and Noah's brother Nate and some of his business associates from Washington.

I could still feel Millie's touch as she handed me Noah's ring. Her smile was a hint of Mama's and Daddy's and Andy's. I got tears in my eyes just looking at her. Seeing the pride in her eyes gave me the slightest hope that they were all there with us and they were proud their girls, me and Millie. Letting go of her hand was more than taking the ring, it was acknowledging that she was grown. I knew she was not my daughter, she would always be my little girl. I smiled back at her knowing that as much as I wanted to marry Noah, this was the last piece of letting Millie go.

In my mind's eyes I could still see the arrangements of white star gazer lilies and lavender rose. Mrs. Weatherby had supplied the flowers from her garden, cut them herself and spared no effort in arranging them. I'd never seen a professional job that was better. From the topiaries, bouquets and boutonnieres, they were more than I hoped for.

Millie and Gabe supplied the guest favors. When we remodeled the barn we found Daddy's home brew, Scuppernong wine. Through a distributor Gabe knew from the club, they had the ten cases we found in the barn repackaged and labeled. The labels read, "Mr. and Mrs. Noah Walden . Vintage 1997. Twenty years in the making." From where I was perched in the window I could see a bottle that had been left behind.

My day was amazing, everything I dreamed of right down to the black patent leather tuxedo shoes that Noah had on. It was perfect including the bout of nausea I had when the preacher pronounced us husband and wife and Noah kissed me and the churn my stomach took when the wave of aroma from the food at the reception hit me all at once. I covered the first round, but Noah noticed the second time. He especially noticed the fluttering of my eyes and squeamish ways I responded when he offered me a shrimp from the display of shrimp cocktail.

"No, thank you," I replied with words broken by my heaves from my stomach.

"Are you alright?" he leaned in and whispered.

"I can't say for sure." All the symptoms were there and had been there for a week. "I don't want to give you false hope, but..."

Noah's voice wasn't as low when he interrupted me. "Are you pregnant?"

I'm not sure who else heard, but Aunt Dot and Uncle Jim were behind us in the reception line and I knew they heard.

"See, I told you she had a bun in the oven. I have a nose for these things," Aunt Dot punched Uncle Jim and then wagged her finger. "You always doubt me, but a woman can tell."

I don't know how long I would have continued to reminisce about the day, but I was pulled back to reality with the whisper of my name.

447

"Mrs. Walden," Noah wrapped his arms around me and I leaned back into him. "This is the way things were meant to be. I love you."

Dear Friends and Readers,

As always, I hope you enjoyed the time you spent with the Andersons and thank you for giving your time to my writing.

Some readers have said that while reading the books, they felt like they are making new friends and became personally invested in the characters' lives. When finished reading, they reported that they miss their "new" friends. Readers said they laughed and they cried at the carrying-ons of the characters. As a writer, this feedback lets me know that I am doing my job.

If you would like to comment on how I am doing, please feel free to contact me via my website www.tsdawson.com, like my author page on Facebook TS Dawson or leave me a review on Amazon.com. I appreciate all of your feedback.

Lastly, please do not be disappointed, I am going to take a break from The Port Honor Series. Already in the works is the first book in The Hunt Club Series. I hope you will look forward to this series as much as I am looking forward to writing it.

The first book in The Hunt Club series deals with the life of Lucy Meeks of Thomson, Georgia. In the book **When I Was Green**, we find Lucy inexperienced in life and love, but the year she turns sixteen all of that changes. Things she thought were true are not. Things she should have known she does not. She is about as green as the gelding that is on loan to her as she takes riding lessons from the new hand at the stables of the fox hunting club.

Thank you again and I look forward to hearing from you.

Sincerely,

T. S. Dawson

The Port Honor Series

<u>Port Honor</u>

I can't hardly wait for the next book from TS Dawson! I love the character development and the detail she adds to the setting. If you love Mary Kay Andrews, Nicholas Sparks, or Haywood Smith, you will love TS Dawson!

-Rachel Noah

As a first time novelist, Dawson exhibits a natural instinct for the craft of writing. She uses familiar language and realistic dialog to draw the reader into the intriguing tale of a young college student's journey into adulthood. Dawson breathes new life into a decade that vanished right before our eyes. But, this is more than a mere reminiscence of the 90's for members of Generation X. It's a mature story of love and loss; about sex and secrets, and coming to terms with one's past while fighting for tomorrow's dreams.

-J. Meeks

Dawson's Port Honor is descriptive in a way that allows you to imagine the characters as well as the scenery, locations, etc. for an excellent visual of the events as they unfold. The story line is not predictable, as so many books are, and leaves you with a cliff hanger that makes you anxious for release of the next book in the Port Honor Series, In Search of Honor.

-P. Aycock

In Search of Honor

I have thoroughly enjoyed both books. The style of writing is very captivating- easy to read & hard to put down! I'm eager to see what the next book will bring! It is full of emotions, made me cry at times, made me angry and made me laugh. You can tell by reading these books that Ms. Dawson has put her heart and soul into them. If you have not read the first one, please buy it and then get the second one. You will enjoy them. Totally awesome.

-T. Bryan

TS Dawson, you have done it again! Wonderfully written and just as captivating as the first one. I purchased it the first day out and finished it on the kindle last night. I loved the characters and how you wrote it from Gabe's view. I can't wait to read the next book. I have truly enjoyed your books and I'm sure I'll reread them over and over. You have a wonderful way of keeping the reader's interest - the pages kept turning so I could discover heartache, love, and laughter. Thanks again for sharing your talent! I'll read any book you publish!!

-A. Cundy

37233585R00254

Made in the USA
Lexington, KY
22 November 2014